Seeing Pink

Seeing Pink

Erin O'Rourke

Five Star • Waterville, Maine

First Edition
First Printing: September 2003

Set in 11 pt. Plantin by Al Chase.

Printed in the United States on permanent paper.

Library of Congress Cataloging-in-Publication Data

O'Rourke, Erin, 1972–
    Seeing pink / Erin O'Rourke.—1st ed.
        p. cm.—(Five Star first edition expressions series)
    ISBN 0-7862-5632-X (hc : alk. paper)
    1. Women—West Virginia—Fiction.   2. Family violence
—Fiction.   3. West Virginia—Fiction.   4. Vigilantes—
Fiction.   5. Wife abuse—Fiction.   6. Revenge—
Fiction.   I. Title.   II. Series.
PS3615.R585S44 2003
    813′.6—dc21   2003052852

to Mom
for giving me all the words of the dictionary,
save one

"The stone was at the bottom of the hill and we were alone."
—Albert Camus

Chapter One

Under the blue glow of the bug light, Jo held the compress to the woman's bruising face, wondering if the bastard had raped her.

Not that it was much of a compress. A dishrag, really. One of those with the checkerboard pattern that she'd picked up at a garage sale last spring and had never dreamed would one day serve as a field dressing. But that's how it went with the little objects around her house; all her life, Jo had been making do. Daughter need a halo for the school play? Here, use this clothes hanger. Run out of glue? Try a little flour and water. She lifted the corner of the dishrag from Penelope's pulpy lip to see if the bleeding had stopped.

"Ice cream," Nin said.

Jo looked from Penny's blackening mouth to Nin, and then to the other women standing guard around Penny in her folding lawn chair, surrounded by dirty paper plates and half-empty beer bottles and the tiptoeing smell of smoke.

"At least"—Nin crossed her ample arms over her chest—"butter brickle with fudge topping always works for me."

Jo looked back at Penny without a word.

"I'm sorry," Penny said. She pinched her eyelids shut, her hair listless strings in her face, and a second later she was melting. She bent over, her delicate hands balled in her lap, snorting back the tears.

"Shhh." Jo leaned close to her, so that their foreheads touched. Penny's skin was hot.

"Do we need more ice?" Hannah asked. "I should get more ice."

"Stay put, girl," Lucy told her. "We got more than plenty

7

here in the cooler." Jo didn't have to look up to distinguish their voices. She knew them too well. These aimless, mystic women. *Mom's Crazy Coven*, her daughter called them.

Jo sensed someone crouch down beside her. She turned, pivoting her forehead against Penny's.

Tamaryn Soza's face looked otherworldly in the blue light. "This ain't right."

Jo closed her eyes, then opened them slowly.

"I hate not doing anything about this," Tamaryn said.

Jo searched around inside of herself, but couldn't find the words.

"Someone needs to be responsible this time, Jo. Someone needs to *pay*."

The only thing Jo could think of was something she'd read in one of her mother's magazines a long time ago: *We abide through life's hardships, and when we can stand it no longer, we abide some more.*

Tamaryn inched forward, so that Jo could clearly see the freckles scattered across her nose, a constellation of dangerous stars. "Are you listening to me, Jo? We let this slide again, we'll be sliding forever. You hear me?"

Jo wanted to say yes, she heard her. But that wasn't entirely true. For the most part, all she could hear was the man on the radio this morning, telling her that it was going to be what he called a kite-flying, lovemaking afternoon, and she should have known he was lying when she ran out of tape and could no longer keep her world from coming unstuck and falling to pieces at her feet.

With the last of the tape from her junk drawer, Jo fastened an elephant to Wednesday.

The paper elephant covered the little square on the calendar completely. The month of June was now almost entirely covered in cutout pachyderms. Jo had once heard that elephants were renowned for their patience, their tolerance, their acceptance of circumstances. The next day she'd bought a pack of elephant stickers and, in a moment of exceptional stress, made about a hundred photocopies. Ever since then she'd been fixing them over her calendar to keep track of something she couldn't quite explain.

"*. . . and with temperatures in the upper eighties, it looks like it's going to be another kite-flying, lovemaking summer afternoon here in the Mountaineer State. For those of you making the commute to D.C. this morning . . .*"

"Play some music already," Jo said as she dropped the empty tape dispenser into the trash and pushed through the screen door to the backyard.

The pink sheets hung without spirit from the clothesline. Chuck had built the now-sagging line two days after they'd bought the place on an afternoon that felt like 116 years ago to all parties involved but was probably more like twenty. Of course he went by *Charles* now and was happily remarried and owned half the town of Belle Springs. Two summers ago the line had given way and deposited Caroline's favorite skimpy blouse in a mud hole the dog had started and the rain had finished off. Caroline had screamed like they'd amputated her arm. Jo had loyally set upon the shirt with bleach and a few home-brewed stain removers she'd read about in the *Farmers' Almanac*, secretly thanking the mud for the favor.

It's not the end of the world, Jo had said, working at the thing with a stain-stick. *Do you have to wear stuff that shows off so much of yourself?*

So much of myself? They're called boobs, Mom.

Ah. Thanks for the update.

Since then Caroline had utterly reversed her opinions of spaghetti straps. And she called them breasts instead of boobs. She was now so much a seventeen-year-old Puritan that Jo found it amazing that the girl had Woodstock genes in her blood.

She checked her watch on the way to the line. Quarter past eight. Still too many things to do, and God still not putting enough hours in the day to do them. Work at nine o'clock would find her back at her vigil over a time bomb. At one end of the fuse was the Washington crowd. Developers from D.C. wanted land for a golf course and a place for the lawmakers to chopper over for quiet deal-making and a bit of R and R in what their press people were calling *a cradle of bucolic Appalachian tranquility*. On the other side were the old townies, entrenched in tradition and refusing to cede even a single acre. If we give them an inch, and all the rest. Half of Belle Springs was wearing T-shirts that read WE ARE NOT SUBURBIA, as if that place were some kind of Sodom and they were afraid of what happened to Lot's wife if they were to look upon such a city, while the other half had gotten pen-happy, their letters flowing to the *Belle Springs Symposium* like the promises that flowed from the lips of the politicians they were defending. Or, more appropriately, like nitroglycerin leaking from a bundle of dynamite. Jo just hoped to keep it all from exploding before the big vote Tuesday night.

She took the pink sheets down from the line and bundled them in her arms.

If she made it to five without a detonation, she'd have to hurry to the market because she'd miscounted the number of buns in the pantry. Though it was only the twenty-second of June, she was hosting her Independence Day gala two weeks early because it was one of those hectic years when half of her friends had out-of-town plans for the Fourth. Nin said to expect about forty people, including kids. Nin always included kids. Probably had something to do with the fact that she had six herself.

Jo stopped midway across the yard. Already the tables were laid out, borrowed from churches and neighborhood gin rummy nights. The lid of the barbecue grill was up, the charcoal waiting. The citronella candles had matchbooks standing by. The entire yard had an air of anticipation about it. Even the big sugar maple with the unused tree house was holding its leaves as if they were its breath.

"You know I'm going to Sarah's tonight."

Jo pulled her eyes from the tree. Caroline stood on the other side of the screen door.

"Did you hear me?" the girl asked.

Jo sighed, a boxer at the sound of the bell. "You know it wouldn't kill you to make a cameo appearance."

"Who's going to miss me? There's not going to be anyone else here my age."

"I can't talk you into one hot dog?"

"I'm a vegetarian, Mother, remember?"

Jo knew that. Of course she remembered. The hot dog comment had sort of come out of its own volition. Her daughter taught Sunday school to third-graders and collected college brochures and didn't eat anything with a face. Jo studied her through the screen: her pale rainwater eyes, Chuck's dimpled chin, her blonde hair barely touched with the heirloom red that was her mother's only spar in an otherwise sinking world. Jo had cut her famed red tresses to shoulder-length when she turned forty, but that was as far as the scissors would ever go; hair wasn't much of a handhold, but sometimes it was the only thing she had to keep her afloat.

"What are you staring at?" Caroline demanded.

"Can you do me this one favor, please?"

"Mother . . ."

Jo marched toward the door. "It's a lousy stupid thing for

11

me to ask, I know, like torture to your young undeserving body, but it will only take twenty minutes—"

Caroline turned and disappeared into the house.

"—and then you can leave all of us old folks here to talk about dentures and bladder-control problems." Clutching the sheets against her with one arm, she snatched open the squeaking door just in time to see a strawberry-haired spirit slip around the corner. *"Caroline."*

"I've got to go!" the girl called from the other room. "I'm giving swimming lessons today, and I don't want to be late. I'll see you later."

Jo hurried after her. "Honey, please."

Caroline grabbed her duffel from the back of the sofa without breaking stride on her way to the front door. "I'll stop by your office this afternoon."

"We need to talk about this."

"Later."

"Now."

Caroline headed outside. "Please, Mother, don't start."

"Don't you walk away from me, Sweet Caroline."

The girl halted abruptly, half in and half out the door. She spun around. Red circles colored her cheeks. "And don't call me that. I can't stand it."

"It's your name."

"Don't remind me."

"Then what am I supposed to call you?"

"Don't you get it?" Caroline's face went through a series of tremors until finally settling on a curl of the lip and a narrowing of the eyes. "Don't you *see?* You and I are not the same person, okay? And what you just said should *show* you. You named me after a *song*, for Pete's sake. A song I don't even *like.*"

She turned, let the door bang, and raced down the sidewalk to her car.

Jo took a single, wooden step toward the porch, but that was all she could manage. She pulled the bundle of sheets tightly to her chest as the sun crept higher in the West Virginia sky and divided the lawn into planes of light and shade. *"You used to like it!"*

Caroline's car jerked out of the driveway and sped away.

"You used to like it," Jo said again. No one heard her but the pink sheets, and they didn't seem in the mood to offer a rational reply.

When next she became aware of her surroundings, she was standing with the phone against her ear, because it was either call someone or break down. And right now, with so much depending on her stability, she couldn't afford the luxury of crumbling.

The second of the station's four phone lines started ringing.

Hannah Jessler punched the button for line two and rattled her standard, comma-less greeting into her headset: "Good morning Clayton County Sheriff's Department my name is Hannah how may I direct your call?"

A brief pause, a smile like the dawn, then:

"Hey, Jo. Calling to remind me to bring the bug light?"

She listened for a few moments, then shook her head. "Don't worry about it. She'll get over it. Yeah, I know you're going to say that I'm not that much older than her, but hey, those seven or eight years make a big difference, could you hold on a sec?"

In response to a crackle of voices on the police-band radio, Hannah grabbed her mike and said into it, "Copy that, six, I'll let him know. And six? Your wife called. Ten-twenty-one at your convenience."

She put the mike down and rolled across the floor to her

13

stash. She kept her chocolate-glazed peanut clusters in the cardboard box the volunteer firemen used for donations at Christmas. She never gained a pound, regardless of how often she donated to the cause of fattening up. "I'm eating again, Jo, just thought you'd want to know."

She paused, then laughed. Her eyes glittered. "I'll keep that in mind. But hey. The girl'll be okay, trust me on this one because I've been in her shoes and you probably have too on more than one occasion. I mean, you fought with your mother, I'm sure. You did have a mother, didn't you, or did someone just find you under a rock?" She swallowed the last chunk of her candy, then licked her lips lavishly. "Okay, you go get them today, knock them dead and all that stuff, all right? Don't let this town come apart at its silly seams. Okay. Sounds good. I'll be early to help with whatever, Terrell might be late because he's on duty, but I promise to get along at least for awhile without him." She kept smiling. "Right. Good. Ciao."

She pushed herself back toward the phone.

Someone intercepted her halfway there, grabbing her chair from behind.

"Got you!"

Hannah yelped.

"Heard you taking my name in vain," Terrell said as he rolled her clear of her workstation and toward the hall. "Now I reckon we'll have to settle this, for sure."

Hannah twisted around to face him. "Am I being abducted? Because if I am then I have to warn you that I'm a government employee and we demand very high ransoms, so I hope you're up to the task."

Terrell pushed her into the hall and leaned down and kissed her when she puckered up at him. "That Jo?"

"Who else? Aren't you supposed to be cruising for

speeders, shaking down innocent civilians, that sort of thing?"

"I was in the neighborhood." A little recklessly he rounded the corner and aimed her down the passage that led to the station garage, then stopped. "You sure I can't just wheel you away from all of this?"

She was still turned around in her seat, looking up at him with her teeth beaming through her smile. She put her hand on his, white against black, then interlaced their fingers so that they resembled piano keys. "Can I be serious for just a minute?"

"You don't have much precedent for that."

"I know."

"Should I sit down for this?"

"Terrell . . ."

"Sorry." He knelt in front of her. "What's up, sweetness?"

Hannah checked the hall over his shoulder. She lowered her voice, and for once her smile slipped away, a cloud across the sun. "I heard Sheriff Cantrell talking with the city manager. I think it's real this time. There's just not enough money."

Terrell studied the semi-clean floor tiles. Hannah loved to watch him when he was doing nothing but thinking. His lips slightly parted, his stone-dark eyes pensive yet alert. There was something exotic about him when he wrapped himself in silence, like a Muslim looking east in prayer. *My hushed hero,* she thought, wiggling her fingers more comfortably between his. There were times when she wanted to blend utterly into him, the way the rain is absorbed into the thirsty desert floor.

"So they want one of the deputies to go," he said.

"They like to call it downsizing."

"And I'm the low man on the totem pole."

"Really, babe, this is not the place to talk about your pole."

He gave her the best smile he could muster. "So the serious minute is over."

She put her free hand behind his head and pulled him into a brief kiss. "There are other places than Belle Springs, that's for sure, you know that, right? I hear there's this thing, they call it a highway, supposedly there are real live *towns* at the other end of it."

His leather belt with all of its loops and pouches creaked when he stood up. "We'll talk about it."

"It's not fair, you know."

"Never has been."

"I'm being serious again."

"I know."

"I mean, come on, let's be rational." She pulled her hand away and spun her chair so that she was facing him. "For someone who hates being serious, babe, I'm the Cleopatra of reality."

"Sweetness . . ."

"Look at me, Terrell. I want to come with you, wherever you end up, you get it? And a little voice inside tells me that maybe you'd have already gone off to bigger and better things if you weren't bolted down to the ground because of *me*."

"Nobody's bolted me anywhere."

"So what do you call *this?*" She grabbed the big rear wheels of her chair and shook the hell out of them.

"I call it a wheelchair," he said softly. "It's maybe my favorite thing in the whole world."

She stared at him, then squeezed her eyes shut and turned away.

The phone rang in the dispatcher's office.

"I've got to go." With a brusque shove of her hands against the wheels, she rolled herself down the hall.

"Here, let me." He stepped around behind her.

"No." She sped up, paddling faster. "That's okay. You'll be at Jo's tonight, right?"

"Should I bring anything?"

She looked back, smiling tightly. "Just you." She winked. "And your pole." She left him standing there and went to answer the phone. "Good morning Clayton County Sheriff's Department my name is Hannah how may I direct your call?" After she hung up, she remembered her van was getting its tires rotated and she was going to need a ride this evening. Tamaryn had a pickup truck, which made things easier, because they could throw the chair—*the goddamn chair*—in the back.

She punched line three and dialed.

Tamaryn Soza ironed with her left hand and answered the phone with her right. She was a southpaw, and when Roy cut her some slack in the summer she pitched coed softball. Every team in town wanted her. Her claim to mediocre fame.

"Yeah?" She clamped the phone to her chin with her shoulder and snagged the cigarette from the empty tuna can that was her ashtray. If she ironed ashes into Roy's company shirt then she'd never hear the end of it. "Hiya, Jessler. Hold on a sec." She put the phone and iron down, gave the Pest-B-Gone Exterminators shirt a snap in the air, hangered it, retrieved the phone and headed for the boys' room at the back of the trailer. "Okay, I'm here. What's up?"

Hannah asked for a lift to Josephine's shindig, Tamaryn said sure no problem and wondered what was eating Happy Hannah but didn't ask. After they said their goodbyes, Tamaryn crushed out her cigarette because she tried not to smoke back here. It was one of her Good Rules. No drags around the munchkins. At least when she could avoid it.

"All right, you monsters." She waded through the toys

toward the bunk beds. She checked the top one. Empty. Not surprising. Down below, two fuzzy-headed forms were mummified in the sheets, several plastic action figures sharing the bed with them. Tamaryn sank down on her haunches and watched them sleep.

Brady was six and fearless. Matthew was eight and tried to be.

"Arise, sweet princes." Tamaryn lowered herself over them so that her face was nested between theirs. She breathed twice, filling her lungs with their scent.

Then she pressed her open mouth against Brady's cheek and blew hard enough to make a silly honking noise.

"*Mom . . .*" He screwed his eyes shut and batted a limp hand at her.

"Up, up, up, you varmints." She nuzzled against them and tickled them but not too much, and they rolled under her like a pair of baby rabbits. *Gimmie these few seconds every day,* she said to whoever might be listening, *and I can put up with all the other hours of muck and crud.* "I. Said. *Up!*" And she pitched herself fully into the bed and wrestled them until they were both hooting and poking, and everything went bump-free from there, no hitches in her morning as she shod them in hand-me-down sneakers and fed them Pop-Tarts and sang only more loudly when they asked her to please be quiet because they were trying to watch cartoons. She pirouetted into the little living room, dancing in front of the television until they shouted *"Ma-ohm!"* enough times, then she did herself up in the bathroom and thanked Jesus offhandedly that she was still built like the athlete she remembered being in high school ten years ago, and thus inspired she couldn't help but feel a little invincible as she got the boys out the door and onto the front porch, where everything turned to shit.

"Dammit, Tam." Roy slammed his truck door. His camouflaged fatigues were caked with grime. "Thought you was going to mow the lawn last night."

She didn't look at him. "Okay, squirts, head 'em up and move 'em out." She herded them down the steps toward her Toyota with its rust-eaten fenders. She watched their feet leave damp impressions in the wet grass. "Can't be late for Nin's prize-winning French toast."

"You knew I was gonna be out all night."

She opened the driver's door. "Here, just get in on my side. But keep your shoes off the seat."

"So you ignoring me now?"

She glanced at him sideways. "Please, Roy."

He hooked his dirty thumbs in his belt, which was festooned with ammo pockets and joined below the small slalom of his belly with a NASCAR belt buckle. "Grass is damn near ten inches high, Tam. City ordinance has got rules about upkeep of personal property."

"Get on up there, Mister T-Rex." She helped Brady into the cab as he roared like a dinosaur, clutching a plastic reptile in each hand.

"They're gonna come mow it with a tractor and send us the bill, for Chrissakes."

"I was busy," she said, when she could stand it no more. "You had all last night to get it done, if you were so worried about it."

"It was your *turn*."

Tamaryn went rigid, her hand frozen to the door frame. She reminded herself that she was actually listening to a thirty-two-year-old. For a moment there she might have been talking to Brady.

"You knew last night was a coyote hunt," he said. There was a truculence in his voice that she would have expected to hear from one of the boys. He wasn't drunk. Not this time.

Which somehow made it worse.

"I'm going now," she heard herself say. "I've got to get them to daycare."

"Yeah, sure. Can't have fat Nin wondering what's keeping you." He reached through the truck window and extracted a rifle. His father's .223. The one Tamaryn called his Psalm 23, because it was the rod and staff that comforted him.

Tamaryn bit her teeth together and cranked the key. She pumped the gas pedal up and down until the old engine finally caught. She didn't bother backing out of the driveway, just turned a circle in the alleged ten-inch grass, telling the boys to get their seat belts on and realizing when she made the street that her eyes had never left her husband's gun. He carried it into the house without looking back. Tamaryn stared at it until it was out of sight, then fought the urge to reach for her cigarettes all the way to Nin's.

Nin Ryan never heard the truck pull up. She was buried alive.

How many layers this time? Oh, kids first, no doubt about that. A couple of parents had already been by this morning, which meant it was time for mathematics: four extras, ages one through five, plus her six minus Lee who'd stayed the night at a friend's and Dorothy who'd gotten her first period yesterday (*My God*, Nin thought, *already?*), and that made eight. Right? Eight, with help on the way in the form of one of Dorothy's friends who made two dollars an hour for helping Nin breathe beneath all the layers.

Layer two: her lists. Including grocery, laundry, and to-do, none of which was even partially completed. So she was buried in schedules and children. Submerged.

And she loved it. Couldn't, in fact, get enough of it. If the Lord had put her on this dingy little planet for a reason, it was the children. She carried herself into the living room, baby on her arm, 10,000 toys like land mines on the floor, waiting to trip her if she wasn't careful. Despite her size, she'd gotten adept at traversing this delightful terrain without turning an ankle; it was a dexterity exclusive to mothers. Already the place was alive with their voices. Nin wouldn't have known what to do in a quiet house. It wouldn't have seemed right.

You poor woman, she'd been told, always with a supportive smile. Everyone in Belle Springs seemed to admire her, even if they occasionally took her for granted with their bake sales and school functions. Secretly they surely said better her than me.

But as the only Eskimo in town, maybe in the whole state of West Virginia, Ningeogapik Ryan figured she had license to be eccentric.

She saw the little light above the door blinking.

She wove through their hands and shining faces. "Watch it there, mister. Yes, Rachel, that's lovely. No, sweetie, you can wait until breakfast."

She always kept the door locked for safety. She'd grown deaf to the doorbell, so she had the light installed six months ago.

Tamaryn stood on the porch, along with her two lifelines, Matt and Brady. Tamaryn was in a hurry so Nin let her go. A wise woman knew better than to ask.

More math. Eight plus two is ten. Divided by one—her— was still ten. Where *was* Dorothy's friend, anyway?

More importantly, where was the mail?

Nin poked her ringless fingers through the blinds. Nope. No Lucy with her blue satchel.

Would it be today that she got the notice?

She knew it was coming. Her marriage was nearly a year dead. A body no longer cooling in the morgue but honestly buried for good, under the unexcavatable dirt of divorce. Yet Dan Ryan, who'd rescued her from Alaska with his southern gentleman's good looks, had made it known on more than one occasion that the graveyard and the soiled shovels weren't enough. He wanted the kids. He wanted her blessed layers. He wanted all the math that added up to who she was.

Were there termites in the walls? Dirty dishes in the sink? Every morning she waited with a deepening sense of dread for the letter that would tell her the Department of Health and Human Resources was paying a visit to investigate certain rumors.

It was the French toast that saved her. Something mundane. She loved her ordinary things. Polished them like ceramic charms. She warmed up the griddle, Dorothy's friend arrived, and the children filled the house with vital sound.

Lucy finally pulled up in her little square white truck and poked a few envelopes in the box, but Nin was inside, laughing with them all at Nickelodeon.

"Sugar," Lucy said, "if I was going to read somebody's mail, don't think I'd trouble myself with yours. Nobody else wants to waste time with *Women of Mudwrestling* magazine."

The old man laughed gamely, causing starlings to take flight from the sidewalk trees.

Lucy smiled. "Now you best get back inside before you stop traffic." She nodded toward his naked chest, which sprouted a dying garden of white hairs. "Man like you, out here half dressed . . ." She shook her head.

He chuckled and saluted her with his mail. "See you tomorrow, Miss Campbell."

"Not if I see you first." She waved and chased her shadow down the walk.

She'd left the truck at the corner by Nin's place. It would

only slow her down in this neighborhood, what with all the stops she had to make. And besides. It was a fine morning, and her bones could stand for some sun.

"How you doing, Charlotte?" she called into the next yard. Charlotte was pushing eighty, but no soldier shined his boots with more verve and dedication than old Charlotte Wilson tended her hibiscus. "Got some red-hot post here for you today." She opened Charlotte's tidy mailbox and wedged in a loaf of letters. "Have a good one!"

Off again. Next house. Greet the kids on their way to swimming lessons. Next one, tell the dog inside the fence he's tempting pepper spray. Next one, wonder what Gail Cratch is doing getting a letter from the Wiccan Potions Company. Turn the corner. Lift the hand because everybody loves to wave at the postwoman. Bend over to hitch up knee-high black sock. Straighten up in time to see a police cruiser cross the intersection and wonder if that's Terrell. Marvel at the way that little brothers make us proud without so much as trying.

"Well, well. Penny's got herself a lingerie catalog. Girl's life must be a helluva lot more exciting than mine." Lucy wrapped the catalog around the rest of Penny's mail, tugged a quick rubber band over it, and bustled between two wretched lawn gnomes to the front door.

It opened in her face and almost knocked her down.

"Uh, hi there," the man said, obviously startled to find Lucy standing on the steps. He was white and twentyish with an Ivy League complexion. Must have been his Jaguar in the driveway.

"Hi yourself," Lucy said. "Got Penelope's mail here."

The man ducked into the house. "Pen?" His slender belt was probably alligator skin, but Lucy noticed that he'd missed a loop. She didn't bother telling him. He turned back around, smiling like an anchorman. "She's coming. Have a nice day." He skipped down the walk, tossing his keys.

"You too." She watched him drive away.

When she looked back to the door, Penny was just appearing. She wore a bathrobe and her hair was piled up. Her elfin features looked even more fragile without makeup. "Any sweepstakes notices today, Luce?" She yawned.

"You still seeing him?"

Penny crossed her arms over her chest and leaned in the doorway. "*Him* has a name, you know."

"Yeah, and it begins with *t-r-o* and ends with *b-l-e*."

"*Jed,* Lucy. His name is Jed. You can get to know him tonight at the cookout. You'll love him. Got time for coffee? I have a fresh pot."

"What if you marry that fool boy? Won't you get tired of all that glitzing around with all the plastic people, listening to all their plastic jive? Most of them folks have more agendas than a cat has lives."

"Your point?"

"Point?" Lucy made a face as she stared at the empty place where the car had been parked before disappearing down the street. She twisted her mouth like a seer trying to read illegible tea leaves, then shrugged. "Hell, no point. But why anyone would want to date a senator's son, I'll never know."

Chapter Two

The party started with a cat catching fire.

The big tabby—one of those itinerant salesman tomcats that no one claims yet everybody feeds—leapt up to investigate the dill and onion slices trapped under cellophane beside the grill, and when his tail went up like a torch, you could smell it from across the yard.

The flames sputtered out as the cat ran screeching under the fence. A question mark of smoke rose up from behind Jo's anemic rosebushes.

"I hope that isn't an omen," she sighed. Her watch said ten after six. The masses were due to converge around seven. "It's already been one of those days. A cat-burning isn't what I need right now."

"And what is it that you need?" Nin asked.

That stumped her. She spent a few moments considering it. So far only Nin had arrived, or Nin and Company, as they liked to say. Five of her flock were adventuring around the perimeter of the yard, hooting for the singed cat to return. A fence in need of paint kept them corralled. The baby, Marky, pendulumed back and forth in a crank-powered swing in the shade. The oldest, Dorothy, had taken a cue from Caroline and begged for a stay of execution, which Nin had granted. Four tables were positioned about the grass, covered with mismatched tablecloths. A fifth stood at the porch near the grill, already burdened with condiments and a dozen varieties of chips and salsa. They'd borrowed Caroline's portable stereo and Nin had tuned it to a Christian music station, which they both knew wouldn't last five minutes past seven.

"Why does all of this seem so normal?" Jo wondered.

"Should it not?"

"I don't know. I spent all day as the unwilling mediator between two war parties. I guess I could use a bit of normal."

"No deals yet?"

"Hardly. The Washington consortium has cut back its request to one hundred and ten acres. The opposition says they'll die if they relinquish so much as a dirt clod. They've got two hundred names on a petition. The consortium's got the lawyers."

"The lawyers usually win."

"True, but you haven't heard the twist in the plot."

"Oh?"

"Enter the opposition's secret weapon, Pete Musket."

"Who?"

"He owns exactly two-point-seven acres right in the middle of the consortium's future country club. Apparently it's old Indian ground. Shawnee, I believe. Musket says he'll sell when the wind spirits come and tear the flesh from his body and his organs are consumed by crows."

"Ouch."

"So normal is good."

"I am glad I came early."

"Me too."

The women sat hip-to-hip on the porch. For awhile they watched the children. Nin fanned herself with a church bulletin she'd retrieved from her van. "Do you remember the caboose?"

Staring out over the grass, Jo smiled.

"Just wondered," Nin said.

The caboose was what they were going to live in one day, because last year when Dan Ryan decided he was better off as a solo act, Nin had said while crying on Jo's sofa that she'd always felt like the back end of a train. The Dan Ryan Express, dragging her along, with the kids all the little cars in between. That was the first night Jo had been drunk since college, and the first time for Nin *ever*. At some point during the passing of the peach schnapps, Jo announced that one day they'd open an underwear store in an old caboose and call it Ass Ends. Nin had laughed so hard that she'd bit her tongue and bled all over her glass.

"You hear from him yet?" Jo asked.

In response, Nin rapped her knuckles against the planks of the porch.

"You know the story of Damocles?"

"Vaguely." Nin fanned a bit faster.

"Think I'm going to call him *Dan*ocles. He's waiting to drop the sword on you, Ninny. It's just a question of when."

Nin began to rock back and forth. "Truly, truly. Maybe when Pete Musket has finished with his wind spirits, I can talk them into doing me a favor. You think they hire out?"

As the minutes passed, the air settled more comfortably around Jo's shoulders. Being with Nin did that to her, the way that gravity brings all things to rest, given time. Jo had more than once observed her own habit of adopting the nature of whoever she happened to be with at the moment. That's why she sometimes felt so self-righteous around her daughter, and so mercurial next to Tamaryn. Nin, though, was what the pillow was to the sleepy head.

"Yo! Did somebody here order a bug light?"

Jo stood up as Hannah came around the corner bearing said lantern in her lap, Tam behind her, muscling the wheelchair through the grass.

Jo extended a hand to Nin and helped her up.

"Damn, we're early." Tam's tight black curls jiggled when

she shook her head. "And here I was trying to be fashionably late."

"Did you bring the pies?" Jo asked.

"In the truck. Hey." She let go of the chair, sniffed twice. "Is something burning?"

"Only feline flesh."

Hannah rubbed her stomach. "Mmmm. You shouldn't have."

"Just wait till you see what's for dessert. Nin, you might want to give Marky's chair a few more cranks. Looks like he's winding down. Hannah, you can open up some boxes of our fine plastic flatware, and Tam, you'll need a stepladder from the garage to hang the light from the rain gutter there. I'll get the pies."

While the others attended her suggestions, she shoved her hands in the pockets of her khakis, dodged the Ryan kids as they collided noisily with Tamaryn's pair, and made her way to the truck, wishing she could carry Nin's emotional anchor around her neck. *At least for a few hours every day,* she thought. By nine o'clock the stereo was playing Jethro Tull and Jo was floating around the islands of after-dinner conversation, without an anchor to be had.

". . . at least until he outgrew me and started hitting back," Lucy said.

General laughter. Glass bottles tinkling. Terrell rolling his eyes and pinching Hannah on the shoulder when she giggled at him.

"That's the trouble with brothers," someone said. "Big sisters never stay that way for long. Puberty always roots for the boys. In more ways than one."

"Amen to that," Lucy agreed.

"I don't remember hitting her," Terrell said, affecting a

look midway between contemplation and offense. "But let me tell you about the welts that girl gave me . . ."

"Sorry, babe," Hannah said. "No sympathy from this crowd."

"You best watch him," Lucy advised her in a stage whisper, "he *loves* pity."

Terrell looked around for help. "This isn't good. I'm outnumbered. But I've got bruises. Really. I can show you."

"Oh, believe me, Luce," Hannah said, "I've already learned."

"And no tolerance for pain either, let me tell you. Boy always thought he needed a Band-Aid, even when there was nothing bleeding."

"The wimp."

"Boy wimp turned adult hypochondriac."

"Hello?" Terrell was getting desperate. "I'm being ganged up on here! Jo?"

"Don't look at me," she said as she walked by with both hands full of empty beer bottles. "I just work here. Wimp."

"Hey!"

Jo went to the overflowing trash can and added more to the pile. She compressed it as best she could, then drifted to the next table.

". . . but what do you expect from a freshman quarterback?"

"*Red-shirt* freshman."

"Whatever. Guy still plays young. I don't think Tech has much of a chance this season."

"We'll see."

"What about you, Jo? Miami or Virginia Tech for the National Championship?"

Jo raised an eyebrow. "What, you expect me to bet against my Nittany Lions?"

The men traded grins. The lady was a player.

"Coach Paterno could stand to wear his pants a little longer," she said, "but I'd put him up against the hefties anyday. Shula, Landry. Even big Vince."

The men laughed. They were too easy. "Good enough. But let me ask you something."

Jo crossed her arms and tipped her head slightly to the side. "Shoot."

"What the hell's a Nittany Lion, anyway?"

"Ah." She nodded slowly. "Sorry, old campus secret. They give us these cyanide pills upon graduation, just in case we ever succumb to the temptation to talk."

"In other words, you have no idea."

Jo smiled, but her eyes weren't in it. "If you're finished with that plate, I'll take it off your hands."

Bearing the bones of barbecued chicken, a few forks and crumpled napkins, she passed through the thinning crowd toward one of the louder circles along the back fence; handsome Jedediah Whitecross had them eating out of the palm of his manicured hand.

She was almost there when her alarm went off.

Maybe she'd heard a whispered word, sharp as a blade. Or perhaps the radars of her ESP were dialed to their most delicate settings of late. Whatever her warning, she looked into the blue shadows under the clothesline and saw Tamaryn and her husband so close together that their faces nearly touched. Tam's hands were shoved into her back pockets, as was her wont when her fires were stoked. For his part, Roy had one hand curled into a fist and the other jamming a finger at Tamaryn's face.

Jo didn't move. Only stared.

Tam wore cutoff shorts, white running shoes, no socks. Her hands were buried in her pockets, hugging her rump.

Roy had on an old pair of dungarees with the cuffs rolled up, because he'd never been the tallest suspect in the lineup, and besides, he liked to show off his flat-toed boots with the polished buckles.

Tam shook her head vehemently. Roy's lips pulled back against his teeth.

Go, Jo told herself. *Just go and do something for a change.* But her knees were locked in place, and Caroline was right: Jo could vacillate with the best of them. If there was a fence within walking distance, Jo would find a way to ride it.

Roy caught her watching. "Something I can do for you, Adams?" She'd never heard him call her by anything other than her last name. He raised his volume a notch higher. "Or would you like a goddamn camera to take a picture?"

Heads turned at the sound of his voice.

Tamaryn, as mortified as ever, mouthed the words, *I'm sorry.*

Jo told herself that she was just being a proper hostess by walking away. The show must go on, and all of that.

Bravo. Way to put your foot down.

As she joined Jed's congregation on the far side of the yard, she realized that she was clutching the paper plates so forcefully that her fingers were carving little half-moons into them.

". . . though my father says the bill is sure to die a quick death on the Senate floor."

"What about that congressman from Indiana?" someone asked.

Jed Whitecross grinned. Jo thought it the kind of smile that you dreamed about as a girl in English class in junior high but weren't so certain of when it was leaning over you in the backseat in high school. He wore a tight T-shirt and dark slacks, his tanned face only half visible in the shadows. When

31

he lifted the bottle to his lips, his watch flickered goldly. He wiped his mouth with the back of his hand and said, "Do they have congressmen in Indiana?"

Jo hated herself for chuckling along with the rest of them.

"Killer party, Jo," Penny said. She was fastened to Jed's side like a woman afraid of breaking contact for fear of disappearing. "Great food."

"I have to concur," Jed said, directing his attention to Jo for what she realized was the first time since he'd started coming to town a month ago. The others nodded their agreement. "My specific compliments to whomever is responsible for the corn on the cob."

"I'll let Nin know you liked it. I guess nobody can boil corn like the Eskimos."

"Have we met?" he asked. "Formally?"

"Depends on your definition of formal."

"You work for the town council, right?"

"I'm a real estate agent on loan. Something of a hired peacekeeper. But to be honest, Mr. Whitecross, I feel more like a referee."

"Call me Jed." He said it as if he meant it. "May I call you Jo?"

No, she wanted to say. *No, because I've got at least fifteen years on you and I voted for your father because he's old school and minds his grassroots instincts but I'm afraid your Rolex is too gold for grassroots and no, again, you may not call me Jo.*

"Sure," she said.

"Great. Pen, grab me a beer. I might as well take advantage of Jo's hospitality. And make it an import, if there's any left, and not one of those domestics you brought me last time." He never looked away from Jo as Penelope smiled and dutifully went to the ice chest. "So, Jo, we were just discussing the sanitation bill. What's your opinion?"

"Oh, well, I'm all for sanitation." She displayed her plates and chicken bones. "Some nights more than others."

He chuckled. "Do you mind if I ask your party affiliation?"

"Why, Jed, haven't you heard that I'm notorious for my nonpartisanship?"

"She's registered independent," Penny said, returning with a beer and wiping it dry on the hem of her shirt. "Or should I say *undecided*."

Jo smiled reflexively. "I've never been much for labels."

Jed took a long pull and licked his lips. "To each his own, right?"

"Something like that. Here, let me get those plates."

"To the nonpartisans," Jed toasted. He received several *hear hears,* and bottles clicked against teeth.

As soon as she had the chance, Jo made a strategic withdrawal toward the nearest trash can. *What time is it, anyway? Is it as late as it feels?* When she looked back, Jed was pantomiming a golf swing while the others clung to his oration and Penny stood behind him like a unnoticed caddy waiting to be called onto the green.

Around eleven one of Jed's crew called out for fireworks.

"Yeah, Mom!" The cry was taken up by Nin's tribe, quickly amplified by Matthew and Brady Soza and at least five others belonging to various parents around the yard. "Can we Mom please Dad just for awhile Mom it's not too late Dad . . ."

"What are you sprites *thinking?*" Nin asked in mock surprise, silencing them all. "The Fourth is nearly two weeks away, don't you know that? *Surely* you know that. I don't think anyone here even *has* any fireworks yet. I don't think you can even *buy* them yet."

A dozen little voices argued otherwise.

"Don't you sprites know that it's against the *rules* to pop firecrackers when it's not the Fourth of July? Haven't you learned *anything* in school?"

Her rebuttal only stoked the fires of their demands.

Nin, smiling not unlike a child herself, turned to Jo.

Jo took the cue and hollered across the yard. "You hear that, Sheriff? The natives are demanding fire."

"Yes, ma'am, so they seem to be." Bandy-legged Sheriff Bo Cantrell, known throughout the county as Bottle, stabbed his stubby thumbs in his pockets and strode as close as he dared to the children. "Well, normally I don't cotton to citizens making up the laws as they go along, mind you"—he cast an old warlock's eye upon the kids—"but seeing as how it's a special occasion and all—"

The children sang his praises. Bottle's cheeks lit up like Roman candles.

They only caught the yard on fire once, but Terrell was quick enough with the garden hose that only a single table leg took damage. Jo was reminded of the cat. She looked out into the impenetrable darkness, wondering where it had gone.

Shortly after midnight, the yard lay warm and empty, as if exhaling. The music had been replaced with the constant *reeee!* of cicadas. The crickets had come, and other night things. An echo of charcoal smoke curled through the humid air. The occasional crackle from the bug light signaled another kamikaze mission had ended in defeat.

The five women surveyed the vacant battlefield.

"Wasn't so bad," Lucy said.

"Food was good," Nin agreed.

"What about my banana crème?" Hannah asked. "You sure it was edible?"

"Edible enough that nothing's left but a dented alu-

34

minum pan," Lucy replied.

"Oh. I guess that's good."

"Nah." Lucy shook her head. "Drunks'll eat anything."

Hannah pulled her chair back an inch and looked over at Tamaryn. "You okay?"

Tamaryn sucked on her cigarette, nodded briskly.

"The jerk," Hannah said.

Tamaryn shrugged and took another drag.

Jo shook herself gently from her reverie. She brushed an errant curl from Tamaryn's face. "Help me with the dishes?"

Tamaryn dropped the butt into an empty bottle. "Just waiting for the starter's pistol."

"Bang," Jo said.

Tamaryn broke a butter dish and cursed.

"Now, remember that the Lord is listening," Nin reminded her, picking the shards from the sink.

"I hope so."

"Meaning?"

"Meaning sometimes I wonder."

Nin cleaned away the shattered pieces, used a checkerboard-pattern dish towel to wipe down a counter that was already clean, and set the towel aside with several damp others of its kind. "You can stay with me tonight, if you'd like. Matt and Brady are already asleep in my van."

"No, I'll get them. Roy'll be asleep when I get home. It'll be okay."

"Whatever you think is best."

"I don't think *best* has anything to do with it." She smoldered for a moment, but then brightened suddenly, her eyebrows arching high on her forehead. "But before I dash away, there was one thing I was wondering." She leaned back against the counter. "Hey, Jessler. I have a question."

Jo, Lucy, and Hannah were making room for the remnants in the fridge. Hannah rolled back and forth, delivering lidded bowls in her lap. "Go ahead and ask, but since I already know it's got something to do with Terrell, then I'm not obliged to answer, unless of course I'm really feeling charitable and it's probably too late in the day for that, got it?"

"How long have you two been together?"

"That's your question?"

"Three months?"

"Almost four."

"He's stayed at your place a few times, hasn't he?"

"Watch it now," Lucy spoke up. "That's my baby brother you're talking about."

"So what if he has?" Hannah said. "Yeah, we watch a lot of movies, we stay up late, we read together, it's not like we can go dancing."

"Can I take a guess at something?"

"Could I stop you?"

Tamaryn pointed directly at her, then closed one eye and peered down the length of her arm as if she were sighting a gun. "You haven't slept with him yet. Have you?"

Jo glanced at Hannah, smiling distantly. Of her Crazy Coven, Hannah Jessler was the purest. There was still so much springtime in her, when Jo knew that the rest of them often woke up in the night and had to reach for extra blankets because of the winter in their dreams. Hannah suffered her moments of frustration—being a paraplegic made that hard to avoid—but her innocence was like an elixir for Jo's soul.

"So maybe I have," Hannah said. "I mean, maybe *we* have, together. Done it."

Lucy looked up, scowling.

"I think it's nice that you haven't," Tam said. The mischief in her eyes gave way to soft admiration. "In fact, I think it's about the most wonderful thing I've thought about in a long time."

"Who said that we haven't done it? I never said that."

"Sure you did."

"Well, so maybe we haven't, but you've got to understand that he's not like other guys, Tam, he's what you call shy, you know. Remember shy?"

"So . . . it's not that you don't want to sleep with him. You just haven't."

"It's not that important to me."

"Liar. You want it to happen, don't you?"

"No."

"Excuse me, Miss Pinocchio, but something seems to be growing out of the middle of your face. Let me ask you again. You want it to happen, don't you?"

"On certain days."

"How about days ending in the letter Y?"

Hannah grinned, her face opening like the petals of a flower. *"Desperately."* Then she looked at Lucy and quickly stowed her smile and glowered humorlessly. "But now that I consider it, I'm a ferocious opponent of premarital sex, and I don't even intend to hold Mr. Campbell's hand until we're securely joined in the holy act of legal marriage."

Lucy burst out laughing. Everyone joined her.

Something moved beyond the window.

Hannah didn't notice. She giggled and made a wide-eyed face at Tam. Nin smiled and shook her head.

Jo stood up.

"Don't know if you'd call him shy," Lucy said, "or just plain afraid of messing up."

Hannah patted her leg. "Ah, Luce, he's just old-fashioned."

Jo opened the screen door.

"Boy is fond of tradition, isn't he?"

A June bug flew into the kitchen.

"Jo?" Nin pushed herself away from the sink. "Jo, what's wrong?"

Silence.

A figure separated itself from the shadows. The first thing Jo heard was the crying.

Is it one of the kids? she wondered.

Then she saw the blood.

"I'll be okay now," Penny said. She held fresh ice against her gummy jaw.

The six of them stood on the front porch. They hadn't spoken much in the last half hour, and in their wordless empathy they'd said and understood it all. The quiet telegraph of their thoughts, the Morse of their touch—these were enough. There was a light brushing of fingertips on skin, a moving of hair from damp eyes, a communicating weight in the air.

"I can take you home," Tam offered.

"No, you can't," Jo said. "You've got Hannah and the boys. Let me just—" *Just what?* She felt like extending her arms outward for balance. Step right, fall. Step left, same result. She wanted to say that Nin's van was full and Lucy was driving her mail truck because her car was in the shop again so it was left to Jo, and there, she supposed, you had the crux of the matter. *It's left to me.* All of her life, it was always left to her. The groceries, the checkbook, raising Caroline, planting the garden, touching up the bathroom paint, the bills. And somehow she'd always managed to walk a middle line through it all, which might have made her weak on the stand-up-for-yourself meter, but the groceries got bought and the bills got paid, so there.

"Let me do it," Lucy said. "Her place is on my way."

Jo hesitated only a moment, then acquiesced. It was the most logical plan.

Logical, she thought. *Logical and rational and sensible, and damn.*

Tamaryn said a soft benediction to Penny before leaving. Hannah squeezed her hand. Nin enveloped her in a hug. Jo watched them depart, Tam fitly lifting Hannah into the cab, Nin cooing to her chicks when the sound of the opening van door woke them up.

Lucy and Penelope went to the little mail vehicle, with its steering wheel on the wrong side. It was about the only thing Lucy drove anymore, regardless of whether or not she was an on-duty agent of the Postmaster General. It was the only postal truck in town, and Lucy said as long as she was putting her own gas money in the tank, they'd let her get away with driving it. She slid the rectangular door on its track and guided Penny through. "Find yourself a place there in the back, girl. It's a lot more comfortable than it looks."

Jo watched Tamaryn's taillights fade into the night. Nin's vanished in the opposite direction.

Lucy returned to the porch and folded her arms tightly across her chest, cocking her head one way and her hip the other. "So what are we going to do?"

Jo tried to get another look at Penny, but she could make out nothing through the truck's windshield. *And when we can stand it no longer, we abide some more.* She was surprised it was so difficult to meet Lucy's stare. The woman's eyes were un-relenting. Jo touched her lightly on the face. "It's late, Luce. For now, we sleep."

Lucy pushed her tongue around behind her cheek, as if waiting for more. Then she got in the truck and started the engine. It idled in the driveway, its diminutive engine sputtering a complaint every few seconds. Lucy put it in gear and leaned out the door. "Thing about sleeping, Jo, eventually you always wake up."

She pulled into the street and drove away.

Chapter Three

"Want the good news or the bad news?"

The question hit Jo in the face the moment she walked through the fingerprinted glass door of the Belle Springs Chamber of Commerce. It was Thursday morning and she was late because of Penelope's lip; she'd rolled endlessly in bed last night, seeing the blood and the bruises in the way that mariners must dream of storms when they try to sleep in a tossing ship. Though she hadn't eaten breakfast, the usually welcome scent of donuts in the lobby made her stomach clench uncomfortably.

She deposited her briefcase on the nearest desk, followed it with a stack of worn manila folders, and picked her fingers through her hair. "Good to see you too, Felix. How are we for coffee this morning?"

Felix deflected the question with a wave. "Good news or bad?"

"I hate it when people ask that. Why don't they just spit it out?"

"Drama, I suppose. Humanity lives for it. Especially tragedy. Now be a sport and play along."

"*Hola,* Jo," Carmen said, whisking by in one of her trademark skirts. Did they still make size threes? Apparently someone did.

"Morning, Carmen."

"*Washington Post* is on your desk."

"Thank you. I hope they left us alone today."

"That you, Josephine?" Martin called from the next room.

"No, Marty, this is her stunt double."

"The mayor called."

Jo frowned. "The mayor called *me?*"

"It was your phone that I answered. And it was the mayor on the other end. So yes."

"When?"

"Ten minutes ago. Are you late again?"

Jo closed her eyes for a moment to realign her compass, but that turned out to be a bad idea because there was Tamaryn hunkered down behind her eyelids, telling her that someone had to pay. She opened her eyes and Felix was still there. Even in his alligator-skin boots, he stood barely five and a half feet tall.

"So how about it? Which do you want first? The lady or the tiger?"

"I give up. Give me the good, please. Call me strange, but I'm not much for tragedy."

"The good news," Felix said, relishing it, "is that the consortium's team, which is meeting out at the site this morning, didn't bring along any media."

"There are people out at the site?" Her stomach only got worse.

"So I understand it."

"Right now?"

"Five or six drove over from D.C. before the sun was up. They stopped for something to eat at Sally Fong's diner. Sally called the moment they left."

"That's the *good* news?"

"You still here, Josephine?" Martin stuck his graying head around the corner. He looked like a newspaper editor in the middle of a big story. "I want you to get out there to the site and see that everyone makes nice. Bottle's already on his way."

"Get out where, specifically?" Jo gestured indistinctly. "What do you want me to do, Marty? Drive out to an empty field and watch people in shoes from Saks traipse around through the mud?"

"No empty field. Pete Musket's place."

"Wonderful." She put her hand on her mouth to hold back an oath. She had promised Caroline that she'd stopped swearing.

"Felix," Martin said, "get a thermos of coffee. Go with her."

"As you command, my lord."

"What's the bad?" Jo said through her fingers.

"Excuse me?"

"The bad news, Felix. I'm on the edge of my seat here."

"Oh, right. Seems that old Peter Musket has himself an Indian."

"Come again?"

"A Shawnee, evidently. Near as I can tell, Musket has scrounged up an honest-to-Geronimo tribal personage. As in Native American. A true aboriginal individual, pejoratively known as a redskin or injun. As of yesterday, this man has been living out there on Musket's land, right around where the tennis courts are supposed to be. Or is it the sauna?"

"You've got to be kidding me."

"It gets better."

"Felix, please . . ."

"The guy's living in a wigwam."

Jo stared at him incredulously.

"And he's asking for a TV crew."

Jo shook her head slowly. "Shit."

"Our feelings exactly."

"Marty?"

"Yes, dear?"

"Call Hannah. Ask her to radio the sheriff and tell him we're on our way."

"Got it." He ducked around the corner.

"Carmen?"

"Ma'am?"

"I need a new poll. We vote Tuesday on this mess. That's five days from now. And we have a community meeting the Monday before. I want to know where the town stands right now so we can compare it to the numbers after whatever happens with our Shawnee friend. Word of this is going to go grassfire before the day's over, and everybody's going to have an opinion. If Monday's meeting is going to turn into a wrestling match, I want to know about it beforehand. Can you rustle up enough volunteers from the election board to do that for me?"

"*Sí.*"

"Good. Thanks. You're coming with me, Felix?"

"So the sultan has commanded, my lady."

"Okay. Get a camera. And do you still have that little tape recorder?"

"Of course, amateur spy that I am."

"Bring it along."

He dashed to do her bidding.

"Felix, one more thing. You better make that *two* thermoses of coffee."

"Why? Are you having some kind of premonition?"

"Just get the coffee." She picked up her briefcase. "And grab the funnies page while you're at it. I never have time to read the comics anymore."

She went outside to wait for him. The sun was doing its thing to the Appalachians, adorning the red oaks with crowns of gold. Belle Springs lay in a valley surrounded on three sides by hills thick with buckeye trees and patches of dogwood and laurel. Jo had played in these places as a child, but she hadn't roamed the wooded corridors in years. She tried to concentrate on one particularly bright memory of watching a gray fox give birth in the scooped-out insides of a fallen log, but thoughts of Pete Musket kept intruding.

Enough, please, she thought, halfway between a surrender and a prayer. *My already cracked and leaking cup runneth over.*

And if it wasn't Pete distracting her then it was Penelope, and the way the blood bubbled from her lip when she tried to talk.

Whenever Jo told someone that she drove an import, she wasn't referring to a Mercedes or anything from Asia. She meant an Opel. The scrappy sedan had been in her care since she graduated college, the only expensive thing she'd ever bought new in her life. Twenty years later the Opel looked like it had survived atmospheric reentry. Sometimes Jo felt that way herself.

"You think it's the weather?" Felix asked. Papers were bundled on his lap.

"What do you mean?"

"The heat. This bloody nightmare of a summer. Everybody's fed up with it. Global warming, they say. The government finally admitted that, you know. The polar ice caps are melting, the Atlantic is rising, and fairly soon our quaint little town will be oceanfront property."

"Terrific. Then I can sell my beach house for an exorbitant amount and move somewhere sane."

"Is there such a place?"

"I'll send you a postcard." She drove through Belle Springs' modest business district along Meridian Avenue, the street that bisected the city into two nearly evenly sized halves. Centered around the historic yet secretly dilapidated county courthouse, the downtown area wasn't breathing without assistance; if not for the steady influx of tourists like serum through an IV, the little bookstores and antique shops would have flatlined years ago.

But then there was the Potomac. A mere six-mile drive, a mini-mecca for tourists. The result of this fortuitous geographic layout was the region's continued economic heartbeat. Beyond the river lay a thin ribbon of Maryland, and then you had Pennsylvania and Gettysburg and all the Americana a person could stand. Belle Springs was the crossroads between towns that sold Quaker quilts and the town that ran the world. The president's house was only a hundred miles away.

I'll be okay, she heard Penny say again.

She tightened her fingers around the wheel and pushed a little harder on the accelerator.

They left the city limits doing seventy.

"Let the billboards begin," Felix announced.

And so they did. Stabbed into the dirt on the shoulder of the road, nailed to fenceposts and utility poles, the signs appeared about half a mile out of town and thickened as the highway neared the war zone. DON'T SELL OUR HERITAGE.

DEVELOPMENT + CHANGE = THE FUTURE.

KEEP FREE OF DEE CEE.

VOTE YES FOR YOUR TOMORROW!

And then, somewhat enigmatically, PUSH LIFE.

"Like Burma Shave signs gone mad," Jo said.

"Burma what?"

"Nothing. Before your time."

They rode in silence for a minute, then Felix said, "My mother thinks I'm gay."

Jo looked over at him quizzically. "What are you talking about?"

"It's because of Lisa. You remember Lisa? Sandy hair and

dimples? I haven't dated anyone since her. Alas, she perforated my heart. That was almost three years ago."

"Three years? So I'll be gay along with you if that's the deciding criterion."

Felix flushed. "I apologize. I don't know where that came from."

VOTE RURAL, the next sign implored.

"What about Carmen?" Jo suggested. "Isn't she available?"

"Carmen? You're jesting, right? In case you haven't noticed, my lady, the dear señorita bears every characteristic necessary to obtaining employment as a photographer's dream. As they say, she is somewhat out of my league."

"That's the trouble with people these days, Felix. Too many leagues."

CONGRESS KEEP OUT.

She let up on the gas, signaled left, and guided the car off the highway. Before the opening bids had been made on the acreage, the road servicing this undeveloped glade had been nothing but hard-packed dirt built on a convenient upthrust of limestone. Since the consortium had made its play, however, the county had graveled the road. Now little orange surveyor's flags dotted the grass. The land itself, of which the consortium was asking 110 acres, was legally owned by three separate and unrelated parties. Clayton County claimed about a third, and almost twice as much belonged to Sheridan Industries. The Sheridan execs had already gleefully embraced the sale, and the county would hand over its share if next Tuesday's vote went the way of current polls, which showed that voters thought the influx of Washington cash too lucrative to ignore. So all that was left to fight over was a thin slice of weeds belonging to Pete Musket, who had somehow managed to stay out of the drunk tank long enough to find himself at the center of the storm.

"How about that coffee?" Jo asked.

Felix handed her a cup.

Several trees in a copse of elderly basswoods were tagged with fluorescent paint—the mark of death. The basswoods would have to give way to a parking garage. When word of a potential chainsawing got around, the local environmentalists rallied to the cause of the opposition. But the copse wasn't much of a woodland, perhaps no more than three dozen members strong, so it wasn't as if the consortium could be accused of deforestation. Nevertheless, some green-minded bard had put up a sign that read FOR EVERY LEAF THAT ISN'T THERE, WE LOSE ANOTHER BREATH OF AIR.

"Looks like the party's started without us," Jo observed. Five vehicles sat in the clearing at the end of the road. Jo recognized three of them: Musket's disco-age El Camino, the Sheridan rep's pampered '57 Thunderbird, and Bottle's police cruiser. A flatbed pickup was nosed up behind the El Camino. Beside it was a black SUV with tinted windows. Jo parked several yards away. The Opel coughed twice and died. They sat there and listened to the engine ticking hotly.

"Tell her you're dating me," Jo said.

"Who?"

"Your mother."

"You think it would help?"

"She's probably not much older than I am. I don't know if it would help, but at least it would be safe. I'm middle-aged and harmless." Her stomach still rocking uneasily, she climbed out of the car. She brought her briefcase along, if for no other reason than to look official. Sometimes it helped.

"Safe, as in you wouldn't try anything on me?" Felix wondered, trailing her toward the small knot of people. "That doesn't sound very exciting."

"Exciting I'm not. I have life insurance, I don't eat excessive amounts of red meat, I'm usually in bed by eleven, I floss. God, do I floss. I'm a mother's perfect daughter-in-law. It's kind of amazing that they're not fighting over me. You'd think they'd be lining their sons up outside my door. Good morning, Sheriff."

Cantrell nodded as she approached. "If you say so." He eyeballed the strangers in the suits who stood about twenty yards away in the open grassland. They were pointing here and there and talking too low to be heard. One of them took notes on a Palm Pilot. "Spare some of that coffee?"

Felix handed him a thermos. "I've got some extra cups in the car." He ran to fetch them.

Jo followed Cantrell's stare. "What's the situation here?"

"Well, you know what happens when you turn up the heat really high under a pot of water and leave the lid on too long?"

"Yes."

"That's the situation. Exhibit A, five representatives of the developers' deal-making team, led by the one in the funny suit there, the one with all the wrinkles in it. What's it called?"

"Linen. It's supposed to have wrinkles. It's the style."

"Yeah. Swell. That's what I get for letting my subscription to *GQ* expire. The man's name is Ashcroft. Mike or Mark or something like that. He's some sort of bigshot for the company that'll have controlling ownership of the country club. And from what I can tell, he's also slicker than pig snot on a steel floor. Exhibit B, Musket's new sideshow, Earnest Paul Tenfeathers, hailing from parts unknown."

Jo looked toward the homestead. All that remained of it was a barnlike structure made of river rock, with a flat roof and a few windows of thick, grime-coated glass. The somber gray stones had been quarried from the banks of the Potomac, their irregular shapes cemented together with black mortar that had been holding strong since long before the Depression. Wild geraniums crawled around its base. The place had a sad, lost look to it that Jo, in her present state of mind, found unduly depressing. The house that had stood beside it was now so much dust, along with the family that had built it. Originally constructed as a birthing barn for livestock, local legend claimed that the building had been used as a way station along the Underground Railroad that smuggled slaves to freedom during the Civil War. Since then it had served through the years as a horse stable, toolshed, and most recently as a flophouse when Musket went on a weekend binge.

Musket himself sat on an overturned produce crate. Tenfeathers, a gaunt sixty-year-old who would have looked only minimally Indian had it not been for the turquoise beads woven into his long gray hair, occupied a sagging lawn chair, smoking a pipe.

"Exhibit C is the wigwam," Cantrell said. "It's around back of the barn."

"Can I talk to him?"

"Who, Tenfeathers?"

"Someone has to. Better me than a television crew."

"You've got a point. I'll introduce you."

"Where's the Sheridan rep?" she asked as they made their way toward the old men.

"Taking pictures of the wigwam."

"Pictures? What for?"

"That way he can show everyone how ludicrous the damn thing is so they won't hold it against him when he puts it to the torch. Can't say that I disagree with him. This whole operation is one bearded lady away from turning into a carnival. Pete, you know Ms. Adams here."

Pete studied her with his rheumy, watchful eyes, then nodded. "Greetings, ma'am."

"Hello, Pete," she said. "Care to introduce me to your friend?"

Tenfeathers didn't look up. He smoked his pipe in silence, playing the role of the inscrutable shaman.

"You gentlemen aren't going to make my life very easy, are you?"

Neither of them replied.

"They do that a lot," the sheriff said.

"Charming."

Felix arrived with both thermoses and half a dozen cups. Upon Jo's suggestion, he scurried over to offer some to Ashcroft's people, who greeted the gift with sincere appreciation.

Peace offering, Jo thought. *If only all wounds were so easily healed.* She was considering the logistical feasibility of sending Felix on coffee runs to Israel, Northern Ireland, and various warring African states when she smelled the cologne.

She turned around to find the Sheridan representative standing behind her.

"Fancy meeting you here," he said.

She noted his camera. "Since when were you a shutterbug?"

"The company thought it would be a good idea. Documentation. For the record, just in case. You never can tell how these conflicts might unfold over time." His voice was still like the Appalachians themselves, deep and rolling, at times intimidating but always bursting with life. "I thought it must be you when I heard the car backfire. Surprised that old beauty's still running."

"Winter mornings are a challenge," Jo admitted.

"How's Caroline?"

"Wonderful and spiteful. Nothing new. Planning for law school. I'd tell you that you should be proud but I know that you already are."

He smiled softly and half-closed his eyes. "One more reason to love the old Opel. We might not have Caroline without it. If you ever get a hankering to sell it . . ."

"I won't," Jo said, more sharply than she'd intended. "Sorry." She looked from Pete Musket to Tenfeathers, then out to Ashcroft's gang and all the orange plastic flags snickering in the breeze. Though the scene was unthreatening, even placid, Jo wasn't fooled. The ocean looked the same way only hours before a hurricane. "Please don't let this turn into a firefight, Chuck."

Charles Adams brought the camera to his face and snapped her picture. "I'm afraid that's like asking the matador to spare the bull. I want this deal, Joey."

"Pardon me, but you no longer have nickname privileges."

"Fine. But this sale is going through, firefight or otherwise. So do us all a favor and stay out of the way." He took another picture of her, then left her alone.

She could do nothing but stand there in the weeds and wish she had the audacity to give him the finger.

She bought more tape on the way home that night.

It was already sundown when she pulled into the driveway beside Caroline's convertible Beetle. She shut off the car and sat there with her hand on the key, uncertain if she could move without melting. Had it not been for her skin, her bones would have been puddled on the floorboard between her feet. How many phone calls had she made today? Her ear ached and was letting her know about it. How many miles had she racked up? Her feet were in cahoots with her ear. How many smiles had she faked and instructions had she issued and white lies had she spoken? Her mouth joined the revolution of offended body parts, leaving no willing piece of her behind to keep her from falling.

Still, she managed to make it to the house. Hot baths were her only solace these days.

But elephants first.

She formed a length of tape into a loop and fastened an elephant onto Thursday.

Earnest Paul Tenfeathers hadn't turned into a problem. Yet. He asked her for a bit of air time, ostensibly to voice the grievances of the collective American Indian peoples, but actually so he could bag a few bucks and get on with his life. A TV tabloid was bound to pay to see him chain himself to the ground on the day the bulldozers arrived. So call it extortion if you like, but Jo was asking the town council to put up a little quiet money to get the man on his way. Better a thousand dollars less in the Belle Springs petty cash drawer than a protest march of every disgruntled native within a three-state radius, all bedecked in traditional plumes and leathers for the benefit of the viewing audience. Too many people these days were looking for a reason to rouse the rabble. Jo was a holdout believer in the peace pipe.

On her way to the bathroom at the end of the upstairs hall, she paused outside of Caroline's room. Music played quietly inside. Jo lifted her hand to knock—

No, check that. Caroline was probably studying. She was attending a summer course of college-level algebra to earn a few credits ahead of time. She had her study-music playing. Jo placed her palm flat against the door.

Can you hear me, Sweet?

Part of her said open it. Just open the door and say hi. Like you used to. Like Caroline was still seven and it was okay to barge in on her. But the other voice knew better. It gave her a preview of the ensuing conversation:

Hi, honey. Whatcha doing?

Mom. That's called a door. It was shut.

So that's mothers for you. We're beasts sometimes. Are you busy?

Only if you call preparing for my future busy.

Yeah, algebra. Whew. I know how it is. There was this time in school when I—

Do you want something, Mother?

Jo took her hand off the door. Yes, she did want something. Now if only a kind person would tell her what that something was, she'd be fine.

The only thing she knew for certain was that she was in no mood for a fight. She left Caroline to her future and drew a steaming bath.

Later, in one of the few moments she could spare for reflection, she'd looked back and tried to remember what she was doing at the moment the call came through. Though she wouldn't be able to recall the details, as it happened she was talking to the Pope.

Darkness had fallen upon the world hours ago. The town settled down to rest, the heat of the day leaking from the bricks of its antebellum buildings. The streets were cooled with the coming of the moon. Jo's sofa was her desk, strewn with forms both signed and unsigned, documents read and unread, phone numbers called and uncalled. The results of Carmen's impromptu poll showed that fifty-nine percent of registered voters thought having Washington power brokers around was a good idea, the numbers split fairly evenly down party lines. A few folks didn't like the idea of the proposed helipad, its choppers stirring up a racket in the middle of the night when Congressman So-and-So arrived with his mistress for a midnight tryst, but they said they'd still vote *yea*. And only a third wanted to tack on a half-percent sales tax to pay for the necessary road improvements. But as for the deal itself, it appeared to be in the bag.

Jo looked up from her work to the television. What station was this? She scanned the room for the remote, noticed that it was at least four feet out of reach, and decided it wasn't worth the effort. One of the big news channels was doing an exposé on the Vatican. She hadn't seen a shot of the Pope lately. He seemed to be giving Methuselah a run for his geriatric money.

". . . yet the Catholic church," the reporter proclaimed, "views itself as neither behind the times nor gender-biased in defending its traditional stance of not accepting women into the ranks of the priesthood."

"Of course not," Jo said to no one in particular. "That way the men can keep all of those great hats to themselves."

The Pope was saying something about the vital role of the female species.

Jo wondered why he reminded her of Pete Musket.

Now the Pope was blessing all women in general.

"Save it," she said. "Hock that ring and feed a small nation for a month."

She felt the ire as it came, but did nothing to divert it. It wasn't this good-intentioned Polish priest that pulled the tide of her anger, nor any religious doctrine in particular, but something deeper. Something restless that couldn't be pointed at and named with a *There, that's the trouble*. The trouble, whatever it was, had lived in her too long and was too elusive to grasp. Like old wind.

"And while you're at it," she said, ignoring the open folder in her lap, "get yourself into the twenty-first century and give homosexuals a break, because I think Felix really is gay and I don't want his mother condemning him because she's Catholic and you told her to."

Stop. Wait. What was she *doing*?

Freaking out, if you don't mind. You couldn't blame her, with everything steam-cooking inside of her like it was. The land deal had been a boon for her in many ways—a salary hike, a ton of respect, and more than a small booster shot to her reputation—but she'd paid the price.

"You know how much vaccine the Vatican is worth?" she asked the pontiff, who wisely chose not to respond. "If you melted it all down and traded it for medicine to be shipped off to the Sudan—"

The phone rang and Jo reached for it without a hitch in her commentary.

"—then we could wipe out malaria and take a big chunk out of HIV as well. Just a suggestion you might want to consider the next time you're polishing the flatware in the holy kitchen. Hello?"

She always answered the phone with a heady note in her voice, a sound almost of expectation, as if this caller might be different—someone she thought lost in a war or a storm, or someone she'd known for a night in a foreign city. But it was only Hannah.

"Jo, it's me, and I didn't want to be the one to have to call you but the others made me because that's what I do, I'm a phone person, I'm sorry."

"Hannah, slow down." Jo sat up, displacing her files. Her eyes focused, her thoughts cleared. She forgot about the Pope. "What's the matter?"

"The others are already at the hospital"—Hannah's voice was glass, ready to break at the next hitched word—"and I asked Esther if she could cover for me if you want to pick me up on your way . . ."

Jo lunged for the remote and shut off the TV. Hannah's tone, her obvious fear, chilled her skin. "Please, Hannah. Tell me what happened. Who's hurt?"

Silence, then: "Penelope."

The room darkened. She reached out for the sofa and found it just in time.

"It's bad this time, Jo, really bad, so maybe if you could throw a few things in a bag for her, she'd appreciate it, because you know how yucky those hospital gowns are."

"Yeah. Yucky." Jo swallowed a constriction in her throat. "I'm on my way."

She barged in on Caroline, who protested only until she heard what had happened and then hurried to lend a hand in whatever way she could. A sense of solidarity snapped back around them like elastic that had been pulled for too long without release. And for that, at least, Jo was thankful. She didn't bother dragging out her carry-on, but grabbed the nearest makeshift sack she saw, a pillowcase from the set of pink sheets, and stuffed it full of socks and hairbrushes and a pack of mint gum, because nobody wanted to be trapped in the hospital with bad breath.

She dropped Caroline off at Nin's to help Dorothy with the kids, and tried to drive like a woman still in control of her small edge of the world.

Chapter Four

Thank God the chair was collapsible.

Even still, it barely fit in the trunk. The angle was all wrong. Jo forced down the lid, pressing on it until it clicked. She got in the car and slammed it into gear, causing the Opel's tires to chirp against the pavement.

"So what happened?" she asked, hitting the lights.

Hannah sat on her hands to keep them still. She normally gestured in the same manner she spoke, as if this frenetic motion compensated for not being ambulatory. Earlier she'd been wearing her Rapunzel hair in a bun, but it had jiggled loose when Jo lifted her into the car, and now most of it hung in her face. She shook her head repeatedly.

"Hannah, get a grip. It's going to be okay. It's *always* okay with us, don't you know that? It always is. We're always safe. So just settle down." Jo used the voice she thought of as her English nanny tone. Though edged with concern, it was also a stony voice, a let's-not-go-overboard voice. "Were you the one who took the call at the station?"

Hannah's hair moved up and down when she nodded.

"Who placed the call?"

"Her brother." Sniff. "Joshua."

Jo slowed down at one of the town's few stoplights, but the dark intersection was deserted so she rolled through without stopping. "Where did it happen?"

"Huh?"

"*Where?*"

"I sent the . . . the ambulance to the Riverhouse."

"He hit her in a public place?"

"No. Yes. I don't know." Hannah finally slid her hands out from under her legs. She fished a pack of tissues from her purse and blew her nose. "I'm not sure. It could have been anywhere. The bathroom. Maybe in the parking lot. Jo, things like this aren't supposed to happen to people we know."

"Did anyone see it? Were there witnesses?"

"I don't know."

"Did Josh at least beat the shit out of the guy?"

"I don't know that either."

"Is she pressing charges? That girl will never learn, will she? Remember that guy a year ago, the one who about caused her to starve herself to death because he only liked skinny women? Why is she always drawn to bullies? Is Terrell or Bottle or someone at the hospital taking her statement?"

"Jo, please . . ."

"Did anyone call since then to let you know how she's doing?"

Hannah put her hands over her ears and leaned her head back against the seat. Jo glanced over and read the body language: *Enough, please. Just drive.*

Jo drove.

Clayton County Hospital was still five or six blocks away. *Nighttime runs to the hospital are either pregnancies or trouble,* Jo thought, taking the corners too fast and paying the stop signs only token respect. The bastard had smacked Penelope again. Jo checked her mirror to make sure a city cop hadn't jumped her for speeding. The bastard had smacked her and this time Penny was in trouble. When the hospital came into view, Jo's pulse quickened. Jed Whitecross was a law student at Georgetown, his father was chairman of the U.S. Senate Committee on Armed Services, and how did you butt heads with a man who owned a yacht?

"This isn't going to be easy," she said.

Hannah sniffled again. "What did you say?"

"Nothing."

She swung up to the emergency room under all the glaring lights.

She wrestled the wheelchair out of the trunk. Hannah opened her door and Jo guided the chair into position. And here they were again. She would have liked to say that she'd gotten used to this. This helping. This lifting and positioning and good-natured grumbling, but somewhere in the front of her mind was always this *remembering*. Hannah on horseback. Hannah kickboxing. Just Hannah.

Now *just Hannah* was this contraption. The chair itself was sporty, the cutting edge of technology and all that crap, but even the fuzzy dice Tamaryn had tied to the armrest didn't dull the blade. The knife worked in their hearts whenever they let it.

"Closer," Hannah suggested. It was one of those words that becomes a fixture in the vocabulary after an accident. Jo had thought of making a list of those phrases and reading it aloud whenever she found herself taking life for granted: *closer, careful, gently, thanks.* They were good words to use. She leaned down and Hannah put her arms around her neck. The door was open as wide as it would go, Jo was stooped halfway inside, and the chair was wedged awkwardly between them. It was never any easier.

Jo bent even further, smelling her friend's skin and the lingering scent of her expensive perfume. Hannah wasn't frivolous with her money, but her weakness was Bulgari. Jo hadn't bought any perfume since the previous century. She started to lift.

"Something's wrong," Hannah said, adjusting herself.

"You're not doing something right."

Afraid of further sharpening the edge in Hannah's voice, Jo tried a different approach. She put one arm high on Hannah's back and the other under her knees. Nothing but dead weight down there. Jo had seen too many movies where the hero dragged a body around as if it were a mere inconvenience. That was such a laugher. No one knew how cumbersome all that water, muscle, and bone really was until they had to help their crippled friend out of a low-riding import.

She lifted.

Her back immediately cried out.

Hannah hung on, the look on her face an alloy of annoyance and resignation.

Hefting her burden as best she could, Jo backed up heavily, hoping the chair was still behind her. Now the pain really sank its teeth into her lower back. She swiveled around. It was plain that Hannah wanted to help but at the same time she gave herself up as half a woman. Jo bumped Hannah's feet against the door. Then her own shin hit the chair, causing it to roll at least two feet before it stopped.

"Great," Hannah said. "You forgot to set the brake."

Jo couldn't reply. Her teeth were too tightly fixed together. She straightened up as best she could and took a single, clumsy step toward the chair.

"You can't try to put me in without the brake."

"We'll see," Jo hissed through rigid jaws. She aimed her burden at its target, and then all at once bent down and released her load and simultaneously stepped toward the chair, fresh lightning bolts sizzling up her spine.

It almost worked.

Gravity took over in a rush. The chair moved. Hannah's slender butt missed the seat. Jo tripped, tried to snag the chair, but that meant letting go, which she did reflexively—

and Hannah went down. Hannah released her hold on Jo's neck in time to break her fall. She didn't land hard, but Jo swore at herself anyway, angry at her own inability to perform a task that every Hollywood schmuck handled with such aggravating aplomb. Though Hannah was now sitting on the ground, Jo hung on to her flaccid legs while simultaneously groping for the chair. She was quickly losing her balance.

Hannah swiped at her. "Just let go of me!"

"I'm sorry."

"Get that thing over here where I can reach it."

Jo lowered her legs and jumped after the chair. "It was my fault."

"You're right. Here, I'll do it." She slammed the brakes into place over the wheels with practiced ferocity and dragged her lower body closer like a mermaid across the beach.

Jo stood behind the chair, holding it so tightly that her fingers turned white, feeling ashamed and not knowing exactly why. "Let me help you . . ."

"Just . . . stay . . ." Hannah hauled herself up with a growl. ". . . *back.*" She twisted as she settled herself in her seat, then used her pant legs as handles to jerk her feet onto their aluminum rests.

When she was finally situated, she sat there staring at the dual doors of the emergency entrance, breathing coarsely.

"Are you through?" Jo asked.

Hannah answered her by flicking off the brakes.

Jo handed her the bulging pillowcase, then pushed.

The doors parted as the women broke an invisible detector, and the air that rushed out to greet them was several degrees cooler than that outside. Though Jo had been bracing herself for it, the hospital's sensory blitzkrieg caught her off-guard nonetheless: the gleaming tiles, the smell of freshly washed surfaces fastened over layers of other, less pleasing scents, the sounds of a distant television and all the cookie-cutter wall art that must have come from a factory that mass-produced psychologically nonthreatening prints for medical facilities and mid-range hotels the world over. Jo realized that somewhere, someone was actually paid to produce such ersatz art. At least plastic plants gave the illusion of life.

They got directions to Penelope's room and headed that way without a word.

Steering the chair with one hand, Jo gave Hannah's shoulder a squeeze.

Hannah reached up, found Jo's fingers, and held on.

There is no such thing as the human eye. Nor the brain. Jo concluded this the moment she pushed Hannah from the elevator. Retinas and cerebellums are the cheap cameras and computers of the body, one to snap the picture and the other to process it. Really there is only the heart. It doesn't matter what we perceive. Nothing is real until the heart makes it so. Though existing as nothing but metaphor, it filters and judges, relishes and revolts, cringes and exalts by extremes. For all intents and purposes, the heart is the torch for which the rest of the ungainly human sconce is built.

There were five of them outside Penny's door.

Not the smallest piece of a second elapsed between the instant Jo saw the people gathered around Penelope's room and the flooding of her body with all the history and emotion and other nonsense those faces carried with them. There were pages inside of her for each of them, countless volumes for some, mere Post-it notes for others. There was dear Nin. She sat with Penelope's parents, speaking softly to them in that steady, soothing way of hers. She wore one of her usual shapeless housedresses and her whalebone earrings. Lucy Campbell stood with her back to the wall, working at her nails with an emery board, which was a secret code for barely holding herself together. She was Jo's age to the day, almost to the hour; they always celebrated that event together, minus the year that Caroline had been in the hospital in Baltimore with pneumonia. Lucy hated not being there, but there was that old saw about the postman that kept her from leaving work. Through sleet and snow and all of that. Lucy claimed there wasn't a mail carrier alive who didn't curse the dead soul of whoever coined that aggravating little bromide. Tamaryn Soza was at the vending machine, wearing sweatpants and a halter top. Jo had no doubt that Tam was sockless inside her tennis shoes. As for being pantyless under her sweats, that was fifty-fifty. Tam slugged the vending machine with the heel of her hand, and apparently her violence paid off, because she snatched her plunder from the slot and tore it open with her teeth.

Jo kept rolling.

Hannah held her hand tighter.

Everyone looked up.

Jo didn't know much of Penny's family. They were the kind who'd lived in town all their lives and contentedly raised honest West Virginian children and kept their lawns in good repair. Invariably they had a relative who'd died of black lung disease. If you lived in Oklahoma, Jo supposed, your heritage was the wheat field. In the Appalachians it was the coal mine. Penny's father bore its mark in the wrinkles around his mouth. Jo had a few notes concerning the man jotted down in her mind, but nothing worth capital letters.

Tamaryn came running.

"How is she?" Jo demanded, bracing herself on the wheelchair.

"Don't know. Doctor's supposed to give us an update any minute now."

"Is it bad?"

"They didn't carry her in on a stretcher if that's what you mean."

"She walked?"

"More or less. Joshua brought her."

"Where is he now?"

"Lucy sent him for food. Said all of his pacing was driving her nuts. He's really strung out by all of this. God, Jo, they won't let me smoke in here."

"How did you find out what happened?"

"Suzie Switchboard here." She nodded down at Hannah.

"You haven't spoken with anyone yet? A nurse or someone?"

"I haven't been here that long. Roy threw a fit about staying with the boys. Said he was supposed to be at the lodge tonight. Whatever." She started to say more, but then the tendons in her neck went taut and her eyes flared. "Whitecross put her in the *emergency room,* Jo. He could have *killed* her."

"Maybe so." Jo thought better of trying to douse Tamaryn's flames. Yes, Jed could have killed her, so odds were strong that anything Jo said at this point about taking it easy would only have the opposite effect.

"I mean Jesus Christ, Jo, we're standing around here with our thumbs up our asses and *he's still out there.*"

Nin stood up when Tamaryn's voice took on new volume.

"Am I the only one who sees something wrong with this picture?" Tam wanted to know, looking around at the rest of them. "Huh? Where the hell's the sheriff at?" This last bit she directed at Hannah. "If he's not here, then I assume you sent him to make an arrest."

"No one's pressed charges yet."

"Pressed charges?" Tamaryn blinked dramatically, as if she were standing amongst cave dwellers and unable to make herself understood. *"Pressed charges?"* She turned a full circle on her toes, made a fist, pressed it to her lips, and breathed deliberately.

Then Nin was beside her. Immediately Tamaryn leaned against her.

"I dropped Caroline off with the kids," Jo said, determined to remain rational.

Nin put an arm around Tam's waist. "Thank you. She is real good with them."

"Do you know anything about what happened?"

Nin considered it. She seemed unfazed by the chaotic energy passing into her from Tamaryn by way of spiritual osmosis. To Jo's renewed amazement, Nin sublimated whatever coarse feelings she might have had the way a farmer turns hard earth to make way for tender new seeds. "I spoke a bit with Joshua. But he didn't have much to offer." She turned her head just enough so that she could look Tamaryn in the eye. "You want to sit down, honey?"

Tam nuzzled her head against Nin's shoulder. Just like that, the fight had fled her. "No. I'll be okay."

Jo looked past them. Lucy stared at her, still leaning on the wall. Telepathy happened:

You seeing all of this, Josephine Adams?

Yes.

You looking real hard at it?

Yes. Shut up and get over here.

Lucy pushed herself away from the wall and joined their congregation.

"How are you?" Jo asked her, because those were the kind of stupid things you found yourself saying at times like this.

Even to people who knew that wasn't what you were thinking. "Never mind. Dumb question."

Lucy pointed at Hannah's lap. "What's that?"

"Some stuff for Penny. It's Jo's. Clothes and things."

"In a pillowcase?"

"I was rushed," Jo said.

"Happen to bring any food?"

"Didn't cross my mind."

"Here." Tam broke her chocolate bar in half.

"Normally," Lucy said, accepting the offer and taking a bite, "I'd refuse on the grounds of needing to maintain my girlish figure, but . . ." She didn't finish, just chewed.

"Has anyone been out to the Riverhouse lately?" Jo asked.

"You kidding?" Tam shook her head. "Come on, Jo, we've got families. My bar-hopping days are behind me."

"I have never been there," Nin said. "I don't believe I ever had any bar-hopping days."

"What about you, Jessler?" Tam asked. "You and Terrell ever give the place a try?"

"No. I'm not much of a dancer. Two left feet."

"Right."

Lucy licked chocolate from her fingers. "What difference does it make?"

Jo shrugged. "I just thought someone might know some of Jed's friends, not that knowing such a thing would help . . ."

Tamaryn balled the candy wrapper and tossed it in the general vicinity of the wastepaper can. "Yeah, I know who his friends are. You got your law school frat boys, your Capitol Hill lobbyists, and your groupies who get off by hanging out with a senator's son. Oh, and of course your everyday, garden-variety young millionaires who think it's cool slumming it in suburbia. Just your regular, all-American crowd."

Jo remembered one of the signs: *Keep free of Dee Cee.*

"Maybe we should all sit down," she suggested.

"Maybe we should all stand up," Lucy said. She refused to look away.

"Maybe. We'll talk."

"When?"

"Later. This isn't the place. I want to say hello to her parents."

Lucy stepped aside to let her pass. But she kept staring.

Jo wished she had the answers they were demanding of her. Since when had she become everyone's Buddha? Already she'd played the likely scenario in her mind: Bottle gets wind of what happened but says he won't touch the case unless Penelope makes the request herself or the D.A.'s office files charges on her behalf. For his part, the D.A. deflects the choice back at Penelope, because he's got too much to consider lately, what with the consortium breathing down one side of his neck and the opposition steaming up the other. Not to mention the fact that he's an elected official and the Whitecross household isn't one you want on the wrong side of the trenches when the votes start flying. The Whitecrosses barbecue with the Kennedys on Labor Day, for crying out loud. So nobody cries foul. The bad guys walk. The good guys suck it up. Life in the Milky Way goes on.

Would Penny still cling to her relationship with Jed? Or had he crossed the line? Even if she didn't raise the proverbial hue and cry against him, at least she could get the hell out of the line of fire. But the stories were usually true. Every day more violence went unreported. Cheeks were turned. It happened all the time. Hush-hush, now, don't let the cops take my husband away because then who will support my babies and besides, call me a dumbshit but I still love him.

"Hope Chinese is okay."

Jo turned around as Penny's brother emerged from the elevator. He had her same ceramic-colored skin and timid walk. His arms were full of white paperboard pagodas.

"Not a moment too soon," Lucy said, homing in on him. "And yes, by the way, Chinese is perfectly okay."

"Any word yet?"

"Only from the good Lord, and He says that everything's going to be fine. So don't you worry. Sweet and sour chicken alright with you, Jo?"

Jo was just about to say she wasn't hungry when she heard the shoes.

So did everyone else. Conversation broke off. The shoes got louder. Jo looked up to see a silver-maned woman with her hands in the pockets of her white coat. As the woman steered toward Penny's parents, the others closed in from behind, forming a half-ring around her when she stopped.

"Good evening, all of you. I'm Louisa Cole."

Penny's father stood up. "Is she alright, Doctor?"

"I've listed her condition as guarded."

"I've never heard of that before," Jo said, drawing the doctor's attention. "What does guarded mean, exactly?"

"Exactly? There's nothing really exact about it, I'm afraid, but it's our best layman's term for a status between good and serious. And you are?"

"Jo Adams. Penny's friend."

"Ah."

"So she's going to be okay?"

There was a mouselike hesitation before the doctor's response, and Jo, in a moment of empathy, read it perfectly. *Okay? Damaged psychologically, fractured emotionally, and pummeled physically. No, not okay, but hopefully one of these days.* "With a little time," Cole said, "I think she'll be fine."

A grand exhale, a collective release. For every heart that is broken in a hospital hallway late at night, there is another that sings with relief.

"Her lower jaw is broken. She has quite an assembly of bruises, but there are no other fractures. Her left arm, however, was dislocated. And several fingernails were torn off, which in my estimation is probably a more painful injury than her jaw and arm combined. There's no sign of internal bleeding, which is always our greatest fear in battering cases. But we'd like to keep her overnight as a routine precaution."

"Yes." Penny's father nodded dully. "Yes, of course."

"Can we see her?" Hannah asked. "If we're really quiet and promise not to make her laugh so she doesn't hurt her mouth, could we go in and talk to her?"

"I'm sorry. It's late. She's sleeping right now, and I think that it's best if she remains that way for awhile. I'm sure you understand."

Hannah lowered her head.

"It's okay, Jessler. We can go outside and get drunk in the parking lot." Tam gave Louisa Cole a madwoman's grin. "Don't worry, Doc. I won't let her operate her chair while she's intoxicated."

Her left arm, however, was dislocated. Jo shivered. A dislocated arm seemed far more gruesome than the broken jaw. She didn't know why. The thought of being pulled apart struck too many chords at once. "Thank you, Dr. Cole."

"You're welcome. I'll be around for a few more hours if you have any more questions."

She spoke with Penny's family for awhile, but Jo didn't hear what was said. When she looked down at herself, she realized she was rolling Hannah down the center of the hall. Lucy fell into place on her right, Nin and Tam on her left. They said nothing, just let their shoulders occasionally touch as they walked. At the end of the hall stood a door marked

CHAPEL. There was a single glass window looking in and the heavy red curtain was open, but the room was dark. Without a word, they filed inside.

Chapter Five

No one said a word. Jo eased Hannah over the burgundy carpet. Lucy drifted between the few rows of pews, touching the smooth wood. Tamaryn strode boldly down the central aisle, stopped before the altar, and looked up at the large cross affixed to the wall. The cross was lit from behind, giving it a hazy aura. The sanctuary wasn't very large, capable of seating no more than twenty comfortably, but the closeness of everything and the abundant shadows gave the place a *nestled* feeling that Jo found mildly stabilizing.

Nin sat down in one of the pews closest to the altar. Briefly she closed her eyes.

Jo parked Hannah beside her.

When Tamaryn turned around, she appeared no more at ease for having gazed upon the cross. Her eyes were a volatile chemistry of accusation and contempt. Lucy finished her exploration and stood next to her, leaning back against the altar. The five of them looked everywhere but at each other.

So now what? Jo asked herself.

She didn't have a fitting response. She kept thinking about the doctor's term for Penelope's status: *guarded.* So much depended upon that single word. Had Dr. Cole listed her patient as *good,* well, then there was nothing to worry about and let's just go home and resign thoughts of Jed Whitecross to a locked cellar door in our minds; all is well. Conversely, if she'd said *serious,* now that was a call to action. Get a specialist in here. Somebody find Bottle and get Jed's ass in jail. This is serious. No more looking the other way. And, heaven forbid, if the doctor had used the word *critical,* then all there was to do was pray.

But Penelope was in guarded condition. That seemed to imply that she was protected, watched over. Shielded. Maybe it was just an argument of semantics, but when a person was guarded, weren't they under the vigil of a ready defender? If you were guarded, wasn't there someone prepared to throw their body between you and a bullet?

Was it that term alone—*guarded condition*—that made her finally speak up? She never knew for certain. But that's how it began. With her finally opening her mouth. "I guess . . . I guess this is when we examine our options."

There. That wasn't so bad. Her voice sounded like her own, even in this darksome room with its conspicuously non-denominational ambience. But no one replied, so she stumbled ahead. "Penny's going to be as healthy as a horse, that's the main thing."

"Amen," Nin said quietly.

"Yeah. Amen." Jo's heartbeat ticked in her wrist. "Do any of you really believe that she's going to turn him in? Is he going to be held responsible for what he's done?"

Everyone but Lucy kept looking at the floor. Lucy had never been a floor-watcher or a foot-shuffler. Her eyes were relentless.

"I don't know what I'm supposed to say," Jo admitted, wiggling under her friend's scrutiny. She took a step away from them, her footfall soundless on the carpet. "I don't know what you *expect* me to say."

"The truth," Lucy ventured.

Those two words hung in the air. Jo imagined she could see them. She wished they'd dissipate like smoke, but the only way she was going to banish them was by chasing them off with words of her own. But what to say? On impulse she decided to part with a personal secret, an anecdote she'd kept to herself until now. She figured it couldn't hurt. "All right. The truth. You all know what a clapboard house is?" She didn't wait for an answer, just rushed ahead before she had time to reconsider. "Clapboard is a kind of siding. I'm sure you've all seen it a thousand times. It's simple, and it's common, and every novel I've read, someone is always living in a house made of the stuff. It's a good, middle-class kind of material. You see clapboard houses all over the place in this country, wherever you go, and there's nothing noteworthy about them. You never look twice at them, though you're sure that real people live inside. Well. I have a clapboard life."

Did that sound as foolish to their ears as it did to Jo's own? The heat seeped into her cheeks and she hastened on. "I know I'm unique, just like everybody else. Humans are just like snowflakes. I know there are things in me, unexpected, *valid* things that you don't find in anyone else. But no one is aware of that stuff when they see me shoving a shopping cart across the parking lot to my car, or when they drive by my house in the morning and see me standing at the window in my old woman's bathrobe. Do you get it?" She held out her hands, inviting them to indeed get it. "To them I'm just the same as the forty-year-old woman in the next house and the forty-year-old woman in the next town, and the next state." She bit her lip. She was glad it was dark so the others might not notice the color in her face, though she was sure they did. She was afraid to meet their eyes, but she forced herself to look.

They all stared at her. But not in the curious way she'd expected, but with a tacit message of affirmation. *Keep going. We need this.*

Well, Jo wasn't certain that any of them actually *needed* her cockeyed perspective on the world, but she kept rolling, just because it would have been too awkward to stop now.

"I don't mind being that way, just another face in the crowd. I have a decent and currently rather interesting job, and my daughter is strong and smart as hell. But." She let the word roll across her tongue, and liking the way it felt, she said it again. "*But*. Do I think that maybe I'll do something about what's happened here tonight? Yeah. I might. Something that the forty-year-old down the block wouldn't do. Like pick up the phone, for starters. I'm not sure who to call . . . one of Terrell's friends in the FBI. A reporter. Somebody. I know that's not much, but it's more than I was doing yesterday."

Nin nodded a silent blessing from her pew.

Hannah, bright-eyed as ever, looked around at the others expectantly.

Lucy remained an inscrutable black sphinx.

"Tamaryn?" Jo felt the heat leave her skin, replaced by a sensation a few degrees colder. Something in Tam's face . . . "Tam, what is it?"

"That's not enough," Tamaryn said.

"I don't understand."

"Sure you do." Tam pinched the words as they left her mouth. "I know you, Jo. You understand plenty. You understand that I am sick of this. All of it. Of talking my head off and not being heard. We let one black eye go"—she shrugged—"doesn't make any difference to anybody. Shit happens, right? Then a friend ends up with a broken bone and her arm pulled out of its socket. Okay, we can live with that, too. But you know what happens next, don't you?" She encompassed all of them with the question, lacing it with an indictment. "No, Tam, we don't know, please tell us how our friend goes crawling back to him and the next we ever hear of her she's dead."

"Easy, honey," Nin warned.

"I'm tired of easy, Ningeogapik."

"Easy never did anyone any harm."

"It never did any good, either. Can't you see? That's what's wrong with the whole town, the whole *country*. It's not that there's some evil little group of people in the government plotting against the rest of us. It's that there's not a *good* little group of people standing up. And why aren't we standing up, Nin? Because it's *easy* not to."

"So what do you want to do then?" Hannah asked. "I can see your point, Tam, really I can, but Jo's right about Terrell having friends in the Bureau. One of the deputy directors there is really fond of him and he's even hinted about giving him a job, so it's not like we don't have any options, but other than calling the FBI or the welfare office or the state police, I'm not really sure we can do anything, unless you want us to go put on our brass knuckles and rough him up."

"Damn, Jessler, that's the best idea I've heard in a long time."

Nin was already shaking her head. "Violence is never the best idea."

"Sometimes it's the *only* idea, can't you see that?" Tam held her arms out at her sides. "Can't any of you *see?* The system sucks, okay? We call the cops, nothing happens. They can't do anything until either Penny or the district attorney tells them to. So we call the newspaper and convince them to run a story, *bam!* Two days later Jed's daddy sends an army of lawyers and PR people to town, and we get squashed and come out looking like a bunch of idiots."

"Come on, honey . . ."

"And Penny *still* goes back to him and then he's *really* pissed at all the nasty things we've said about him, so he smashes her head in with a bottle of one of his goddamn imported beers."

"We're not going to send the media after him," Jo said.

She tried to keep her tone as low and reasonable as she could. But she could feel the momentum flying entirely out of her hands, and all she could do now was hold on. "And we're certainly not going to attack him."

"Why not? Huh? It's called justice, Jo."

"It's called vengeance."

"Sometimes there's no difference."

"Sure, fine. I admit that Jed Whitecross deserves to get his jaw cracked in return. And his arm dislocated. I have to agree. But what would you have me do, Tamaryn? Put on a black mask and carve a big Z on his chest?"

"His chest wasn't the part of him I was thinking about carving, but yeah, that's what needs to be done."

"Lucy . . ." Jo looked at her as if she were reaching for a lifeline. "Help me out here, please."

"I think," Nin said, drawing their attention by the pleading note in her voice, "that all the help we really need is right here." She held up a Bible she'd found on the pew.

To this, Tamaryn had no response.

"I'm not so sure about that." Lucy eased away from the altar. Now that she had finally spoken, heads turned to follow her. Her dark skin provided her with camouflage in the gloom. "Now, don't get me wrong, Nin. And don't you look at me like that. I know that book is full of truth, each and every chapter in it. I don't guess each little story is true when you get down to who said what, but the details don't really matter much. That book in your hand points us in the right direction. This world would be a lot better off if folks spent more time with it and less with the gossip magazines. So you're right. We can find a load of answers between those covers."

The other shoe, Jo thought. *Here it comes.*

"But truth's got lots of faces," Lucy said. "Different

shades of it, you might say. You get a lot from talking to older people, folks who've been there before. There's much to be said for advice from someone who's made the mistakes. That's truth." She nodded, as if in deep agreement with herself. "Then there's the kind from books. Oh, thank the Lord for books. Doesn't matter if it's fiction or self-help or smutty romance or whatever. They've all got something to say, all have little chunks of good judgment buried in them, if you look deep enough. But all of that, books, good advice, even the Bible, all of that is secondhand. It's not the horse's mouth. You know what I've learned, Nin? There's the kind of truth you read about, and the kind you live. The kind you *do*."

She held out her hand, palm up, and then slowly made a fist.

"Don't give me a parable," she said. "Just give me an *hour*."

She studied her own hand, smiled darkly, and relaxed her fist. "Who knows?" She looked at Jo. "This just might be our hour."

Jo felt something shift inside of her. Yet at the same time, she grew very careful. She still thought it best to take things gently. If the air in the small chapel now carried a charge, then she was afraid of moving too quickly, for fear of sparks. "Let's just say," she began, "for the sake of argument, that we choose not to sit this one out. I'm speaking strictly hypothetically here—"

"The hell you are," Tamaryn said.

Jo took a steadying breath. "Let's just pretend for a minute. I'm sure you all remember how we play make-believe. So we walk out of this door. We're Penny's guardians. We walk out of this door, and then what?"

"We find him." Tamaryn put her hands on her hips. "We find him, and then play it by ear."

"What does that mean?"

"We improvise."

"We confront him?"

"You bet."

"Just the five of us."

"*Just* the five of us? Come on, Jo. There's only *one* of him. I'm not much at arithmetic, but damn. Give us some credit here."

"You're right. Credit is given. Five of us. One of him. We find him. Alone."

"I don't like where this is going," Nin said.

"We find him alone," Tam said, taking up the reins, "and we don't beat him up, because I'm sure that Nin's probably right and that wouldn't be a very Christian thing to do."

Hannah nudged her chair closer. "But we scare him."

"That's right, Jessler. We scare the piss and vinegar out of him."

"And he goes right to the cops," Jo said.

Tamaryn wasn't concerned. "So we do it at night."

"That's still no guarantee he won't identify us."

"Maybe I don't care if he identifies me or not."

"No," Lucy said, quieter now, her eyes a bit more predatory than before. "Josephine's right. We've got too much to lose. There are children to consider here. Just imagine how Dan Ryan would react if he learned that Nin had been out on a midnight raid. Those kids would be hauled out of her house by noon the next day. But there might be a way . . ."

Jo had never been more afraid to ask.

"Uh-huh. Might be a way yet. . . ." Slowly, like a woman touching fire, Lucy reached down and lifted the pillowcase from Hannah's lap. Then, with a sudden sound that caused Nin to gasp, she turned it upside-down and dumped everything on the floor. Hairbrush, toothpaste, nightgown—

She pulled the pillowcase over her head.

"Now *this*," she said from behind her pink hood, "would make a strong man wish he'd brought along a second pair of underwear."

Staring at her masked friend, Jo wanted to laugh. *You've got to be joking.* There were many courses of action they could pursue of varying degrees of legality, but this . . . Her laughter shriveled in her throat. There was nothing humorous about it. There was, in fact, a shortness of air in the room, and a darkness not wholly the result of the shadows.

Lucy turned her head left, then right. She was faceless and menacing. "I don't hear anyone talking. I don't hear a damn one of you even breathing. What's the matter, ladies, cat got your tongues?"

Jo at least had to try. Already the current had mingled with her blood. And Lucy was right. It *was* unsettling to look at her like that. "Lucy, listen to yourself . . ."

"No, Jo dear. I'm finished listening. I've heard myself, and myself says take this hour while you've got the chance, before you curdle up in old age and die wishing you'd worn that damn pillowcase out the door." The fabric around her mouth moved in a disturbing way when she spoke. "And if you don't believe that half a dozen ghosts in sheets can scare the holy living God out of a man, then I'm here to tell you that you're wrong. Believe me. You're wrong." She spun around, first toward Tamaryn, then Hannah and Nin, then finally at Jo. "Spooky, isn't it?"

Jo felt herself nod. "I'll give you that."

"Just what the doctor ordered, don't you think?"

"You're saying we make disguises and play a Halloween prank."

"No, neither one. I'm saying we cover up so as to keep our kids safe, and we should decide right here and now that this is no prank, no trick-or-treat. Pranks are played on history teachers who give you a bad grade. This is something else."

"Justice," Jo asked, unable to curtail the sarcasm.

"To some."

"What about to you?"

"Me? It's truth, Jo. It's just my truth, and I'm finally going to do right by it."

And when we can stand it no longer, we abide some more.

Jo didn't realize how frightened she was of no longer abiding until she glanced down and saw her hand. Her fingers were trembling.

No one was more surprised than Jo herself when she looked up from her shaking hand and said, "Well, we better cut some eyeholes in that thing. Kind of hard to follow our truth if we can't see where we're going."

Chapter Six

Nin awoke, roused not by the crying of a little one in need, but rather a murmur from inside of her. She lay there, feeling the rhythmic rise and fall of her breasts, in the fragile darkness before dawn.

Minutes passed. She shoved herself up into a sitting position, wondering why she wasn't tired. The red numerals of the clock told her that it wasn't quite five-thirty in the morning. Early, even for her. Mothers are patch-sleepers, their nights sewn up with little swatches of sleep here and there. Nin had been a patch-sleeper for over half of her life. But after returning from the hospital, she'd fallen into a tunnel of dreamless sleep, and now, having emerged from the other side, she felt . . . different.

Different how? she asked herself. *Silly old thing. Just get up and see what the day brings.*

So she did. She moved through her room, touching all the familiar things to keep herself aligned in the dark. She would bathe first, a rare pleasure. Normally she showered quickly, because children sensed when you were occupied, especially when you were occupied in the *bathroom,* and that's when cups were spilled and sisters pinched and—

Nin smiled.

She pulled her nightgown over her head, thinking that Tamaryn probably slept naked. Nin was thirty-six years old and couldn't remember, though she tried hard while letting the warm water rise around her, the last time she'd slept without any clothes on.

Hmmm. Funny thing to be thinking about.

82

She dressed with a minimum of lights. The house was still and breathless. Though Nin reveled in the sounds that usually filled its drooping eaves, there was something to be said for the silence, for the frail layer of anticipation that settled softly around her. For some reason it reminded her of watching the first snowfall of winter drift down from a hushed sky.

She checked all their round faces first. The kids slept in the senseless positions comfortable only to children and certain cats, elbows here, arms there, legs hanging off of beds and sure to be asleep come morning: *Hey, Mom, my foot's asleep. Watch me try to walk!* She went last to Marky, a soft bundle in his bed, looked after by the same stuffed animals that had watched over his brothers and sisters before him. They were a dutiful troupe, those animals, and dependable. Though dragged and yanked and abused for their efforts, they stood their posts without complaint. Nin supposed that stuffed animals were our best example of angels.

Nibbling a cherry pastry, she went to the clothes pantry for the sheets.

If there was one thing in this house that wasn't running low, it was the supply of covers, blankets, shams, and sheets, picked up at every garage sale Nin had ever browsed. You could never have enough of them, for all the changing of them you had to do when you had kids. Add to this all the friends that stayed the night, all the tents set up in the living room, all the costumes made for Halloween, and you had a big pile of bed-dressing math. With six little bodies to look after, everything in Nin's life came in multiples. She always bought family size. She was Noah's ark to the third power.

She sorted out the twin-size sheets, of which there were many. Twin-size wouldn't do. Grown women needed at least full-size. *And queen-size for me,* she thought, not unhappily.

She carried the sheets to the laundry room, which was really her back porch. The bleach was kept up high, well out of reach. Up there with it were other odds and unlikely ends, including fabric softener, one lonesome sock, a Matchbox car, and several colors of dye. Jeans faded and needed to be blue again. Church pants got grass stains. And thanks to the fairy outfit Melissa had worn for the school play last year, Nin had two boxes of pink on hand.

Soon dawn opened up the sky. Children yawned, some cried. All were hungry.

Nin washed and dressed those that needed her assistance, marveling at how much the others had grown that they could do things for themselves. She fed them cereal from giant boxes. When it was time to walk out to the mailbox for the day's suspense—was this the morning that Dan changed her life?—she didn't go out only as the receiver, but as the giver as well.

Lucy handed her a bundle. "Don't worry. It's not there. I checked for you."

"Thank you." Nin handed over a carefully folded stack of sheets, freshly pinked. They'd dried quickly in the warm morning sun.

Lucy accepted the sheets like a spy taking possession of stolen documents. She hastened to hide them in the truck, then asked, "You're still coming tonight, aren't you?"

Nin flipped through the mail, just in case Lucy had missed something marked with Dan's return address. But she found only bills and a coupon book. "I better get back inside. Marky needs to be changed."

When she looked back through the living room window, she saw Lucy just sitting there in the seat of her boxy little truck, staring at the sheets.

"Mom, I can't find my left shoe!"

"Look in the cabinet, honey. Your brother probably hid it behind the cereal again."

By noon Hannah was wondering how someone bound to a chair could feel like they were climbing the walls.

There were days in this town, and then there were *days*. Like this one. Time grinds to a halt in Belle Springs. No one calling to complain of a stray dog noodling around in their garden. No speeders out on Highway 9. No drunks. Throughout that wing of the county courthouse that comprised the sheriff's department and three-cell jail, the only sound to be heard was the trickle of the coffeemaker and the grinding bump of the Truman-era air conditioner turning on.

Hannah had even given up on TV. Of all her small circle of conspirators, Hannah was the lone television junkie. Nin's tube only showed cartoons and kids' shows. Lucy didn't have cable, but rented videos with all those tall and untouchable actors who didn't know what they were missing by having never met her. Tamaryn owned two TVs, but one was Matt and Brady's domain and the other exclusively showed Roy's tractor pulls and professional wrestling. Jo kept saying she was going to be more informed and watch the late-night news, but Hannah doubted she ever got around to it. Jo was a procrastinator of Carnegie Hall caliber.

But this chair, it affected your mind. It grounded you. And being grounded led naturally to daytime talk shows and—*zap!*—before you knew it, you were into the afternoon soaps and caught up in hokey stories of who was having whose love child, and just how many times can a villain come back from the dead, anyway?

Today Hannah had left the television off. After last night, nothing there seemed real.

So she rolled. Over to the coffee machine for a cup, over to the far counter to dust and pass the time. She went down the hall to where the volunteer firemen kept their trucks, but no one was there. The town police department, an entity unconnected to the county sheriff, was housed at City Hall down the street. That's also where the ambulance service made its home, and probably a lot of other interesting municipal divisions that would have helped her to slug her way through the afternoon. But it was Friday and everyone who could was taking off early. Summer outings, shopping trips to Baltimore's Inner Harbor, long drives into the mountains . . . and tonight, for five imprudent women, a rendezvous near a tavern called the Riverhouse.

"Are you up for this?" Hannah wondered aloud. Forget the chair for a moment. Just consider. Catch a man alone. Scare him, shout at him a bit. Maybe wave a few sticks in the air and threaten to kneecap him. How illegal was such a thing? She understood enough of police procedure to know that the law would consider such an act as assault, without the battery.

She felt the pricklings in her stomach when she thought about it. The Hoofbeats, she called them. Just like in the old days before a barrel race, when her feet twitched nervously in the stirrups and her fingers tightened on the reins in expectation of danger.

"She rolls in beauty, like the night . . ."

Hannah touched her right wheel and turned around. She couldn't help it: she smiled.

". . . of cloudless stars and something or other . . ."

"That's awful," Hannah laughed.

Terrell spread his hands apologetically. "Hey, so I'm no poet. At least I try, right?"

"Good point, men don't do poetry anymore. At least not straight men."

"Who said I was straight?"

"Come here. We'll find out."

He did as he was told. She watched him as he neared her, his thick arms filling his uniform sleeves, the way the pleats of his pants pulled tight when he walked. He bent over her at the same moment that she straightened up, and she smelled him an instant before their lips touched. His scent, along with his breath in her mouth, infused her with warmth. Desire replaced anxiety. No more Hoofbeats. She pressed her mouth harder against his.

He pulled away, feigning whiplash. "Whoa." He licked his lips.

"You're either straight or faking it really well."

"Coffee hot?"

"Yep. I've been drinking gallons."

"That quiet around here?"

"Horribly so. I keep turning the scanner up just to hear the voices."

"I could go out and rob a bank, give you a few calls to handle." He took a sip. "What? You don't find that funny?"

She held her smile in place. "Hilarious."

"Something bothering you, sweetness?"

"What makes you say that?"

"Want to talk about it?"

"Drink your coffee, mister."

"I'm drinking. But here's another question for you."

"I suppose it's about Penny."

"Yeah, how's she doing?"

Hannah went to him, the rubber tread of her tires almost soundless on the tiled floor. She took his hand and held it against her face.

"I hear she's going to be released today," he said.

"Why do people do that to each other?" she said into his hand.

"Know what? I became a cop because I had this teacher in junior high, Mr. Billings, an English teacher. He was my favorite. He got beat up one night. Missed a few days of school. I never heard the whole story. I just wanted to get back at whoever did it. But now look at me."

"What do you mean?"

"I'm a county deputy."

"So?"

He didn't elaborate.

She looked up at him. "Yes, you're a county deputy, and also a college graduate and an army vet, you've been a little busy, babe, it's not like you've been wasting your life up to this point."

"I know. You're right. As always."

"Besides, you're on your way up."

"Watch it. You know what they say about counting your chickens."

"They're my chickens. I may count them as I please. Have you called him yet?"

"Who?"

"Don't *who* me. Lawrence Perez, our favorite G-man."

"Why don't we talk about this tonight over dinner?"

"No, I'm meeting with the girls tonight, so what about it? You've sent him your application?"

Terrell nodded.

"And?"

"And the gears turn slowly with things like this."

"You're asking for Quantico, right?"

"Hannah, please . . ."

"I only want to know so I can look into what all the Quantico women are wearing this time of year, I don't want to be behind the fashion times, you know, when we make our grand entrance into the glamorous world of the Eff Bee Eye."

"Listen to me for a minute . . ."

"Aren't I always listening? Do you think heels or flats for our first Bureau ball? I'm afraid that if I wear heels, I might come off looking taller than you, and we don't want to give them the impression that you're a little guy, because you only get one chance at making them—first impressions, that is."

"I think you're putting the cart in front of the horse."

"Well, aren't we just full of country aphorisms today? First with the chickens and now the horse. You might as well use the one about silk purses and sows' ears, just to get it out of the way—"

"Hannah, stop."

"What?"

He sank down beside her chair. "I'm asking about tonight."

"Yeah, I heard you, stud. But I'm sorry. I'm booked. Ladies' night."

"No. You don't get it. I said I'm asking." He looked at his hands. "About . . . I just thought . . . even if it's not tonight . . ."

Something tingled in Hannah's throat. She decided immediately that she liked it.

"I was thinking that maybe, if you thought it was a good idea . . ."

"You're asking to stay the night?" The tingle spread the length of her arms and down her spine, electrifying every part of her still capable of feeling.

Terrell's skin, as dark as the coal his daddy had spent a lifetime dragging up from the ground, hid the blush that Hannah knew was there. "I don't want to rush things, sweetness."

"Rush them, please. Good God."

"No, it's just . . ." He started to stand up, but she shot out a hand and held him there.

"Look at me."

With an effort, he did.

"I just decided, four seconds ago, that I've never wanted anything more in my life."

Did he look relieved by that? She hoped so.

"And I won't tell you," she went on, "that I haven't imagined it, what it would be like, and you can't lie to me and tell me you haven't done the same."

He grinned like a boy.

"Uh-huh. So you're not alone. But, you sexy thing you, your timing sucks."

"Pardon?"

"I'm committed. You know that Jo's got all this stuff going on right now, and I told her that I'd give her a hand with one of her projects. She's been under an Everest of stress lately, and last night at the hospital I promised her I'd help out."

"Hey, no problem. It's cool."

"Really, or are you just saying it's cool because that's the cool, tough guy kind of thing to say? And don't fib to me because right now I'm a woman on a tightrope and one gust of a fib might be all the wind I need to knock me off balance."

"Do you like jazz?"

"I like everything as long as it's yours."

"I'll bring some tunes. When I come over. Which will be soon."

"You bet your ass it will be."

He kissed her again, and this time she threw her arms around his neck. The feeling of his tongue against hers would have been perfect had it not been for the small voice of the wheelchair-induced pessimist in her. *Tonight,* the voice said. *First we just have to get through tonight. Only then will there be time for jazz and other, more physical, harmonies.*

Only then.

Lucy watched the headlights swing into her driveway. Finally.

She didn't need to look at the clock but did so anyway. Ten-seventeen. Two minutes since the last time she'd checked.

She hefted the sack that contained the sheets that were no longer sheets. She'd finished her mail route eight hours ago, at two in the afternoon. She'd been at the sewing machine ever since.

"Here we go then." She locked the door behind her.

Tamaryn's truck smelled. No muffler. Hell on the ozone, for sure.

"Toss it in the back," Tam said through the open window. It was too dark to see her face.

Lucy lowered the bag into the truck bed. "What's this?"

"What's what?"

"This black duffel bag you've got back here."

"Bats."

Lucy jerked open the passenger's door, filling the cab with light. "*Baseball* bats?"

"Softball. Take it easy, Luce. I'm on a team, remember? I've also got my glove and cleats in there. I never bother taking the stuff in the house."

Lucy didn't like it, but got in anyway. "Well, just the same, sure wish you hadn't brought them." She slammed her door.

Tamaryn cupped her hands around her lighter, took a deep drag, then backed into the street. The dashboard clock said 10:20.

"How many bats you got in there?"

"Five."

★ ★ ★ ★ ★

Jo hadn't ridden in the back of a pickup since she was a girl.

The one thing she'd forgotten was the wind. The wind was different at night. Something about not being able to see, with only the rush against your ears and the throb of the engine in your bones . . . it took her back. The first boy she'd ever dated had owned a truck. Joseph Mitz. And despite Joseph's blue eyes and the blanket he'd brought along "so you won't hurt your back," she hadn't gone further than allowing his hand up her shirt. *Did you let him feel you up?* one of her girlfriends had asked the next day. Jo remembered the careful, tremulous way he'd gone about it, uncertainly testing one breast, then the other, like a man who doesn't know whether to clip the red wire or the blue.

The stars gleamed overhead, forming their safe, familiar shapes.

When she lowered her gaze, she saw Lucy watching her. Nin had taken Lucy's place in the cab, and now Lucy leaned against the bed wall, her knees drawn up to her chest. She'd pulled her hair out of her face and fastened it behind her head with a banana clip. Occasionally the wind caused her eyes to water, and she wiped away the tears. "You know," Lucy said, loud enough to be heard over the gale, "that we're almost eighty-five years old between us."

"We look pretty good for an almost-eighty-five-year-old."

They sat there, feeling the blacktop hum beneath them.

After awhile Lucy shoved the duffel bag out of the way, crawled across the truck bed, and situated herself beside Jo. "They sure don't make these things for comfort, do they?"

"Not back here they don't."

"You're still not sure about this, are you?"

"Are you? Look at us. Look at what we're doing."

"No way for an eighty-five-year-old to behave herself, is it?"

Jo leaned closer so she didn't have to shout. "Do you have any idea what Caroline would say if she knew I was doing this?"

"First thing, there is no *I* anymore. This is *us* all the way. Second, Sweet Caroline would want Jed Whitecross to be punished for what he did."

Jo believed and did not believe that. Yes, Caroline bristled at the thought of the world's malefactors, be they bullies or jaywalkers or thieves, and planned to dedicate her life to prosecuting such miscreants. She was young and her sense of morality was more than a line drawn in the sand. Sand got washed away. Put your finger in concrete, however, and your line was indelible.

"She would disown me," Jo said.

"What? I didn't hear you."

"Nothing. What if Jed's not alone?"

"Then we mission abort, I guess. You bring your mobile?"

Jo removed her phone from its leather sheath.

"How are the batteries?"

Jo checked. "Better than mine." She tapped a finger over her heart.

"Watch it, girl. No backing out now."

"I'm not backing."

"Or getting squeamish."

"I'm not squeaming."

"Good. Because we're there."

The truck slowed down.

Jo had time for one last montage of memories—Joseph Mitz's sweaty forehead, Caroline's hair, Penny's purple jaw—and then Tam pulled the truck to the side of the road.

Jo lowered herself to the ground.

"Nice night," Lucy commented.

"For what?"

"For playing dress-up and acting like fools."

Tam slammed her door, causing Jo to flinch. The sound was too loud, out of place amongst the reedy drone of bugs. They'd parked twenty feet off the blacktop on a dirt track that led over miles of hard country to Protestant Lake. There were fresher, flatter roads that serviced the lake, so no one much bothered coming this way anymore. Ample cover was provided by the moss-covered red oaks that lined the sides of the track. Jo looked toward the highway, anxious about traffic, but she saw no headlights.

"We're not fools," Tamaryn said. "Tonight is the night we stop being fools." She brushed by them and exhaled a long funnel of smoke.

"You've really got a hard-on for this, don't you?" Lucy asked her.

"Just get the robes, Luce."

Nin had already removed the bundles from the truck and held them in both arms, albeit several inches away from her body. "I don't like the word *robes*. It makes it sound as if we belong to some kind of cult. I would prefer we simply call them sheets."

"Sorry, Ninster." Tam dropped the spent butt and heeled it into the dirt. "I'm calling a spade a spade. Robes and hoods is what you've got there. Now let me have one."

One by one, Nin distributed the garments. No words were spoken, but arms were outstretched and dyed fabric taken in hand. Tamaryn got a flashlight from the glove box and passed its beam over the women at random, allowing them to have a look.

Jo held the simple cotton mantle to eye level and inspected it with all the gravity she felt rocking back and forth inside of her. Nin was right. It was just a sheet. And yet it wasn't. She noted the precisely cut circles for the eyes in the hood, the careful hem along the bottom of the robe. "I don't suppose you have this in a size five."

"Girl," Lucy said, "you haven't been a five since junior high."

"Hush. I'm thinking thin."

"Well, if that's what it takes, I should start thinking now. I might make a size five by the time the sun burns out."

Tamaryn turned her robe over brusquely, whipping it about, searching. "You cut any holes in this thing, Luce?"

"Only one for your head. So I made yours extra large."

"Funny."

"What am I doing wrong?" Nin had gotten the sheet over her shoulders, but it was bunched and coiled around her neck. She held out her arms for help.

"Here, let me." Jo pulled what needed to be pulled, draping her friend in what looked like a giant pink poncho. She couldn't stop thinking, *Any minute now I'm going to wake up laughing.*

"Damn, Luce. This fits pretty good." Tamaryn had donned the hood.

Jo froze.

That did it. The mask was too much. It was conical in shape, with two black chasms that swallowed Tamaryn's eyes. In the backsplash from the flashlight, crowned with that distinctive headpiece, Tam didn't look like a prank player at all. She looked like a hater.

Jo splintered. "Maybe this isn't the best way to spend a Friday night . . ."

"Forget it, Josephine Adams," Lucy said. "For once in your life, stay in the race."

"What's that supposed to mean?"

"Nothing."

"Lucy, what is that supposed to mean?"

"Just get dressed."

But for once Jo didn't give in. She recognized this place where they were standing. It was that proverbial point. The one of no return. "Look at her." She pointed at Tam. "Look at her, Lucy, and tell me that doesn't sicken you just a little bit."

"Can't. It sickens me a lot."

"Well?"

"I believe," Nin said, "that being sickened by it is the point."

Jo stared at her blankly.

Lucy wiggled into her sheet, appraised herself when Tam pointed the light at her, and then, with both hands, pulled the hood over her head. The outfit was complete.

"Boo," she said.

Somehow, that put it to rest. Everyone else had made a consensus of things, so what was there to do but vote with the majority? The issue would lay fallow for tonight, and perhaps in the light of morning Jo could take the time to cultivate it again. But nighttime has a certain inertia to it, a kinetic energy that lends itself to deviant behavior. A minute later, Jo had donned her gown.

So this is it. Only a small slice of time out of her life, no big deal. Sure, the entire escapade was juvenile, not to mention frivolous and irresponsible, but she also acknowledged a visceral urge for revenge. Or maybe it was justice, or just a base human need to extract recompense where it was due, but the part of her that wasn't an unwilling participant was quickly growing in stature. *Whitecross deserves it. So just do this and get it over with.* She adjusted her mask so that she could see more or less clearly. Her peripheral vision was rotten, so she practiced turning her entire head to see to the side. She tried lifting her arms. The sheet provided nowhere for her arms to go, so she had to bundle the fabric around her elbows to free her hands. Then, just as she was doubting her own capacity to carry this through, she surprised herself by chuckling.

"What is it?" Lucy asked.

"We're going to have to make the next model with armholes," Jo said, "so that disgruntled women the world over can swing their rolling pins at their husbands without wrinkling their robes."

"Uh-huh. And maybe one of them little trapdoors in the rear so they won't reveal their secret identity when they're using a public toilet."

"Good idea. You better be writing this down."

"Oh, I'm taking mental notes, believe me."

"And I'm afraid these hoods will wreck the hair."

"I'll make them taller."

"Any taller and you'll have to include aircraft warning lights."

"You can't say they're bad for having been put together without a pattern."

"No, actually they're perfect."

"Thank you."

"For a conehead."

Tam yanked off her hood. "Are you two finished?"

"Oh, don't you go getting a bee in your bonnet," Lucy scolded, her warning leavened with mirth. "Have some respect for your elders."

"You're not that *eld*. Now this is serious."

"I'm really quite comfortable," Nin decided, stepping up beside the others. "This isn't much different than what I wear every day. Although I do feel a little like a pink teepee."

Lucy giggled. Jo couldn't help but join her. It must have been contagious, because Nin laughed, a sound like water bubbling over smooth stones.

Tam gave them a crooked smile as she wired an old Tennessee license plate on top of her real one. Earlier she'd scrounged up a bright yellow magnetic decal advertising Quan's Automotive and applied it quite visibly to the tailgate as part of the disguise, so that Jed would have something to report if indeed he went to the cops, which Jo thought unlikely. In this part of the country, most folks would only say he got what he deserved, so he probably wouldn't humiliate himself by admitting that he'd been accosted as punishment for being a woman-beater. "If I didn't know you guys better," Tam said, "I'd say you were smoking something behind those hoods."

"Fools are like that," Lucy said. "As a matter of fact—"

The phone interrupted her.

"Shhh. This is it." Jo hiked up her robe to liberate the phone. She put it to her ear without bothering to remove her hood. "Hannah?"

She listened intently for a moment. "Are you sure no one saw you?"

Hannah launched into one of her scenic-route replies, and Jo was forced to cut her off. "It doesn't matter. We'll talk about it later. You're certain he's alone? Okay. Right. I'll call you as soon as it's over. Be safe."

She hung up, suddenly cold. "He's coming."

"Everybody get in position," Tam said, already in motion. "Time to see if Lucy's stitches can hold up to a little action."

Chapter Seven

Jo crouched in the weeds on the side of the road, wondering about the bugs. Were they crawling up her legs? It sounded like they were everywhere. They probably were.

The road was dark and quiet.

Tam had driven the truck back onto the highway, then nudged it over to the shoulder and thrown up the hood. Upon her instruction, Nin and Lucy had taken shelter just around the bend, hidden in the nook of the dirt track. Jo had crossed the blacktop and waded into the ditch, where she was now hunkered down in a manner she hadn't experienced since she was a little girl and more inclined to hunkering. She realized she hadn't had a good grass stain for nearly thirty years. Maybe it was time. On the tail of this thought came the voices again, one that lectured her about irresponsibility and the general risk of what she was about to do, and the other that was sickened by a society where people got their arms dislocated and were forced to abide.

She leaned on her hands and felt the grime between her fingers and the slightly damp edges of the weeds and the softness of the soil as it gave way beneath her knees. She told herself to breathe as normally as possible. Her breath had gone staccato. She felt it falling against the inside of her mask. When was the last time she'd been so nervous? Must have been the morning six years ago outside the judge's chambers, when it was still up in the air if Sweet Caroline would live with her or Chuck. It was the same feeling. The same pounding.

At least the highway was clear. The road was three miles long, connecting the Riverhouse with the civilized world, and it was a slow night. Only a single car had passed since they'd taken up position in the grass. She estimated how long it would take Jed to get in his Jaguar and reach the point of the . . .

. . . the *ambush*. That's what it was. No two ways about it.

I'm taking part in a trap for another human being. That was the first voice again.

Hell of a rush, ain't it? That was the second.

Tamaryn, for her part, was the bait. She'd parked the truck so that Jed would approach from the rear; the taillights flashed, a Mayday for roadside assistance. Tamaryn stood at the left front fender, obvious to anyone who happened along. She hadn't put on her robe, but wore a pair of denim shorts that Jo figured only about five percent of the adult female population could have fit into without the assistance of a crowbar and half a pound of grease. Tam had brought sandals, saying the more skin, the better, but at the last minute she'd opted for her running shoes. *Just in case,* she'd said. Jo didn't like the sound of that.

Tam bent over the engine, her upper half concealed behind the truck's raised hood. All Jo could see of her was precisely what Jed would see: a lithe pair of female legs.

Wars had, no doubt, been started over less.

Wars by men, Jo thought. *Women don't run the Pentagon. Women don't spend four times as much money on the military as is spent on education. Women don't—*

But that wasn't true. It didn't matter if you called yourself a woman or a Republican or a Teamster or a dyke. Anyone who put up with it was responsible for it. Man or woman, those who abided were agents of the crime.

Headlights appeared.

Jo saw them emerge over a hill fifty yards away, a pair of yellow dots in the darkness. The pitch of the engine increased as the car approached, in direct proportion to her own pulse. She wished a lot of things in the next minute as the car slowed down. She wished Penny would press charges. She wished, crazily, that Caroline could see her now. But most of all she wished for a glimpse of Nin and Lucy because she was gripped by the senseless fear that they'd abandoned her and when she sprang up from her bug-ridden weeds to abide no more, she'd be alone.

The car drew closer and slowed down. It was a two-door sport coupe, silver-white but looking gray in the darkness. Abundant chrome. As sleek as a submarine. The gravel crunched as it pulled to the shoulder opposite Jo's hiding place, splashing the pickup with light.

Jo trapped the next breath behind her teeth.

Tam moved her feet a little but kept herself hidden.

The door opened.

Jo bent even closer to the ground, though it served no purpose other than to make her feel better. She peered through the tips of the weeds at the man-shaped silhouette that got out of the car.

It's him.

She could see him easily enough when he reached the front of his car. The headlights illuminated the urbane good looks that had served his father so well and had undoubtedly aided Jed's own social pursuits. The shadows shifted as he walked through the light, giving Jo rapid glances of his designer blue jeans and his cowboy boots.

Cowboy boots? Kid's never been on a horse in his life.

She inched closer.

Jed hesitated at the back of the truck. He tipped his head slightly to the side. Was he listening? He seemed to be considering, or hearing a siren go off in that part of his black heart where intuition lived.

Jo tensed the muscles in her arms to stop the shaking, but that only made it worse.

And then his voice carried out across the highway, as smooth as wine. "Having some trouble?"

Briefly Jo wondered if he was drunk, and what did that matter? It didn't. He was due, intoxicated or not. Thank the road gods that the blacktop was empty. She waited on the balls of her feet.

"Anything I can help you with?" Jed asked.

As if she'd rehearsed the motion, Tam reached farther across the engine, rising up on her toes and causing the muscles to accentuate her calves. She stood that way for several seconds. Then, slowly, she drew herself free and turned to face him. She wore the pink hood.

"Hello, shithead."

Jed rocked back on his heels.

"Why, Jedediah," she said, the hate in her words as thick as Jo had ever heard it, "you look like something just dribbled down the leg of your pants."

Up! Jo rose to her feet. She felt separated from what was happening, as if the moments were unfolding on the other side of a screen and she was watching them play out from a distance. *Move!* She took a few steps and reached the pavement, her mind on this side of the screen and her body on the other. *Closer!* She approached him silently from behind. All she could see of Tam on the other side of him was the peaked top of her hat.

"What is this?" Jed demanded. "Some kind of damn joke?" He laughed artificially.

"That's right. That's exactly right. Some kind of damn, damn joke." Tam walked toward him. "And you know what?" Just then two robed and hooded figures unfastened themselves from the shadows and appeared behind her. "The joke's on you."

"Hey now, wait a minute." Jed held up his hands, the sight of the three of them loosening the buckles of his bravado. "I don't know what this is about but . . ."

They fanned out around him. Fabric rustled as they walked.

". . . Jesus, take anything you want, take the car . . ."

Jo came on from behind, cringing at the unalloyed fear in the man's voice.

"We don't want your car," Tam said. Without turning away from him, she snaked an arm into the bed of the truck and hauled out an aluminum bat.

Jed backpedaled. "Oh, Christ . . ."

Jo balked at the sight of the bat. This wasn't part of the plan. "Wait a minute," she said, before she could stop herself. "Put that thing away." She wasn't supposed to say anything—Tam was the ambushers' self-nominated talker—but Jed was about to back into her, and her nerves were fraying like split ends from hell. Jed spun around at the sound of her voice, and when he saw her, he yelped like a little boy, and the sound stabbed Jo in the heart.

Tam let the bat drag the pavement as she closed the distance between them: *scrape.* "Don't bother running," she said. "You'll only die tired."

At that, Jed went into full retreat.

But he didn't get far. He stumbled against the car's bumper and almost fell. He was boxed in between the two vehicles, with pink ghosts blocking his escape on either side. He thrust his palms defensively in front of him. "Please, Jesus, I'll give you anything you want, I've got money, you want it and it's yours, I've got it, tons of it, just please don't hurt me . . ."

"Shut up," Tam said.

". . . please . . ."

"Shut the hell up." She lunged forward and waved the bat at him.

That did it. Jo jumped forward to stop her just as Jed slipped in his ill-fitting cowboy boots and went down in a quivering heap. The glare of the headlights turned him white.

Is that what Penny looked like before he slugged her? Though Jo had been in the process of going to his rescue, one hand raised to block the bat, she didn't follow through. She suddenly, irrationally hated him. In his fear he revealed the very quality that he preyed upon. Something about this irony threw a switch, and Jo bit down hard on her teeth to keep from shouting at him. Without thinking she slammed the butt of her hand against his car.

Jed shrieked at the sound. The others turned toward her, plainly startled by her actions. Though their eyes were indiscernible behind their disguises, Jo felt their confusion. But she couldn't have explained her rage had they asked. It had been a long time coming, and acquainting herself with it was like meeting a stranger on the street. She swatted the car again and then jumped at him, arms held high above her head like a child leaping out from behind a door to scare a friend. She even made a noise as she did it, a raw, wordless cry of frustration. It shocked the others into motionlessness and caused Jed to scrabble for cover.

He hit his head against the pickup's tow hitch and howled.

Roused by the man's pain as certain animals are drawn to the scent of blood, Tamaryn pointed the end of the bat at him with renewed ferocity. "How's it feel, asshole?"

Jed blubbered incoherently.

"What did you say, you prick?"

"Do you know who I am?" he screamed.

"Ask me if I goddamn care!" She swung the bat at the car. The lady could hit. She caught the hood ornament with

the fattest part of the bat's barrel—*ping!*—snapping the silver cat from its moorings and sending it soaring out of the light and into the swallowing darkness.

Jed covered his face.

Fight him! Jo resisted that voice, though she couldn't see what difference it would make at this point. The fabric of her mask moved in and out rapidly as she breathed, making a funny little popping sound that Jo found remarkable simply because it was noticeable amidst the flurry.

"This what you want?" Tam hollered at him. "Does it make you feel like a man, crawling around on the ground?" She lifted the bat like a hatchet, ready to strike either the car or the man, her weird, triangle-topped shadow lurching across the ground. "Does it make you feel *strong?*"

Jed was crying now.

Lucy and Nin just stood there, towering over him.

Jo's eyes swept over them, then down to Jed, then up to Tam and the way the veins were visible in her biceps as she clutched the bat. Tam yelled, a primitive sound that sent night birds winging from the trees. Jed cried louder. And half a second later the tides of Jo's anger receded enough that her rational shores could ground her. No more being tugged into Tamaryn's sea by the undertow. She was exhausted.

"Wait." She stepped into the melee and put a hand on the bat, which shook in Tamaryn's grasp. The metal was warm to the touch. "Enough."

"Not yet it's not."

"Yes."

"No, just let me—"

"Someone's coming," Nin said.

Heads snapped. Eyes stared through black holes.

Lights.

Shit.

Jo wanted to run, but the car was too close, coming on too fast. People did that at bars. They drove too quickly, drank too much, whatever.

Jo stood there flat-footed.

The car slowed down as it neared, but just barely, its headlights blinding them, its passengers certainly intrigued by the sight of the cowled figures and the man on the ground at their feet. Though she could see nothing of those inside, Jo sensed heads turning, eyes growing wide.

The car passed them.

The driver, probably scared witless, put the pedal to the floor and the car hurtled away. Seconds later its taillights were eaten by the blackness. Jo thought it was a white four-door sedan, but maybe not. It could have been anybody.

Run!

That, at least, sounded like good advice.

"Come on!" She wrenched at the bat and was surprised when Tamaryn relinquished it. She didn't want to risk anything else by speaking again, so she jabbed the bat at Lucy and Nin, then at the truck. It took them a few moments, dazed as they were by what had transpired, but one more vehement thrust of the bat got them moving. Next she looked to Jed, who was curled up on the ground with his arms shielding his head. He'd stopped bellowing. His fancy jeans were dirty and his legs trembled. But he would live.

Jo waved a hand in front of Tamaryn's face until she broke the spell. She sensed that Tam was about to rip out another malediction, so she took a single step toward her and at the same time put her hand over the place where Tam's mouth was hidden behind her mask. She whispered from hood to hood, "Do this one special thing for me and get in the truck."

She held her hand in place until Tam nodded. As soon as

Jo released her, Tam took the bat and ran to the cab, tossing the metal club into the back along the way.

Faster!

"Right," Jo said under her breath. She pulled herself over the tailgate and swung into the bed, silently cursing the sheet when it impeded her. She tapped on the window for the others to hurry up—Nin was just now getting in, the broken hood ornament clutched in her fist—and why did it seem like everything moved so slowly when you were giving birth and running from the scene of a crime? Tam got them moving, throwing a barrage of gravel over Jed, working the clutch so rapidly that Jo thought her fillings would shake loose. But the ride quickly evened out, and soon the night air was rushing over her, filling her lungs with summer wind.

She tore away the hood and breathed.

Two miles passed before she emerged from her meditation of the stars. Back there a man was lifting himself up off the ground, the first person she'd ever physically confronted in her life. There had been times with Chuck, instances when she was one molecule of self-control away from slapping him, but the Gandhi in her had always prevailed. Until tonight. Her hand still stung from striking the Jag. Violence did something to the body, gave you a fix you couldn't get through any other substance but adrenaline. It was scary. She further observed, with a disturbingly small amount of disgust, that satisfaction was part of the fix. She'd made a stand against a bully. She'd crossed the line for a good cause and felt better for it. But now that the surge was over, she felt washed-out, so frail she might blow over the side of the truck and be carried away, a kite-woman without a string.

The best part was knowing that at least for a few minutes she'd stopped waffling and actually chosen sides. The worst part was the sound: she kept hearing the soft pop—fluttering noise of the hood as it drew in and out against her mouth. It haunted her all the way back to town.

She didn't say goodbye to Nin when they dropped her off. Or to Lucy when she slipped up her dark driveway and vanished into her side of her duplex home, the neighbor's half of the lawn cut as short as artificial turf and Lucy's side something of a rain forest. Jo took her place in the cab. Tamaryn smoked like Phillip Morris was coming to dinner. Orally occupied, she didn't have to speak. For this, Jo was thankful. With her costume coiled beneath her arm, she got out when Tam stopped at her curb. She wove between the Opel and Caroline's convertible like a woman coming out of a maze. At least she hoped she was coming out. She went straight to her room, sequestered her disguise deep in the closet, and sat down on the bed with the phone.

She dialed Hannah. For once, Hannah shut up and let Jo do the talking.

Twenty minutes later, she went to Caroline's door, found it closed, then systematically patrolled the house, checking all the locks. She slept that night with the lights on.

Chapter Eight

Hannah's life was made of ramps.

She'd decided shortly after the accident that ramps were what divided the walking world from the rolling one. Inclines and declines, that's what it was all about. No quick steps, but a gradual rise and fall.

Hannah had never been one for gradual *anything*.

"Radio," she said, pushing back the sheets and sitting up in bed.

The morning news program filled the room.

"Music."

The deejay kept talking. No music.

"It was worth a try." She yawned, squinting against the light that slanted through the French doors on the east side of her room. Though it was the middle of summer and even at night the heat was fierce, she'd disdained the air conditioner and instead opened the windows before she went to bed, welcoming the strong breeze that kept her chiffon curtains billowing while she slept. The room itself was devoid of every piece of furniture but the bed, with broad drop cloths covering most of the polished hardwood floor. She was in the middle of painting. Sealed cans awaited her attention. Rollers on long poles leaned against the walls.

The curtains swayed.

She said her quick morning supplication—"God thanks for another day and the many blessings You've given me and let me not mess up so badly today that I hurt anyone's feelings or make anyone's day any harder, and one more thing. Thanks for keeping Jo and Tam and Lucy and Nin all safe last night and forgive us all for what we did, especially me because I still say he deserved it and I know that's not right. But most of all thank you that everyone's okay. Amen"—then she got down to the business of ramping her way to work.

Getting from bed to chair was easy, at least it was now, though there had been a time when every tumble she took going from one to the other made her want to lie there and die. Now she accomplished the task with comparative ease. She folded her legs into position, gave the wheels a spin, and rolled smoothly down the ramp that led from her room to the hall. At one time, the hall had been carpeted.

Hall to bathroom, next ramp. Here, everything had been rearranged, a home-repair project conducted by various men from local churches who were good with plumbing and anxious to lend a hand. The sink was a foot lower than when she'd bought the house. The toilet was bracketed by shiny bars. The bathtub had been swapped for a shower stall with an extra-wide door. Hannah missed the luxury of a long soak with the bubbles up to her chin. If you ever started thinking how macho you were, just try getting out of a bathtub without using your legs.

"Lights."

The lamps on either side of the room flickered to life. She didn't use overhead illumination anymore. If you thought the bathtub stunt was tricky, there were lightbulbs in the ceiling to be replaced.

She squirmed out of her nightshirt and fought her way into the shower.

Always a battle, the shower. Hannah squared her chair in front of the door. Stainless steel tubes ran at two heights around the inside of the shower. Taking a tube in each hand, she pushed her bare bottom off the seat and sort of hovered there, balancing with her elbows locked like a gymnast on the parallel bars. Her arms, as always, strained from the effort. She hand-walked into the shower, having long ago gotten used to the sight of her legs dragging uselessly below her, her feet bent at weird angles as she tugged them along the shower floor. But the one thing she'd never truly gotten used to, at least not late at night when the memories fluttered around her with black wings, was the unshakable feeling that her lower half was not a part of her at all but rather an interloper that sought only to oppose her. She couldn't feel Terrell's hand when he touched her thigh. One night she'd asked him never to do it again, because she couldn't stand seeing his fingers against her skin without being able to know their fire.

Besides, there were plenty of other places for his hands to roam. And those places were *quite* capable of sensation, thank you very much.

Halfway to the plastic chair, she smiled. She poised there, remembering his charming, adolescent manner when he suggested that they spend the evening together. In that instant he'd been both inept and sexy, and the mixture of the extremes was an aphrodisiac surprisingly complete in its power. It left no part of her wanting. Terrell was the whole thing, the child's heart and the man's enveloping soul. Hannah grinned when she pictured the bashful way he looked up at her through his eyelashes. Why was it so hard to tell a woman how you felt?

"Timid men vex me," she announced. Then she swung herself onto the chair.

After showering, dressing was relatively easy, and she took the ramp into her kitchen with time to spare. Everything here was windows, and all of them were open. She loved to see the curtains blowing. Automatic coffeepots were third on the list of civilization's great innovations, falling behind the telephone and, near and dear to Hannah's heart, the wheel. She reinvented it in her daydreams, making it more efficient every time. She drank two cups of coffee and ate a bowl of Cheerios because she'd loved them ever since she was a girl, then took another ramp outside and let gravity usher her to the sidewalk.

At eight-thirty the sun was perfect. From a pocket on her chair Hannah removed her gloves, the padded, fingerless kind used by bicyclists, and pulled them on as Larry Koger trundled by in his tow truck and honked at her in salutation. Hannah smiled and waved, then got moving. She took her normal route, yelling hellos at the usual faces. When the school bus went by, borrowed by the Parks & Recreation department to haul students to summer swimming lessons, she stuck her tongue out at the kids, who loved her for it and gleefully returned the gesture. True to form, Mr. Fisk came jogging around the corner of Freedom and Seventh streets, his graying hair pasted to his head, his Yale T-shirt splotched with isosceles stains of sweat.

"Morning, Hannah."

"You ever going to finish this race, Mr. Fisk?"

"God, I hope so."

"See you tomorrow."

"Yep."

Hannah turned on Seventh and gave an extra effort to surmount a hill that at one time had daunted her but now went nearly unnoticed. She used to resent Mr. Fisk. He was seventy and a rich retired doctor and probably took his morning run for granted. Just like the aerobics instructor Jennifer Atwood, who pressed the pedals of her cutesy little BMW without a second thought; Jennifer waved big as she passed, and Hannah smiled genuinely when she waved back. Hannah's own car had no pedals. Instead there were levers attached to the steering wheel. She didn't drive much when the weather was nice, except when she was heading to her beautician's out on Red Oak Road or spying on scumbags at the Riverhouse.

Her smile faded.

Last night she'd sat in the parking lot at the bar and waited for Jed Whitecross. Part of her had hoped that he wouldn't be alone, because then she could have buzzed Jo and called it off. But he'd come out at one a.m., tossing his keys in the air, completely by himself, so Hannah had sent the all-clear and then drove home with her finger light on the gas lever.

Thinking about it, she felt the Hoofbeats stir. They bothered her all the way to work. "Nothing good can come of this," she said to a bluejay pecking at the grass. She was met at the door by the courthouse custodian, a former star offensive tackle for the Mountaineers whom everyone called Big Lane, as in what you made for a running back when you were All American. He was a giant and could have gone pro until he tore his ACL, which was football shorthand for retirement.

"You don't need to hold the door open for me every day," she told him as she rolled up the handicap ramp, her smile blossoming again.

"Wouldn't be right if I didn't."

"You're a gentleman and a scholar, Mr. Lane."

"Don't know about that."

"When was the last time I baked cookies for you?"

"A week. Why?"

"Do you have any left?"

He laughed.

"That's what I thought. I'll work on another batch this weekend."

"Nah, you don't need to do that. . . ."

"Too late," she said over her shoulder, zipping down the

waxed tiles. "Your order has already been processed and will be delivered shortly by Meals on Wheels." She let the right tire rub against the palm of her glove, which caused the chair to turn and deliver her into the dispatcher's office with faultless timing. "Hi, Esther. Am I late?"

Esther put her newspaper aside, blinked groggily and looked at the clock. "Is it that time already?" She was forty-nine and, according to her, had been such for at least five years now. "Sure flies when you're pretending to have fun."

"So it was a slow night?"

"What? Didn't you hear the news?"

Hannah jammed her fingers into the spokes, stopping cold. *Here it comes.* The Hoofbeats practically trampled her. "What news?"

"About last night."

"What about it?"

Esther stood up, rubbing her back. "Old Robert Mason's mangy bluetick dog jumped the fence and killed two of his cousin's prize-winning cottontails."

Hannah sighed like a woman who's just been told the test results came back negative.

"Should've seen poor Mason, tossing out apologies like confetti."

"Yeah." Hannah sent a silent thank you toward heaven. "Sorry I missed that."

"You feeling under the weather? You look a little pale around the edges."

"No, I'm fine. There are just some days, you know."

Esther nodded as if she understood, though it was evident that she didn't. Esther was one of those people who didn't really know how to handle someone with a disability; it was like finding a horse with a game leg and not being sure whether to send it to the vet or put it out of its misery.

Hannah chided herself for such thoughts. Esther didn't mean any harm.

"You need to duck into the ladies?" Esther asked. "Or are you ready to settle in?"

"I'll take it." She accepted the hands-free phone and put it over her head, too distracted to fret over what it did to her hair. "Has Terrell checked in yet?"

"I thought it was his day off."

"It is. But he's got a meeting out of state this morning and I know he's planning on leaving early. Thought he might have left a message."

Esther gathered her things. "A meeting on Saturday? Shame on him. When I was your age, Bud and I never missed a Saturday night rendezvous."

"So there wasn't a message?"

"Can't say there was. But he's a man, right?"

Hannah waited for Esther to expound on this statement, but apparently there wasn't a punchline. The inability of men to leave notes was clearly one of those truths that were held to be self-evident.

"Alrighty then, dear, I'm out of here. Hold the fort. You know how wacky people can get in the heat. It's the weekend, and you never can tell."

Normally such a statement wouldn't have sounded as ominous as it did.

"And when Big Lane comes looking for donuts, tell him that it's Saturday and the shop is closed. He always forgets."

"Sure."

Esther slid into her shoes—none of the dispatchers wore them when pulling the graveyard shift—and slipped around to the civilian side of the counter. "See you Monday."

"Yeah. See you."

"Oh, I almost forgot." She dropped her card in the time

clock, held it for half a second while the machine thumped a number against it, then slotted it in the rack beside her name. "If the Gibson boys show up today with some mixed-up story about white supremacists, don't pay them any mind."

The Hoofbeats surged again. "What do you mean?"

"You know how they are. It was Friday, and it's in the Gibson genes to get wasted on Friday night. They can't help it. They're good boys at heart."

Hannah wheeled up to the counter. "What happened?"

"I'm not exactly sure, they were too many sheets to the wind when they stumbled in about two in the morning talking about how members of the Aryan Nation or some such thing were setting up shop in Clayton County."

Hannah felt herself blink. "I don't understand."

"It's nothing, dear. Don't worry about it. I just wanted to warn you, in case they were still hallucinating this morning. The oldest one, Shawn, he was the least drunk of the two, and he came in last night jabbering about seeing a gang of men in pointed hats. I called Bottle to ask if I should lock him up for public intox, and he said just to call the boys' sister to come and get them. But then Mason's coon dog made a midnight snack of the neighbor's rabbits, and I was too busy to see if the sister picked them up or if they just drove off by them- selves. I'm sure I would have heard if they didn't make it home all right."

"Yes, I'm sure you would have."

"Well, then I'll see you in a couple of days."

"Right. Bye."

Esther left.

The entire building was as quiet as the stone of which it was built.

Down the hall, Big Lane whistled as he mopped.

Hannah had never been more thankful for the sound.

116

★ ★ ★ ★ ★

Tamaryn hung up the phone, stared at the splotch her greasy hand had left on the receiver, and decided, after an iffy internal battle, to wipe it off. She was in such a mood that she almost left the stain there just so the next person to pick it up would pay the price. But there was another one of her Good Rules: no smoking around the boys, and no taking out her frustration on innocent phone users. Or anyone else for that matter. Despite the satisfaction it would bring.

She snorted at herself and cleaned the phone on her apron.

"You still here?" Sally Fong asked from the far side of the window that separated the dining area from the kitchen. "Thought you said you were leaving."

"Are you trying to get rid of me, Sal?" Tam untied her apron as she pushed through the gray metal door. She pitched the apron in the vicinity of a cardboard box bound for the cleaners. "Because I don't get paid enough to take this kind of grief."

Sally cackled, vaguely witchlike. "You give more of it than you take, sunshine. Big stuff going on with you tonight?"

Tam grabbed her Gatorade from the walk-in fridge and her purse from the top of the bun rack. "Big stuff like what?"

"You and Roy painting the town red?"

"Hardly."

"You two into that Latin dancing that everybody's doing lately?"

"That'll be the day."

"So he's more of a candlelight-at-home kind of guy?"

"Yeah, right."

"Maybe he's there fixing you dinner right now."

"Enough with the grief-giving already, Sal."

Further laughter, even more full of broomsticks than before.

"You're lucky I'm in a good mood," Tam said, shoving through the swinging door.

"This is a good mood?" Sally called through the window. "They say Lizzie Borden had good moods like this."

Tamaryn didn't reply, but dashed between tables that she'd grown so weary of seeing for the last three years and plopped down into the corner booth at the back. LOVE MUST LAST was carved into the tabletop.

"So?" she said. "Did you hear anything?"

Lucy looked up from her paperback. "The tomatoes on my BLT are soggy."

"Yeah, the help in this place really sucks. So what about it?"

Lucy put her book aside and hunched closer. At the same time, it was as if a new presence sat down at the table with them, one that changed the look in Lucy's eyes and altered the quality of her voice. It was the specter of conspiracy, conjured at the moment illicit affairs were spoken of, and it carried its own allure.

"I didn't do my route today."

"I know. It's Sabado. Your day off, you lucky crumb. So what?"

"But I walked anyway."

"Since when did you exercise?"

"I ran into Thelma Babcock, out watering her grass."

"Do I know her?"

"Her son is dating Becky Gibson."

"Okay . . ."

"Becky Gibson picked her brothers up from jail last night."

"Wait a minute. I know this story." Fresh color rising in her freckled cheeks, Tam pinched a corner of bread from Lucy's sandwich and said while she chewed, "Jessler just called. She said somebody reported seeing a gang of rednecks in bedsheets hanging around the road to the Riverhouse."

"That would be Kyle and Shawn Gibson."

"So we must have made an impression."

"No, a gang of rednecks in bedsheets made an impression."

"We got people talking. That's good. Gives them something to do."

Lucy leaned closer, her voice falling to a whisper. "The last thing I want is to stir up rumors about white-power patriots going around scaring people. This country needs as little of that as it can get. There's enough racism going around as it is."

"I agree. We should have stopped that car and explained to the Gibson brothers that, no, we're not dumb Caucasian men with an inferiority complex, if you don't mind, we're just five pissed-off women, now will you please spread the appropriate gossip."

Lucy removed one of the tomatoes from her sandwich and handed it over. "Here, see for yourself. Have you talked to Jo today?"

Tamaryn took a bite of the tomato. "She likes to spend the weekends with Caroline. I try not to bother her. You're right. This scores a six-point-nine on the soggy scale."

"Well, Caroline hasn't been much for spending time with her mother lately."

"It's a phase. You went through it too."

"That doesn't make it any easier on Jo."

"You think she regrets what we did last night?"

Lucy shrugged. "You'll have to ask her that yourself."

"Come on, Luce. You know her better than anyone."

Lucy thought about it for a few seconds. "The truth?"

"Lie to me."

119

"I think she's proud of herself and ashamed of herself at the same time."

"Hmmm. Not me. What about you?"

"The jury's still out."

"Would it make any difference then if I told you I had a plan?"

"A plan for what?"

"Our next secret mission."

"You mean a sequel to last night's misinterpreted white supremacist sighting?"

"You didn't spend all that time making those outfits for nothing."

Lucy looked at her skeptically. "I'm afraid to ask."

"Then don't. Just meet me at Jo's tonight. We'll talk about it then."

"Why her place? Caroline might be there."

"I don't know. I guess it doesn't matter."

"But it just feels like the place to be."

"Yeah, actually, it does."

"You know she won't go for it."

"She hasn't even heard the plan."

"Doesn't matter. I haven't heard it either, and I'm not sure if *I'm* going for it."

Tam helped herself to a long drink of Lucy's iced tea. "How does seven sound?"

"As good as any time for people like me without anywhere better to be. I was planning on spending the evening with Danny Glover and a remote control. You're looking to push this, aren't you?"

"I ain't *looking* to do anything. It's like you said at the hospital."

"Sometimes I talk too much. Never know when to keep my mouth shut."

"Let me ask you something, Luce."

They were still bent over the table, their faces only a few inches apart. "What?"

"It felt good, didn't it?" Tam took another slurp of tea, then slid out of the booth. "Don't answer that. Just think about it. You can tell me tonight at Jo's."

"And where are you going between now and then?"

"First home to get the boys, then over to Martinsburg."

"What for? I thought Matthew's last soccer game was a week ago."

"Shopping."

"You hate shopping."

"Yeah, I know."

"Then why do you look so excited about it?"

"I'm not shopping for groceries, Lucy Campbell." Tam ducked down and kissed her on the forehead. "I'm shopping for paint."

"Pardon me?"

"*Pink* paint. Catch ya on the flip side." She snagged a cold french fry from Lucy's plate and stepped out under the sun.

It felt so good.

Chapter Nine

It was shortly after four when Jo left Penny's house, thinking about the sound.

Huff-pop, huff-pop.

That was how she spelled it in her mind, the sinister little noise of the dyed cotton rasping against her mouth when her breathing sped up. All day it had been there, like that itch in your inner ear you can never reach no matter how ardently you work the Q-tip or how many times you swallow. It's still there. Sticking its tongue out at you.

She and Caroline had stopped in at Penny's to check up on her, as she'd been released from the hospital last night and was home convalescing.

"Thanks for coming," Penny had said, leading her and Caroline through the house to her music room in the back. "You remember Jed?"

Jed Whitecross looked up from the piano.

"How could I forget?" Jo replied. Her guts turned to sludge. Had she known Jed would be here, she wouldn't have come. Yet she couldn't flee without giving herself away. The last time she'd seen him, he was lying on his back in the gravel.

Jed pushed himself lazily from the piano bench, his smile leading the way. "If it isn't my favorite party hostess. Jo Adams, right? How are you, Jo?"

Jo was glad he didn't offer his hand. That would have been too much. "Fair to middlin'. And you?" In her mind she heard him begging, *Just please don't hurt me.*

"Doing okay, all things considered." He put his arm

around Penny's waist. Her shoulder was heavily wrapped. "Things were a little touchy there for awhile, weren't they, babe? But we're getting along fine now. They say that time heals, am I right?"

Jo wanted to sit down but was afraid to ask. Penny had taken him back. Jo had hoped to hear Penny's story, and by listening help her get rid of Jed Whitecross, like lancing the pus from a blister. Yet here he was.

Even after what he'd done to her. Here he was.

"Are you going to introduce me to your friend, Jo, or just make me stand here and suffer?" Jed trained his blue eyes on Caroline. "You must be Jo's sister."

Caroline beamed.

Jo suppressed a groan.

"This is Caroline," Penny said. "She's Jo's daughter."

"Daughter? No way. You're fooling, right? I wouldn't have guessed it." If he'd been terrified last night, it didn't show at all this afternoon.

"It's good to meet you," Caroline said.

"The pleasure's mine, believe me. Can we get you ladies a drink? Jo, is it okay if I offer your daughter a beer?"

Even after the sheets, Jo thought. *Even after the words we yelled at you in the dark. Even after the softball bat. You're still flashing those white teeth.*

"Just kidding, of course," Jed said. "No alcohol for minors, even if they *do* look twenty-one." He winked.

The encounter hadn't gotten any better from there. Jo said get well soon, Penny said she was working on it, and then Jo left her there with Jed's hand on the small of her back and his eyes stealing glances at Caroline's legs.

Jo drove home with both hands on the wheel.

"That's my reason for law school," Caroline said from the passenger's seat.

Jo sensed the trap in her daughter's tone. There should have been a sign: WARNING, PARENTAL MINEFIELD AHEAD. She was glad that Caroline had been home and willing to come along to check up on Penny. Hadn't there been a time when Saturdays had been their meeting place, their common ground? There had been picnics and trips to the mall. Jo was sure of it.

"I'm afraid you'll have to explain that," she said.

"Law school isn't about all the things they make it about."

"Care to be a little more cryptic?"

"C'mon, Mom, didn't you see them in there? Penelope got beaten up. Her arm's in a sling! And now she's back with the guy who did it and pretending like nothing has changed. We're just supposed to act normal and not bring it up. But think about what would happen if she went to court."

One step ahead of you, Jo thought. She'd already whittled that twig in her mind, and its final shape wasn't a promising one. There were attorneys that normal people had and then there were the Olympians, the quasi-celebrities that kept movie stars from prison and went up against the Department of Justice without concern. If you had Jed Whitecross's kind of money to throw ceaselessly at your defense, you could win a case by attrition alone.

"I see what you're saying, Sweet, and I wish there were something we could do about it."

"Maybe there is. That's what the law is for, isn't it?"

"I suppose so. At least in theory."

"Robert Kennedy once said that there is no basic inconsistency between ideals and realistic possibilities."

"Did he?"

"Yes."

"Well, he said a lot of things."

"What's that supposed to mean?"

"Oh, nothing, I guess. You just need to remember that part of politics is getting elected. And that's hard to do without compromising yourself every now and then."

"I don't think he was like that." She turned and looked out the window.

"I didn't know he'd become one of your role models." And that was the crux of the issue, wasn't it? Not only had Jo accidentally steered her daughter into another closed-up silence, she'd admitted an ignorance of a matter that was obviously near to Caroline's heart. Robert Kennedy? Who would have thought? *Damn. Sometimes I can't win for losing. Whatever the hell that means.* "What else did he say?"

Caroline kept her eyes outside. "Who?"

"You know who. Bobby."

"It doesn't matter."

"Doesn't it? You're planning on going to law school, you darn sure better know a little something about one of the most important attorney generals in the history of this country. So how about it?"

"He said the world's hope was to rely on youth," she related with little feeling.

"That's nice. I like that. I have to agree."

"He said there is no greater need than for educated men and women to point their careers toward public service."

"Okay."

"He said that it's not enough to allow dissent. We must demand it. For there is much to dissent from."

"Now *there's* a motion I'll second every time."

Caroline looked at her suddenly. "Where were you when he died?"

"Probably out dissenting somewhere." She smiled, but mostly to herself. "No, that's not true at all. I never once took part in any passive resistance. I never got arrested for handcuffing myself to the black man or the Jew beside me. I never heard Robert Kennedy speak in person."

She felt ashamed. Sitting here beside Caroline made her feel inadequate for having passed up the opportunity to hold a placard, or shout a slogan. Until now, it had never bothered her. But between the lingering ozone of last night's lightning strike and the laser beam of Caroline's stare, she was burned.

"It's okay," Caroline said. "None of my friends' mothers set fire to their bras, either."

"You asked them?"

A grin touched Caroline's lips. She shook her head. "I just wish there were some way to help Penelope. She keeps getting stuck with rough guys like this. She's not going to do anything about it on her own."

Jo agreed without saying so, simply thrilled to have evoked a smile, however partial it might have been. She scored another point by keeping the conversation nonconfrontational all the way across town. For the first time since she'd stood up in the roadside weeds in her pink kimono, she thought about something other than *huff-pop, huff-pop*. When she asked if Caroline was considering joining a sorority when she got to college, her daughter opened her mouth and poked a finger down her throat. She pulled a disgusted face and made a retching sound she hadn't used since she was twelve years old. "Please, Mom, *gag* me!" And she laughed, a hill down which Jo would have gladly rolled any day. They tumbled down it together, quipping about the social elite and making sundry noises of repugnance at the mention of each new combination of Greek letters.

Jo was in such spirits that she even fingered a borderline flirtsy wave in Warren Dearborn's direction when she saw him washing cars in front of the Autoporium. Warren, a widower who'd asked her out once or twice, looked startled to be on the receiving end of the gesture, and he let his hose get away from him and took a shot of water in the face. Caroline saw it all, and she burst out with laughter. Jo filled herself with that sound; she would have traded the air in her lungs for it.

When she got home, she was just about to suggest they send out for veggie pizza when Caroline played back the messages. It was Nin. They were coming over at seven. She said that Lucy had called her and sounded strange. Nin sounded a little strange herself.

"What's that all about?" Caroline asked.

Jo groped around inside of herself, but the amusement that had danced there only minutes before had fled. "Nothing. Just a bunch of wannabe bra-burners trying to make up for lost time." As soon as she said it, she wished she hadn't. No need to plant any seeds in Caroline's brain. "I'm sure it's not important. We can go out, if you want. See a movie?"

"Nah, the Crazy Coven needs its fearless leader. Besides, I told some friends I'd see them tonight."

"Any friends in particular?"

The shrug that Caroline gave her was evidence that the wall was up again. Parents to one side, please, friends on the other. "Is midnight okay?"

"It's Saturday," Jo said, in the tone she couldn't help but use when facing the wall. "You know midnight is okay on Saturday."

Caroline might or might not have heard her. Flip a coin.

In a moment she vanished upstairs.

Jo stood in the center of her living room surrounded by her familiar, accumulated things. If she'd ever found comfort in them, for the life of her she couldn't say why. She closed her eyes and imagined an empty house, a house with only beds and bathtubs and maybe a beanbag or two so that a mother could sit on the floor with her daughter and have a little room to breathe.

She tried to watch the evening news but couldn't. She thought about calling Martin to make sure everything was ready for their presentation at the town meeting on Monday, but even thoughts of work and business couldn't distract her for long, which was evidence enough that something was wrong. She vacuumed the living room and watered her needy plants, all the while being nibbled on by razory teeth. But she wasn't able to give a name to her discomfort until seven o'clock. That's when Tamaryn started talking about the paint, and Jo realized the teeth were the mouth of dissent, waiting to be fed.

There came a moment that evening—Nin tried to put her finger on it but she couldn't say just when it happened—that their eyes all *matched*. That was the only way she could describe it to herself days later, in one of the rare moments when she was able to stop sanely and think. It didn't last long, that second, but like the aligning of the planets, it was impossible not to notice if you were looking in the right place. Nin sat in the center of the sofa, watching them, and when they finally decided to act, they sealed the pact not with any words but with their eyes.

Tam had started it.

"So can we stop with all this Elvis stuff and get on with it?"

"I'm just asking," Hannah said, "if anyone has any suggestions on what albums to buy, because Elvis has so many of them out there and I want to make sure I get one with a lot of good songs on it, and I don't just mean all the popular ones you hear all the time."

"I didn't know you were a fan," Jo said, leaning in the

doorway between the living room and kitchen.

"I'm not, or at least I wasn't, you know I usually listen to country, mostly, but Terrell is really into jazz and I realized that I like a lot of it, so I thought I might give some other types a try as well. Broaden my musical horizons."

"I'd let you borrow some of mine," Lucy said, "but all I have are those old albums. The kind you play on a turntable. I wouldn't know how to use a CD if you handed me an instruction book in five languages."

Nin, quiet observer that she was, looked beyond their words. So often people spoke to fill up space. Nin had never understood that. Instead of talking of what they felt, or simply letting the silence give them room to think, they rattled on about the silliest things. Elvis! Nin smiled inwardly. Her grandmother had taught her the medicine of smiling, and how you could get away with doing it even when no one knew. She thought about the hood ornament she'd rescued from the grass, and she stopped smiling. She'd taken the shiny little cat ostensibly to clear up any sign that the attack had taken place. She thought it best to clean up the evidence. Actually she wanted to look at the object when she was alone, to confirm that what they'd done was real. She reminded herself to throw it away as soon as she got home.

She turned her brown eyes on Jo. Always her gaze went there first, when she was watching the other women, as she so often did. Clothes were clues. Jo wore blue jeans and a white button-down shirt with the tails untucked and the sleeves rolled up. This was her usual weekend attire. *But.* She wore hiking boots, laced up high and tight. And no earrings. Nin nodded to herself, and that only amused her further, because she envisioned her grandmother nodding in the same, knowing manner. Oh, how glorious were the hand-me-downs from one generation to another.

"I might even have some old eight-tracks if I dug deep enough," Lucy said.

At the sound of Lucy's voice, Nin examined her, not critically, but the way you admired a painting that has hung on your wall for years yet continues to please you every time you look at it. Nin knew all of Lucy's wrinkles (a few more around the eyes than there had been last year), all the issues that lit her fire (gas prices, child abuse), and all the things that gave her pause (bringing people letters that made them smile, the sight of a kitten, the mere thought of Sean Connery). But something in the way she sat tonight was not Lucy Campbell at all. Perhaps, Nin thought, it was because she was experiencing all three of those things at the same time. What they had done to Jed Whitecross gave her wrinkles, it inflamed her, it brought her peace. No wonder she couldn't sit still.

"But if you have any suggestions other than Elvis then let me know, because I'm not sure where to start, but I thought about Sinatra and Nat King Cole . . ."

And then there was Hannah. Oh, Hannah. The Lord had instilled in her a wellspring of optimism, hadn't He? Nin's grandmother would have adored her. There were times when the fountain lost some of its *umph,* when Nin wondered if the girl's love affair with life had finally gone dry, but the sweet water always returned. The chair was brutal. But it hadn't shriveled her. At least not yet. With the exception of Tam, who made no effort to ignore her emotions, Hannah was the easiest of them to read. She was also so delightful with the children. Earlier in the evening she'd converted a dish-soap bottle into a water gun and chased the kids into the backyard. Now she bounced Marky in her lap. "Or maybe a show tune from Broadway . . ."

"Hey!" Tamaryn stood up. "Can we please cut the crap?"

No one said anything, but their faces changed.

"I bought some spray paint today. Lots of it. I thought I might find someone willing to help me put it to good use, but now I'm not so sure."

Still she received no reply, so she began to stalk the room. "Look at us, will you? We finally do one decent thing and now we're too scared to talk about it. I thought about it all day, and I want to keep going. We got to get people talking. And no, Jo, before you ask, I don't know what good that'll do. It probably won't help at all. But I don't care. It sure beats going around numb all the time."

Numb? Nin asked herself whether or not she agreed with that. Well. People were a little dumbed-down these days, true enough. But *spray paint?*

"Let me tell you a story," Tam said. "Matthew has this music teacher in school. You know how kids are in music class, more concerned with making farting noises than learning the scales. But anyway, they got this new music teacher last year. She decorated her room with the usual mug shots of Beethoven and people, and I guess she tacked an American flag to her piano. So what, right? Big deal. But Matt comes home and tells me the principal made his teacher take the flag down, because one of the mothers saw it and complained. She said it wasn't respectful to hang up a flag like that, with tacks poked through it. So she called the school and griped." Tam threw up her hands. "Will somebody please tell me what the hell's wrong with this picture? We've got kids who can't read, kids who don't even have enough to *eat,* and some stupid bitch is complaining about *flags?*"

Here comes Jo, Nin thought.

"How does vandalism alleviate that situation?" Jo asked, as predicted.

"It doesn't, Josephine. It doesn't at all. It just says that I am sick and sad and through hanging out on the sidelines while the people with the balls to speak their minds are the ones with nothing positive to contribute."

"So what are you proposing that we paint? This woman's house?"

"Hell no. I'm taking my frustration out on men." She smiled wickedly.

"And what is it that you want to deface?"

"Why, Jo, I thought you'd never ask."

Nin swung her gaze back at Lucy, who didn't seem surprised by any of this. Had Tamaryn already discussed these matters with her? Lucy would vote for the paint, Nin was sure. Of the five of them, Lucy had the least to lose. She risked her job, but had no children to be taken from her, no boyfriend to disappoint and no teenage daughter to estrange. And Hannah? How would she vote? The brightness still lit her eyes, but it shared space with trepidation.

And Jo?

That one was too close to call. Twenty-four hours ago it would have been easy, but now, with the hiking boots . . .

"Roy and his friends have this cabin," Tamaryn began.

"Hold on." Jo went to the back door, glanced around, then returned. "Sorry. Go ahead."

"You think we're being spied on?"

"Caroline comes in the back sometimes."

"Does talking about this make you that nervous?"

"The cabin. Roy and his friends. Go ahead."

"Right. It's on the north side of Protestant Lake. They use it when they're hunting over the weekend. Fill it with beer, shoot deer all day, come back and tell dirty stories, et cetera. Same old thing. But they hardly ever use the cabin during the summer, because the good hunting seasons aren't open yet."

"You want to go out and graffiti the cabin?"

"They love to play that stupid paintball," Tam continued,

as if she hadn't heard the question. "I can't get Roy to fix the washing machine, and he's out playing cowboys and Indians in the woods."

"Boys will be boys," Lucy allowed.

"Yeah, and that's always been a piss-poor excuse for letting them goof off while we try to make ends meet. Do you know Stan Morris? His wife works herself to death with me at the diner, but does Stan make do with second-rate hunting equipment? Are you kidding me? I can't believe I live in a world where men spend thousands of dollars on guns and mud tires when there are families in the Appalachians a hundred miles away who eat just one meal a day. Some of those kids are *barefoot*, for God's sake."

"So what do we do?" Jo asked her, though Nin suspected she already knew the answer.

"I don't know. Let off a little steam, if nothing else. You tell me. We can't start a revolution. Or I would."

"You say you already have this paint?"

"Eight cans. I bought it out of town so no one would make the connection if they asked somebody at the hardware store."

"Will the cabin be empty tomorrow morning?"

"That's the impression I got from Roy."

"Do you really hate him that much, Tamaryn?"

Tam scoffed. "Don't start, Jo. He's not the same as he used to be and you know it. He doesn't do anything with his life. He just plods along, and honks his horn when someone cuts him off in traffic, and gripes at the politicians on TV, and that's it. I just want to wake him up."

"This will only make him angry."

"We'll see."

"Okay, another question."

Tam crossed her arms. "Go ahead."

"I've been meaning to ask. Last night, that line you used on Jed. 'Don't try and run, you'll only die tired.' " She grinned. "Where on earth did you ever come up with that?"

"Yeah," Lucy chimed. "Girl, you had me rolling my eyes."

Tam looked offended. "I thought it sounded tough."

"You *said* that?" Hannah asked, a smile breaking across her face. "You actually told him that he'd only die tired?"

"Yeah, Jessler, so what? I didn't see you out there saying anything better."

Hannah laughed so hard she almost dropped Marky. "Oops! Whoa, there, little fella." She hugged him close and, getting more tickled by the second, laughed some more.

Nin was not surprised when the laughter infected her. And that, she supposed, was why she would go along with whatever madcap notion Tamaryn had in mind. Shared laughter was the shortest route to unity. Did the thought of committing vandalism titillate her? Perhaps. At least in a childish way. But excitement played little part in her decision. There was truth in what Lucy said the other night at the hospital, and there was truth in Hannah's laugh.

Tamaryn finally smiled in spite of herself.

"So we're really going to go through with this?" Lucy asked, when their mirth had subsided.

Tamaryn deferred to Jo. "What do you say?"

"I say you're crazy."

"It's about time somebody was."

"Maybe so," Jo said softly. "Maybe so."

And then it happened. Though she was certain the others didn't notice it, to Nin it was as clear as if they'd extended their hands to the center of a circle, one on top the other, and swore a musketeer-style oath. Then a train of kids chugged into the house, tooting about being thirsty, and normal life resumed.

It wasn't until nearly nine-thirty that Nin caught Jo alone. They were standing on her front porch, watching the others leave.

"May I ask you something?"

"Of course," Jo said. "Anything."

"Why are you doing this?"

"What do you mean?"

"Well, as for me, I feel as if I am just along for the ride, like any minute now one of you is going to need a soft place to land, and I hope to be there. The others have their reasons, and I think I can guess most of them. Except for you. What's this all about? What are you thinking when you imagine yourself out at the cabin tomorrow?"

Jo was quiet for a long time, her eyes on the stars, and Nin started to think that she wasn't going to reply. But then she said without looking down, "One of these days, ask me to tell you about the answering machine."

Though intrigued, Nin had to satisfy herself with that, because not only was it apparent that Jo wasn't going to divulge any secrets, but it was late, and there were the children to consider, always the children.

Nin eased herself down the steps.

"See you tomorrow?" Jo asked.

"I'll bring the pastries." If she couldn't divert them from this potentially destructive path, at least she could keep them well fed along the way.

Chapter Ten

Less than twelve hours later, Jo stood in the sun. Dawn was breaking. New warmth touched her face, then spread its hands down the length of her body as if getting to know her all over again. It was true. She hadn't watched a sunrise in how long? She couldn't remember. It was one of those things that everyone talked about in passing but nobody ever bothered doing. At least nobody that Jo knew.

She added it to her checklist of fresh feats accomplished: Assault a man on a dark highway—check. Watch the sun come up—check. Trash a perfectly innocent cabin—

"Give me time," she said over the rim of her Styrofoam cup. She watched Hannah through the steam of the hot coffee.

Hannah owned a van and hated it. A van—for someone who used to turn heads in a ragtop Camaro, hair flying like a blonde banner in the wind. Jo stood patiently and sipped her convenience-store coffee, remaining surprisingly steady, while Hannah backed her chair onto the mechanized ramp. *A ramp for the vamp,* Tamaryn had said when they'd tried it out for the first time. Had it been three years ago? Four? *This lift makes me miffed,* Hannah said a few days later. With the press of a button, the ramp ascended, conveying her into the van. Jo didn't look at her face. She never could, during this part. Hannah was a good sport, but please; sometimes the ramp just got old.

An elevator for the—what rhymes with elevator? Tam asked.

Alligator, Jo supplied.

Alligator, elevator. That doesn't rhyme.

136

Okay. How about spinach-hater?

"This isn't really an inconspicuous getaway vehicle," Jo said as she nestled herself into the passenger's seat.

"I'll park in the trees, but you don't really think anyone will be out there at this time of day, do you? I know that during deer season there are men there pretty much all the time, wearing their bright orange vests and all that, but Tam said in the summer the place has a tendency to go to seed."

"Which justifies their annual cleaning slash keg party weekend."

"Yeah. The heathens. Are you nervous?"

"About painting the boys' fort?" She sipped and shrugged. "As far as social deviance is concerned, this doesn't rate very high. But I know what you're asking. So yes, maybe a little. Like I told Caroline, I don't have a lot of practice at being arrested for protesting the death penalty and that sort of thing. My social activism skills aren't very finely tuned. Although I seem to be learning quickly."

Hannah used her thumb to work the accelerator, guiding them into the quiet street. Rolled newspapers lay unclaimed on lawns. Dew still jeweled the grass. "Do you think Tam's doing alright, I mean, on the inside is what I'm talking about, because she's a lot more . . . I don't know, *angry* than she used to be."

"You would be too if you lived with Roy Soza."

"He hasn't done anything to her, has he? Like hit her?"

"Not that I'm aware of. At least not yet. Good thing for him. I'm sure he'd be in for a fight."

"Yeah, she'd knock his block off."

"Or worse."

"Uh-huh." Hannah stopped the van at Lucy's house. "That's what worries me."

★ ★ ★ ★ ★

Jo gave up her seat to Nin and settled into the back of the van with Lucy and Tam, finding a place next to the chair. True to her word, Nin had brought breakfast. They'd picked her up in the church parking lot. Nin's usual schedule on church mornings involved getting all the kids to their proper Sunday school classes at Belle Springs First Baptist and Marky to the tireless ladies in the church nursery. Once a month she delivered the scripture lesson in her own class; last week she'd opened up a discussion on the tribulations of Job. Now, playing hooky, she sat in her knee-length hose and flowered Sunday dress, a set of carefully folded pink sheets between her knees.

"All this crusading is hell on my diet," Lucy said, putting away the last of her jelly donut.

"It will keep your energy up," Nin promised.

Only Tam had declined the sugary sins, an indication that she hadn't gone entirely off the deep end. Though being a mother and a waitress and a maid to her husband didn't leave much time for exercise, she burned a lot of calories between the three roles, and she still clung to her regimen of hard-body foods. Jo studied her through the wheelchair frame, trying to decide if the glaze over her eyes was the result of antagonism or simple lack of sleep.

Either way, she's ready to snap.

Tamaryn caught her staring and stuck her tongue out at her.

That put Jo somewhat at ease, but ten minutes later they reached the lake, and ease became a thing of the past.

Protestant Lake was serviced by three roads, only one of which was paved. That was County Road 12, a two-lane blacktop kept more or less in decent repair, a straight shot from Belle Springs. CR 12 saw the most traffic, usually trucks with bass boats attached and, come autumn, the same trucks with dead bucks tied to the grill.

One of the back roads led a roundabout way to the Riverhouse; Friday night they'd parked at its opposite end while they dressed in their lady Robin Hood attire. This morning, Hannah took the third road simply because it was the shortest. Nin only had until noon, when church got out and the nursery gals would expect to see her.

When they were close, Hannah drove into a bare spot between the trees. The entire lakeside was heavily wooded with white oak and the occasional beech, the sweet-smelling hills thick with azalea and the goldenrod that Jo collected as a child and wove into her hair. The yellow buds entwined in her red locks had always pleased her mother.

Tam rolled the van's side door open before the vehicle had fully stopped. She pounced down into the grass and shimmied into her robe. Since the encounter with Jed, they'd cut armholes in the robes and sewn on billowing sleeves, permitting them more freedom of movement. "Time to dash into the phone booth, girls. Let's make this quick."

The others followed suit with varying quantities of enthusiasm. Jo's hands fumbled over the fabric. She supposed her hurriedness was due to honest exhilaration. Between the caffeine, the scent of the woods, and the echo of Caroline's words of dissention, she felt *light*. No longer so firmly rooted to the ground.

Nin unfolded her garments with deliberation. "Now that I think about it, it becomes even more important to me that we're not seen. I don't believe it would be difficult to recognize us. And I am certain it wouldn't be difficult to recognize *me*."

"You?" Hannah snorted humorlessly. "I think I've got

you beat in that department."

"A fine and undeniable point," Lucy said, already dressed and unloading the paint cans. "This daylight business could get us into serious trouble. Somebody could drive up on us, and then what would we do? We'll have to be extra careful. And fast."

"We're fine," Tam said, ending the discussion. "Here, give me that box."

The mechanical ramp lowered the chair to the ground. Jo helped Hannah get the sheet settled over her body, tugging, adjusting, and smoothing, and when she looked up, Hannah was grinning.

"Don't start," Jo warned.

"This is fun."

"It's not fun."

"It's nuts."

"I'll give you that."

"Normal people don't do this kind of thing."

"Sure they do. When it's all they have left."

Hannah put on the hood. Then she laughed.

"What is it now?"

"I don't know. Just us."

"Jessler, you be sure to stay on the road, got it?" Tam put on a pair of gloves, then hefted the box of cans and started toward the cabin. "Don't get into the dirt. Roy's cronies may be stupid and mean, but they can damn sure tell a doe track from a wheelchair rut."

"Aye, aye, General." She saluted.

"Let's go, then."

"Lord be with us," Nin said, and they followed her through the trees.

Jo had never seen the cabin before today, but it was a

dump. It stood about fifty feet from the lake and the tumble-down pier that reached out over the water. The porch had seen some recent attention, as its lumber was visibly newer than the rest of the shanty, but the paint on the window casements was flaky and the roof was decidedly bowed in its center, probably the result of last winter's accumulated snow. Brown-tipped weeds grew high around the baseboards. A blackened fifty-five-gallon metal drum served as a burn barrel. The ground around it was embedded with nonflammables, mostly beer cans so faded that you couldn't tell one brand from the next.

Jo took two even breaths. An unidentified woman in her head said something about abiding. She looked at the cabin. One of the windows was cracked like a crooked smile. Jo tried not to take that personally, but she couldn't shake the feeling that the cabin was intentionally mocking her.

"Give me a can," she said.

Tamaryn placed the cardboard box on a tree stump used for splitting wood. Jo went straight to the stump, thrust her hand into the box, and liberated a can with a pink plastic top. After putting up a fight, the top popped off, and Jo shook the can vigorously. The metal bearing inside made a satisfying sound as she pumped the can up and down.

"So is there a method to this madness?" Lucy asked. "Or do we just start in however the spirit moves us?"

"The window's mine," Jo said. She mounted the porch, still shaking the can, the lightness permeating her body. She felt about three seconds away from floating. *My superheroine persona, Helium Lady.* She stopped before the window, tried to peer through it but the dust was too thick. She batted the confining sheet out of the way and watched as her arm drifted up and brought her weapon to bear. *Able to leap rideable fences in a single bound.* She painted a pink slash across the glass.

The dam broke. The women spilled forth.

Tam sprinted up the steps and threw her shoulder against the door. The padlock held but the hasp broke away from the jamb. The peak of Tam's hat bent against the door frame as she rumbled inside.

Hiking up her gown, Lucy ran to the nearest corner and began painting broad arcs of color, one under the other, forming a pink rainbow.

Nin used the handrail to ascend to the porch, but she nevertheless moved with uncharacteristic alacrity. Clucking to herself, she cleared her arm from the sheet and applied a tidy circle of paint to the cabin, stepped back to appraise her work, then added another spot of color beside the first.

Hannah, careful to remain on the gravel, could go no farther than the burn barrel that stood within arm's reach of the path. She raked the can back and forth in the barrel's direction without regard for design, pausing only long enough to adjust her finger on the nozzle.

The sound of hissing cans filled the woods.

Jo was only dimly aware of the others. She coated the entire window, her nose cringing in response to the rising paint fumes. The thought of someone walking through the forest and catching her in the act only reinforced the sensation that she was hovering miles above her own body. *Is this what it feels like to be a criminal?* She'd never run from the cops as a teenager, or attended a college frat party that was raided by campus police, or even performed a little harmless shoplifting in the candy aisle of a convenience store. *Is this how all the non-abiders feel?*

She paid extra attention to the casement. "Needs a paint job, anyway."

"What did you say?" Nin asked, looking up from her work.

"Nothing. Just keep your can moving." She stepped

backed and sneezed. The window and much of the wood around it now appeared as an uneven pink rectangle. Good enough. The lightness carried her into the cabin.

Tam was wrecking the place. She'd overturned a card table and knocked a stack of enamel camping-style bowls onto the floor. In huge letters above the rusty steel sink she'd written GIRLZ RULE.

Though little sunlight filtered through the grimy windows, Jo could see well enough to spot the calendar that was pinned to the back door. She levitated toward it. February boasted a woman wearing only red heels and a fireman's hat, straddling a hose. Jo covered her hand with the sleeve of her robe and lifted the page. March wore a pinstriped tie and a briefcase, but nothing else. Jo restored the woman's modesty by covering her in paint.

A bottle shattered against the counter.

Jo didn't even turn around. Tam was hunting down anything smashable and expending her anger in the shards.

The lightness carried Jo to the fireplace, in which lay mounds of dead ashes and an iron poker. Still keeping her hand in her sleeve, she fished out the poker, painted it pink, then placed it atop the mantel amongst a confusing assortment of trophies: the skull of a small animal, a football, a plastic hula girl that shook her grass skirt when you nudged her hips, a pair of shot glasses turned upside-down, a figurine of the Virgin Mary, and a condom stretched over a toilet paper tube. She was sure there was a code in this assembly, a riddle that—if deciphered—would unfold the mysteries of an entire gender. But the longer she stared at the curios, the more their message seemed as inscrutable as Mayan hieroglyphs. She considered swatting the entire lot onto the floor, but then again, setting the pink poker between them seemed to be enough.

Outside, Lucy was singing.

And what was that other sound? An approaching car?

It must have been the wind.

Jo drifted. Around the room, painting this and that. Watching the tip of her finger change colors from such close contact with the nozzle. She reminded herself to wash her hands the first thing upon returning home, but her thoughts were insubstantial and she doubted she'd remember.

They'll catch me pink-handed. She smiled.

"Shit." Tamaryn banged her empty can against the corner of the mini-fridge. "I need more ammunition. How about you?"

"I'm fine. But thank you for asking." She watched through a mental fog as Tam bolted through the door, back into the sunlit world. Jo blinked twice behind her mask, stared at her hand until it again felt connected to her arm, then returned to the calendar and covered up a few more of those poor women.

Should have let Joseph Mitz do his worst. Would that have changed her life somehow? *Should have stretched him out on the blanket he brought and made him see stars.* She painted a lightning bolt across the wall and the gun rack that was bolted there. *If he were here now, omigod, how that boy would be in trouble.* She found a bullet resting on a shelf below the gun rack, its brass casing dull with dust. She picked it up, wiped it clean on her robe, and rolled it around on her palm.

Tam burst in with a can in each hand. She went to the only wall left unscathed and gave it a double shot, like a villain in a western letting loose with both triggers.

Jo turned her hand over. The bullet seemed to drop sluggishly through the air, as if sinking in water, and finally settled to the floor.

". . . unless we want to end up spending the night in the pokey."

Jo tugged her head up. "Excuse me?"

"You freaking out on me, Josephine?"

"I'm trying, but I keep getting interrupted. What's the matter?"

"I said we better scat, unless you want Terrell bringing us dinner through bars. I thought I heard an engine or something out there. Like a boat out on the water. Go get everybody rounded up while I finish up in here."

"Sure. Right. You just . . . finish up in here." She left the cabin and was thankful that her hood shaded her eyes from the sun. She should have been running, but she couldn't. An engine? Coming this way? She stood on the edge of the porch and breathed unpainted air. After half a minute, her feet became feet again, her bones no longer buoyant.

She turned to Nin. "Hey, Picasso. Are you about finished?"

"I believe so. I wasn't certain what to paint. I am afraid I haven't contributed much to our effort."

"What the hell is it supposed to be?"

"I intended it to resemble a woman's body."

"Are those tits or eyes?"

Nin leaned back and surveyed her own work. "Is it that bad?"

Jo shrugged. "All great artists have to start somewhere. But, no, I don't think this one is worth signing your name to. Lucy?" she called. "Are you around here somewhere?"

"No, I've been abducted by aliens that all look like George Clooney, and I'm not in any rush. Hold your panties."

"Well, hurry up." Everything was snapping back into full speed. "Hannah?"

The burn barrel was completely, entirely, blindingly pink. Hannah had applied multiple coats to ensure a rich gloss and was working her way through her third can. "This sucks, Jo,

Tam gets the palace and I get stuck with the trash."

"You got some on your chair."

"Did I? Oops. Sure enough. Remind me to clean that off."

Lucy cackled from around the corner. "Who would've thought this would be so much *fun?*" When she appeared, she'd folded her hood up so that her face was exposed. "Damn, but we should sell *tickets* for this. Have folks coming from miles around. And not just women either, mind you." She deposited the spent cans in the box. "Kids could come take out their frustrations on abusive parents, employees against their bosses, Indians against the government, everybody against lawyers . . ."

Jo shook her can one last time and gave a parting blast to the porch.

Lucy waved a finger at her. "See there? Feels good."

Jo was again thankful for the mask. She wasn't sure if what she was feeling was *good,* but she felt something. Then she tensed. "Shhh."

"What?"

"Did you hear something?"

"Don't do this, Jo. My nerves can only stand so much."

"She's right," Tam said, hurtling from the cabin door. "We've got to vamoose. Somebody's out there on the lake."

"At this time of morning?"

"Just get going, Luce!" Tam grabbed the box and ran, cans rattling, toward the van.

Hannah spun the chair deftly and stroked the tires.

"Oh, my," Nin said, and set off at a lumbering gait.

Lucy looked back at Jo. "You waiting for a personal invitation?"

Jo stared at the water. Any moment a waterbike or outboard fishing boat would motor around the bend in the shoreline. The buzzing sound grew louder.

"Girlfriend, you know what they say about she who hesitates."

Jo tore the hood from her head and shook out her hair. "What the hell are we doing here?"

"Right now? Running." Lucy broke into a jog.

Jo followed her for want of a better course of action. Immediately the lightness returned. It was the feeling of being chased, the fear of being caught, the anticipation of what she'd do if that happened. And it wasn't so bad.

Halfway to the van, she let out a yelp.

The others looked back to see if she'd fallen.

She took advantage of their surprise by flying past them, shouting over her shoulder about the last one there being a rotten egg. She considered slowing down to let Hannah catch up, then laughed away her charity and let the wind tangle her hair.

Chapter Eleven

When her alarm went off the next morning, she wondered if it all had been a dream.

She stopped the clock from buzzing, then lay there staring at the hazy light of dawn that outlined her bedroom window.

"Helium Lady," she said to the darkness. *Helium Lady?* She started to giggle, so she pulled a pillow over her face and decided to forego the coffee. She was already giddy enough.

She made decaf instead. It wasn't until she was at the front door with her cup in hand that she realized she wasn't wearing her robe. Just underwear and an oversized T-shirt. Nothing decent for porch-sitting and watching the town shake itself awake.

"So let them talk." She went outside and sat down on the steps.

Her street was quiet, except for Mr. Fisk two houses down, who was tying his shoe before his run. The grass was pearled with dew. Jo pulled her shirt over her knees as far as it would go, put her coffee aside, and removed the rubber band from the morning's *Symposium*.

TOWN MEETING TONIGHT.

Beneath this, ominously: HEATED CONTROVERSY CONTINUES.

"You're telling me," Jo said. Aside from a few hours spent in the guise of her superheroine alter-ego, she'd dedicated the last three days to preparing for tonight's gathering. Though the mayor and city council were technically in charge of things, Jo's presentation was the centerpiece of the discussion, and she dreaded the idea of the warring factions making the most of such a convenient target.

TELEVISION MEDIA EXPECTED TO ATTEND.

"Marvelous." The TV crew from Baltimore was something she could have done without. Yet, now that she thought about it, the promise of all that attention didn't bother her as much as it had twenty-four hours ago. She blamed it on the residue from Helium Lady, this new and timid bravery that had her sitting half-dressed on her porch and tossing her hair in the face of reporters. "I hope the camera gets my good side."

She scanned the story and all the familiar names. Chuck would be glad to see that he was mentioned as early as the third sentence. He'd never been a second-paragraph kind of guy. Bottle was quoted as saying that extra officers would be in place to ensure that events didn't degenerate into a brawl.

Then Jo did something she never did. She ignored the rest of the important stuff and skipped to the funnies.

At least, she tried to. A headline on page three snagged her eye:

VANDALS ABUSE HUNTING LODGE

Sheriff Bo Cantrell confirmed Sunday that a Protestant Lake retreat owned by Belle Springs resident Owen Selvey was the object of a weekend vandalism attack. A favorite gathering place of county sportsmen, the lodge was allegedly entered illegally and "partially covered" with graffiti on interior and exterior walls. Sheriff Cantrell said that the nature of the graffiti resembles what is often perpetrated by college freshmen during "rush week." With fall classes scheduled to begin in less than a month, certain fraternities and sororities of area universities have already begun the rigorous initiation process that is a part of their tradition. In the past, students have been responsible for various misdemeanors within city limits, including destruction of public property, indecent exposure, and littering. Cantrell said that at this time his office had no leads in the case. Mr. Selvey was on an out-of-state fishing trip and unavailable for comment.

Jo stared at the page for several seconds after finishing the article. The words blurred, causing her eyes to water. She blinked away the moisture and slowly read the story again.

"Lodge?" Talk about euphemisms. "That shithole isn't a *lodge.*"

She laughed suddenly, but shut her mouth as soon as she realized how she looked. Still, she grinned over her coffee cup. *Lodge.*

That was almost as bad as *sportsmen.*

When she pictured sportsmen, she thought about those dashing gents from Yorkshire who trailed foxes and were always home in time for tea. The men who hung their guns in Owen Selvey's beer shack smelled of snuff and said things like *I'll bet you could hit that hole if there was hair around it* whenever one of them tossed a crumpled can at the trash barrel and missed.

"Sportsmen? Who writes this crap?"

What was worse was the thought that, after tonight's public gathering, those same hacks would be penning prose about *her.* She was glad to find that she didn't care.

"Go get 'em, Mr. Fisk!" she called.

"I'll give it my best!"

She watched him chug down the sidewalk. She finished her decaf, stood up, and left the newspaper lying on the porch.

Lucy pulled the mail truck into her half of the duplex's

driveway. Tam's muddy Toyota was parked at the curb. Not a good sign.

"What have we gotten our thimblewit selves into now?" she asked herself, continuing the conversation that had begun the moment she lifted her head from her pillow this morning and realized she was a criminal. "Oh, nothing to get excited about, I reckon. Nothing they didn't have coming." She slid open the door and noticed how tall her side of the lawn was getting. "All of this sunlight sure is good on the grass, isn't it? Yep, have to say that's right. Going to have it up to the windowsills unless I break down and hire myself a mower."

Tam was sitting on the porch. Her shirt was splattered with dried grease. She stood up.

"Don't mind me," Lucy said, unfastening the top bottom of her uniform, "just chatting with the only person willing to talk back. Woke up this morning tasting something new in the air, and I'm not sure if I like it or not. Spent the day trying to talk some sense into myself. Now, why am I not surprised to find you here?"

"What do you call a chicken crossing the road?" Tam asked.

"Aren't you supposed to be at work?"

"I took off an hour early. I called Nin. She's got the boys till five. So what do you call a chicken crossing the road?"

Lucy looked back at the street. The fingers of paranoia brushed her neck. "How about we repair to the drawing room, as they say. I'm getting the heebie-jeebies out here, and I'm not sure why."

Tam followed her into the house.

Lucy sat down in the nearest chair. It was either get these shoes off or buy crutches. As she unlaced them, she was aware of the unusual clarity of her actions, as if everything were outlined in white, the edges crisp, the colors vibrant. So it had been all day long. "Something to drink?"

"No thanks."

"You've heard what they're talking about around town?"

"I work at a diner. I hear it all."

"And?"

"What do you expect? They think kids did it. Why, what have you heard?"

"The same, pretty much. Dumb punk kids messing with other people's property, teenagers don't respect their elders anymore, what's the world coming to and all of that."

"Gerald Fawles came in for lunch. He was way upset about it. Every time I walked by his table, he was bitching about all the work it was going to take to fix it back up."

"He spend a lot of time out there?"

"He's a friend of Owen Selvey and the head of the county rod and reel club."

"I see. Mad, was he?"

"Hugely. But he also has five kids from three different mothers and never bothers to go see any of them, so I don't really care how mad he is. He's one of the most irresponsible men I've ever met."

"Well, he's no saint, I'll give you that."

"The creep gets handsy with married women, Luce. Believe me, I know."

Lucy massaged her foot, trying to restore a bit of life. It was a sad thing that body parts wore down the more you used them but there wasn't an easy way to mend them. What was needed was a sort of home-repair store for joints, a lumberyard full of new bones and fresh, arthritis-free fingers. Just tell us your size, ma'am, and our employees will be happy to custom fit your heel to stop that aggravating plantar fasciitis and swap out those flat arches for ones with a teenager's bounce. "You might as well go ahead and say it, Tamaryn. I can see there's a banshee in your eyes, and I can't stand the thought of keeping her locked up."

Tam went to the window and looked out between the blinds. "I want to make a move."

"A *what?*"

"A move."

"I'm not following. Or maybe I am and I just want to hear you say it."

Tam turned around. "It's two-thirty right now. That gives us two and a half hours till I have to be at Nin's. But ever since last night this has been on my brain—"

"Mine, too."

"—and I don't want us to miss our chance."

"Our chance to what?"

"Gerald Fawles has got this place west of town . . ."

"Oh, no you don't."

"Just listen to me, Luce, please."

"I'm listening, girl, trust me." She waved her hand as if batting away a bad smell. "But if you think Jo will consider dressing up in the middle of the afternoon and taking it to Gerald Fawles on the very day of her big to-do at the town meeting, then you're crazier than I thought. And I thought a lot."

"I'm not going to ask Jo."

Lucy narrowed her eyes.

"This is just you and me, Luce. Two of us, hitting him real quick, then getting out of there. We're starting to get people talking and I don't want to let up now. Gerald owns a rental house two miles west of here, but nobody's living there right now. That's where he takes his girlfriends."

"How do you know any of that?"

"I don't. Not really. I heard his wife talking. She's not

sure. She just suspects. But we all know Gerald."

"Yes, yes, we all know Gerald and his philandering ways."

"He has no respect for anyone, Lucy. Not his wife. Not his kids. Not even the men he calls his friends. He takes advantage of everyone who gives him half a chance."

"So the man's not worth a squashed bug on a windshield. What's that got to do with us?"

"Think about it, will you? If there were fewer people like him in the world, we'd be a lot better off. Too many are just here to live off the refuse. They wouldn't recognize their own soul if you pulled it out of their ears and smothered them with it. The Geralds of this country don't vote, they don't contribute, they don't make themselves part of the solution."

"You want to terrorize a man for not voting?"

"You know what I'm talking about."

"Yes. I suppose I do."

"What we started the other night with Jed Whitecross ain't about one sex stepping on the other," Tam said. "It's not a man or a woman thing. Maybe it was at first, but not anymore. It's a *people* thing, people who've spent too much of their lives not saying *hey*." She cupped her hands around her mouth and shouted at the ceiling. *"Hey, I'm part of the human race and I think there's a better way!"*

Lucy let the words ring off the windows, almost expecting them to echo. When she was certain that a ghostly version of Tam's voice wasn't going to repeat the pronouncement, she sighed. "Since when is anger a better way? Isn't that what gets this country in trouble in the first place? We stomp another country into ashes because we were stomped first. That doesn't end the stomping, Tamaryn darling, it only perpetuates it."

"Whatever."

"I'm serious. This won't help anything."

months. We're causing ripples in the pond."

"Pushing our luck is what we're doing."

"We'll see."

Lucy changed out of her postal service garb and shoved the pink outfit into one of her larger handbags. All the while she tried to avoid meeting Tamaryn's eyes, for fear of absorption: in putting on the sheets, she sought a place of truth to leave her footprints, but she suspected Tamaryn's motivation was much simpler and thus harder to resist. Rage was an easy lover and had a way of seducing you into going all the way.

"Do you still have that gun?" Tam asked suddenly.

Lucy almost dropped her handbag. "Come again?"

"You showed it to me one time when we were cleaning. It was your father's."

"Yeah, I know what you're talking about, Tamaryn Soza, but I can't believe you're even thinking such things. Ought to be ashamed of yourself."

Tam looked all too calm. She checked her watch. "Never mind. Forget I mentioned it. Let's just get out of here."

"Forget you mentioned it like hell."

"We need to go, Luce."

"What on earth would possess you to take a gun along?"

"It doesn't matter."

"I asked you a question."

"I was just thinking about waving it around if someone tried to stop us."

"People get killed with guns, Tam."

"Yeah, you're right."

"We're not taking any gun."

"Okay."

"Jesus."

"Can we just go now?"

Lucy, muttering to herself, got the rest of her things to-

Erin O'Rourke

gether and reluctantly put her shoes back on. She didn't bother locking her front door and wondered why she ever worried about it at all. Her highest dream was of a world without keys.

She climbed into the pickup and held her nose against the heavy exhaust smell. "You ever hear of carbon monoxide poisoning?"

"It's not so bad once we're moving."

"Couldn't be any worse."

Tamaryn drove past the city limit sign, then said with a smirk, "So . . . what do you call a chicken crossing the road?"

"I don't know. Lay it on me."

"Poultry in motion."

Lucy tried to fight it, but she smiled. Tamaryn smiled too, and a second later, they both laughed.

"Good afternoon Clayton County Sheriff's Department my name is Hannah how may I direct your call?"

"Hello, is this the police?"

"Sir, this is the sheriff's office, can I help you?"

"Uh, maybe. I want to report something."

"Can I have your name, sir?"

"Uh, yeah. Archie Hall. I own a herbicide service in Hancock. I fly a plane."

Hannah wrote *Archie Hall* in the log beside the time. "Go ahead, Mr. Hall."

"I just got through dusting Scarborough's orchard six miles outside of Belle Springs. And I saw something strange."

Hannah drew a few doodles around his name. "What did you see, Mr. Hall?" *Extraterrestrials,* she thought. *He saw the mother ship collecting apples in its tractor beam.*

"Well, I know this may sound weird, but I was making my last pass and I saw a couple of people at an old farmhouse

158

running around in red robes." s hand.

The pen turned to stone ir

"Uh, you still there?" please repeat that last state-

"Yessir, I'm still here, ment?"

"Listen, I know w uldn't have been more than a hun-
what I saw. My altit't taken a drink in going on sixteen
dred feet, and I at least two people going in and out of
months. There know what they were up to. Maybe it was
the house. I st the same, I wanted to let someone know.
nothing, but
You might nt to check it out."

"Mr. H , you're saying they were wearing *robes*."

"Uh-hu. And hats, too, so you couldn't see their faces."

"And these robes were red?"

"Well, *light* red. Could have been more of a peachy color
or even pink, but I was a little way off the ground and the sun
was behind my wing, so I'm not sure. You believe me, don't
you?"

"Where did you say this happened, Mr. Hall?"

"At the Scarborough orchard, just next to the Fawles place."

Hannah asked for a number where Hall could be reached
because she'd been trained to do so, even though she had no
intention of calling him. She thanked him for his information
and wondered why Jo had pulled off an escapade without
telling her. Betrayal, that's what it was. It was the same way
she often felt toward her legs. But even worse was the fact that
they'd been caught in the act.

"We'll be in touch, Mr. Hall."

She almost tore the page from the logbook and threw it
away. Instead, she dialed Jo's cell number. The Hoofbeats
were so intense that her fingers shook as she stabbed the buttons.

Ch... r Twelve

Jo watched the auditorium
bombs.   h people, thinking about

The entire meeting hall was on.
week now she'd been listening to the ing to happen. For a
morning that she'd awakened and not It wasn't until this
She wasn't entirely sure why things had chan able to hear it.
pected.   d. But she sus-

"More of them than I anticipated," Martin sa. He and Jo
shared a long trestle table with the six members of the city
council. The table was positioned near the edge of the stage,
awash in bad theater lighting. "I've never been very good at
speaking in front of crowds. There must be a thousand here
already. Talk about feeding the multitudes. You sure you
have enough fishes and loaves to satisfy everyone?"

"Satisfied?" Jo said. "I'm afraid there are a few hotheads
here who won't be satisfied until they see someone crucified."

"I suppose you're right."

They'd decided on the high school auditorium when it
became evident that the basement of the City Hall wasn't
going to provide enough chair space. Dozens of eager voters
milled about, dressed in their ball caps and summer clothes,
fanning themselves with the flyers both factions were handing
out at the doors. Jo listened to the drone of their conversa-
tions and the rustle of the mayor's papers as he nervously rearranged them too close to the microphone. *Girlz rule,* she
thought randomly, and then decided that every heart was a
bomb as well, and sometimes an explosion wasn't such a bad
thing.

They're already clanning up," Martin said, quietly
ιough that only Jo could hear him. "See there? The
Sheridan team and the consortium on one side, the not-so-
silent opposition on the other. Lordy, this could get ugly.
When was the last time you talked to Chuck?"

"Why?"

"Well, I was hoping he'd given you an assurance that his
people would play by the rules. Call me a party pooper but I
don't want things getting out of control tonight."

"Nothing's out of control, Marty."

"Yet."

"Trust me. Here, have some water. You're starting to
sound hoarse."

"Thanks. If you don't mind my saying so, I'm glad as hell
that you're doing the talking. If I wasn't so broke, I'd give you
another raise."

Jo muttered a noncommittal reply, distracted by more
thoughts of bombs and then of planes, because Hannah had
said the crop duster had spotted a pair of figures that could
have only been the Soza-Campbell hit squad running an un-
authorized sortie against another deserving foe. At first Jo
had been irked at the news. What right did Tam and Lucy
have to put the others at risk? She'd resisted the urge to call
and harangue them. What could she possibly say that
wouldn't be entirely hypocritical? At least they'd chosen an
apt target. Gerald Fawles had once helped himself to a
handful of Jo's boob in the produce section of the grocery
store. Right in front of the iceberg lettuce. His wife had been
no more than two aisles away, innocently shopping for Gerald's dinner. That kind of thing happened every day across
the country, turning people into tiny quiet victims. So whatever message the girls had painted on the man's bungalow, it
was probably accurate and definitely deserved.

"Is this going out live?" Martin asked, trying to look natural in front of the camera crew. "The broadcast. Do you think it's live?"

"I doubt that very much. We're not newsworthy enough to be live. I'm sure they'll give us thirty seconds on the eleven o'clock news, but unless the furniture starts flying I wouldn't expect any more than that."

But the plane. Damn. Why did they have to get themselves *seen?*

"If everyone could please take your seats," the mayor said into the microphone. A squeal of feedback punctuated his words. The talk faded. The mayor tapped the mike. "We'll get underway as soon as we're all seated."

Jo searched the crowd. She caught sight of Tamaryn just slipping in the back, her boys in tow. Presumably Lucy was here as well. Jo would deal with them later. Her eyes settled on Penelope and her brother, Josh, three rows from the front. Their faces, nearly identical, were impassive. Penny wore sunglasses, though the room wasn't bright. "Don't be afraid," Jo told her from afar. "Remember, you're in guarded condition."

"I didn't catch that," Martin said.

"Just talking to myself. Do you vow on your life that the overhead projector is going to work? I only ask because I'm counting on my visual aids to make up for my lack of public-speaking ability."

"The machine's fine. And you will be too."

"You're right. I will be."

Why hadn't she felt that way until now? Glancing down at her hand, she saw a small half-moon of pink paint coloring the tip of her index finger. More people took their seats. More little bombs ticked behind rib cages.

"Ladies and gentlemen," the mayor said, his voice resounding off the walls and bringing a final, if uneasy, silence to the crowd. "Ladies and gentlemen, if I could have your full attention, please, we'd like to begin tonight's proceedings."

Full attention. Jo realized she'd been lacking that for months now. Too often she had dragged through her days with her attention at half-mast. Then Lucy had put a pillowcase on her head.

"Considering the special nature of this evening's meeting," the mayor continued, "we're going to table several unessential issues until next month, including the new waste ordinance and the matter of repainting the parking lanes at the courthouse. Now, to keep this as fair and as orderly as possible, we're asking that all parties honor the platform we've set up to ensure that everyone has a chance to be heard. Anyone who has something to say will get the opportunity to say it, but you'll have to be patient. First, we'll get all the facts out so that we're all clear on the numbers. So at this point I'd like to turn the floor over to Jo Adams, who you all know is serving as county liaison for this issue. She'll bring us all up to speed on the status quo. Jo, if you could, please . . ."

That was her cue.

She'd been anticipating it for days.

Dreading it, even.

She stood up and walked to the podium, fearing nothing.

". . . which brings us to the final adjusted figures as shown on the bottom of the graph." She indicated the numbers with her pencil, her actions transferred in silhouette to the big screen by way of the overhead projector. She paused for a moment to adjust the microphone clipped to her collar. With the house lights dimmed, she couldn't see the faces. But she knew they were watching her. She knew they were listening.

Now's the time to call them all cowards.

She took a sip of water. "Could I have the lights, please?"

Now's the time to tell them about the dangers of abiding.

The lights came up. People blinked. A few rubbed their eyes.

"So what we've just seen is a comprehensive overview of the entire proposal from its initial stages to its financial ins and outs. The pros and cons, if you will." She gripped the sides of the lectern, aware of the way her voice carried throughout the hall. Though she was in the middle of possibly the most important moment of her career, to be seen on certain televisions tonight and read about in newspapers in the morning, she was being sidetracked, pulled off course by the need to cry out against complacency.

Say it.

"Now with that taken care of, I'd like to open a short question-and-answer period before we hear from the representatives of the two parties."

Shout it.

No, she thought back. *They'd have me escorted from the building.*

"There, in the fourth row." She picked the first hand in the air. "Go ahead."

A man in overalls stood up. Jo had seen him around town but couldn't conjure his name, which wasn't surprising considering her current state of mind. "I was just wonderin'," he said, "if Sheridan was guaranteein' that its construction contract would go to a local company."

Jo never hesitated. She was prepared for the question. She'd studied every aspect of the issue and had compiled a list of over fifty likely concerns, committing to memory a politic answer for every one of them. "The Sheridan executives have assured me that the physical development of the complex will be exclusively a contract belonging to a Clayton

County–based firm. However, they do reserve the right to employ architectural agents from other areas. So I believe the answer to your question is yes, the workforce will be one from this county. The jobs will be ours."

More hands. Jo pointed.

"Will the highway have to be renovated to accommodate the increase in traffic?"

Almost without thought Jo said, "We anticipate nothing beyond minimal adjustments to the surrounding infrastructure, mainly dealing with water flow, but nothing out of the ordinary." It was too easy. She was an actress with her lines stitched to her tongue. Meanwhile, as if her mind were an overhead projector of its own, an image flashed between her eyes: the assembled townspeople marching on Washington to demand justice for the underdogs of the world, with their leader, the pink-clad and intrepid Jo of Arc, leading the way. "Next question. You, sir, near the door in the back."

Had it not been for the lights in her face, Jo would have recognized him. Then she could have called on someone else. There were plenty of raised hands. No one would have guessed that she was intentionally overlooking him. It wasn't until he spoke that she realized her mistake.

"This don't have nothing to do with why we're all here," he said, loudly enough that his words carried across the auditorium, "but my name is Gerald Lester Fawles, and I want to know who defiled my personal property this afternoon."

Silence.

Jo dug her fingernails into the lectern's wood.

There was a soft murmur from the crowd. Jo waited for the mayor to say something, to lean toward his mike and *say something* because he was in charge and that was his job, but nothing happened. All of the anxiety that Jo thought supplanted by her newly discovered courage came rushing up her throat like bile.

Gerald Fawles stood in the aisle with his hands on his hips.

Jo said, "Mr. Fawles." The volume of her voice surprised her.

No one came to her rescue. The thousand faces were a dark and unreadable sea.

"Mr. Fawles," she managed, "I'm not sure if this matter pertains to our discussion."

"I'm not saying that it does, Ms. Adams. But after what happened at Owen Selvey's place yesterday and my rental house today, I think we should all be a little concerned."

"Really, Mr. Fawles, I'm sure that if you discussed this with the authorities—"

"It's women behind it, you know."

Jo knew her mouth was open and she consciously closed it. She also knew the camera was still rolling because there was always one around at the worst times, and she wondered if her face was as wickedly warm as it felt. The lights glared hotter and brighter. She heard the sound again—*huff-pop, huff-pop*—and thought about taking a drink but feared that she'd drop the bottle.

The murmur had become a buzz. The council members looked at each other like idiots. Jo had no choice but to blunder ahead. "Again, Mr. Fawles, I don't believe this is the proper forum to voice a grievance you might—"

"Let him talk!" a voice shouted from somewhere in the middle of the audience. "Every ass has to let out hot gas now and then."

Laughter rippled through the auditorium.

"Who said that?" Gerald demanded.

Heads swiveled toward him. The camera found him. So did one of the narrow-beam spotlights, and Jo got her first good look at him. He wore a wide checkered tie, his shirt-sleeves rolled up to his elbows. His gaunt cheeks looked deathly pale in the harsh light.

A camera flashed.

"Please, Mr. Fawles . . ."

"What did they paint on your house, Gerald?" the voice sneered. It was a woman, and whoever she was, she was now on her feet. The heads swiveled again. "Tell us what they wrote."

"Was it *you*, Luisa?" Gerald demanded, his voice hiking up another notch. Now the crowd was spellbound. The buzz had faded, the flyers had stopped fanning. The camera team moved closer. In the back a few people stood up to get a better view.

Stepping around in front of the lectern, Jo said, "If everyone would just settle down for a moment, I'm sure we could work this out . . ."

"Yes, Gerald, it's me. The mother of the three-year-old you never see."

A tremor passed through the auditorium.

Sheriff Cantrell sidled between the rows, closing in.

"Why don't you tell us what they wrote?" Luisa yelled.

"You vandalized my personal property?" Gerald shouted back.

Others came to their feet. More lights splashed across the combatants.

Jo leaned against the lectern to keep from falling.

"Adultery pad of the deadbeat dad!" Luisa screamed.

Gerald reeled as if he'd been struck in the face.

"That's what it said, Gerald! I drove up there to meet you just like you asked, and I saw them leaving!" She leaned over the heads of those seated beside her and pointed at him. "You're a sick nympho ass-wipe, Gerald Fawles!"

A burst of applause.

Cantrell reached Luisa and said something inaudible amongst the scattered cheers.

"I will not keep it down!" Luisa backed out of the sheriff's reach. "I'm gonna find those painters and join up! You hear me, Gerald? *I'm signing up!*"

"You tell 'em, girl!" It was a woman's voice, anonymous in the crowd.

And then another: "Sign for me too, Luisa!"

Huff-pop, huff-pop.

Cantrell lifted his arms like a priest bestowing a blessing. "Yo! Everyone quiet down!"

"You're a crazy bitch, Luisa, you know that?" His mustache twitching, Gerald started to push his way toward her through the masses, but then he noticed the camera lens aimed at him and he ducked behind his raised hands. "Get that damn thing out of my face!"

Luisa was practically standing on one of the orange-padded chairs. *"Adultery pad of the deadbeat dad!"*

Random knots of people stood up. More voices joined the din.

Jo heard each one of them individually, as if she could see through the wild tapestry of sound and make out each separate, needy strand. Though incapable of action, trapped by the swiftness of the eruption as an animal is pinned to the road by headlights, she spent those few seconds seeing herself in motion. Lunging out to them. Touching their white-knuckled fists.

"Order!" The mayor's amplified voice boomed off the walls. "We will have order!"

"Not now," Jo said, though no one could hear her. "Not anymore."

Luisa kept shrieking.

Concerned men bookended Gerald and held him back.

All 1,000-plus people stood up, pushing, jostling, many just trying to get the hell out. Tamaryn was surely down there, protecting Matt and Brady but not wasting the chance to lend her war cry to the fray. Children cried. The mayor called again for order. Something fell over and shattered with the sound of breaking glass.

Jo saw Chuck. Her eyes homed in on him.

He was laughing.

Both sets of doors rocked open as pieces of the frightened mass escaped. Others followed, but the angry sounds didn't diminish: Cantrell and the mayor, Luisa and her sudden supporters, Gerald and a few opportunistic bigots.

Chuck found it all abundantly funny.

Cantrell and a handful of helpful souls—Jo thought they might have been volunteer firemen but she never knew for sure—finally inserted themselves into the path of greatest resistance and through sheer force dispersed the insurgents toward the doors. By then Luisa had vanished, either swept to safety by allies or forced out by foes—something else that Jo never found out. It was the last time in her life she ever saw the woman.

"Please leave the building in an orderly manner," the mayor said, his command sounding much more like a plea. Other members of the council had given up the ship; only three of the six chairs were occupied. Martin looked like a man suffering from acute food poisoning.

The thousands dwindled to hundreds, but these were the hard-liners. Insults fell like mortar rounds. The land-sale proponents fired at the opposition for being ignorant hayseeds, the opposition shelled the Washington attorneys for abusing the spirit of the law, and a gang of old hippies in the back cursed at the cops on general principles.

Thank God for the lectern. Without it, Jo wasn't sure

she could have kept her feet.

That wasn't true.

Perhaps it would have been true a day ago, or two days ago, but now she glided. Down the riser steps that led from the stage to the auditorium floor. Across the floor and into the riot. Through the riot toward the doors. Shoulders bumped her. The scent of perspiration assailed her. And then she was in the lobby and two steps later, outside.

She grabbed a black wrist.

Lucy gasped.

Jo put her hand on the back of Lucy's head and pulled her close. "Going somewhere?"

"Running for my life, thank you very much."

"See what we started?"

"Ray Charles could see that, Josephine."

"I mean, *holy shit.*"

"Yeah." Lucy looked startled. "If I didn't know you better, I'd say you were *proud.*"

Jo kissed her on the tip of her nose. "Just wait till they see what we do next."

That said, she shoved her way back through the mob, because someone had to find a paper bag for Martin before he got sick all over the mayor.

Chapter Thirteen

Midnight.

Hannah sat before a mirror two feet lower on the wall than it used to be. She pulled her lips back in an exaggerated grin, searching her teeth for remnants of dinner.

How mortifying that would be.

She checked the Garfield clock. One minute after twelve. The night beyond the window was deep and moonless. From the other side of the bathroom door came the sound of pounding water. Hannah closed her eyes and imagined the cascades sluicing between his pectorals, running down his thighs. . . .

"Shame on me." She grinned again, this time for real.

A touch of her wheels carried her across the room. Should she try and look busy? Should she occupy herself with some contrived pastime so as to appear indifferent when the water shut off and he appeared in the doorway?

"That depends," she said, "on whether or not he's naked."

Now, there was food for thought. *Food!* Naughty girl. Nevertheless, she bet he'd come out dressed. Terrell was modest in a world where modesty was out of style. It was an adorable quality, really, as long as you weren't someone who daydreamed of being ravished by him.

Twelve-oh-two.

What was taking him so long? He'd been late getting here as it was, what with the calamity at the town meeting and all. Poor Jo. She'd worked so hard for this. It was dreadful to think of how she must be feeling right now. At least no one had been arrested.

But back to being late. Tomorrow was Tuesday—the big

171

election day—and Hannah was going to pull a double shift at work. So sleep would have been the smart thing to do. Hannah was not so starved for Terrell's touch that she couldn't have waited till the weekend; it was enough just to have him spend the night on her lumpy couch. But now she had Lucy to answer to. Not the Lucy of real life, but the Lucy in her mind, the one that kept telling her *just give me an hour.* That was a Lucy who didn't sleep. She lived. She gathered her rosebuds. She *carped* her *diem.*

The telephone rang and scared her so much she laughed.

Thankful for the diversion, Hannah swung her hair out of the way and put the phone to her ear. "Hello?"

"Were you awake?" Jo asked. "You sound awake."

"Very much so, why, what's up? And I'm sorry about the meeting, I heard what happened and let me just say that I guess it could have been worse."

"I'm fine, Hannah. Don't worry about the meeting. It was fine, too."

"But Esther said that—"

"We'll talk about what Esther said in the morning. How are you for a stealth mission?"

"Now? Like *right now?*"

"Can you drive us? Nin's staying with the kids. We need a getaway car."

"Jo, you know I'd do anything for you guys . . ."

"Good. Come pick me up. I'll fill you in on the details along the way."

". . . but now is maybe the most inconvenient moment of my entire adult life."

Jo only paused for a second before saying, "You're kidding me."

"Nope."

"Tonight?"

"He's in my bathroom right now, Jo, in the shower as a matter of fact, and I can't really call it off at this point, unless you absolutely couldn't do it without me, because I'd do anything for you, Jo, you know that, don't you?"

"He's staying the night?"

"He's stayed the night before, you know."

"That's not what I mean."

"Yes, I know what you mean, but I can't answer that. Maybe he is and maybe he isn't." She looked over her shoulder when she realized the water was no longer running. "This is an important one, isn't it, Jo, what you're doing tonight?"

"Yes."

"It has something to do with what happened at the town meeting, doesn't it?"

"Yes. Look, Hannah, just forget that I called. If the rest of us actually had lives, or at least better offers, we wouldn't be going out pinking tonight. You have my full endorsement. But call me in the morning, okay, and spill your guts. I want details."

"No, wait." Hannah cupped the receiver in both hands. Suddenly everything was all mixed up. Jo's voice was different. After what Tam and Lucy had done this afternoon, Hannah had assumed that Jo would call the whole thing quits. They'd pushed it too far. But now it sounded as if just the opposite had occurred. And the bottom line was that Hannah didn't want them risking their foolish necks without her. And she and Terrell had plenty of rosebud-gathering evenings in front of them; her lumpy couch wasn't going anywhere. "Give me half an hour, Jo, I'm on my way."

"Hannah, no. Not if Terrell is there."

"He's not. See you in a bit. Bye."

She hung and hated herself in advance, just to get it out of the way.

"Hey." He stood in the doorway. His feet were bare. He wore faded jeans. His shirt was unbuttoned halfway down his stomach. God.

Hannah kept her gaze steady. "Don't be mad at me for what I'm about to tell you, baby."

"Uh-oh. Should I sit down?"

"I have to go."

He stared at her without speaking.

"I am so horrendously sorry, but that was Jo and she—"

"Jo? You mean the other woman? The one you're always running off to?"

"Please, Terrell, don't make this any harder than it is."

He held up his hands. "Okay."

"Don't say okay if you don't mean okay, because I can tell by the way you say it that it's not."

"Hannah, it's all right. I'm serious. After being in the middle of that freak show tonight, I'm sure Jo could use a friend." He said it and meant it—*could this guy be for real?*—but his eyes were evidence enough of how he felt. How much could one man be expected to put up with?

"Baby, I'm so sorry . . ."

"Let me make it easy on you," he said, disappearing into the bathroom long enough to find his boots. "I'll go. You get to Jo's. Just be sure and tell her that she's on my list."

"Are you sure?" She rolled in front of him before he could make the front door. "I want you to know that you are without a doubt the single most understanding man I have ever in all my life had the pleasure of knowing, and one of these days very soon I will make all of this up to you in all manner of creative ways."

"You don't have to make anything up to me. But I'll

hold you to that anyway."

"Deal. Sure you're alright with this?"

"Very."

"Promise?"

He drew a cross over his heart.

"Good. Now kiss me like I'm getting on a plane to leave Casablanca forever."

He dropped his boots and put his hands on either side of her face. He stared at her, and for the first time since she'd known him, Hannah was uncertain of the look he was giving her. There was sadness there, like a dark pool whose depths had yet to be measured. Hannah crushed her mouth against his. But even that was different, and when he broke away and headed for the door, he didn't reply when she called goodbye, only held up a few fingers and waved.

"Turn left at the next corner, and be sneaky about it."

"We're in a van, Jo. Vans don't sneak."

Jo heard the edge in Hannah's voice but thought it best not to comment on it.

"Are we there yet?" Lucy said from her seat in the back. And that was the last thing they needed. A smart-ass.

"If anyone wants any Gatorade," Tam said, "I brought a jug."

Jo almost asked for some. Not because she was especially thirsty, but it was one a.m. and every word spoken in the van's gloomy interior had a weird resonance about it. Knocking back a sports drink would have added a nice touch to the surreal atmosphere.

None of them had been asleep when she phoned. As if they'd known. As if they'd been putting off their pillows because they sensed her need. And what need was that, exactly? She would have liked to say the need to better humanity, or the need to uphold those too weak or underprivileged to uphold themselves. And maybe that was indeed one ingredient in her recipe for misadventure, but the final mix was more complex. There had been a feeling in the auditorium. To hear those voices raised and know that she was at least partially responsible for the raising . . . she had tasted it and wanted more.

Break out the riot shields and the stun guns, there's a new outlaw in town.

"Did you see his face?" Tam asked.

Hannah turned left. "Whose face?"

"She means Gerald Fawles," Jo explained.

"Thought he was going to blow a fuse," Lucy said. "If I'd known he was going to come unglued like that, hell, I would've pinked him a long time ago."

"I can't believe everybody started yelling like that," Hannah said. "I'm sorry I missed it, because, wow, that's not something you see all the time. Did you recognize any of the other women? The ones who were yelling at him?"

"It wasn't just women," Tamaryn told her. "There were a few men whooping it up as well. You should've seen them, Jessler. They were all so *pissed*. It's like the dike finally cracked. It was amazing."

Amazing? That wasn't quite the word Jo had in mind, but it would suffice. A connection had been made tonight, a tacit agreement between strangers that it was finally within the rules to voice a complaint and toss out a threat. Maybe not amazing, but certainly contagious. An entrepreneur with a truck full of pink spray paint could have hung a SOLD OUT sign on his bumper in half an hour.

"You still haven't told me where we're going," Hannah reminded her.

"You'll see. Turn left again here."

"Aren't we going in circles?"

"Squares, actually. Have you seen any headlights behind us?"

"We're trying to throw off a tail? Is that what we're doing?"

"She's a spy all of a sudden," Lucy said. "Better watch out. She might frisk you to make sure you're not wearing a wire."

Jo had to smile. "See anything?"

Hannah checked her mirror again. "Nope. All clear."

"Then take Pike Avenue out of town. And go a little faster."

"You got it."

"Sure nobody wants a shot of Gatorade?"

"You talked me into it," Jo said. "Pass it up."

Tam handed the drink to Lucy, who in turn handed it to Jo. "You know," Lucy said as their hands met on the bottle, "they don't have to be right behind us to see where we're going. If you want to be paranoid, they can watch us with satellites these days."

"I don't think we rate the satellite stage quite yet."

"Me neither. But I don't like the look in your eyes."

"You can't even see my eyes. It's too dark."

"Haven't you ever heard that old white wives' tale about black folk being able to see in the dark?"

"No. Is it true?"

"It depends on who we're looking at."

Jo believed it. Blindfold them both, it wouldn't matter. If you were lucky in this life, you met one person who could read the Braille of your soul by touch, without judging you for all the bumps.

"Pike Avenue," Hannah announced. "And still no bad guys behind us."

"It won't be long now," Jo said. "We might as well get dressed."

She waited for the next wisecrack, but she heard only the rustling of sheets. With the unfurling of the robes, there was no room in the van for small talk. Only big talk. And big risks.

Jo unfastened her seat belt in order to settle the sheet around her. The fabric smelled of laundry soap, having been freshly cleaned that afternoon. Even the washing had been a clandestine affair. If Caroline found out that her mom was moonlighting as a vigilante, the gulf would only widen between them. Jo desperately built bridges whenever she had the chance.

"How did Nin take it when you told her?" Hannah asked.

"Like she always takes it. With more grace than the rest of us put together."

"Did she try to talk you out of it?"

"No more than usual. I think she accepts that I'm a lost cause. I'm sure she's just hoping that eventually I'll get it out of my system. But I hate to tell her that she's got it all backward. I'm finally getting it *into* my system. Slow down a bit. See that sign? Turn there."

"There? But that's . . . oh. I get it."

The sign read SHERIDAN ENTERPRISES.

Tam slid up between the front seats. "How positive are you about security?"

"What have they got to secure?"

"That's no answer."

"There are no guards, if that's what you mean. I suppose there might be an alarm protecting the main offices, but that shouldn't have any bearing on what we're doing. Hannah, swing right just inside the gate. That leads to the garage. They keep the company cars there."

The van's lights splashed across the low brick wall and the building's glass front as Hannah made the turn. Jo got a glimpse of the carefully planted rhododendrons, then the darkness claimed them. "Don't pull into the grass. We don't want to leave any tracks."

"Right. No tracks. Gotcha." Hannah kneaded the wheel with both hands. "Talk about the Hoofbeats."

"The what?"

"Nothing. Just nervous to the fourth power, that's all."

"Ah, Jessler, ain't nothing for you to be worried about. If we get caught, Terrell can always pull a few strings and get you off. Doesn't some federal big shot owe him a favor?"

"Hey now, Mrs. Soza," Lucy said. "If my baby brother is calling in a marker on anyone's behalf, it better be for me. I'm too old to do hard time. Young things like you and Hannah, though . . ."

"Nobody's getting caught," Jo said. "Just put your hoods on. Hannah, pull up there at the garage doors."

Hannah did as instructed. "I trust you when you say that, Jo, that we're not going to get caught, but if we keep it up, sooner or later something bad is bound to happen, and I don't mean to jinx us by saying that, but it worries me. The only sure thing about luck is that it always runs out. Is this close enough?"

"Perfect."

Hannah shut off the engine.

"Be ready," Jo told her.

Hannah nodded.

Jo pulled the hood over her head, adjusted the eyeholes, and stepped out into the night. If not for the dim yellow glow from the sodium-vapor lights at the front of the building, visibility would have been nil. Even the stars seemed weaker tonight, like candles in a distant room.

Lucy and Tam exited through the van's rear door, and Jo again realized how chilling they looked dressed in these outfits, like the ladies' auxiliary of the KKK. She tested the batteries of her flashlight. "Lucy, I put a pair of bolt cutters back there under Hannah's chair. Could you get them out, please?"

Lucy unearthed the big orange-handled device. "Bolt cutters? What on earth are we doing with bolt cutters?"

"Cutting bolts," Jo said. "What else?" She calmly took them and headed toward the garage.

The steel teeth chomped through the chain.

Jo made an exasperated sound and lowered the cutters, her weary arms tingling from the strain. "That's a hell of a lot harder than it looks."

Tam knelt at the base of the garage door and pulled the chain free, doing her best to muffle the noise. "You sure it's in here?"

"With the exception of his marriage to me, Chuck has always hated change. He's been keeping it here for years."

Tam heaved the door up a few inches, then stopped. "Too loud?"

"Can't be helped. Just lift."

Tam raised the door until it was waist-high. Jo bent down and shot the flashlight beam inside, sweeping it from one side to the other. "It looks okay to me."

"Famous last words," Lucy said. "Are you sure Hannah's okay with this?"

Jo inspected the vehicles that were lined up in the garage until she located Chuck's 1957 Thunderbird. As soon as she saw its spotless pearl-white paint, she stopped moving the flashlight. "I don't think she's going to cave in, if that's what you're implying."

"I don't know what I'm implying, really. She's just different than us, that's all. *Better,* I guess. I keep waiting for the shine from her halo to give us away."

"Let's talk about this another time," Tam whispered. "Now what are we waiting for?"

"Good question." Jo crouch-walked under the door. The others followed.

And that was the end of the discussion. Chuck's T-bird pulled them like a lodestone. The car was just too clean for its own good, and Chuck had laughed at Luisa's outburst in the auditorium. He *laughed,* and there you had the planet's woes in a nutshell. Jo thought about carving such an admonishment into the car's hood: If you're not willing to reach out a hand to your fellow *Homo sapiens,* then at least have the decency not to ridicule their point of view. If the earth had a suggestion box, Jo would have dropped in a request that said please walk a mile in every person's shoes.

She took out one of her best steak knives and rammed it into the left front tire.

The knife was part of a matching set that hadn't really been matching for several years now. Kitchen utensils, like comprehensible lyrics in a Bob Dylan tune, come and go. Jo had selected this particular blade because it was sharp and not serrated, the better to skin apples and puncture whitewalls.

The sound of the expelling air was lost to the sibilant din of paint cans in action.

"Now you mind your spelling, Tamaryn," Lucy said as she worked her way around the trunk. "Don't make me come over there and copy edit your ass."

"It's not too hard to spell *dick.*"

"That's not what you're supposed to be writing," Lucy reminded her.

"So now you're censoring my graffiti?"

Jo let them talk. At least they were being fairly quiet. They each held a flashlight in the hand that wasn't busy with the paint, and the three beams jumped randomly about the garage, stirring up the shadows. Jo went to the next tire and repeated her attack. Like using the bolt cutters to split the chain, poking a kitchen knife through a real live tire was not as simple as it seemed. It took her three tries to get the blade in deep enough to do any appreciable harm.

"I still say we should set this thing on fire," Tam said.

"Out of the question," Lucy fired back, trying to keep her voice down. "Too much chance that somebody would get hurt. Like a firefighter or cop. Don't get yourself so worked up about it. You sound about ready to spit flames yourself. Then the damn car *will* catch on fire."

"Good. Can I put a few certain people inside of it first?"

"Girl, sometimes you worry me."

Jo did a third tire and decided that was enough. How long had they been here? Five minutes? A compulsion to run crawled down her skin like goose bumps. "Shut up and let's get out of here. We've done enough."

"But, Jo, I thought we—"

"Enough."

"Okay, jeez, don't get your bra in a knot. Lead the way."

Jo slid under the garage door. She wouldn't have been surprised to see half a dozen squad cars lined up parallel to the building and snipers taking aim from the trees. *Throw down your kitchen knives and put your hands where we can see them.* But there was only Hannah's van and the cutters lying on the concrete beside it. Jo gave the signal.

Hannah started the engine.

Jo was sweating behind her mask but resisted the urge to remove it. She tugged open the passenger's door, tossed the cutters and the knife on the floorboard—

"Jo, wait."

She turned around.

Tam stood five feet away, unmoving, her eyes nothing more than two black dots. Jo was just about to tell her that they didn't have time for more antics, but then Tamaryn raised her left arm. She looked like a student waiting to be called on by her teacher, except that her fist was clenched. The sheet slid down to her elbow. Tam aimed her flashlight at the exposed skin.

"You see this shit, Jo? This is what he did to me."

Jo, suddenly afraid, stared at her friend's arm but saw nothing.

"I never planned on having Matthew," Tam said.

"What are you talking about?"

"Now I'm so glad he was born, but I didn't always feel that way. Because Roy raped me that night."

"*What?*"

"But hell, you can't rape your wife, right? Date-rape, sure. But spouse-rape? He flushed all my pills down the stool, said he wanted lots of kids. So you see this?" She slashed the flashlight beam across her arm. "I had them stick a Norplant in my arm. They implanted this damn *device* in me, Jo, so my husband couldn't knock me up whenever he wanted."

Jo sank back against the van. "Tamaryn . . . I am so sorry. . . ."

"So excuse me for my general bitchiness," Tam said, whipping her arm down and clicking off the flashlight. "I just thought you should know."

Lucy held the door open for her as she climbed into the back, seeking out her Gatorade and guzzling the last of it. The darkness made the silence feel even deeper. Jo pulled herself inside the van, feeling small and exposed. Though she'd intended to rip the hood from her sweaty head the moment they were safely away, she ended up riding all the way home with her eyes staring through the too-narrow holes.

She wished, at the very least, that she'd slashed the last tire.

Chapter Fourteen

If the others are out wrecking antique cars, Nin thought, *then the least I can do is vote.*

She moved through her morning house, wearing only a towel. So it was a *beach* towel, true, and she'd never imagined as a little girl that her body could ever take this shape, but her blood pressure was fine and she was happy. She walked through the kitchen, her bare feet cool against the linoleum. She almost always wore house slippers.

She almost always did a *lot* of things, but she'd blinked awake an hour ago and there was Jo again, telling her about the sound the air made when it was leaving Chuck's tires, and how it would never make up for the sound of his laughter last night in the auditorium. Nin knew it wasn't right, destroying things to make a point. But she also knew what kind of laughter Jo was talking about.

"Forgive me, Father," she said as she walked toward the television. "But Jesus threw the money changers out of the temple, now didn't He?" She should have been ashamed, comparing Christ's anger to her own, but shame seemed like a good waste of emotion.

She bent down and turned on the TV, aware of the air against her bare skin. It was a rare thing to change stations, away from the cartoons to the local cable channel, where she hoped to catch the exit polls and see how the early-bird voters were responding. If you wanted the scores of area football games on Friday night or information on the coming county fair, you tuned to Channel 12. The station manager, Wayne Dubbins, also happened to be the youth minister of Nin's church, and what would a righteous, tie-wearing man like Wayne say if he knew Nin was involved in pinking up the town?

Pinking. Jo had coined that crazy verb and now all of them were using it.

And there was Wayne himself, sitting behind the news desk on Channel 12's no-frills film set, while the exit poll results scrolled across the bottom of the screen. Nin turned up the sound.

". . . but it didn't take long for word of last night's altercation to reach Washington," Wayne reported, "where the radical feminist group AGNES has already seized upon this issue with the apparent intention of turning it into a rallying point for their cause."

"Heavens, that's all we need," Nin said. Her towel started to slip and she pinned it against herself with her arms.

"An increasingly vocal lobbyist group, the Activists for Gender Neutrality, Equality, and Solidarity released a statement on its Internet website early this morning calling for a closer examination of unreported acts of domestic oppression. The group's frontline spokesperson, Rita Dawn Ingersol, said that AGNES intends to send a representative to the Belle Springs area to, quote, 'Shine the light of truth on a problem we'd all rather keep in the dark.' Ms. Ingersol was arrested twice in the last year for disturbing the peace and destruction of public property."

"Well, she'll fit right in." Nin thought about calling her and asking for her sheet size.

The exit polls showed a dead heat.

Wayne went from domestic oppression to livestock futures.

Nin threw open her towel and flashed him.

Wayne seemed unimpressed, and Nin, smiling terrifically,

sauntered back to her bedroom.

Sally Fong's diner was a cultural crossroads. Here the boot-wearing, bacon-eating crowd intermingled with the briefcase-toting, bagel-eating crowd and together solved all the world's troubles by ten a.m. Tam liked to think of the restaurant as the United Nations building, only greasier.

She bustled between the tables. Chatting here and there. Snatching up plates. Sloshing coffee. Palming tips. It wasn't the kind of job her classmates talked about at the annual high school reunion. But that's what you did when you had two kids and no college credits and, besides, it burned the calories like rocket fuel. She might not have an office but she could still fit into her prom dress, so screw 'em.

"Can you get table five for me?" Jan Morris asked. "If I don't pee I'm gonna need gills."

"Did Harvey leave you a tip at table eight?"

"Yeah, why?"

Tam grabbed the next two plates of hash browns off the rack before Sally could even ring the bell, placing one in the crook of her elbow and the other flat on her palm. "I thought so. I have this theory about how the window at table eight puts him in a better mood. From there he can see Belinda Stokes out walking her dog."

"Belinda Stokes must be ninety years old."

"So what? I think it's sweet. Now go to the bathroom. And let's make sure we seat Harvey at eight every chance we get."

What jugglers practice behind closed doors, waitresses must learn in public. Tam seldom dropped anything, navigating the tables with reckless aplomb. But today her mind wouldn't switch to autopilot, and more than once she had to pause and adjust a plate to keep it from tipping. She'd hardly slept after Hannah dropped her off at home. She felt like a junkie in need of a fix. And to compound her agitation, any minute now Penelope would come in on Jed's arm—they were vegans and unwavering members of the bagel crowd—and then so much for the plates. Maybe Jed had missed the point when Tam waved the bat at him. Or maybe he was just so arrogant that he believed himself untouchable. Hell. He probably was.

". . . voted no, personally," someone was saying.

". . . thought I'd wait till the crowds thin out . . ."

". . . you hear about what happened over at Sheridan?"

". . . sorority girls, my ass . . ."

Tam was tempted to hover nearby to hear how that particular dialogue played out, but then the diner door opened yet again and six more hungry customers came in. Tam was halfway to their table, coffeepot already in hand, when her eyes focused on them and she realized they were neither bacon people nor bagel people. In fact, she didn't recognize them at all.

A few heads turned, stared at the strangers, looked back.

Shit. This is the last thing we need.

They were Native Americans. Or American Indians. Or indigenous peoples, or whatever the hell they called themselves these days. They weren't dressed in deerskins but clearly they were aboriginal nonetheless. They were all men, but other than that, they appeared to have little in common. One wore a blazer, while another had a pack of smokes rolled in his sleeve. Tam wondered if Pete Musket had enlisted them or if they'd heard about his plight and come unbidden to his aid. Either way, what they brought was a fresh bag of trouble. They sat without speaking, studying their menus.

"Morning," Tam said. "Coffee?"

They all looked at her with haunted, polished-stone eyes.

★ ★ ★ ★ ★

Hannah caught Terrell on his third pass through the office. County employees were everywhere, clipping up and down the hall. Even the dogcatcher had already been called out twice this morning. "Hey you! Black stallion!"

"Can't chat," he said, pecking her on the forehead. "Do I look okay? This shirt feels tight."

"You're as immaculate as usual, you know what men in uniform do to me. Did the sheriff tell you that there are Indians on their way out to the site?"

"He mentioned it. I've got to go, sweetness. I'll try to meet you for lunch."

"Sounds wonderful, but I won't hold you to it. Are you mad at me for running off on you last night?"

"Not one bit."

"I don't believe you. Call me when you get the chance and we'll talk about it. Oh, and Terrell?"

"Yep?"

"Did you guys . . . out at Sheridan . . . find anything?"

He shook his head. "Nothing was stolen. That's all I know. We got some prints, though. I'll see you later."

"Prints?"

"Yeah, off one of the Thunderbird's fenders. I'll call you." He puckered up and blew her a loud kiss, and then he was gone.

Hannah bit her knuckle, wondering which one of them had been caught.

Lucy swerved to miss the dog.

"Out of the road, you mangy mongrel!"

The mail truck swerved into the opposite lane and she fought it, but the shitty thing didn't handle worth a damn and she bumped the curb.

189

"Dammit!" She pressed on the gas, lumbered completely onto the curb and then off again, cranking the wheel until the truck realigned itself. A car shot by in the opposite direction, at least twenty miles over the speed limit for a residential area. "Slow down!"

The big tub of mail had slid forward and was now leaning against her leg.

"Back, fool thing." She shoved it away, and the sun broke free of the treetops and blasted her in the face. She snapped the visor down, and now she was officially an hour behind schedule.

Somebody waved. Lucy saw the hand and tipped her head back, but that was all the greeting anyone was getting this morning. She'd slept too late. The rush of breaking and entering, of pinking and avenging, had socked it to her body, and she'd shuddered awake feeling several new categories of aches in her knees, shoulders, and neck. She'd tried to laugh it off at first, muttering something under her breath about spring chickens, but the pain wasn't fooling around. She'd downed four aspirin, and if the pain was some kind of sign, then she fully planned on ignoring it.

School bus.

Lucy planted both feet on the brake. The truck jerked hard. The seat belt tightened against her chest, and a fresh current of agony surged up her neck.

The bus passed. Children grinned and carried on.

Lucy barely noticed.

Let the damn truck die where it was. She got out, fetched her bulging mail bag, and headed up the nearest sidewalk to whoever lived at this address. She couldn't remember.

Just match the numbers, she advised herself. *Match the envelope with the house, that's all. Just like they teach the rookies.*

Lucy was no longer a rookie *anything*. She was, as they said

190

of ancient football players, a *wily veteran*. Whatever good that did her.

She stared at the numbers in her fist until they made sense. She dropped them in the box and plowed through the grass to the next house.

Come on, Dobermans. Where the hell you at today when a lady is itching to Mace somebody's ass?

She left wet dew tracks on the porch, matched the numbers, and that's how it went the rest of her route, except she noticed a lot more traffic running about and even a helicopter churning up the sky. She picked up her pace and dodged the usual talk with joggers, making up for time spent in bed, her heart pounding harder than it should have and her brain, hell, her brain filled with images of kitchen knives and thoughts of capture and incarceration. Still, she did okay till she reached Nin's house, where she was four feet from the front door when she saw the return address on the envelope: DEPARTMENT OF HEALTH AND HUMAN RESOURCES.

"Oh, God." Lucy stopped, wooden-kneed, on the sidewalk. She stared at the letter. It trembled in her hand.

"Are you all right?" Nin asked from the doorway. "You look a fright."

"What is that you're wearing?" Lucy returned.

"A towel."

"That's what I thought."

"Are you feeling okay, Lucy?"

"Not really."

"Do you want to come inside? I have Froot Loops."

"Froot Loops sound just about perfect." She told her legs to move and they surprised her by complying. She wanted to tell Nin about the letter, but the wily veteran said to hold her tongue. Trusting its advice, she followed Nin inside, cramming the letter into her bag.

"So much for the thousand bucks," Martin said.

Jo hung up her desk phone—her tenth call of the morning—and said, "What do you mean? I thought the mayor approved it. I know some might construe it as extortion but—"

"He's not alone anymore."

"Who?"

"Your pal Earnest Paul Tenfeathers. Looks like he's got himself a tribe."

"Marty, this is not the day you want to be kidding around with me, I promise."

"It's almost eleven o'clock. The polls have been open for three hours and it's still anybody's war. The last thing we need right now is a pow-wow happening in the middle of the battlefield. A thousand dollars no longer buys us peace. We have to convince those people, whoever they are, that it's in their best interest to leave Pete Musket's place alone."

"We as in *me,* is what you're trying to say?"

"Find out what they want. I'd go with you if I could but . . ."

"I'm already out the door, Marty." She grabbed her purse and saw Tamaryn shining the flashlight against her arm. "Where's Felix?"

"That's half my problem," Martin growled. "Felix called in sick. I told him that he better be on his deathbed if he's calling in today." He ran both hands through his silver hair. "I swear, Jo, I'm going to need a pacemaker after all of this."

Jo looked around. "And Carmen?"

"Huh?"

"Carmen. She sick too?"

Martin turned his head slowly to the right, then left. "Well

. . . damn. In all of this ruckus I guess I didn't even notice. Hey, Bess!" he shouted. "Where the hell is Carmen?"

Jo didn't wait to find out. She left the building.

Maybe Felix isn't gay, after all.

That thought occupied her until she reached her car, then a police cruiser rolled by and she lowered her eyes automatically, wondering if she should get rid of the knife. Could they match the blade to the tires? She'd left the knife in the glove box of the van. Should she destroy it instead of simply returning it to her kitchen? Throw it away?

Forget the stupid knife. Think about Chuck's face.

Yes, that was pleasing, at least momentarily. Jo pumped the Opel's gas pedal until the carburetor quit resisting and did its thing. Chuck's face when he saw the T-bird. Chuck's face.

BE NICE, they'd painted, in mostly neat letters on both doors. That was it. Nothing profound. Nothing obscene. Just be nice. It was the most hopeful advice that Jo could give anyone. Tam had voted for *Suck my dick,* which was eye-catching but missed the point.

Be nice.

Jo drove across town.

Were there more cars in the street than usual? Jo turned on the radio, turned it off again, caught a glance of herself in the mirror and realized that she hadn't put on any mascara today, saw Tamaryn's arm again—*They implanted this damn device in me*—then she ran a red light, and wasn't that how the cops always nailed you? They stop you for a traffic violation and the next thing you know they're finding the heroin stashed under the seat or the empty can of pink paint under the spare tire in the trunk. A little bad luck was all it took.

She was telling herself to relax when she saw the pony.

That's what you called a Mustang when you were hip. A

pony. The racy yellow dynamo sat on the edge of the Autoporium lot with three balloons tied to its antenna. Its wheels were chrome and its windows tinted as black as the sky had been last night when Jo led the raid on the garage.

Someone honked behind her.

"Yeah, I hear you." She turned into the car lot. Tenfeathers and his new fan club could wait.

Warren Dearborn smiled a little sheepishly as he approached her. Jo leaned against the Opel's fender with her arms over her chest, sizing him up. He wore a blue denim shirt under a dark blazer. A few of the curls in his hair were losing their color, but the gray gave him a rugged look that wasn't unbecoming. His wife had been dead for three years. Jo had played bridge with her. Back when playing bridge still mattered.

"Don't tell me," Warren said, hooking his thumbs in his pockets. "You're finally parting ways with that old soldier."

"Among other things. Actually it's sort of an impulse purchase."

"I never knew anyone who bought a car on impulse."

Jo laughed before she could catch herself.

He looked at her quizzically, then grinned. "It's nice to see someone in such a good mood. My last customer was an eighty-two-year-old ex-schoolteaching marm who kept calling me *Sonny* and said that car dealers who rolled back odometers went to hades to live with the devil and crooked pharmacists."

"Crooked pharmacists? She actually said that?"

"Apparently they've been overcharging her for her diuretics."

"Ah, those wicked Philistine druggists. Any reason in particular why she'd accuse you of odometer sabotage?"

"Not at all. But I have this 1939 Packard with six original

miles on it, if you're interested."

"Uh-huh. Sounds dubious to me."

"I'm a car salesman. What you call dubious, I call *like new*."

"Oh, is that how it works?"

They both laughed.

"I'm suddenly very glad you had an impulse," Warren said. "Did you have a certain model in mind?"

"Did you hear the sirens this morning, Warren?"

"No. I live out of town. But I assume you're talking about the break-in."

Jo dismissed the subject. What was she *doing?* "Have you voted yet?"

"I'm not registered."

"Really? You're the only one in town without an opinion on this earth-shattering event?"

He shrugged. "It's not so earth-shattering."

"No. It's not, is it?"

They looked at each other for a few seconds, then Warren, blushing faintly, gestured across the lot. "So, you're really thinking about getting something new?"

"Not thinking, Warren. Doing."

"Well, we've got some good deals on sport utility vehicles . . ."

"Save your sport utilities for the next impulse shopper. I want the pony."

"Pardon?"

"The Mustang. Yellow. Polarized windows. Shiny wheels."

He flicked his blue eyes toward the car. "You mean it?"

"I know what you're thinking. Midlife crisis. And though that has nothing to do with it, I don't have time to stand here and try to explain it, at least not without sounding like a total flake. So just lead me inside and dazzle me with paperwork. I have a band of Indians to antagonize."

"Hey, you're the boss."

They walked beside each other toward the office, the sun on their faces.

"That Mustang's a stick shift, isn't it?" Jo asked.

"Yes."

"Good."

Chapter Fifteen

The AGNES team pulled into town in time to catch the ladies of the St. Joseph Catholic Church in the closing hour of their Get Out And Vote complimentary luncheon. They happened upon the event by chance, their nondescript brown sedan cruising the streets in search of the perfect place to pitch their tent. They were on their way to the Brittany House Bed & Breakfast when they saw the sign. Rita Dawn Ingersol herself, who had been seen in the company of certain nationally televised talk-show hosts, led the way into the church's fellowship hall and was greeted warmly all around.

Word spread when one of the St. Joseph women dashed home to retrieve her copy of Ingersol's book. Before returning to the church to get an autograph, she made a phone call, and that was that. The Brittany House gave them their rooms free of charge, and the mayor's wife sent an invitation to dinner.

"A dinner party?" Jo asked, the phone pressed against her head as she drove. "They've been in town three hours and someone's already planning a party?"

"So the grapevine tells me," Martin said. "Now what's the story with Tonto?"

"Please, Marty. No name-calling."

"My apologies. I'm a little strung out here. Exit polls are not an exact science. And neither is indigestion. So what's he say?"

"Who?"

"*Tenfeathers.* Jesus, Jo, stay with me here."

"I'm sorry. Look, Marty, I'll call you back."

"Now wait just a minute—"

She broke the connection and tossed the phone on the seat. The *leather* seat, mind you. The smell filled the car. She'd yet to try the stereo, but it had a CD player and more speakers than your average rock concert. She'd become so accustomed to the Opel's uncertain chug that the throaty sound of the Mustang's engine was disconcerting. She tried to summon some nostalgia for the old clunker, all the days it had dropped Caroline off at school, all the spilled drinks, the loose change, the crumbs. But the past broke apart in her fingers every time she tried to grasp it.

She turned off the AC and rolled down the windows, just to feel the wind. And maybe it was something in the breeze, but she was struck by the desire to turn around and drive to Penelope's place and tell her everything, tell her what they'd done, tell her to slam the door on Jed's winsome face and live a little. But even this notion couldn't captain her thoughts. By the time she pulled up behind Pete Musket's El Camino, her hair was a disaster. She combed her fingers through it and briefly examined herself in the mirror.

So is this it? Hannah had asked last night on their way back from the Sheridan garage.

It?

Yes, Jo, our last mission. I think it's important that we decide now.

I think it's important that we get some sleep.

You know that if we pink something else, then it's going to have to be even bigger.

Bigger how? Did you have a particular target in mind?

Well, I don't know, I was sort of thinking that maybe . . . it's stupid, but . . .

Spit it out, Hannah.

Okay, fine, I'm spitting. I was thinking we should do the sheriff.

Jo winked at her reflection. "You're right," she said. "It *is* stupid."

Yet she hadn't said no.

She got out of the car, wondering how she could convince these obstinate Indians that it was in their best interest to give up Musket's land to a group of white developers. More importantly, she wondered how she was going to advocate a position that she was no longer sure she believed in.

Hannah drummed her fingers against her spokes, staring out the window at the troublemakers on the courthouse lawn.

"What are they again?" Esther asked.

"AGNES."

"Like, a woman's name?"

"It's an anagram, or an acronym or whatever it's called. Something about gender equality."

"Left-wingers, eh?"

"With a lot of money and influence."

"From Washington?"

"They're the NRA of women's rights."

"Is that so? You're awfully quiet this afternoon. You and Terrell have a fight?"

"No. But now that you mention it, I don't think he's very happy with me right now."

"Did you give him reason to be that way?"

"Probably."

"Well, shame on you, Hannah Leigh Jessler. That's one man that you don't want to let slip through your hands. No, ma'am. I've seen them come and go, and he's a keeper."

"I know. I'm dirt."

"Now, I wouldn't go that far. Buddy and I have been married thirty-one years come November. It's not always been easy. We still fight. Like wildcats, sometimes. But a woman can learn to back down if it'll save her marriage."

Hannah watched the women position their sound equipment around the gazebo. One of them passed out pamphlets to people on the street.

"But Bud and I will be a mite better off as soon as he's back to work," Esther said.

"He's still sick?"

"As a dog, Hannah, as a dog. It's frustrating, you know, that he and I have worked all our lives and we can't even afford to go to the doctor. Just doesn't seem right."

"No, it doesn't. Esther, can I ask you a question?"

"Go ahead. My raggedy old life's an open book."

"If you could do something about that, about not being able to pay the doctor, and I don't mean doing something like winning the lottery, but really *doing something,* then what would it be? What would you do?"

"Other than rob a bank?" Esther struck a contemplative pose. "Call the president. Tell him that it's his job to make life fair. So that if I work fifty hours a week till I'm a senior citizen, then fairness says I should be able to have surgery without putting my family in debt for the next decade. That's what I'd do. Call him and tell him to make things fair. Why do you ask?"

"I don't know. Just in one of those moods."

Out in the grass, the women were setting up a video camera.

"It's hard," Hannah said, "making things fair."

"Well, if you ever manage to do it, you let me know."

Hannah looked up at her. "I will."

The consortium was winning.

By four o'clock the exit interviews were giving a ten percent edge to the developers from the nation's capital. A small party of their supporters had gathered at the site, and they were standing in an open field about thirty yards from Pete Musket's birthing house and Earnest Paul Tenfeathers's wigwam when they started celebrating. One of them fetched a bottle of champagne.

Jo heard the cork pop. Samuel Grady heard it, too.

Grady was the spokesman for the informal congregation of aboriginals who'd parked a Winnebago in Musket's grass. Jo had spent the last several hours playing the diplomat, a role toward which she was becoming increasingly ill-disposed. She expected a little give-and-take, but she found Grady unswerving: "Mr. Musket owns this land, Ms. Adams, and he's rightfully not giving it up, on account of it being old Shawnee ground."

Jo had offered a token argument because it was her job, not because her spirit was especially inclined to care one way or the other. Grady had already contacted the *Post*. They were sending someone to hear his story. Jo didn't recognize the reporter's name, but upon calling Martin with the news, he'd moaned like a man dying and said the guy had once been nominated for a Pulitzer.

Jo stepped out of Grady's humid motor home and glanced toward the festivities being held under the pavilion with the Sheridan sign stuck into the ground beside it. Chuck was nowhere to be seen. He was either still sweet-talking townspeople on their way in to vote, or raising hell about his car.

Should have pinked him a long time ago. Should have just told him to be nice.

The Nin in her heart argued otherwise. *Violence begets violence.*

Begets? Nin, I don't even know what begets means.

I don't believe that for a moment, Jo. You went to college.

"And what do I have to show for it?" she asked herself, not

201

caring if anyone heard her talking to herself. "A diploma, a lackluster transcript, and not a single night in jail when the police raided a party."

Hannah had said they'd found fingerprints. Jo wasn't overly worried, as her prints weren't on file, except the one they'd taken when Caroline was born; did the police have access to that? And hadn't Tamaryn gotten in trouble in high school? A drunk-driving arrest after a concert. Wasn't that the kind of thing they erased after you turned eighteen?

She got in the Mustang and took the long way home.

At six-fifteen Channel 12 proclaimed the defeat of the opposition. And if that wasn't excitement enough, a rally was to be held tonight on the courthouse yard, for those wanting to hear more of something being called domestic-oppression awareness. The event was to be webcast live on AGNES's official Internet site, with a book signing to follow.

"We're going to that, aren't we, Mom?"

"You're eating dinner with me first, aren't you, daughter?"

"You mean you cooked? Something other than macaroni out of a box?"

"I raised you on macaroni out of a box. You've turned out all right."

"Miracles happen, huh?"

Jo picked up a pillow from the couch and threw it at her. "Evil girl."

Caroline followed her into the kitchen. "Dad called."

"Oh?"

"You heard about what happened with his car?"

"A little."

"He says it was Rita Ingersol."

"Who?"

"The head of AGNES. Dad said she was out to get publicity by sabotaging the land sale. Then he called her a meddling dyke, so I hung up on him."

"You hung up on your father?"

"He shouldn't have said that."

"I agree. Good for you."

"Besides, they finally have people taking notice."

"Who's they?"

"The women in pink. They're dissenting, you know, like we talked about on the way back from Penny's. Hey, you made primavera!"

"Hey, I did." Smiling, Jo took two plates from the cupboard, lit a pair of candles, and ate dinner with her daughter.

Lucy reached the courthouse at half past seven, just as one of the choir members from St. Joseph's broke into the second verse of "America the Beautiful." Lucy guessed there must have been nearly 300 people gathered on the lawn, and one by one they stopped singing along, because once you got past the purple mountain's majesty, nobody knew the words. Lucy shouldered her way through them as if she were racing a sniper's bullet to the podium.

"Sorry, sir . . . my fault . . . pardon me, please . . . come on, Jo, where are you?"

She stood on her toes for a better view. The scent of hot dogs was everywhere. They'd set up a concession stand beside the big statue of Booker T. Washington. Lucy hadn't eaten all day.

There. A swatch of auburn hair in the crowd.

Lucy hurried in that direction. She still wore her USPS uniform, although her shirt had come untucked and her socks were chafing her ankles. Her poor feet. This was really all for them, right? All of this sneaking and pinking and lawbreaking? Each stride she took from here on out carried the possibility of change. Whether they knew it or not, these people were gathered here because of her. AGNES had descended upon the town because she—Lucy Campbell—finally stepped where stepping counted. Suddenly what she did with the hours allotted to her *mattered*.

"Sounds nice, don't it?" she said to herself, and then she saw Jo standing under a shade tree with Caroline and that guy from the Autoporium, Warren Dearborn. Her hand went to her back pocket, where the letter addressed to Nin burdened her like an iron weight.

". . . so that we might raise our *voices*," Rita Ingersol said through the loudspeaker, "with as much dedication as we raise our *children*, and then maybe, just *maybe*, we'll find the strength to raise our *hands*."

Applause, a whistle or two.

"And once we have those hands in the *air*, once we have them *so high* that the world can't help but *see*, then we can wave them as *one*. And let me tell you something, ladies and gentlemen"—a moment's pause—"enough of us start waving as one, we can stir up one hell of a wind."

Cheers, shouts, one or two *amens*.

"She's a firecracker, isn't she?" Lucy observed.

"She's a professional," Jo said. "This is what she does for a living."

"Get folks ticked off, you mean?"

"It sells a lot of books."

". . . though that *fight*, that hand-waving *struggle*, begins nowhere else but our own homes, our own houses, in the middle of our very own families. Let me ask you something, folks. Can I ask you all something?"

"Do we have a choice?" Lucy muttered.

Several people shouted for Ingersol to ask away.

"I want to *ask* you, and think about this seriously when I

say it, how long do you think our government would put up with a foreign despot who blatantly, routinely, and shame-lessly oppressed the citizens of his country? How long?"

"Do we have to stand here and listen to this?"

"We've got no one to blame but ourselves," Jo said.

"We need to talk about that."

"I know."

"Where's Caroline?"

"Warren's buying her a smoothie."

"Since when did Warren get elevated to smoothie-buying status?"

"Is that what you want to talk about?"

"No. You know it's not. But still. Warren Dearborn?"

Jo grinned with half her mouth. "He's harmless."

"Sure. I used to think the same thing about us."

". . . yet our government *refuses,* or better yet *ignores* the plight of millions of oppressed women and children in our own *country.*"

Jo noted that several dozen onlookers, mostly coed types with trendy hair and legs that were tanning-bed brown, had pressed closer to the gazebo. They were the most vocal mem-bers of the crowd, yelling words of encouragement and nod-ding continuously.

Yet how many of them would've had the chutzpah to stand up? she wondered. *How many would put their pink where their mouth is?*

But it was easy to let them off the hook, because courage wasn't the point. Pinking wasn't about guts, it was about your rope, and the choices you made when you were at the end of it.

"Can you get away tonight?" Lucy asked.

"I don't know. Sweet and I are having a good day."

"Then by all means, let me do my best to ruin it."

Jo resisted the urge to look away from the podium. She kept her eyes on charismatic Rita Ingersol and talked from the corner of her mouth, realizing as she did so that inmates in the prison yard spoke like this when discussing plans for escape. "Please don't tell me that they got a fingerprint match."

"Not yet, thank the Lord. I stole a letter. From someone on my route. First time I've ever done that."

"Explain."

"It's Nin's. From the state."

Jo crossed her arms over her chest. "What does it say?"

"You're accusing me of opening it?"

"What does it say?"

"It says they're inspecting her in a week. It says they've had . . . reports."

". . . that some of us are *tired* of the oppression, and just like the slaves of old, we're raising our *voices* and then raising our *hands,* and then—"

Jo squinted, stared at the podium . . . "Oh, Lucy . . ."

"—then we're raising our *flag!*"

On cue, Ingersol's assistants ran a piece of cloth up a twenty-foot pole planted beside the gazebo. It was a banner of solid pink.

"There's a time for wallflowers!" Ingersol hollered. "And a time for *vigilantes!*"

The flag caught a breeze and fluttered. The coeds roared.

"The hell you say . . ." Lucy whispered.

Jo closed her eyes and then opened them very slowly, as if the mirage would vanish in the interim. But the flag remained, as pink as the sheet that had draped her body only a few hours before. "Lucy, what have we done?"

"Started a war by the looks of it. Damn, just listen to them."

Jo was listening. And seeing. And feeling the vibration in her legs when the crowd began to stomp.

"Let the word go out from this time and place!" Rita Dawn Ingersol's voice rang across the town square. "An old shackle is released! A new movement has begun! May all of the oppressed, the homemakers, the battered children, the elderly locked away in their rooms, may they all fly the flag to let the world know that there is another way of doing things in this country! A way of *liberty!*"

The coeds thundered their hands against the gazebo. Parents with small children headed for their cars. Hecklers let loose a salvo of boos. Currents of movement flowed across the yard.

Caroline and Warren appeared, holding their smoothies and wearing similar looks of amusement, equally surprised by the sudden upswell of emotion and noise. "Mom! Pretty radical, huh?"

"Not my exact thoughts, but yes, I agree."

"See? You finally get to attend a rally, after all!"

"I can hear the ghost of Bobby Kennedy cheering me on. Lucy, Warren, we all better vamoose. I'm not especially fond of the tenor of tonight's peaceable gathering."

"Good idea," Lucy said. "God knows we don't want to get involved with any vigilantes."

"No," Jo said, shooting her a look. "We don't. I'll call you when I get home."

"You do that."

"Warren, I'm sorry, but I think it's best if we cut the evening a little short."

Warren, clearly overwhelmed by the spectacle, nodded dully. "I understand. We can always get together another time. Maybe next week?"

"Wonderful," Jo said. *If there is a next week.*

Caroline held up her cup. "Thanks, Warren. You're alright."

"My pleasure. See you around, Jo."

"You bet." She gave him a parting smile and then led Caroline through the grass toward the Mustang, which was an occasional yellow gleam on the far side of the town square.

I can't believe you actually bought this car, Caroline had said. *It's not really you. It's just so . . . cool.*

Better cool late than cool never, Jo had replied.

Though Ingersol still shouted into the PA system and voices were still being lifted in support or opposition, Jo's thoughts were fixed firmly on her little girl, who wasn't so little anymore and in many ways wasn't even a girl. It occurred to Jo for the first time that she had raised a *woman.* And not just a woman, but a *person.* That was something big. A vital, uncontainable force.

Jo stopped in the midst of the commotion, bodies pushing and shoving around her, took her daughter by the arm, and pulled her close. "Caroline, I want you to promise me something."

Caroline's eyes widened in concern when she saw the look on her mother's face. "Sure, Mom. Anything. What?"

"If I ever stop riding the fence, you'll be proud of me just for choosing. Whichever way I decide."

"Uh, okay . . ."

"Swear it."

"Yeah, of course, I swear, Mom. I swear it."

Jo studied her for a few seconds, then nodded. She dug the keys from her pocket and gave them a jingle. "So you want to see what she's got?"

Caroline grinned warily, as if suspecting a trap. "Are you serious?"

"More than you know."

They drove until nightfall, stopped once for gas and junk food, and didn't circle back to town until the moon rose above the trees. By then Jo was anxious but tried not to show it, because she sensed that with the coming of the darkness, her day had only just begun.

Chapter Sixteen

She left home at eleven, bound for Penny's house to disclose the secret of the sheets. From there she'd head to Lucy's to talk about Nin, because one of Mom's Crazy Coven was in trouble, and Mom was no longer abiding.

But Penny first. It was one thing to run around displaying all this messy bravery, and another to make someone clearly understand your motivation. Penny had to know a few things. Jo enumerated them as she drove. One, it was okay to get beat on; people were ships and ships were built to take a drubbing from the waves. Two, it wasn't okay to get beat on forever. Three, Nin was right that violence begets violence, but four, we did it anyway so please forgive us.

"Five," she said, pulling up to the curb. "We even kind of enjoyed it."

Oh yeah, and six: this car kicks ass.

She gunned the engine twice before turning it off.

She even walked quicker up the steps. She noticed the difference in her stride. Usually she was on her way to bed by this hour. Thinking about Wednesday morning. Work. Telephone calls. Maybe bowling afterwards if Martin could talk her into it. But now there was air. Different in her lungs. Every breath a meditation. Cicadas stirring in the dark trees.

The front door was open.

Not just a few inches, but open all the way. Light spilled across the porch.

Penny?

Jo stopped with her hands held in front of her, like a mime

running into an unseen wall. But she was no longer comfortable with hesitation, even for a moment, so she jumped up the steps and threw herself through the doorway.

Lamps burned on either side of the living room. A june bug buzzed erratically around one of them. The television was on but the sound was muted. The sliding-glass door that led to the backyard was open about eight inches. Jo smelled sandalwood and saw a guttering candle oozing smoke across the room.

"Penelope?"

Penny was out back, of course. Lying with Jed in the hammock. No, she was in the shower. *They* were in the shower, because that's what people their age did on Tuesday nights instead of going to bed with thoughts of work and bowling. No, there was no sound of running water. So they were taking a bath instead. A quiet bath with bubbles and—

Jo ran down the hall. "Penny, answer me!"

But Penny didn't answer, and that was only normal because she'd gone for a walk. Jed was an ogre but he was trying to change, and he'd invited her for a stroll to talk about forgiveness. You see, Pen, I had this epiphany the other night after leaving the bar. These five maniacs with a softball bat kindly showed me the error of my ways, like five pink Ghosts of Christmas Future pointing Scrooge toward the grave, and we're taking this walk so we can discuss it.

They wouldn't have left the door open.

"Is anyone here?" She flicked on the light in the guest bedroom. Grainy pictures of Penny and Joshua's ancestors stared down at her from the walls, their faces gaunt, their eyes mineshaft empty. The bed was neat and the room smelled unused.

Jo rushed to the end of the hall and the master bedroom, where the door was shut and no light seeped from beneath it, and had she been wearing her hood she would have heard it as she put her hand to the cold knob—*huff-pop, huff-pop*—and when she pushed her way in and hit the switch, she was bracing herself for . . .

. . . nothing. There was no one here.

"Penelope, where *are* you?"

She shouted the words again: *"Penny, where are you?"*

She waited for a moment, as if she might receive a reply. The only sound was the gentle hum of the air conditioner and the strident knocking in her ears.

Back to the hallway. Running. Wishing for hammocks and showers and strolls. Hearing Tamaryn say that someone had to pay. Tasting fumes in the air as Owen Selvey's cabin filled with paint. Feeling Caroline's soft skin, the wind in her own hair when she drove the new car, the sizzle of excitement when AGNES ran that flag up the pole. Seeing Warren Dearborn's timid smile and the way his shirt stretched across his chest when he moved just so. Still running. Reaching the bathroom at the far end of the house. Groping for the light and finding it. Blinking. Blinking . . .

Falling to her knees.

"Oh, God, Penny."

Penelope lay on her back. Blood leaked from her ear. It puddled on the floor and stained the neck of her bathrobe. It dried in droplets on the silver chain around her neck. It speckled a jar of fingernail polish lying beside her. Her toes were painted the same color as the smears on her thighs. A red handprint blotted the white lip of the tub.

Jo had never seen or smelled so much blood. Blackness pressed down around her eyes. Her stomach heaved. She closed her mouth and swallowed the vomit as it came up her throat.

A scarlet bubble formed under Penelope's nostril.

Jo stopped thinking. She bent down and touched Penny's

chest and then her face, getting her fingers sticky with blood but not noticing. Bubbles meant breath and breath meant *alive*. Jo put her ear close and heard the ragged respiration. She looked for the source of the blood but, shit, there was so much of it that it was impossible to tell. Penny's head, somewhere, it came from her head, and Jo remembered reading that head wounds were the worst kind of bleeders but that said nothing for the gore between Penny's legs, and there she went, thinking again, so stop it. Just save this person's life.

Jo hooked a towel from behind the door and bound Penelope's head in it, as tenderly as time allowed. *Live, goddammit.* She parted Penny's bathrobe but saw no lacerations, which meant the blood spigot was in her skull. *Live and see what I do to this bastard.* Again she shoved her ear to Penny's face and listened until she was sure lungs were still pumping and air still flowing. *Live, you hear me?*

"Live," she said, then clawed for the sink and used it to pull herself up. She sprinted down the hall to the phone.

Her fingers had never been so cold. She punched the buttons for Hannah's emergency line, and realized that she had never dialed those three numbers before. So this was how it felt to use them. They were a code for life chiseled to its finest tip.

She panted into the phone.

Her hair was bloody from hanging in Penelope's face and it left long strings of red on the receiver. She tasted it, briny and sharp, when she licked the sweat from her upper lip. The lightness coruscated through her veins, last seen carrying her across the wood planking of a certain run-down cabin and now returned to detach her from the world, while back in the bathroom Penny died a little bit more.

"Please just pick up the stupid pho—"

"Clayton County emergency services, may I please have your name?"

"Hannah. It's me. I'm at Penny's. I need an ambulance."

"Jo? Jo, what are you—"

"Send a goddamn ambulance!"

She hung up and raced back to the bathroom.

She knew she should have stayed on the line, let Hannah talk to her, maybe get some first-aid advice over the phone. That would have been the response of a sane person, a logical, coolheaded person, but instead, Jo sat down and cradled Penny's head in her lap, breathing the inescapable scent of blood. She tried to focus on the bottle of spilled fingernail polish, but her eyes kept slipping to Penny's legs. Already bruises were forming there.

Jo rocked back and forth, singing to herself and to Penny, until her song gave way to the alien cry of sirens.

So it wasn't a wineglass. Nin had never owned any. Nor had she ever carried a brown bag out of a liquor store. At least not until today.

The scented water came so near to the top of the bathtub that Nin had to move slowly to keep from splashing it to the floor when she brought the chardonnay to her lips. She sipped, savoring the unfamiliar flavor, then returned the glass to her tub-side table, which looked suspiciously like a toilet draped in a bath towel.

"So many candles . . ." She smiled like a woman slipping into a dream. Her hunt for candles around the kitchen hadn't produced more than a half-package of the birthday variety, so she'd bought ten white tapers and a box of tealights after procuring the wine. The tealights were the best. They floated. One of them bobbed between her knees, flickering. . . .

Her eyelids grew heavy. She wondered what it would be like to fall asleep in this warm, soothing water. There was little chance of her slipping under the suds and drowning herself; her body filled the tub too completely. How rare and sensuous it would be to drift away, wine on her lips, the candle burning between her knees.

Someone pounded on her front door.

The sound jarred her, causing her to shift suddenly and send water rocking over the rim.

The hammering stopped. Then, muffled, came the voice: "Nin, are you awake?"

"Tamaryn," Nin breathed. What was she doing here at this hour?

"Nin, unlock the door!"

The aftertaste of the wine turned sour in her mouth. Something dreadful had happened.

The blade of fear sliced through the cobwebs of drowsiness. "Oh, Lord, please . . ." She put a hand on either side of the tub and shoved herself out, without regard for the water that ended up on the floor. The flame of the floating tealight was doused.

She wrapped a towel around herself as she tromped through the dark house toward the sound of Tamaryn's voice, the noise of her heavy footfalls causing her children to stir in their beds.

Tam drove the pickup into Lucy's yard. "I'll only be a minute."

"Let us pray that a minute is not too long," Nin said.

Tam jumped out. Her sneakers sank in the moist grass.

Don't scream.

She commanded that of herself as she vaulted the railing and struck the butt of her hand against Lucy's flimsy screen door. God, she needed a smoke. Dummy, running off without her cigarettes. *Don't scream just don't scream try to maintain at least a little control.*

"Lucy!" She kicked the door, denting the thin metal. She wanted to tear the walls from the house and drag Lucy through the hole, just to speed things up. And here, back again, was the fire. The *fire.* The hotness that fueled her when she fought with Roy. That drove her into a slide to beat the throw to second base. That had gotten her into so much trouble as a kid. That had caused her to implement the Good Rules in an effort to quench the flames. Roy had knocked her around a few times, and on those occasions when the fire engulfed her, she hit him in return. She'd blacked his eye once. He'd called in sick to work the next day so his friends wouldn't see.

"Lucy, get your ass out here!"

The neighbor's light came on.

"Go back to bed!" Tamaryn shouted at their window.

She walked to the end of the porch. The truck idled loudly, the headlights bathing the front of the house. This is what you got for sticking to your Good Rules. Punched in the teeth. Punched in the teeth and left to fend for yourself. But the cops and preachers and social workers didn't understand that you could only get pushed so often and left alone for so long before you either died quietly or survived loudly.

She heard the screen door open. She spun around, blowing the curls from her eyes.

Lucy stood in her pajamas. Her hair was loose, her arms held stiffly at her sides. The look in her eyes was that of a woman expecting the worst. She lifted her chin as if anticipating a blow. "Careful now, Tamaryn Soza. I don't want you standing here on my porch and telling me that somebody is dead. I won't have that. No, ma'am, I won't."

"She's still alive. But we need to go. She's in surgery right now."

"*Who?*"

"Penelope."

Lucy closed her eyes. But Tamaryn noticed the way her body relaxed, a brief but definite sign that she was at least a little bit relieved. It could have been one of the others, Terrell or Hannah or Jo or Nin. Tam had experienced it herself, the weird double feeling of pain and relief, spliced together with guilt. It didn't make sense that you could ache for a person yet be silently thankful that it wasn't someone else. It was a shitty part of being human.

"How bad?" Lucy asked.

"Really."

"Where are the boys?"

"Nin's in the truck. She called her sister-in-law and had her come over to look after the munchkins. Told her that Penny had been taken to the emergency room and we had to go see her. I left Matt and Brady there."

"I'll get my shoes."

Tam followed her into the house.

Lucy grabbed a bra from the top of the dirty-clothes basket and her shoes from the hall closet. "Jo's already at the hospital, isn't she?"

"How did you know?"

"Have you spoken to her?"

"No. Jessler was the one who called me."

"Easy does it, Josephine," Lucy said, as if Jo were standing in the room with them. "Don't you do anything drastic until you get my approval." She dumped her keys in her purse. "I'm ready. I'll dress in the truck."

But suddenly Tamaryn couldn't move. "Luce." It had finally overtaken her while Lucy was gathering her things. She wanted more than anything to hustle outside, but she was rooted to the floor. Beads of sweat formed along her neckline. She stood in front of Lucy and tried to convey with her eyes the intensity of the fire, the rage, the bewilderment, the struggle. This is how it had felt when she'd been too weak to keep a man from pulling her pants down. She'd fought him with all the savagery in her. She had bitten him, torn gashes in his skin. But when he clubbed her head against the floor, the strength had fled her arms, and the legs that he parted and the body he injected with his juices were not her own. Surely nothing that helpless could belong to her. "Let's bring it along."

"No."

"Just in case."

"No."

"I'll get it myself if I have to."

Lucy looked away. She lifted a hand, a signal for silence. She held her arm that way for awhile, then touched her forehead, as if she were about to faint. Finally she said, "He's a true son of a bitch, isn't he?"

Tamaryn nodded.

Lucy returned from her bedroom seconds later, carrying a small bundle wrapped in a towel.

Jo lies naked atop the quilt her mother sent her for her dorm room bed.

The music is playing, but not so loudly that the international students in the next room will complain; they are Chinese or Vietnamese or some sort of Ese—Jo has never bothered to ask. But they go to bed early and spend too many hours with their studies. Jo remembers a time when she was the same way, her freshman year and out to master the books or die from Hi-Liter fumes in the attempt.

Now she is a senior and knows better. She squirms a little on her belly, feeling the softness of the blanket against her skin and watching with half-lidded eyes as this impossible boy unbuckles his belt and lets his faded jeans fall to his ankles. She has never known anyone like Chuck. He's the only one of her friends who is sloganless. He supports no causes. He favors no proverbs. Chuck is not a stand-taker. He is a backer. He's always there, watching from the corner of the classroom, only partially interested in the subject at hand until the prof singles out a student for expressing a particularly far-fetched theory. And then Chuck is there, wading in, rallying to the cause not because the cause is his but because he has been sent here by the gods to even the odds for the little people.

His bare body is lean, his ribs as visible as speed bumps. He stands there looking somewhat discomfited at being on display like this. Silly boy. He assumes that women look at naked men the same way that men drip their eyes over a naked woman. And sometimes that's true, but usually what a woman sees travels through the filter of her heart. Men are blessed with the ability to make their filters transparent as it suits them. Chuck stares into Jo's eyes, pleading with her but also looking for her approval. Does she like what she sees?

She smiles. She thinks that Chuck shouldn't be here, but rather outside in a secluded place, perhaps on a deserted island catching fish with his hands. That's how he seems to her. Elemental. Irresistibly she wants him. The tingling in her body becomes an ache. She pushes herself up on her elbows, exposing her breasts.

Chuck folds his lips inside his mouth, wets them. He looks away, and Jo can sense that he's yearning for a cigarette. Usually she hates it when he smokes. It seems like such a contradiction for a boy—check that, a man—*with a body and mind so at ease to depend on such a habit. But then there are certain times—now would be one of them—that smoking makes him look sexy-cool.*

Come here, Jo says.

He studies her for a moment more, then does as she says.

Get down.

He goes to his knees, so that now she can stare at him levelly.

Quiet, she says. The Ese are asleep next door.

And she slides to him, capturing him in her arms and pushing her body, her mouth, her stomach against his. With her clinging to his neck, he falls back to the floor, overcome, and for several seconds he is helpless for the first time since Jo met him. But then he recovers.

Quiet! Jo gasps, and the word escapes her teeth each time he surges against her.

Quiet!

Quiet!

Qui—

—et!

"Quiet," she said.

Hannah looked over at her from the driver's seat. "Nobody said anything, Jo."

Jo blinked. She lifted her head from her arms and stared into the darkness beyond the windshield. Her mouth tasted sour. There was a cottony thickness in her ears.

"You okay up there?" Lucy asked from the back of the van.

Now there was a question. Was she okay? The vapor of the dream still lingered, clouding her vision. She peered through the fog and saw the dashboard clock. Three-twenty-two.

That would be a.m., she thought. The last thing she remembered was standing outside the operating room, watching Tamaryn pace a trench in the floor. Hannah had been pacing, too, which was even worse: roll twenty feet down the hall, pivot, roll back. Repeat until madness ensues.

The vapor thinned.

The ambulance ride had been nothing but a montage of

shifting sounds, bright colors, and the acute need for a glass of water. Once at the hospital, she kept making trips to the water fountain, holding her hair out of the way and drinking until her stomach sloshed when she moved. Terrell had been the first to arrive. He folded her against his chest and said all the right things. Nobody said all the right things anymore. If Hannah let this man get away then Jo was going to punch her in the nose.

As long as Terrell's on our side, we'll be all right. Come what may.

And what was coming?

Her vision finally cleared and she was looking at the courthouse. The back side. Where the cop cars were parked and the entrance to the county lockup was illuminated by a bulb inside a protective wire cage. They had taken Jo's statement and helped her clean the blood from her hands. Swatches of it stained her shirt. Her knee was dark where she'd knelt in it on Penny's floor. Though it seemed like the events of a past life, Jo recalled her anger. She had yelled at them to bring him in, just go find him and bring him in. And they had. A highway patrolman pulled him over twenty miles outside of D.C., politely requesting that he turn around and answer a few questions back in Belle Springs. A few questions. That sounded unreasonably sane.

"You didn't answer me," Lucy said.

"The opposite of okay, Lucy. Whatever it is, that's what I am."

Other than the police cruisers, only three cars were parked behind the courthouse. One was Esther's. She'd taken over at the dispatcher's desk when Hannah's double-shift finally ended at midnight. Car number two belonged to an attorney who'd arrived looking far too neatly pressed and formidable for this time of night. He even brought along an assistant. But the third car, that's where Jo's eyes kept straying. It was minus the chrome cat on the hood, but other than that, it looked new.

"How long we going to sit here?" Lucy asked.

Jo didn't look away from the car. "Did you bring your mailbag like I asked?"

"I do everything you ask."

"Good. Nin?"

"Yes?"

"Nothing. I just like to hear your voice."

They sat in silence and waited for Jed.

The door beneath the caged lightbulb opened.

"Look alive, ladies," Tam said.

Jo stared through her eyelashes across the parking lot. So much for erecting some kind of plan. She'd been sitting here in silence, trying to build a scaffold that would support the weight of her rage without collapsing. But hell. Nothing worked.

The lawyer's assistant came out first, a notebook computer under her arm and a phone against her ear. Already the legal team was seeking the strings, pulling as necessary. The attorney followed her, talking as he came.

Jed Whitecross was beside him.

"Shit, Jo, they didn't even arrest him!"

"I can see that, Tam."

"To arrest him," Hannah said, "they need something called evidence."

"Up yours, Jessler. Nobody likes a smart-ass."

"Or a bitchy backseat driver," Hannah fired back.

"Please don't do this," Nin said. "We will not fight amongst ourselves. Not when there is such a need for our energy elsewhere."

Jed said a few last words to his attorney, then started his car with a touch of his key-ring.

"So what do we do?" Hannah asked. She tapped her fingers on the steering wheel. "Someone tell me what to do here, do I follow him or wait or what?"

"Jo." Lucy sidled up between the front seats. "Jo, it's your call."

"Since when?"

"Since always."

"You know how I am about choosing."

"No, I don't. Why don't you tell me?"

"The D.A. will have to file charges."

"Yes, I suppose so."

"And the tabloids will be all over it."

"I'm sure they will, considering Jed's daddy and all."

"His life is trash."

"Could very well be."

Jo finally vocalized the essence of her thoughts. "The problem with justice is that it's always retroactive. By definition it happens too late."

"What are you saying?"

"I want a new word, Lucy. Justice sucks." She looked down at herself and fingered her robe. "Hannah, when he pulls out, follow him."

Chapter Seventeen

They drove through a black tunnel of trees.

Jed didn't stop after parting ways with his attorney at the sheriff's office. His taillights flashed briefly at the all-night filling station on the east side of town, and Jo thought he was going to pull in for gas. Perhaps he considered it. But then he sped by, leaving the safe glow of civilization behind. Jo fastened her eyes to the two red fireflies a hundred yards ahead in the darkness, afraid that if she looked away, she'd lose him.

"Don't get too far back," she advised.

"I'm trying, Jo, I'm really trying, but I've never tailed anyone before."

"Real people don't do this kind of thing," Lucy mused.

"We ain't real people anymore." Tam's lighter flicked. "Scoot over, Luce. I need to be close to the window."

"Do you think he sees us, I mean, should I get closer, because there's no one else out here and I don't want him to get suspicious and stomp on the gas. We'll never catch him if he does."

"Should've brought the pony," Jo said, mostly to herself.

"Huh?"

"Forget it. Speed up a little bit."

"How much is a little?"

"Just go, Hannah."

Jo felt the van accelerate. Strange, but her pulse wasn't doing the same thing. There were no debilitating bodily functions, no wet underarms. What was happening to her?

"Would it be wise to telephone the hospital again?" Nin asked. "Penelope should be out of surgery by now. I'd like to know how she's doing."

"That's a good idea. Here, use my phone. But if anyone asks, you're at home."

"I understand."

Jo turned around in her seat and extended the phone into the darkness. When she felt Nin's fingers, she grabbed her hand. "You don't have to do this, Nin."

"If we turn around now," Nin reasoned, too calmly, "then he will get away."

"Shaking a bat at a man is one thing, and using it is another. I think that's what we're intending here. You shouldn't be a part of it."

Inexplicably, Nin laughed.

Jo let go of her hand. "What did I say?"

"Why, Jo Adams." Nin slapped her knee, chortling like an old woman. "Do you assume that I am unacquainted with the stick?"

"Pardon?"

"The stick. I have more than once in my life felt its heat. I've taken my share of bruises, Jo, the good Lord knows that I have. *Stripes,* He calls them. That makes them sound noble, doesn't it? As if you're getting the stick for a worthy cause. Do you know I was sixteen years old when I married Dan? Guess where we met. Go on, guess."

"I don't know, Nin. Tell me."

"Behind a bowling alley in Juneau. My boyfriend was punching me in the stomach because I had just told him I was pregnant. He was trying to get me to miscarry. Dan came along and broke his jaw with a tire iron. So you see, Jo, the stick and I go way back."

"I . . . I didn't know."

"Of course you didn't. But here I am. It didn't work, by the by."

"What didn't work?"

"The attempted abortion by punching."

"Dorothy isn't Dan's daughter?"

"He adopted her. It was a gentlemanly thing to do."

"Yeah. I guess it was." She could barely see the shape of Nin's face in the gloom, but she assumed there was a look of contentment there, if not downright serenity. "So, uh, do you want me to nominate him for the Nobel prize for good fathers?"

Nin laughed again. "You do that, Jo. And tell him I said that he can shove it where flowers don't grow."

Jo smiled in the dark. But then she turned around and they were close enough to the Jag that she could read its license plate. *Here we go.*

Looks that way, an inner voice responded. *Want to reconsider?*

Yes, but I won't. Too late.

"How fast are we going?" she asked.

"Almost seventy."

"Pull up beside him."

Hannah flashed her a look. "You sure?"

"Do it."

Hannah complied. She thumbed the gas lever and swung into the left lane. The speedometer needle crept higher. Trees blotted out the stars.

"I think I'm going to be sick," Lucy said.

Jo kept her eyes on the Jag as the van moved up alongside of it. Soon both vehicles were motoring through the night at nearly seventy miles an hour, side by side on the narrow blacktop. She could see nothing of Jed inside the car except for the outline of his hands, backlit in the dim green light of the dashboard.

"Okay I'm next to him now what do I do?"

"Faster."

"Jo, you've got to remember that he can outrun us easily . . ."

"Pretend this is a barrel race, Hannah. Go like you used to go back then." Was that the first time she'd ever mentioned Hannah's former life? In all of these years, had she never scraped up the courage to talk about the accident? Without looking away from the car, she said, "That is, if you still remember what it was like."

"Remember?" Hannah laughed, a rueful, raven-like sound. "If you only knew."

The van took on speed.

"Jo?"

"I'm still here, Tam."

"There's something you should know."

"Make it quick."

"Lucy's father had a run-in with a pack of racist thugs back in the sixties . . ."

"Tamaryn," Lucy warned.

"They kept harassing him on his way to the mine. So he took his best pair of shoes into town one day. His wingtips, the only expensive thing that he owned. And he traded them for a gun."

"Cut in front of him, Hannah."

Hannah signaled right and changed lanes.

"Good girl. Are you ready for this?"

"What's she talking about, Jo?" Hannah asked.

"Never mind her. Can you do this or not?"

"I promise to try."

"What's this about a gun?" Nin asked.

"Now, Hannah!"

Hannah shoved her palm against the brake.

The tires pinched shrilly against the pavement. Jo's seat belt locked hard. She braced herself with both hands against the dash.

Hannah let up momentarily. The van shuddered and fought her, its back end trying to spin out of her control. She jerked the wheel against the vehicle's momentum, then leaned again on the brake.

Tires whined. A horn blast pierced the night behind them.

The van swerved.

"Hang on!" Jo yelled.

Hands reached for something solid to grab, voices cried out, lights cut across the trees. Hannah steered away from the ditch, the rear wheels ripping over the rocky shoulder. She released the brake and then applied it again, whispering, *"Oh shit oh shit oh shit oh—"*

Jo saw a pair of red eyes in the trees—a raccoon or possum or some poor frightened creature—then the van spun completely around.

Suddenly the Jag filled the windshield, coming right at them, fishtailing, the smell of scorched rubber stinging Jo's nostrils. . . .

The van rocked to a standstill. Jo's head snapped back against the seat. With an effort she kept her eyes open, watching the Jaguar slide toward them—

It stopped four feet away.

Smoke spiraled up from hot tires. Dust swam in a sea of headlights.

"Bit my damn tongue!" Tamaryn spit on the floor.

Jo lifted a hand in front of her face, just to check, but her fingers weren't shaking. She unfastened her seat belt. "Hoods!"

Fabric fluttered as they masked themselves.

"Lucy, get the stuff!"

"Got it."

"Let's do it." Compelled by a force that she no longer attempted to comprehend, she jumped out without waiting to see if the others would follow. For a second she was blind in the glare, then she stepped around the front of the car and she saw Jed inside, holding his head. The car's engine was still running. Jo had to get to him before he backed up and left her standing there, her new spiritual thirst unquenched.

She ran around to the driver's door, not so clumsy in her sheet as she'd once been. She'd adapted to the restrictions of the hood, having learned to turn her head in such a way to compensate for lack of peripheral vision. It took less than three seconds for her to reach the car and grasp the door handle. She pulled the door open.

Jed turned to look up at her. A line of blood creased his forehead, plainly the result of an impact with the steering wheel. His shirt collar was open, his sleeves rolled up. A fabulous jewel of a watch lay against his wrist. He hadn't shaved since this morning, but his hair was neat. His eyes were blue wells of fear. "Oh, God . . ."

"Get out of the car."

Jed shook his head rapidly, like a disobedient child.

"I said get out. *Now*."

"*No!*" He fumbled for the gearshift.

"Lucy!"

"Here!" Lucy thrust something at her. "Take it!"

Jo grabbed the can of pepper spray and—hardly bothering to ensure that it was pointed in the proper direction—fired an extended burst into the car.

The first part of her shot caught him in the shoulder, but she quickly adjusted, blasting him across the face.

She hadn't expected such a reaction.

Jed went into a seizure. The thousands of tiny heat units contained in the spray acted as a kind of mini-napalm when applied to body tissue. Jed opened his mouth to scream but the poison poured into him and set his throat on fire. His hands flew to his face, gouging at his mouth, his eyes, his ears, as if to tear the searing flesh from his bones. Vibrations rippled through him, and a sound like a small animal being strangled rose from the gaping pit of his mouth.

Jo stood there holding the can, stunned.

"What the hell are you waiting for?" Tamaryn shoved her aside.

Jo conceded her position at the door, allowing Tam to duck into the car and grab Jed by the shirt. She wore her softball batting gloves, bright red against Jed's crisp white shirt. "Hey, dickhead, remember me?" She unfastened his lap belt and shook him viciously. "Now come out of there!"

But Jed was still convulsing, flailing against the seat, and wasn't going anywhere easily.

Undeterred, Tam released his lapels and locked her hands around his upper arm. She was the most physically adept woman Jo had ever known personally, and had her life taken a different turn, she might have earned a living as an athlete. She lowered herself for leverage, her sneakers visible beneath the hem of her robe, screwing themselves against the pavement for traction. With a violent grunt, Tamaryn tore Jed out of the car.

He didn't even try to break his fall. His hands were too busy clutching at his eyes. He landed on his side in the middle of the highway, coughing now, brutally enough that Jo wouldn't have been surprised to see bits of his esophagus spewing through his teeth. His feet drummed against the asphalt. One of his leather loafers flew into the weeds.

Jo shook out of her trance. "Lucy! Tape!"

Lucy held out the roll of duct tape and Jo took it, trading her for the can of pepper spray. It had been her idea, the pepper spray, the best way she could think of to subdue the man. Nin had expressed her reservations but she'd come around in the end. Lucy said that she'd only had to use the stuff twice in her career, both times in self-defense against misanthropic mutts, and she wasn't sure how effective it really was on people.

The answer to that question was *very*. Jed howled as if in his death throes.

"Hold his legs," Jo commanded.

Tamaryn hitched up her robe and straddled him.

Jed made a wet gurgling sound.

"You two give her some help!" She didn't wait for Lucy and Nin to thaw out and get into action. The lightness was in her veins and Helium Lady was moving. She dropped to her knees at Jed's feet and wound the tape around his ankles. Four, five, then six times she passed the roll under his legs, the heavy tape shackling him more effectively than any pair of manacles could have done. The tape proved too resilient to be torn with the hands, so Jo slipped her mask up long enough to apply her teeth to the task. "Get his arms!"

She slid off Jed's legs just as Tamaryn slugged him in the face.

"Bastard!" She hit him again, a second left cross to the nose. She drew blood.

"That's enough," Jo said. "Hold his hands."

Lucy and Nin had positioned themselves on either side of him, and now they each took an arm and wrenched his hands from his tear-streaked, blood-splattered cheeks. He tried to speak, but his words were lost in a paroxysm of coughs.

"Closer!"

Lucy and Nin pinned his arms together. Jo went after him with the tape, wrapping it around and around from his wrists down to his elbows.

Hannah yelled from the van, "Hurry up, you're taking too long!"

"There!" Jo swatted his bound arms out of the way and slapped an eight-inch strip of gray tape over his mouth. She didn't bother blindfolding him. Even if his vision eventually cleared and he saw something he could later relate to the police, such as Hannah's chair, it was Jo's opinion that no jury in West Virginia would convict them. Not with Penny swimming in a coma in ICU. Not with all the sabers AGNES would rattle in their defense. Jo was betting on public sympathy and an army of pissed-off lesbians.

Jed whimpered behind his muzzle and shook his head, his eyes scrunched shut in pain. Jo checked to make sure that she hadn't inadvertently stoppered his nostrils, then shoved herself to her feet. "Let's get him up!"

Tamaryn started lifting him before the others had even established a firm grip. Lucy and Nin took his upper half, leaving Jo with his legs. Her back pinched painfully when she stood up with this burden, but still her heart was as silent and cold as the stars overhead. No more unnerving *huff-pop*. No more goose bumps. Just a steely taste in her mouth, and her mind occasionally inventing a word for justice that didn't occur after the fact. *Preemptive justice?* No, too verbose. *Forefairness?* Close, but not what she was looking for.

"Into the van!" she ordered.

The four of them lumbered their load toward the van's sliding door, while Hannah hissed at them to hurry up and Nin recited the Lord's prayer.

". . . hallowed be Thy name."

Jed floundered in their arms. Jo tightened her hold around

his knees. Her mask was pulled askew and she could hardly see where she was going.

". . . and forgive us our trespasses . . ."

"As we forgive those," Lucy said, joining the rhythm of Nin's mantra, "who trespass against us."

They blundered into the open doorway. Feeling a sudden shift in weight, Jo let go. Jed fell to the floor of the van, mewling, twisting uselessly against his bonds. They shoved him in as far as they could. The wheelchair, clamped to the mechanized ramp, made for restricted confines, but Lucy crawled in after him and dragged him into the back.

". . . but deliver us from evil . . ."

"Tam, get his heap off the road."

Tamaryn bolted for the car.

Jo put her hands on Nin's back and helped boost her into the van. Nin said, "Thank you, honey," and then continued with, "for Thine is the kingdom and the power and the glory."

"Forever and ever," Jo said, and pulled the door shut. "Amen."

Tam drove the Jaguar into the trees. She spun dirt from the tires while getting through the culvert, but the car's powerful engine thrust it easily up the other side. The woods rapidly thickened to a point that made driving impossible, but Tam edged the Jag in at least fifty feet before shutting it off and snuffing the lights. It wasn't much, and Jo figured the car would be easily seen from the road come daylight, but if it even bought them an extra half an hour, then hiding it had served its purpose.

"What's taking her so long?" Hannah wanted to know. "Someone could come along any second now. Jo, we really really need to make like a goalie and get the puck out of here. Right now, please."

Tam came running at a full sprint, the peak of her hood bent back in the breeze. Jo held the passenger door open for her. Tam leaped into the van with feline grace, then worked her way to the back.

Jo shut the door.

Hannah pressed three fingers on the accelerator, bent over the wheel, and piled on the speed. She engaged her high beams and looked from the road to her wing mirror and back again with whiplash frequency.

"How's he doing back there?" Jo asked.

"I think he pissed his pants," Tam announced.

Hannah was chanting again: "Oh shit oh shit oh shit—"

"Don't you hyperventilate on me," Jo warned.

"But Jo we just *kidnapped* someone."

"Hush. Just get us to the lake in one piece."

"The lake. Okay. The lake. I can do that."

Jed screamed as best he could behind his gag.

"Welcome to my parlor, asshole," Tam said.

Jo started to rebuke her, or at the very least ask for her restraint until they reached the water, but then her mind struck gold, and the new word tinkled like a coin onto her tongue, freshly minted.

Antequity.

Justice was something you enacted to heal wounds, make amends, placate the aggrieved. But combine the prefix *ante* with *equity* and you could provide for a situation *beforehand*, so that a problem never arose. Justice was a cure. Antequity was a prevention.

So now I'm a walking dictionary. She straightened her mask. *Add that to my ever-growing list of titles: midwife of lost causes, den mother to vigilantes, icon of the oppressed, and budding wordsmith.*

They drove to the lake.

Chapter Eighteen

Tamaryn Soza, like a woman rolling a bundle of carpet, shoved Jed Whitecross from the van. Unable to brace himself against the fall, he landed heavily, his back and skull bearing the brunt of impact.

He resumed sobbing at once. Though muffled by the gray band around his mouth, his sounds were clearly audible in the otherwise undisturbed night air. Every few seconds he expended another burst of energy and thrashed against his trammels, but the tape held.

Without waiting to see if the others followed, Jo slogged through the damp grass and cattails to the water's edge. Reflection turned the lake into a second sky. A black field of stars lay at her feet. At the horizon line, the two firmaments met seamlessly, so that it was impossible to tell where water ended and space began. Jo measured this vastness against the size of her anger.

Except it wasn't anger.

Not precisely, anyway. What filled the hollows of her bones and swelled her veins was not so much outrage as it was her own fed-up spirit. For too long she had lain dormant inside of herself, with all of her that mattered compressed into a manageable, polite package. You didn't step on any toes that way, you didn't offend, you didn't tack a flag to the piano in your classroom. But over the course of the last week, she had unfolded. The presence she felt lightening her body wasn't helium, not really, but the expanding atmosphere of her soul, making skies where before there had been only the routine between day and night.

A scent tickled her nose.

She turned around as an imposing pink-robed figure assumed a position beside her.

Nin. Her hood made her seven feet tall.

"Is that a new perfume?" Jo asked.

"Do you like it? I bought it this morning at the pharmacy."

"Pharmacists go to hell when they die," Jo said. "To live with the devil and car dealers."

"Is that so?"

"That's what Warren Dearborn told me."

"He seems like a nice man."

"So far. Are you okay?"

"What? An Eskimo can't even buy a new bottle of perfume without causing a clamor?"

"You could have bought a lot of Froot Loops with the amount you paid for it."

"You are truly right about that, honey. I wonder how many boxes of them I could buy with the amount a person might pay for a canary-yellow Mustang."

"Thousands, I'm sure. And it's not canary."

Nin found Jo's hand in the darkness and pressed it into the warmth of her own. "You sure don't seem upset enough to be doing what we are about to do."

"You either."

"I have learned to keep it hidden." She shook her head. "Oh, how I have learned."

"Penelope might die, Nin. I'm not letting Jed walk away. I've told you already that you don't have to be here. No one's forcing this on you."

"Now, that's where you're wrong," Nin softly admonished her. "I am a prisoner on the Jo Adams Express. And it's running too fast to jump off. I can't control the destination, no ma'am, and I can't slow it down. So I just have to hold on and try to keep it from running off the tracks."

"So can I cut him loose or what?" Tam hollered.

Jo started at the sound of her voice. To Nin, she said, "It's not really like that. Is it?"

Nin patted her hand. "You remember the caboose, don't you?"

"Sure. Ass Ends. The engineers of underwear."

"Ever since that day, I've been stuck to you. There's no unsticking now."

"Quit your bawling!" Tam yelled at Jed. She unwound the tape from his arms. "And if you try to so much as breathe on me, I swear to God I'll tear your throat out."

"Don't try to run," Lucy said to him. "You'll only die tired."

Tam glared at her from behind her mask, then got to work on Jed's legs.

Keeping her hold on Nin's hand, Jo made her way back to the van. "Walk with me."

"Always."

After ripping away the last of the tape, Tam backed off. She packed the tape into a sticky ball and pitched it into the van. On an unspoken cue, the four of them formed a ring, the headlights fully illuminating the man who was sprawled at their feet. The four became five when Hannah eased her chair into the circle, her tires making deep scores in the soft earth.

His coughs subsiding, Jed dug at his eyes to clear the moisture. He tore away the gag, sniffed up a ball of snot that was roosting on his upper lip, and took several long, painful breaths until his body began to settle. He blinked and, still on his back, looked straight up. At the sight of the robes, the hidden black eyes, the silhouette of hoods like mountain peaks against the night sky, he buried his face in his hands. *"Please, no more."*

"I'm going to crack a rib," Tamaryn stated. "At least one." She spoke with no inflection, as if she were commenting on the weather or an old pair of shoes. Without looking away from him, she said, "Jo, that's what I want to do. I want to crack one of his ribs."

A chill kissed the back of Jo's neck. The tone of those words . . .

Suddenly Lucy bent down and grabbed him by the hair. "You sick, unhappy little boy!" She shook his head so hard that Jo heard hair tear loose at the roots. "That's what you are! A sadistic vain horrible *bully!*" She pulled straight up, yanking out a clump.

Jed screamed.

From behind her chair Hannah produced a familiar aluminum bat, official size and weight of the Women's Pro Softball League, and silenced him with a single, splintering blow to the knee.

The cry was swiped from Jed's open mouth. He curled up, grabbing his leg, and at that precise point, the last strands of Jo's life as a normal, unoffending person came finally to an end. The bigness inside of her fell out into the world. She removed her hood even as she descended, letting her hair fall loose on her neck, and then she smelled him, a revolting potion of cologne and urine. Her hand went to his face not as a fist but as an open-fingered, talon-like embrace. She pressed her nails into his cheeks and chin, leaning into him and forcing his head to the dirt, and when she was inches away she spit at him, spit between her splayed fingers and into his eye and—

Jed punched her in the ear.

Whiteness blared across her eyes.

The attack had come too quickly. She reeled. And then Jed was fighting, alive and reckless and strong. He rocked

238

onto his knees and swung at her again as she tipped backward. His knuckles grazed her chin, snapping her head to the side.

She flailed, fell, caught herself—

Jed scrambled to his feet, seething. Spittle flecked his lips. His back was hunched, his hair in his face, and in the yellow shine, his skin looked jaundiced. He stepped left and hit Lucy in the chest.

It was a straight jab, rapid as a piston. It caught Lucy just below her neckline. She made an airy, punctured sound and went down.

Sitting on her butt in the weeds, Jo opened her eyelids as wide as she could. *Don't you pass out,* she told herself. The fog cleared her eyes in time for her to see Hannah swing the bat again.

But Hannah's angle was all wrong. She was too low, too far away, unable to muster any kind of power at all. Jed took the bat in the right thigh without pausing in his lunge toward Nin, the biggest of his attackers. He was nothing but raw instinct now and went at her undaunted. Nin lifted her arms to cover her face.

Jed aimed for her stomach.

This isn't happening.

Nin, to her credit, didn't cry out. She doubled over with a soft grunt, her arms dropping immediately. But she was not unacquainted with the stick, and would not be so easily subdued. In the half-second Jo spent getting off the ground, Nin took two aimless, loping swings at Jed, and though he dodged easily, it bought them a little time.

Jo stepped toward him, into the witches' circle of flattened cattails and tromped-on grass. She didn't know what to do with her hands because she wasn't a fighter or a martial artist and in her life had only hit one person—Chuck, one night when she couldn't stand his unkindness—but then Jed's eyes locked with hers and recognition stopped him cold.

"Jo Adams?" His face twisted almost comically. "I don't get it. Why are you doing this?"

"Tam," Jo intoned.

Tamaryn, from behind, kicked him between the legs.

Another twist of his face, this one not so funny. In fact, it was the most tortured expression Jo had ever seen on another human being, a grotesque *rumpling* of the skin on his face as a bolt of agony shook his muscles loose from his bones. In that abrupt yet timeless moment, with Nin and Lucy gasping for breath, with Hannah poised for another swing of the bat and Tamaryn in a psychotic rage, Jo knew that it was over. Jed was beaten. The Crazy Coven had won the battle, and there would be a rib or two cracked, and maybe worse.

She transformed her hand into a fist, thinking not of Penny's mangled lips but of the word antequity, and then something must have gone wrong because Jed's face hardened and he pivoted at the waist and crashed his cocked elbow into Tamaryn's jaw.

She dropped like a stone.

Jo, mystified by this turn of events, blinked once. She recovered almost instantly and aimed what she hoped was a telling blow at the bulge in his throat.

Too late.

Jed dodged, his reflexes uncanny, his riposte too quick. Jo felt a grenade explode in her stomach, and this is what it was like when they talked about the wind getting knocked out of you.

Jo had no air to breathe. She was on her knees without feeling herself fall.

"Jo!" Hannah rested the bat in her lap in order to shove herself deeper into the fray. Jed saw her coming but here also was Nin, a giant in a pink executioner's hood, and Jed turned to meet her, blocking her clumsy swing with one hand and popping her twice in the face with the other. Nin's head snapped back in response to the blows. She lost her balance, teetered, then collapsed.

Jo pulled as hard as she could for a breath, even a small one. A needle-thin bit of air pierced her lungs, but nothing more.

Hannah brought the bat down on Jed's shoulder.

Jed arched his back in obvious pain, reaching behind him like a man trying to remove a knife from between his shoulder blades.

Hannah lifted the bat and shouted again, this time a word that made no sense to Jo. Something about hooves. The metal club shone brightly in the van's headlights. When it moved, its fat tip trailed across the sky like a shooting star.

Jed flowed to the side. The bat hit the ground.

Jed shouted and stomped on the bat, tearing it from Hannah's gloved hands.

A jarring burst of air rushed into Jo's body. Feeling returned to her limbs.

"Why the hell are you doing this?" Jed shrieked, and then he whipped at Hannah's head, not as an attack, but a demasking.

He looked from the hood in his hand to Hannah, squinting, as if he didn't believe what he saw. Hannah's face was wet with tears, her long hair matted to her forehead, her eyes holding not a trace of the rose-colored gleam that Jo so loved. Hannah held up her hands, palms out, as if to plead for clemency. But then she slowly turned her hands and gave him the double-barreled bird.

Jed dropped the hood. "Why you stupid crippled whore—"

Jo marshaled another breath and dove for his legs.

241

She collided with the back of his knees, driving him into the chair. Hannah tried to shove him away as he fell, but he found purchase on the armrest where the fuzzy dice dangled, and the chair tilted, one wheel lifting off the ground. Hannah lunged against the momentum in an effort to keep her balance, but then Jed rolled, Jo on top of him, and the chair went with them.

Ejected from the sanctuary of her seat, Hannah landed on top of Jo and Jed, the two of them locked in a sudden, noisy grapple. Hannah's legs flopped about as she tried to crawl out of the melee. Wallowing on her belly, she attempted to pull herself along by using tufts of weeds as handholds.

Nin got up on her hands and knees, panting.

Jo realized that Jed was trying to break her neck.

He'd managed to get his forearm around her throat. They both lay on their sides in the soggy undergrowth, Jo's back against Jed's chest, like lovers in bed. She felt his heart striking against her spine, his hot breath on her face.

"Tell them to back off," he hissed in her ear.

Jo entrenched what was left of her fingernails into his arm. She felt them sink into his skin. He made a dry rasping sound but held on. He was choking her, but worse than that, he brought his other arm over her head, gripping her in such a way that he could twist her head around farther than it was designed to go, the way little boys did with their sisters' dolls. What had once seemed inevitable a few seconds ago—Jed a huddled, whimpering puddle at their feet—was now turned upside-down. Jo was dying.

"Get them away from me or I'll kill you."

Jo tried to nod in compliance, but her head was clamped in a vise. The strength seeped from her hands until she was unable to apply pressure to his arm. Though she felt blood moistening her fingertips, she knew he wasn't going to release her. But if she acquiesced, if they let him get away swelled with such hate and triumph instead of reduced to pliant obeisance, they were finished. Ruin would tumble upon them from Washington. Jed and his family would bury them in a legal avalanche. Prison. Children taken away and put in foster homes. Lives reduced to rubble.

But still. It was either that or feel her neck bones splinter.

It wasn't much of a choice.

Let the bastard kill her.

"Say it," he told her. But she didn't. *"Say it, Adams, or I'll find that virgin daughter of yours before your dead body is even cold and help myself to that tight ass of hers."*

"Jedediah Whitecross," said a voice.

Click.

Jo peered up through the water in her eyes to see the glint of gunmetal in Lucy's hands.

Lucy held her daddy's revolver in a two-handed stance, her legs shoulder-width apart. The hammer was already pulled back. She sighted down the barrel.

"I'm gonna dust your ass on the count of three," she said.

No one moved.

Jed snorted. "You won't do it."

"You're right," Tam said, putting her hand on the gun until Lucy let go. "But I will." She took the gun in a southpaw grip and pointed it at his head.

Hannah, propped up on her arms, looked back over her shoulder. Nin, still hooded, still on her knees, clasped her hands in prayer.

"So let's count to three," Tam said. There was a vacuity in her eyes that Jo had never seen before. "One."

Jo felt the arm go a little slack around her neck.

"Two. You think I'm kidding?"

Jed let go.

Flushed with relief, Jo sprang to her feet, swallowing as much air as she could, surprised that her legs had the stamina to support her.

"Three." Tam pulled the trigger.

"No, wait!" Jo brought her hand down on the gun just as the hammer snapped forward. It pinched the webbing of flesh between her thumb and index finger against the firing pin, as painfully as if an animal with sharp teeth had bitten her. "God, that hurts!" She tore the pistol from Tam's hands with so much force that the gun flew ten feet to land between Hannah's legs in the mud, taking a little piece of Jo's skin with it.

Tam still stood in her shooter's posture, staring down at Jed.

Jo vigorously shook her hand, trying to fight off the pain. Nin, whispering to herself, crawled toward Hannah. Lucy shielded her eyes against the intensity of the headlights.

"Jesus, Tamaryn." Jo sucked on her hand's sore spot for a moment, then flexed her fingers. "You would have killed him."

Tam stood there in a trance.

"Tamaryn, are you—"

"*Jo, the gun!*" Lucy yelled.

Uttering a savage cry, Jed threw himself toward the gun.

Hannah grabbed it and fired.

The report of the shot silenced the insects. It rang against the tiny fibers in Jo's ears. It carried out across the surface of the inky water like a stone skipping to the far shore.

She noticed the smell first. Having never fired a gun or been in the vicinity of one when someone else worked the trigger, she wasn't prepared for the harsh tang of cordite that abraded the delicate tissue of her nose. It was not unlike the smell of the burning cat when its tail caught fire five days ago in her yard. By that scent, rather than the sound, she knew what had happened. Hannah had lifted the gun, just above the level of her waist, not really very high at all, and reflexively pulled the trigger.

Jed stood up straight. He reached down to adjust his belt, except he wasn't wearing a belt.

Blood spurted from his navel.

The stain appeared on his white shirt and spread quickly. Jo thought it looked like a red cummerbund. Jed smacked his lips together, looking down at himself, his hands fluttering about the wound as if he were afraid to touch it.

Hannah lowered the gun.

Jed's knees buckled. He staggered like a drunk and fell to the ground. Jo had never seen a man's face so colorless. Propping himself up in a sitting position, he used his free hand to touch the spigot his belly button had become. His face was not only talcum-white, but etched with a look of exquisite surprise. "You shot me," he said, mesmerized. "You crazy goddamn bitches shot me."

He laughed sharply, but the sound shriveled into a croak.

"Jo, what do we . . ."

She heard the voice but couldn't place it. Nin? Or Lucy? She was too far away to respond. She could only watch.

Jed attempted to push himself up, but his legs wouldn't comply. He breathed through his mouth, head hung down so that he could examine himself. Whenever he moved his fingers, blood squirted between them. "Crazy goddamn bitches . . ."

"Jo, *do something.*" And now the voice was clear. Nin. Dear lovely Nin.

"Can't do nothing now," Lucy said. She didn't move, but remained a statue cut from black stone, speaking as if her words had issued from a granite-carved throat. "Man's been gut-shot. Can't you see that? Nobody lives for long once he's been shot in the stomach."

"Eat shit and die, nigger bitch!" Jed shouted. "I'm going to be alright, you hear me? All of you! I'm going to be . . . just . . . right as goddamn rain. . . . ." His words petered out and he sucked in a mouthful of air.

Suddenly Hannah dropped the gun like it had bitten her and blurted, "We can save him, Jo, we can save him if we get him to the hospital pronto, okay, I know we can because they do it all the time. So let's please just put him in the van. Jo? *Jo?*"

Jo slowly moved the hair from her eyes and hooked it behind her ear.

Tamaryn stepped up beside her.

". . . crazy bitches . . ."

"Jo!" Hannah shouted. "He's dying!"

"*I am not!*" He looked toward Hannah, his face now streaked with sweat. "I am not," he said again, as if trying to convince her.

"I . . ." Hannah dashed a hand over her eyes. "I don't believe you."

The cummerbund became a loincloth as the blood streamed between his legs.

Watching the man bleed to death, Jo thought about Old Mother Hubbard. Caroline was eight years old and Chuck had just been laid off. There was the mortgage, the dentist bill for Sweet's terrible overbite, Jo working sixty hours a week and still not enough food on the table. She lost twelve pounds for not eating. And then that night when she needed a can of tomato soup for her daughter's dinner and there was nothing in the cupboard but flour and saltines, with payday two days away. She dragged out a footstool to look deeper into the cupboard, looking for *anything,* and she spent that night crying in the bathroom next to the toilet because sometimes all you needed to hold yourself together was one can of tomato soup and even that was too much to ask.

As Nin and Lucy joined hands, Jo searched inside of herself for food to satisfy whatever organ was responsible for compassion. She wanted to nourish it, to unwither it, to make it grow. But just like that night eight years ago, she searched her cupboards and found them bereft. There was nothing to feed that part of her.

Jed coughed up blood.

"Jo," Hannah said weakly. "Tam. Somebody please say something."

"We cannot do this," Nin said. She wept silently, hugging Lucy close to her.

"We're the good guys, Jo, we're the good guys . . ."

"Violence begets violence . . ."

"*Jo* . . ."

Jed stared up at her, his lip quivering. "I'll be all right," he said hoarsely. "You'll see."

He fell over and died.

Nin covered her eyes. Hannah cried so forcefully that her body shook.

After awhile, the insects started buzzing again.

Chapter Nineteen

A breeze awakened in the cat's cradle of stars and yawned sleepily upon the lake, winding through the sedge and plucking at the bulrushes with phantom fingers.

Look, Mom! Caroline laughs, pointing. Corn dogs!

Jo lowers her sunglasses and peers over the top of her book.

Chuck says, She's talking about the cattails. They do kind of look like long, brown corn dogs, don't they? He gives the reel of his fishing pole a few spins and yells, There's mustard in the picnic basket, munchkin!

Can we really EAT them? Caroline wonders, amazed at the prospect.

Only if the egrets will share. Chuck smiles. It is the same smile, albeit years older, that beams from his daughter's face. Again Jo marvels at the magic of heredity. She hopes that whatever traits that she herself has passed to her little girl are worth repeating.

Don't go too far out, Sweet! she calls.

Ah, Joey, let her go. She'll be fine.

I'm sure she will be. But you never can tell what might be floating around out here.

"You can say that again," she said, watching Jed's blood seep into the water.

If any of the other women heard her, they didn't respond.

The sky changed.

Where once was a solid field of blackness, with stars reflecting off the lake's surface to build an illusion of never-ending night, now glimmered a faint and promissory thread of yellow light. It was really nothing more than a pencil line drawn in the darkness, but it alluded to a coming day. Dawn, it vowed, was not far away.

Jo took this as evidence that the planet was continuing to spin. Had the world trundled to a standstill in the last few hours, had the sun commenced smoking like a blown-out candle, she wouldn't have been surprised. Not too much, anyway.

She realized she was waiting for Hannah to stop crying. Eventually she did.

"Tam?"

Tamaryn turned her head just enough to see Jo from the corner of her eye. Jo saw an understanding there, a shared . . . *thing* that now cemented them. The mortar between them wouldn't sunder without tearing both of them apart.

Nin took off her hood and offered it to Hannah, who blew her nose on it.

"I'm with you," Tam said. "All the way. Just tell me what to do."

"We're going to have to be very careful. And fast."

"So?"

"So get rid of the gun."

Tam picked it up from where Hannah had dropped it, and tested its weight. Then she jacked her arm back, paused, and hurled the pistol out over the water as if she were trying to throw out a base-stealer at second. Though the weapon was lost to sight in the gloom, Jo heard it splash.

Tam ran her hand through her curls, bouncing on the balls of her feet. "Now what?"

"Now?" Jo nodded down at the body. "We do the same with him."

His skin wasn't cold.

Of course it wasn't. He'd been dead less than twenty minutes. His body temperature, though dropping, hadn't yet cooled, and neither had his limbs begun to stiffen. But his lips were the color of worms, and that was enough.

She took his wrists. Tam got his feet.

On an unspoken count of three, they lifted him. When they did, his head tipped back, his neck bending to an astounding angle and his mouth falling open.

"Everybody stay back," Jo said. They didn't need to see this.

At least the bleeding had stopped. His body no longer trailed red droplets. That was because his heart had stopped pumping blood through his arteries, right? Or was it the veins that carried the blood and the arteries that returned it to the old pulmonary power plant? Jo could never remember. How did that old song go? *Don't know much about history, don't know much biology. But I do know that you're dead,* she thought. *And I helped make you that way.*

Jed Whitecross got a little revenge by being one heavy bastard.

Though this was the second time she'd helped bear him from one point to another, she swore that the chore was more taxing than it had been before. He may have complicated matters earlier by putting up a fight, but Lucy had been assisting in the effort, while now she stood stone-footed and watched them work. But then again, there wasn't quite as much of him as there used to be. You'd think without all that blood, he'd have lightened up a bit.

That wasn't funny at all.

The ground softened. Jo's hiking boots made sucking sounds every time she lifted her feet. But she was thankful that the smell of mud was so pungent. There were far worse things she could be smelling right now.

And don't forget the footprints, she thought, the next time her boot touched down. *Footprints and splattered blood and who knows how many other clues we're leaving behind.* Movie cops always talked about *signs of a struggle.* How difficult would it be to erase those signs? Impossible. And while she was thinking about it, how many other loose ends had they left untied? The abandoned Jaguar. Skid marks on the highway matching the tire tracks here at the lake. Blood all over the damn place. And no one to vouch for her where-abouts at the time of the . . . the *murder.*

Jo suppressed a shudder.

"What's wrong?" Tam asked.

"Nothing. Keep going."

Nin had been consoling Hannah, but now she stood up. "Stop."

"No can do," Jo said, straining with the load.

"This will not work." Nin stroked Hannah once more on top of the head, then marched over, lifting her robe as dry ground gave way to water. "Jo, you must listen to me."

"So I'm listening." She didn't let go of Jed. "Make it quick."

"I take it that you're planning to put him in the lake."

"That was the general idea, yeah."

"He won't sink."

Jo glanced at Tamaryn, then back at Nin. "You're right. I didn't think about that. I'm open for suggestions."

Nin picked at her robe. "Perhaps a couple of the sheets, filled with rocks . . ."

Tam dropped Jed's legs, and they splattered in the mud. "Good idea." In an instant she'd removed her pink poncho. Her T-shirt was damp with sweat. "Hey, Luce. Look alive and help me find an anchor for this asshole." She jogged back to drier land.

"Nice thinking," Jo said to Nin. Still she didn't release her hold on Jed's pulseless wrists. "But before you say anything else, let's agree right now that we don't have time to discuss what's happening here. Got it? We'll deal with the fallout later on. The sun'll be up in another half an hour, and I want us to be long gone by then. Okay?"

"I understand. But he still will not sink."

"Excuse me?"

"The body, it will not sink. When I was little, my uncle had a sled dog named Bushki, a husky with a coat of silvery blue. A fine, honest animal. But Bushki contracted rabies and had to be put down. The ground was frozen, and much too hard for my uncle to dig a grave. So he took Bushki out in his fishing boat, blessed his spirit, which had been noble and courageous, and put him into the water. I was there. I watched him. But before he sent Bushki to his cold home in the ocean, he took out his belt knife, the one he used to carve scrimshaw, and he punctured the dog's lungs."

Jo stared at her uncomprehendingly.

"This man's lungs are still full of air, Josephine. It is as if he wears a life jacket under his ribs. If you want to ensure that he doesn't rise, you should do as my uncle did."

"Stab him in the chest."

"Yes."

"You've got to be joking."

"I doubt very much that I will ever joke again."

Jo read the truth of that in Nin's brown eyes, along with the evident fear; her children were now at serious risk, the most essential part of her in danger of being torn away. Only Ningeogapik Ryan, woman of the earth, could have stood there and explained the proper way to sink a dead body when the world was breaking apart around her.

Enough contemplation.

"Tam, tell me the good news about those rocks."

"We're trying. There ain't a lot of them around here."

"Hannah, you better get back in the van."

Hannah didn't acknowledge the instruction with any words, just pulled herself blank-faced to her chair, waged a brief war against it, and rolled with dirt-clogged spokes to the ramp.

Jo finally let go, causing lifeless arms to sink an inch into the mud. "So let's deflate this sack of shit. I don't suppose you've got that scrimshaw knife on you."

Nin shook her head.

"Didn't think so. Never one around when a girl needs one."

"Is there something in the van we could use? In the toolbox?"

"Like a screwdriver?"

"I suppose. Do you think that will work?"

Jo looked down at the body. The *corpse*. "I don't know. You're the expert on this. I guess we could give it the old college—wait a minute."

Be nice, they'd written on Chuck's car. After slashing the tires.

She'd left the knife in the glove box.

"Don't move. I'll be right back." Running came more easily now. Perhaps she'd limbered up in the last few days, stretching muscles that had gone unused for years. All the supermarket magazines espoused the benefits of maintaining a healthy exercise regimen for women over forty, although Jo didn't think this was what they had in mind. But it was a hell of a lot more exciting than yoga.

She located the kitchen knife among Hannah's insurance-verification forms and returned full-speed to the body, knowing she shouldn't run with sharp objects but figuring it didn't matter much at this point.

Jo and Tam bound him in the sheets they wore, like two

bags of ballast wrapped around him, secured with endless yards of duct tape. Mummified in strips of pink and gray, anchored with chunks of stone, he lay in the shallow murk and awaited this one final, funerary act.

Jo turned the knife in her hand so that she held it like an icepick, just as she had with the T-bird's tire. She felt the rising sun on her cheek. She was wet from the hips down, covered in lake slime. Tamaryn stood beside her, hands blackened from excavating the rocks, smears of dirt like war paint on her face. Lucy was in a similar state, her hair frizzy with humidity. Nin had declined Jo's suggestion to join Hannah in the van, and now her early morning shadow cast a shroud over the body.

Jo knelt in half a foot of moss-covered water and drove the blade into his chest. It was not so difficult as she anticipated, but rather like stabbing through a watermelon rind. The sound was like that too.

She withdrew the knife.

Sour air wheezed up from a dead lung.

Somebody turned around and threw up. It sounded like Lucy, but Jo wasn't sure.

Concentrating on her work, she sought out the second lung and shoved the knife in.

"Get us out of here, Hannah."

Hannah had no reply. She started the van and drove them away from the lake.

"Now everybody listen up."

Their faces, dirty and silent, were only half-seen in the muggy light of sunrise.

"I'm not going to say all the things you already know. Like be careful. Like keep your mouths shut. And neither am I going to open up some kind of Murderers Anonymous forum talk about what we've done. Hi, my name is Jo and I killed a man and hid his body. Now is not the time for that. So we're all just going to have to deal with our feelings alone. Can we do that? Can we do *alone* for once?" She was glad to see that they didn't lower their eyes when she met their individual gazes. Hannah rocked back and forth a little over the steering wheel, and every so often a fresh tear curled down her cheek, but that was the only indication any of them gave that they weren't hardened felons who'd been taping and sinking men for years.

And as for herself?

Later, she promised. *No soul-searching while leaving a murder scene.*

"Good. Now then. I have one task for each of you. That's four items. Four things we have to take care of to give us a chance of coming out of this intact. Unfortunately, doing them won't necessarily be easy, and if it's easy then it may not be pleasant. But they have to be done. Let's call them our Icky Errands."

She studied their faces again, looking for a sign of uncertainty, a fissure that portended a future, calamitous crack. Lucy sat with her head tipped back against the carpeted wall of the van, her knees drawn to her chest, the whites of her eyes clearly visible in the shadows. Nin sat opposite her, legs extended because she wasn't good at folding them, hands complacent in her lap, as serene as a tribal medicine woman. Tam occupied the wheelchair, flipping the fuzzy dice that were tied to the armrest.

Well, maybe they weren't as gritty as hardened felons, but at least they weren't a blubbering heap of running mascara.

"Okay. So. Here we go. Lucy, you have Icky Errand number one. . . ."

★ ★ ★ ★ ★

Seven a.m.

Clouds began to bar the sky, the sun imprisoned behind them, so that the Mustang cast no shadow as it rolled into the driveway.

Caroline's car wasn't here.

Jo engaged the parking brake, got out, and stood on the oil-stained spot where the Volkswagen should have been. What was today? Wednesday, right? Day after the big vote. Caroline taught swimming lessons on weekdays, but this was a little early for her to be up and about. So where was she?

Jo closed her eyes just long enough to keep her balance. If she allowed herself to sway, she'd think about the state of her conscience, and the signs of a struggle she'd left at the lake, and how she hadn't gotten any sleep last night. She'd stopped at the hospital on her way home. Josh told her that Penelope was stable but still comatose. They'd sewn her up but hadn't been able to rouse her. And the Jaguar was sitting in the trees and there was blood under Jo's nails.

Shower first.

Morning rituals may indicate humdrum and unspontaneous lives, but in times of crisis, the habit of routine often saves us. Jo allowed her body to carry her through the motions, her mind disconnected from the switchboard of her nervous system, so that, without distraction, she dressed and did her hair and burned her tongue on that first sip of coffee. She didn't bother with the *Symposium*. She knew the headlines already. Without a doubt it was the most stirring day of news in recent town history. Here's how the vote went and what both sides had to say about it, here's Rita Dawn Ingersol with her hand in the hornets' nest, here's Samuel Grady, published Iroquois historian and noted thorn under the BIA's saddle.

On second thought, maybe she'd try th... ...fter all. ...ripped out She went outside, picked it up out of the... of it into the the funnies page, and heaved the rem... neighbor's yard.

After the last comic and her ser... ...up of joe, she called Martin. He asked where are yo... ...she said at my kitchen table. Why are you at your k... ...h table and not here? Because, Marty, it's not nine o'... ...ck yet. Who cares what time it is, I've got a situation here... ...th a capital S. What kind of situation? *Indians*, Jo, I'm ...p to my eyebrows in Indians, and I just got a tip from a crony in D.C. that the consortium cavalry is en route to the building site, aka Wounded Knee, the sequel.

"You're right," she said into the phone. "Capital S."

"Jo, for the love of Mother Mary, will you please just get out there?"

Jo hung up.

So the vote had settled nothing.

And still no Caroline, sweet or otherwise.

She scribbled a note, fastened it to the fridge with a Snoopy magnet, and was halfway to the door when she spun around, ripped the calendar with its stupid elephants off the wall, and deposited it without ceremony in the trash.

The natives had multiplied during the night.

When Jo turned onto the newly furbished access road, she found parking to be at a premium. Vehicles were wedged in wherever they could fit, primarily pickups and station wagons festooned with bumper stickers and spotty with fender rust. Tents had sprouted like toadstools in the dark. Some enterprising individual had even imported a phone booth–shaped portable toilet. And like a tailgate party before the big game, barbecue grills were jumbled in front of Pete Musket's stone-

wo...
the sn... house, the scent of pork and biscuits rising on
Jo did... cooking fires.
nition and st... locking the car. She left the keys in the ig-
She wore cream- moment letting the sun caress her neck.
blouse, and mother slacks and a matching jacket, snowy
white gown on the wed... arl earrings. It was like wearing a
wouldn't have felt like suc... ay of your second marriage. She
..ar had she been in a ski mask
and jackboots.

Get them away from me or I'll ki... ou.

It was Jed's voice, as clear as if he were still pressed against her and whispering sour nothings in her ear.

She folded the image up, slid it between her thoughts, and hoped it stayed there until she had time to think.

"Whatever you're selling, Ms. Adams, we don't want any."

"Good morning to you too, Pete."

Musket, Tenfeathers, and half a dozen Amerindians sat in folding lawn chairs between the grills. They'd set up a television, complete with satellite reception provided by a receiving dish mounted on a tripod. Samuel Grady emerged from the Winnebago, which was evidently the mobile command headquarters of this ad lib sit-in. He bore only a passing resemblance to the man she'd met yesterday. His double-breasted pin-striped suit looked straight from the shears of a British tailor. Spread-collar shirt, French cuffs. Only his tie belied his Savile Row purity. More of a talisman than a necktie, it was an odd pair of braids, perhaps woven of horsehair, adorned with carved wooden beads.

Jo immediately looked around for a camera.

Sure enough, a news crew was setting up shop on the edge of Musket's property, just inside the boundary marked by the surveyor's flags. And it wasn't just local Channel 12 this time, but heavy-hitter WJZ, the CBS affiliate out of Baltimore.

And she had thought the town meeting was full of bombs. Apparently that had simply been the opening salvo, making way for the heavy artillery.

She met Grady with a handshake and said with a smile, "You make a mountain out of this pitiful little molehill, I'll find you in the next life and get my revenge."

Grady was taken aback. He tried unsuccessfully to free his hand.

"The media cuts both ways," Jo told him. "Remember that."

Recovering quickly, Grady placed his free hand on top of Jo's. His priestly, red-leather face softened. Keeping his voice low, he said, "Are you my sudden enemy, Mrs. Adams?"

"It's *Ms.*, and that remains to be seen."

He propped a tight smile onto his mouth. "All things in life are circular. My people have come around to this place in time only after long years of silence."

"Your metaphysics don't interest me, Mr. Grady." She added her left hand to the fold, so that now the two of them stood like a couple exchanging nuptial vows. "It's your methods that I have a problem with. When you're orating for the sake of the camera, just remember there's a fine line between rhetoric and truth. If I hear too much of the former, I'll give my own little interview, and all pink-wearing women in a fifty-mile radius will be lending their considerable voices to the effort of getting you thrown out of here." She slipped her hands from his and on impulse added, "I don't live a clapboard life."

She checked her watch as she walked away. Nine thirty-five. Still plenty of hours left in this improbable day, but not enough to allay her sense of urgency. There didn't seem to be enough time to complete all her intended quests; she planned to locate Caroline, deflect a possible border war, conceal murder evidence, and hopefully, if she pushed herself hard enough, have dinner with Warren Dearborn, a man who knew nothing about her save that she liked to work crossword puzzles, took her vitamins, and endeavored to be in bed by ten.

Chapter Twenty

Lucy hated her Icky Errand.

It wasn't messy, just dishonest—which was good, considering she'd had enough of messy to last awhile. But the untruthfulness of it bothered her. Though until recently she'd done little to distinguish herself in this life, she'd always taken pride in being what her daddy called *solid stock*. She didn't lie. She hadn't stolen anything since she was a girl, and that was just five-cent candy and everyone did that. God was like the superintendent of a big apartment building, and Lucy tried to be a tenant who fixed her own pipes and didn't complain when the heating was fouled and said hello when she passed Him in the hall.

But—and this was a damn large *but*—she had provided the gun that had killed a man. Peel away Jed's ugly outsides and you had a dumb kid who bullied girls. Just a kid, nothing more. A spanking was what he needed more than anything. After walking zombie-eyed into her house this morning, Lucy took a bath and broke down right there in the hot water, aching all over for what she'd done.

She was late getting to work.

The men at the P.O. gave her a hard time about her tardiness, but jokingly so, in that sandpapery way men have of chiding each other that they don't understand women detest. And so she told them. "Don't kid me like that, Mike. I know I can dish it out as well as I can take it, but I don't take it as well as I let on. Be easy with me."

Mike had blushed redly. Lucy loaded the last box into her truck and drove away.

And now it was ten o'clock, her mailbag was slung over her shoulder sans pepper spray, and she was afoot. Damn feet. They were responsible for getting her into this fix in the first place. So intent had she been on leaving her tread in the wet cement of life, to dry and stand forever, that now a mother's son was dead.

She walked faster, rattled some letters into the next box, kept moving.

It was a gray morning, cooler than it had been yesterday, with humidity thickening the air. She'd heard someone say they might have rain tomorrow. Lucy had never needed it more than she did now, a silver, cleansing downpour. She rooted herself in her black mood so entirely that she went three blocks without getting on with her Icky Errand.

Then she spotted Charlotte Wilson working the flowers in her yard.

"No solid stock in these shoes of mine," she said under her breath as she made her way across the street. "Just a damn fool human being trying to cover up her tracks, her life in a sure shambles now, uh-huh, and nothing to do but shamble it some more."

"Morning, Lucille!"

"Why, howdy-do to you too, Charlotte. Them hibiscuses look like blue-ribbon winners if I ever saw any. You'll clean regular house at the county fair this year."

"Do you really think?"

"Of course I do! In fact, those blossoms there are so big that sometimes when I walk my route I can smell them from clear down at the intersection."

"You *can't.*"

"Can. Would I lie to you?" Hell. That wasn't the right thing to say. She almost dropped the letters as she handed them over. "Looks like more kindling for your fire today,

262

Charlotte. Nothing but manna from junk mail heaven."

"Oh, Lucille, I read it all anyway, no matter what those folks are trying to sell me. When you get to be my age, you like to think that every envelope was sealed with you particularly in mind. As if this here person at Vibrant Vacuum really knows me and believes their fancy dust-sucker will change my life for the better."

"Is that so? You really read all that?"

"It is and I do, sad to say. Would you like a spot of tea this morning?"

"Love to, but I'm running a bit behind. Say, I was wondering"—and here it came, the prevarication, the magician's patter, the dirty lies—"did you hear about that car they found out on Highway 9 this morning?"

Charlotte instinctively shuffled closer; mail-route gossip was rivaled only by hair-salon hearsay. "Car? Lucille, I'm sorry, but I certainly haven't." The old woman seemed apologetic for her failure to glean this piece of tittle-tattle before breakfast. "What car would that be?"

"You know Senator Whitecross?"

"It was the senator's car? What was it doing out there?"

"No, it belongs to his son. Jedediah. At least that's what I hear."

"Wrecked?"

"I'm not sure. Maybe."

"I didn't hear an ambulance. And I *always* hear them." Charlotte squinted, her thin eyelids lined with blue veins. "What is it that you're not telling me, mail lady?"

That I'm a heel, Lucy thought. She felt like a con artist working the old lady for her life's savings. "It's nothing much . . ."

Charlotte brandished her envelopes. "It's got to be more exciting than reading about vacuum cleaners. So out with it."

"Heard they didn't find anyone in the car."

"All right."

"Heard they think the Whitecross boy may be in trouble."

"Really?"

"Heard there was a pink neckerchief tied to the antenna."

"A what?"

Lucy shrugged. "That's just the grapes, straight from the vine."

"I see."

"Well, you take care of yourself," Lucy said, seized by a suffocating need to get out of there. "Keep them flowers growing tall, and enjoy that mail."

Charlotte called out something in return, but Lucy's ears were ringing too loudly to hear.

Solid stock wouldn't be so cowardly. Solid stock would turn itself in to the authorities and spend the rest of its life grieving for Jed's mother. But Lucy couldn't confess the crime without bringing the others down with her, and the one thing solid stock never, *ever* did was rat on family. And since that day the mine shafts had swallowed her father, all she had was Terrell, until Jo came along and sisterized her.

Every few houses along the remainder of her route, she sowed insidious seeds, and her thumb turned out to be surprisingly green. Plants of deceit grew in the furrows she left behind, sprouting with such flourish as to give Charlotte Wilson's hibiscuses a run for their blue-ribbon money.

—but she was shaken out of her hard, twenty-minute sleep when the phone scared her awake, the irritated voice at the other end asking what they were supposed to do without a dispatcher, because it wasn't like she was a telemarketer with no one's life in jeopardy if she didn't do her job.

"I apologize, Sheriff, I really do, it's just that I spent all night at the hospital and sort of drifted off here at the kitchen table—"

"Get the hell in here, Hannah. Between you and your boyfriend, I don't know which of my underlings is harder on my ulcer."

"Hey!" Hannah stiffened. "What's that supposed to mean? I do my job, Bottle—"

"Don't call me that. It's not my name. Just get here if you still want a job."

"Listen, *Sheriff*, you have no right to—"

She was talking to dead air.

She held the phone away from her face and stared at it, unbelievingly. "You . . . you *pig*." She threw the phone into the living room. It struck the wall, probably broke, but she didn't care. Let it split the foundation and bring the house down around her head. It wouldn't matter now. The backs of her eyes stung from lack of rest and Bottle was under backbreaking stress and not to be blamed for his assholeyness, and Hannah knew she was too unsettled to eat but she tried it anyway, frozen waffles and orange juice, a pedestrian sort of breakfast that normal people ate on normal mornings, but she didn't get very far before her stomach contracted in revulsion.

She worked the wheels frantically, spun around the corner, took the ramp, and barely held it in to the bathroom. She bumped into the toilet, bent over her knees, and belched out a greasy stream.

I killed him.

The vomit burned her throat coming up. She took two breaths, then retched again. Against her will, her insides bunched up, forcing maple syrup and burning bile from her mouth. She coughed repeatedly, hanging on to the rim of the toilet in her fingerless gloves, her hair limp in her sweaty face and a nail file working back and forth in her intestines. She held her mouth open, letting the liquid threads dangle from her teeth until gravity claimed them. This discharge weakened her so much that she could only hang there, half in her chair and half over the john, waiting for the spell to pass.

She wondered what time it was but was afraid to move to check the clock.

"Music," she mumbled through the septic taste in her mouth.

The voice-sensitive system responded to her command and soon Roy Orbison was telling her anything you want, you got it, anything at all. She wished vehemently she could take him up on that offer. But then again, old Roy probably said that to all the girls.

When she thought it was safe, she lifted her head.

The bathroom swam out of focus. She rubbed her eyes, her hands still shaky, and then brushed her teeth and went through two capfuls of mouthwash. She took it easy leaving the house, afraid of tipping the touchy scales of her nerves. If she moved too suddenly, her stomach would slide again, and with nothing left inside of her, she'd probably barf up a rib or two, which she decided wouldn't be good. Let Mr. Crabby Bottle fire her. She still had an Icky Errand to take care of, and getting that over with was worth chancing the unemployment line.

She let the ramp convey her to the van, worked her way forward to the driver's seat, and couldn't remember ever needing Terrell so desperately. It was a physical need, like starvation. Hannah didn't believe in Satan. She'd never seen the sense in such a concept. But she had decided that the true devil was loneliness, because nothing separated people from each other, and people from the divine, so much as the walls constructed by isolation. Terrell was her link. And she couldn't help but feel that, somehow, she was losing him.

She didn't drive straight to work, but to the car wash.

Jo had tasked the others with diverting public attention and establishing an alibi. Just where she'd come across this recent proclivity for such ventures, Hannah didn't know, but her own project involved cleaning up the mess. And that meant the van.

She couldn't stop thinking about the feeling of the trigger under her finger.

After the cleaning was said and done, she spent seven dollars in change scrubbing tires, whisking up possible clothing fibers, wiping down surfaces, hosing off damning lake mud, and adding several layers of disinfectant just to be thorough. It was more strenuous work than it should have been, but she was going without sleep, on a body without nourishment, and rubbing so hard that she could have started a fire had she been using two sticks instead of a sponge and brush.

She bought oatmeal cookies on her way to work and presented them to Big Lane, apologizing that they weren't homemade. When he gave her a hug in thanks, Hannah had to force herself to let go.

Tam stopped on the sidewalk in front of Nin's place, struck her lighter, and inhaled profoundly. She trapped the smoke in her lungs, counted to five, and exhaled twin plumes through her nose.

"Bye, Mom!"

She turned around and waved. "I love you, Brady!"

"Love you too!"

She bit her lip hard enough that her tear ducts got the message. She waved until Brady closed the door. "Be safe, my heroes," she said when he was gone.

She drove across town.

Okay. Matt and Brady were in good hands. So stop thinking about them for a minute. Damn. Talk about a rock and a hard place. Whitecross had gone for the gun, the idiot. Only planned on shooting him in the leg, but that shit had gone south at a high rate of speed, so here we go. Getting it on. Doing whatever it takes.

"It's cool, it's cool, everything's always cool in the end." God, that should have told her something right there. She wasn't prone to talking to herself. That was more Hannah's territory. Girl could flap her jaws, that's for sure. Tam dared a smile. Thinking about Hannah did that to her. Too bad the Wheeled Wonder had gotten involved in this. She was in way over her head.

"I'll watch over you, Jessler. Trust me on this one. I won't let them take you."

Whoever *them* was.

All of Tamaryn's life, there had always been a them. Most recently it was Roy. But there was also the opposing softball team, the IRS, rich people, customers who didn't leave tips, men, and probably now the cops. Nin said that's what was wrong with the world. Too many people using the words *us* and *we.* As in *we* Americans stand together, or don't mess with *us,* we're Yankees fans. When you had an *us,* you always had to have a *them.*

Tam personally didn't give a poodle's penis about debating such philosophies, she only wanted a few less of *them.* Five women versus the law enforcement agencies of West Virginia didn't leave much room for error.

She got out of the truck at Penelope's house.

While lighting one cigarette from the butt of another, she obliquely surveyed the premises. The results of this simple surveillance irked her even further, because there was only a single squad car in the driveway, *one,* when by all rights they should have brought in the state police and a forensics team. Obviously Penny wasn't a priority. She wasn't dead, right? Hadn't even pressed charges. Let's just stand around in a circle jerk until the congressman's psycho son actually kills someone. Maybe if he beats up somebody important next time, we'll send a second car.

Them.

Tam was going to enjoy the hell out of this Icky Errand.

She stormed to the front door. There wasn't even any yellow warning tape, just a note that told her to keep out, by order of so-and-so. Tam tried the door and found it unlocked.

"Ma'am? Excuse me, ma'am, you're not allowed inside."

Halfway across the threshold, she looked over her shoulder. A uniformed deputy was jogging toward her through the wet grass.

"Ma'am, I have to ask you to stay out of there, please."

"Who are you?"

"Jason Reece, Clayton County deputy."

"With the sheriff's department?"

"Yes, ma'am."

"Since when?"

"Ma'am?"

"Jesus Christ, cut the ma'am stuff, I'm not anybody's grandmother."

"Oh, sorry. No problem. Just force of habit." Rosy circles appeared on his smooth cheeks. He took off his hat, revealing a hayrick of blonde hair. "Maybe if you could tell me your name . . ."

"Soza. Tamaryn. Are you new?"

He smiled like a boy asking to carry your books home from school. "First day."

Tam took an intentionally long drag, appraising him. She

kept her eyes on him but blew the smoke to the side. "Cantrell hired you?"

"That's right. Proud to be working for him. He's had a pretty distinguished career."

"Yeah." Something was up. "What about the budget cuts?"

"I . . . don't think I know what you're talking about."

"He didn't let Terrell go, did he?"

"You mean Deputy Campbell? No, not to my knowledge. But like I said, I haven't been around here very long. Haven't even rented a house yet." He smiled enthusiastically, as if imparting this bit of personal lore somehow made them friends.

Tam took a last puff, then flicked the butt through the air. "Let me know when you get moved in. I'll bake you a pie." She went inside the house.

"Wait!" He rushed after her. "You can't do this, ma'am . . . I mean, Miss Soda—"

"I'm not a soft drink, Deputy," she said, moving swiftly toward the bedroom. "Swap your D with a Z, as in zebra. Do you mind getting the light?"

He turned on the light obediently, but continued to protest. "Please, I am under strict orders not to let anyone into the residence . . ."

"Residence? Don't be so stuffy, Deputy. Real people say *house*. And do you know whose house this is?" She noticed an overturned lamp but didn't dawdle over it. "It belongs to my dear friend, Penelope."

"I'm aware of that, ma . . . uh, Ms. Soza, but—"

Tam halted outside the bathroom. Not because she was afraid of seeing the dried blood smeared across the floor. As of three hours ago, there was nothing in this life that would ever scare her again, except the thought of injury befalling her two darlings. But in order to accomplish the mission Jo had given her, she was going to have to be alone, if only for a few minutes, and not trailed by blushing rookie policemen.

With her body facing the bathroom door, she turned her head so that she was looking sideways at Deputy Reece, examining him through eyes half-hidden by curls. No paunch over his belt, just a flat plane all the way up his V-shaped torso, and no hair on the arms visible in his short-sleeved shirt. His shoulders could have used a little beef, but his face was nice. That is, if you liked that Mormon missionary look.

He turned his hat around and around in his hands. "What do you say we talk about this out on the front porch?" he suggested. "I have some coffee in the car." He blanched almost as soon as the words left his mouth and added, "I didn't mean it like that."

"Like what?"

"Uh, like a date or something."

"A date on the front porch?"

He squirmed.

"Hey, it's cool. I know what you meant." She smiled against her will. This goofy guy. "But listen. You know that Penelope's in the hospital. They sent me here to get some of her things. Girls got to have their things, you know. So what I'm going to do, Jason, is go into the bathroom here and put together a care package for her. I'll only be a sec. You can tell the sheriff what happened if you think it's for the best. Wouldn't want you to get the third degree from him on your first day."

"Well . . ."

"And don't sell yourself short, either. From where I stand, I don't see why a girl wouldn't want to drink coffee with you on the porch. Show some confidence, Jace. We like confidence."

He grinned toward the floor, and when he brought his eyes

up, he was nodding. "Don't be long, okay?"

"Cross my broken heart."

True to her word, she wasted no time in the bathroom. From her jeans pocket she extracted a balled-up wad of duct tape. Stuck to the tape were several stands of hair. Jo had used her tire-gouging, lung-poking knife to cut enough hair from the body that the cops would have no trouble finding evidence of Jed's presence in Penny's house—just in case the guy's weasely lawyers tried to say he'd never been here. Jo had surmised that maybe Whitecross had taken precautions to erase himself from the residence, as Deputy Reece referred to it. So Tam was here to provide the state with plenty of proof.

When she was finished administering hairs to the sink, the hairbrush, and the bloodstain on the floor, she threw some random items into a toiletry bag and found the dear deputy pacing in the kitchen.

"Get everything you need?" he asked.

"You bet. Hope I wasn't too much of an inconvenience."

He was quick to shake his head. "Not at all."

"So how about that coffee on the front porch that isn't a date?"

He grinned and nodded, and the coffee was nice.

"Now you play respectfully, Erica. Brady, would you like some more milk? Yes, sweetie, I see, that's a very, *very* nice giraffe, and is that her little baby giraffe? No, you just had your breakfast, and it's not break time till ten-thirty. Dorothy, could you help me with her, please, don't let her put those crayons in her mouth . . ."

"You sure you don't need me?" Ramona asked. "I could stay."

"You've been here all night as it is," Nin said, gathering up plastic cups from around the room. "I appreciate it, but I'm sure you have things to do."

"Nothing that can't be put off until tomorrow. Do you mind if I say that you look exactly like a woman who's spent all night awake at the hospital?"

"So *Cosmopolitan* won't be calling today to request a pose for their magazine cover. Story of my life. Do you mind getting those plates?"

Though Ramona was no longer her sister-in-law, at least technically speaking, they hadn't disowned each other after Dan left, but remained fast friends. She helped Nin transport this latest load of dishes to the kitchen, clucking her disapproval all the way. "If I were your mother, Nin, I'd send you to your room and not let you out until you had at least eight hours of uninterrupted sleep."

Nin forced a laugh because she thought it was an appropriate place for one. "Uninterrupted? That word applies to nothing in my life, watching television, reading a book, and certainly sleep. If I weren't being interrupted, I wouldn't be me. You know, I would probably just fade away. Erica honey, don't tease your sister!"

"Think about the children," Ramona reasoned. "What happens if I leave and you doze off in the middle of the afternoon when they need you? Heaven forbid that one of them has an accident, but say they were outside with a broken arm and you were in here zonked-out. Then how would you feel?"

Nin started to say *terrible*, but that didn't seem to fit. She'd left terrible behind hours ago. Whatever was miles beyond terrible, down in the untrekked forest of dead trees that marked the land of shadows, that's where she was, dragging her spirit behind her as if each minute of her life were cast of iron, forming a chain around her neck. If not for the laughter of the little ones flashing like guide lights in the darkness, she doubted she'd find the will to keep walking.

"I suppose you are right." She stood with the plates in her hands, in front of the open dishwasher, wanting to trade places with Jed. Let him be alive. She'd rest at the bottom of the lake in his stead. Oh, if it wasn't for the children . . .

"I'm not leaving," Ramona said. Without another word, she went back to the living room and plopped down on the floor to join in the latest game of Hungry Hungry Hippo.

For the next fifteen minutes, Nin knelt beside her bed and prayed. She hadn't assumed such a penitent posture since she was young. But now she knitted her thick fingers together and hated herself, though it was likely a sin to do so, and her supplication must have been answered because the balm of sleep washed over her. For the first time in longer than she could remember, Nin napped, miraculously uninterrupted.

She didn't wake up until one in the afternoon, and then she promptly panicked.

She'd forgotten all about her Icky Errand.

She was supposed to call the hospital. Speak with Josh. Set things up. Make things right. It wasn't going to be much of an alibi, depending as it did on Joshua's muddled state of mind and some fudging of the clock, though at least it would have been *something*. But now it was too late, the window of time had slid shut while she slept, and the story that Jo was counting on to save them wouldn't be in place when they needed to fall back on it.

Nin slid off the bed and went to her knees again, but this time instead of praying, she could only put her face in her hands and cry.

Chapter Twenty-one

The red car swung around the corner, cutting her off.

Jo braked in plenty of time, but when her seat belt tightened against her, she realized that she must have been bruised last night when the van slammed to a halt in front of Jed's car. A sore spot on her breastbone flared. It was the least of her worries.

"Mom!" Caroline bounded out of the Beetle. Warren Dearborn sat in the driver's seat.

Jo got out of the car and met her daughter in the street. "Where have you been?" She opened her arms, but Caroline pulled up short. "Sweet, what's wrong?"

"Where have *I* been? What about you? We've been running all over town looking for you. I called the hospital, then Lucy's house, then Nin's. I even had to talk to Roy Soza."

"Ouch. My condolences."

"Is that supposed to be funny? Mom, I was scared to death something had happened to you."

"I know, and I'm sorry. It was totally unlike me to go away without writing a note. But I was commiserating with the Coven. What happened to Penny has been sort of rough on us, to say the least. But you're right. I should have called."

"Yes, that would've been nice, not to mention considerate. I had no idea what to think, you could have been anywhere, with all this craziness going on."

"What craziness would that be, specifically?"

Caroline threw her arms out. "Look around, Mom. In case you haven't noticed, a caravan of cars has been arriving ever since Rita Ingersol made her speech yesterday. Every motel in town is packed with protestors. And they're all wearing pink. Or *super cerise,* as they're calling it. I don't see how you could've missed them."

"No. I saw them." *Not only did I see them, daughter dearest, I CREATED them.* She held out a placating hand. "I'm sorry for not calling. So now you can be the parent and bawl me out. But being a parent, you also have to forgive me. That's one of the rules. Page twelve, paragraph four of the child-rearing handbook. All lectures to be followed with appropriate phrase of forgiveness. So what do you say?"

"I almost called the police, Mom."

"Believe me when I tell you that I'm very glad you didn't." She kept her hand extended.

Shaking her head in perfect parental fashion, Caroline traded her look of exasperation for one of relief. She bypassed the hand and went straight for the hug.

Jo wanted to hang on for as long as she could. *This, at least, is still real.* The older Caroline got, the greater the span between moments of physical contact. Those times came like stepping stones across a river, and Jo had seen too many parents stranded in the rapids because the distance became too great to leap. She'd always resolved to keep those stones close together.

She looked over her daughter's shoulder at Warren Dearborn. He gave her the peace sign.

"So she conscripted you into her maniac mother hunt, I see."

"That was my former line of work," Warren said. "I paid my way through college hunting maniac mothers. It's not something I'm proud of, but you do what you have to do."

Jo permitted herself a smile. Though she sensed her supply of them was diminishing.

"Have you eaten?" Warren asked. "Nothing stokes the appetite like maniac-mother hunting."

"I had a donut earlier. Does that count?" Actually, she'd eaten three donuts, as well as a protein bar she found in Carmen's desk. Her body was blazing away the calories as fast as she consumed them. "I don't have a lot of time. We'll have to make it quick."

"Quick we can do. But I think all fast-food places are probably off-limits. I've spent most of this morning learning the fascinating virtues of nonanimal foods. So I suggested french fries, being veggies and all I assumed they were permitted, but apparently they're cooked in the fat of assassinated cows. And the linoleum in my house, well, I found out that all this time I've been walking around on crushed hooves."

"Alarming, isn't it?"

"Kind of amazing we're not facing a national bovine revolution by now."

"So we'll eat salads. A cucumber revolution sounds a lot less threatening. You two pick the restaurant. I'll follow you."

She drove behind them, the radio off, thinking about burning her shoes.

And other things: pants, blouse, even the underwear she'd had on yesterday, they all faced incineration, along with the three remaining sets of robes and hoods, the ones that hadn't been used as funeral shrouds. Hopefully Lucy and the others were doing the same to clean up after themselves. She hadn't seen any of the women since they parted ways at sunrise, and though less than eight hours had passed since then, she felt amputated. Supposedly you could feel a phantom itch after they cut off an arm. Jo's phantom itch was of the soul, or whatever part of her was stitched to the rest of the Coven. Of course *soul* was too fancy a word for it, too esoteric. The soul didn't get dirt under its fingernails or know the mixed-up feeling of laughing while you cried. If Jo had to invent a term for it—

She stopped inventing terms when the tow truck went by, dragging a white Jaguar.

So it begins.

All day she'd been extrapolating events in her mind, even while she was holding a conversation with Martin or fending off reporters on the phone. From what little she knew of police procedure, the sheriff's department would impound the vehicle and wait around at least a day to see if Jed turned up. After all, he was a charming rogue and notoriously prone to flings; he could have hooked up with a girl last night and was even now somewhere listening to her music, drinking her wine, and secretly hating her cat. This was undoubtedly not the first time he'd left his car unattended so that he might partake of a bacchanalian whim. And with all the other distractions Bottle was having to cope with, it might very well be tomorrow morning before he finally got around to inquiring into the whereabouts of delinquent Master Whitecross.

Next step? If it became clear that Jed hadn't been seen at any of his local haunts, discreet calls would be made. It wouldn't be wise to make any major moves without first seeking the permission of Senator H. Burgess Whitecross. If the senator determined that there was cause for alarm, he would contact those entities he thought most capable of handling the matter, which Jo figured gave her at least until tomorrow evening, perhaps even Friday morning, before an outsider with Washington credentials arrived in town to investigate. By then, the trail would have sufficiently cooled, the *signs of a struggle* obscured by the coming rain, and Jo's odds of Getting Away With It greatly enhanced.

She watched the tow truck until the light turned green.

Of course, she could always turn herself in.

She wasn't sure how she'd live with the knowledge that she'd been party to a murder. Assuming that all went well and her role in Jed's disappearance was never uncovered, she'd live out her days with this secret. Would it grow like a tumor, stealing her sleep, her good health, her sanity?

Could be. For now, though, only the present tense mattered.

She ate lunch and watched the clouds muster, while her dinner companions proved themselves an effective comedy duo, ending their impromptu skit by providing voices for a pair of pickle spears and calling themselves the Dueling Dills. But even Warren's easy smile couldn't scratch the phantom itch, nor Caroline's laugh drive away the fear.

Everything happened at once: Terrell and Sheriff Cantrell rounded the corner in heated debate, the phone rang, newly employed Deputy Reece radioed in to report a fistfight at the Brittany House, the phone rang—line two—the office lights dimmed in a freakish electrical ebb, and Hannah noticed the speckles of mud on her fuzzy dice.

She put her hands to her temples. Paused. Took a breath.

Remember the barrels, she advised herself. *This is no different than rodeo. Don't fret over the clock. Just take the barrels one at a time.*

She wanted to hear what Cantrell was saying, wanted to meet Terrell's gaze because she hadn't been able to see him alone even once today, wanted most of all to scream at the sight of the mud. *The mud.* Instead, she leaned into the mike—"Roger that, car three, stand by"—and answered line one.

"Good afternoon Clayton County Sheriff's Department my name is . . ." She went blank.

Dear God I can't do this.

". . . how may I direct your call?"

It was Robert Mason, he of the rabbit-biting bluetick, calling to complain about all the racket over at the Brittany House Bed & Breakfast; meanwhile Terrell and the sheriff drew up to the counter and Cantrell had this look on his face that made Hannah want to pink him until his flinty little eyeballs floated in paint. But despite her best efforts to divide her attention in half, she still couldn't hear what he was saying. Whatever it was, it didn't look very friendly.

She told Mason she'd send in the SWAT team, then switched to line two.

"Is this Hannah Jessler?" the voice in the phone asked querulously.

"You got it, bud. Who's this?"

"Charles Adams."

Hannah coughed. Chuck was a curve ball she hadn't seen coming.

"You still there?"

"Yes, Mr. Adams. How may I direct your call?"

"Is Bo in his office?"

"One moment, please." She put him on hold and said, "Sheriff, sorry to interrupt, but I've got Charles Adams here, wants to know if you're in. Are you in?"

She didn't think it was possible for Cantrell's face to express any more fatigue, yet the lines in his face deepened as she watched. "I don't get paid enough to handle this three-ring circus crap," he said. "I reckon he wants permission to tear down Musket's wigwam, now that he's won the vote. Ask him if this is an emergency. I'm busy."

"Mr. Adams, the sheriff is in the middle of several important matters right now, as I'm sure you understand. Is there a message you'd like me to give him?"

"Message? Yes, tell him that unlike Gerald Fawles, I'm not letting those criminals get away with assaulting my property. I may be in the middle of a victory celebration here, but that doesn't prevent me from acting on my own behalf if you people are too busy to help me."

"I'll be sure to relate that to him."

"And tell him that I know who destroyed my car."

Hannah barely checked herself before she coughed again. "You do?"

"Yeah. Rita Lesbo Ingersol and her left-wing disciples. Goodbye, Ms. Jessler."

Hannah allowed herself to breathe again. "Yeah, bye." She was glad she hadn't eaten anything, for fear that her stomach would launch another revolt. For a second she'd thought the game was up—there'd been a hidden camera at the Sheridan garage, or someone had seen her van cruising the neighborhood—but thankfully all eyes were now on AGNES. She clawed two more antacid tablets from a rapidly shrinking roll. When she looked up, Terrell was leaning on the counter, watching her. Cantrell was gone.

"Hey, hotshot," she said.

He'd pulled a ballpoint pen from his shirt pocket and was clicking it with his thumb.

"Am I supposed to be reading your mind?" she asked. She wasn't up for any sparring.

"Wish you could."

"Me too. But is it okay if we just try it the old-fashioned way? Like talking about it?"

"Later. I only wanted to say hello. I haven't seen much of you lately."

"I know. What did you do last night?"

"Worked. Went home. Crashed. How's Penelope?"

"Asleep. Maybe forever."

281

"Is that what the doctors said?"

"They didn't say much of anything, except pray. That seems to be all we do around here anymore, pray, I mean. And I for one am tired of making prayer a last resort, but that's probably not what we need to be talking about right now, so what can I fix you for dinner tonight?"

Terrell studied his pen.

Hannah pushed herself as near to the counter as she could, peering up at him, waiting for his radar to lock on to the signal she was sending him, searching his face for an indication that the gulf she sensed between them wasn't as unspannable as it was starting to feel. Why couldn't he intuit the codes, fired from her eyes like arrows? Or did he simply not know how to respond?

"How about fried mushrooms?" she offered, her voice tightening. "I know your fetish for portobello mushrooms. I could pick some up on my way home."

"Can't."

"Sure I can. It's easy. They have this place, it's called a supermarket, see, and they have all this food there, and if I bring in something for trade, like either money or maybe an animal pelt, they'll give me stuff in return, in this case portobellos, and maybe if your stars are in order, I'll also barter for a bottle of wine."

"I've got to work."

"Okay, later then . . ."

"Probably all night."

"Please don't shut me out, Terrell."

"I'm not shutting you out. I'm supposed to meet with a unit from the state police."

Hannah carefully put her hands on her knees. "The state police?"

"Yeah, they're due in town this evening. One officer from

the Latent Print Section and a couple from Trace Evidence. They're going to take a look at the Whitecross car, most likely open up their own file on him, if not take over the case altogether."

"Already? I mean, the guy's only been missing since . . . when? Last night? God, Terrell, he's probably out hungover somewhere, or running for his life for what he did to Penny."

"Possibly so. But if he's running, then he's doing it in only one shoe."

"Huh?"

"I found his shoe in the ditch."

"His shoe . . ."

"We weren't going to call his father until Whitecross had been gone for at least twenty-four hours, but the shoe sort of decided things for us. It's too blatant a clue to put off until tomorrow. The sheriff's on his way right now to Washington to meet personally with the senator and apprise him of the situation, see how he wants to handle it."

For once, Hannah was almost glad she was sitting down. She felt faint. How did that old saw go, the one about the kingdom and the nail? Their lives could be turned into a mud slide because they'd overlooked one patent leather loafer. Jo had dazzled her by constructing a plan on the fly and dictating the specifics of its execution. By now all the other pieces were in place. Lucy had started the grindstone of the rumor mill, Tam had made Jed's presence at Penny's house indisputable, and Nin had erected a tenable alibi. But now Terrell had found a shoe.

"So you found something, big deal." She was glad Terrell wouldn't look at her, because she couldn't have met his eyes. "Like I said, Jed's freaked over what he did to Penny and now he's on the lam, and he dumped the shoe to throw off the dogs."

"In his statement last night he said he didn't do it."

"What do you expect? The man's a stinking, lying puncher. I hope he rots in hell."

Terrell stepped back from the counter, finally lifting his head. "You don't mean that."

"Every last word."

"That's not the Hannah I know."

"Well, pleased to meet you."

"Is this about us? Is that what this is all about? Because if I've done something wrong, then just tell me. Don't play games with me. My life doesn't have room for games right now."

She still couldn't look at him. But there was nowhere for her eyes to roam that she didn't catch sight of the dice. They seemed to be everywhere. Jo had all but promised her that at least thirty-six hours would pass before they had to deal with a major inquiry into Jed's whereabouts. So much for that. Hannah could think of nothing to say that would encapsulate her emotions. "I don't want to lose you, baby."

Terrell was around the counter and crouching beside her in an instant. "Tell me what to do, Hannah. That's all I ask." He touched her leg, but took his hand away quickly, latching on to her arm instead, a part of her that could feel the intensity of his grasp. "I've got this strange feeling these days, like I'm going to turn around and you'll be gone. You know what I'm saying? We've got to get through this, Hannah. Get through it, or give up. All right? You decide. I'll be here waiting for you, whichever way you choose."

"Don't leave this up to me," she said into his shoulder.

"I think that's what you want."

"It's *not* . . ." The words came out in a squeak. She buried her face deeper in the warm hollow of his neck.

Terrell stared through her hair, blinking back the wetness in his eyes.

"It's not," she said again. She hit him feebly in the chest. "It's not what I want. Got it?"

He cleared his throat. "Can I change the subject for a second?"

"No."

"Sheriff says I should take my paperwork to Quantico first thing Monday morning."

Only now did Hannah raise her head. She sniffled. Tears clung to her eyelashes. "He fired you?"

"He made a suggestion."

"Why would he want to get rid of a good cop?"

Something different happened to Terrell's face. In her distress, Hannah couldn't interpret what she saw. Nervousness? Or something deeper? Fear? She put her hand against his cheek. "Baby, what did he say?"

Terrell moved his mouth indecisively, then whispered, "I think he's had about all he can stand of working with the resident nigger."

Hannah felt as if she'd just been slapped. She forgot about Jed. "Did he *say* that?"

"Not in so many words. But Mama Campbell didn't raise a blind son." He tried to say more, then apparently either lost the words or grew too frightened of using them. "Forget it for now. I want to see you before Monday."

Hannah nodded.

"When?"

"Now," she said. "Right now. Let's just leave and—"

He put his fingers over her lips. "I'm busy. I may be high-tailing it out of the county come Monday, but until I'm gone, I'm doing my job. Yes, I agree that Whitecross is nobody's saint, and off the record, there's no doubt in my mind that he's guilty and deserves the deepest pit we can find to throw him in. But if that lost shoe wasn't just his attempt to mislead pursuit while he skipped town, then that means he's in trouble."

"And you're Captain Trouble-Fixer."

She said it hoping to evoke a smile, but Terrell just said, "Something like that." Then he stood up. "So when?"

"Tomorrow. Thursday night."

"Where?"

"My house. Ramp heaven."

"I'll be there by eight." He turned to leave.

"Terrell, wait!" She wheeled toward him. "Kiss me, dammit."

But instead of bending over her and knocking her out with a whole-mouth whopper, as was his custom, he only took her hand, pressed his lips against her knuckles without catching her eyes, and then left her there, alone with her dice.

Jo had never seen anyone in a coma before.

The slack facial muscles. The tubes.

"Dr. Cole make an appearance while I was gone?"

Caroline shook her head.

Jo had spent the last five minutes in the restroom, which was a misnomer. There'd been nothing restful about it. She'd done what she could with her makeup, wondering why she bothered. While washing her hands, she'd become enthralled by the sight of the water spiraling down the basin.

"What time is it?"

Warren extracted a pocket watch, the kind on the chain used by railroad conductors of a bygone age. He flipped open the brassy cover. "I think it's ten after five."

"You think?"

"The glass is cracked. It's hard to tell. So it's either ten after five, or it's tomorrow already." He didn't say this with any hint of mirth, but Jo sensed that he was trying his best to calm her waters. Caroline had phoned him this morning, asking if he knew anything about a certain mother in a yellow car, and he'd been tagging along ever since, in his faded corduroy sport jacket and cowboy boots. He'd even taken the day off from work. "It's okay," he'd assured them during lunch. "I'm on good terms with the owner."

And all this time, Jo had thought he was merely the hired help.

"Where to next, boss?" he asked, shutting his watch.

If only he knew what he was getting into.

"I have to check in with Marty. The mayor isn't letting us relinquish our public-relations duties until after this Pete Musket business has been settled. So I'm still an adjunct city employee, looking after my fellow citizens." She went to Penelope's bedside, smoothed the hairs from the woman's bandaged face. "Not doing so swell with my end of the bargain, though."

"Bargain?"

"I had her in guarded condition," she said, mostly to herself. Penny's skin wasn't as warm as it should have been. "And now look at her."

"Mom? Visiting hours in this part of the hospital ended ten minutes ago."

"I know. We'll go. I don't want to break any rules."

Goddamn crazy bitches.

She almost gasped. Had the door rattled open, broken from its pneumatic hinge, and a water-rotted ghoul ambled across the threshold, trailing streamers of duct tape, she wouldn't have found it strange at all.

Definitely time for some sleep.

She patted Penny lightly on the head. "Sweet dreams, you. Do me a favor and just keep on resting until . . ." The television distracted her.

Mounted on the wall, sound muted, the TV depicted the evening news. The on-site reporter was notable for two things: one, her heavily sprayed hair didn't move a single strand despite the prairie grass that waved in the wind behind her, and two, the Indian standing stoically beside her was a regular fashion plate.

"Could you turn that up, Warren?"

He touched the volume button.

". . . but as you just heard Mr. Grady attest, his supporters will not leave this piece of ground until asked to do so by its rightful owner, and that owner, Mr. Peter Musket, has said he won't sell regardless of the price. Now we're sending you across town, where Lyle Ortiz is standing by. Lyle?"

Jo found herself looking at the façade of the Brittany House Bed & Breakfast.

"Thanks, Ginger. I'm standing in front of what has recently become the second point of contention in the usually sleepy town of Belle Springs, West Virginia. Known for its serene atmosphere and quiet streets, Belle Springs is now a growing hotbed of civil unrest. Yesterday, Rita Dawn Ingersol, author, motivational speaker, and nationally known founder of the civil rights group AGNES, proclaimed Belle Springs the temporary nerve center for her renewed campaign against what she is calling domestic oppression. Though Ingersol denies any connection to recent acts of vandalism against alleged perpetrators of this oppression, she has also made it perfectly clear that, quote, 'AGNES will not denounce any act that weakens the grasp of social subjugation.' Though Ingersol vows to maintain her organization's policy of nonviolence, many Belle Springs locals are expressing concern, due to the dramatic influx of outsiders into their community. We've also learned that at least two nearby counties are sending in police officers to help curtail the possibility of this public demonstration escalating into an all-out riot. This is Lyle Ortiz, reporting live from Belle Springs, West Virginia."

Jo, incredibly, felt like laughing.

Doom had a breaking strain. Heap too many serious matters on the heart at once, keep adding layers of unrest, and sprinkle on enough panic, and soon it would snap. Joy always rushed in to fill up the space. Standing there with one hand on the foot of Penelope's bed, with the machines beeping and her eyes aching for want of sleep, Jo gave way to a tiny need. It wasn't much, just a rather smallish chuckle, but it seemed to get the blood flowing again.

"Mom? We have to go before they kick us out."

"Turn it off, would you, Warren? All this talk of social subjugation is . . ." Her words trailed away as intuition fired up a flare and drew her attention. *That's it.*

"Yoo-hoo! Mother!"

"I'm coming, Sweet. It's just . . ."

"What? Spit it out already."

"I need to make a phone call before supper," Jo said, wondering if this was what you called inspiration and, if so, then what kind of misguided muse was watching over her. "I think I have a mission for Rita Ingersol. We'll see how super her cerise really is."

Chapter Twenty-two

Lucy woke up at half past midnight.

"What day is this?" she asked the darkness, her mouth sticky, her eyes cornered with sand.

The darkness didn't say.

"Could be Thursday. Is this Thursday?" She decided it must have been, because Wednesday she had helped kill a man, and had killed him redundantly in her dreams. He sank only to rise again, each time varying the details of his death with the courtesy of a man afraid of boring his audience. In one episode he bled out quickly, his flesh dissolving instantly in water. Later he held on for hours, conversing with her about the rising cost of postage stamps. *Did you know that the adhesive on stamps in Israel is certified kosher?* he asked her. Several versions later, he died while pointing accusingly at her feet.

"If every night is gonna be like this," she said, "think I'll just stop sleeping altogether."

Not all of her dreams had centered around Jed Whitecross. Terrell had made an appearance, dropping in between shootings to ask her why Daddy wasn't coming home tonight. It had taken them five days to dig his body out of the collapsed shaft, so they'd had a funeral without him. Lucy had looked at all the men in suits standing with their hands clasped in front of them, gazing down at her father's empty box, and she'd hardly recognized them, as it was the first time she'd seen them without their faces caked with coal dust. The next dream in which Terrell materialized, he was grinning like a simpleton, hooking a thumb over his shoulder at the gorgeous white girl in his squad car. She wore a bridal veil, and her eyes were shaped like wheels.

"Little brother. Have to see my little brother. Been too, too long."

She got out of bed and dug around for clean clothes. She'd fallen asleep as soon as she'd finished her mail route. That was nearly eight hours ago. And a lot could happen in that short stretch of time. Was Penelope awake yet? Was Hannah's van hosed out and spit-shined? Had Sheridan's grumpy old executives given the boot to the Shawnee squatters?

"Should have set my alarm. Whole damn town's likely gone to hell, and here I am, as bad as Nero."

She drove to the courthouse, the windows of the mail truck rolled down to let in the rain-scented night air. Clouds blotted out the stars. Every so often, lightning opened up the sky, still miles away but steadily drawing closer. Strange vehicles occupied the courthouse parking lot, two navy blue sedans with government plates, along with what looked like a furniture mover's truck. The truck bore no markings of any kind except for a discreet row of numbers stenciled along the bottom of the door.

"Smells like bad news, even from here." She went inside to find Terrell.

The lights inside were as harsh as ever. Lucy let her eyes adjust, listening. At this hour the building was nearly deserted. Upstairs, the D.A.'s office and the courtroom were empty, as were those chambers housing the county assessor, the health department, and the election board. Only the first floor exhibited any sign of life. Lucy said hello to the night dispatcher, and then she heard it, her brother's oil-smooth laugh, and though she couldn't say what inspired his joy, the sound of it scared away the last filaments of her Jed-heavy dreams.

She found him in the employee lounge, sharing coffee out of stoneware mugs with a woman in a hunter-green business suit and oversized hoop earrings.

"Sis?" Terrell looked surprised to see her. He lowered the front legs of his chair and started to stand. "What's happened?"

"Don't get up on my account," she said, waving him down. "And nothing's *happened,* so just sit back down and relax. Since when did you start thinking of your one and only sister as the bearer of bad tidings, Terrell Othello Campbell?"

His grin floated back to his face. He resumed his seat. "Ever since the day you told me that you flushed my pet frog down the stool because he was giving you warts."

"Thirteen-year-olds have a thing about warts. Sorry. I'm sure the frog survived the trip."

"So you couldn't sleep?"

"Something like that."

"Penelope's going to pull out of this."

"We'll see."

He took a drink of his coffee and patted the chair beside him. Lucy sat down, but not after mentally noting again how handsome he looked in his uniform, how completely *grown up*. The transformation had happened when she wasn't looking. She'd stopped being taller than him the day before his sixteenth birthday. Now he was over six feet, and the muscles moved under his shirtsleeves the way a thoroughbred's rippled beneath its skin.

"Lucy, I'd like you to meet Sergeant Charae Smith of the West Virginia State Police Forensic Laboratory. Charae, this is my guardian angel. And the flusher of my favorite frog."

When the woman's hand came across the table, Lucy reached for it with trepidation. Forensics? What were the state snoops doing here already? In the second it took to extend her hand, she lived through a dozen tiny panic attacks—the chill in her fingers would give her away, the guilt in her eyes would overflow, the lies would contradict themselves, the fear would—

"Hi, I'm Lucy."

"Hello, Lucy. Please ignore all that sergeant stuff and call me Charae."

Lucy broke contact. Was her hand shaking? Her palm sweating?

Charae smiled. "I can see the resemblance."

"Not possible," Lucy said. "Someone left him on my parents' doorstep."

Terrell shook his head. "See that? What did I tell you? This is the kind of abuse I've been putting up with all my life."

Charae said something about siblings, how lonely she'd been growing up as an only child, and Lucy decided that this woman passed the paper-bag test, flat-out. Back in the day when skin color and caste were inseparable, colored folk stood a lot better chance of being accepted if their flesh was lighter than a paper bag. Charae's complexion was the soft and radiant tone of caramel. By contrast, Terrell's was the color of the stuff his daddy used to haul out of the earth.

". . . at least that way, you always have someone to dry your tears when you're young."

"Or *cause* them," Terrell said. "Not a day went by that I didn't get pinched, poked . . ."

"You're cruising for a pinch and a poke right now," Lucy warned him.

". . . scratched, bitten . . ."

Charae laughed. "Oh, Terrell, it couldn't have been that bad." Her smile lit up her face.

Lucy growled inwardly. She couldn't sit here any longer, as she was afflicted with an unexplained dislike for this cosmopolitan lady from cities tall and bright. She stood up. "Well, it's late, and I should be getting back home. I was just out to the convenience store for some microwave popcorn to go along with the late show. Thought I'd drop in and say hi to my poor, put-upon brother, maybe pinch or bite him a few times for old times' sake."

Charae said it was nice meeting you, and Lucy must have returned with something halfway funny, because everyone laughed, though she was only partially aware of the words coming out of her mouth. Idle talk no longer made sense to her. Chitchat was meaningless static on the edge of her mind.

Terrell walked her to her truck. "One of these days, you going to tell me what's eating you?"

"One of these days."

"How about now?"

"I don't think so. Charae, though . . . she seems likeable enough."

"Sure. Does this mood of yours have something to do with Penelope?"

"No. No, I thought it did at first. But honestly, I don't think so anymore. How long have you known her? And I don't mean Penelope."

"Charae? She got in town around six."

"Mmmm. Six hours, huh? You two get along like old war buddies."

"Whatever it is you're steering at, Sis, don't go there. I hardly know the woman."

"Thick as thieves, as they say."

"You going to ride me about this? Because I've had a rougher day than usual, and I don't need this kind of talk right now. I've got Whitecross on one half of my brain and . . . other things. And for your information, Sheriff Cantrell is suggesting that I move on to greener pastures."

Lucy wasn't surprised by this at all. "I figured he would, sooner or later. Always knew the man was a bigot. It was just some of the things he said, the little remarks, the locker-room humor. She likes you, you know."

"Who? Charae? Sis, we just *met*. Will you just give it a rest?"

Lucy slid open the truck door and settled herself onto the squeaky seat. "Do me a favor."

Terrell put his hands on his leather tactical belt and spread his feet, as if bracing himself.

"Keep me in the loop on the Whitecross case."

"Why?"

"Because I'm Penny's friend." She held out her hand, index finger extended.

After a little consideration, Terrell linked his finger with hers. "We make a promise, we make it true."

"You for me and me for you." Lucy felt her eyes misting up, so she rapidly started the engine and put it into gear.

"Sweet dreams," Terrell said.

"Yeah." She drove away.

Nin got the shakes for the first time at seven that morning. Ever since waking up after her nap yesterday and realizing that she'd failed them, she'd been teetering on the cusp of a breakdown. What did she have in this life but her wee ones and her friends? Jo had depended on her, and she'd overslept. *Overslept*. Now when the police came to question them, as Nin was increasingly certain they would, then their alibi would not be in place.

She leaned against the doorjamb between the hallway and

a bedroom full of sleeping children, the excess flesh of her arms and thighs jiggling as if a current were passing through her.

And she was supposed to be the strong one.

Our bedrock, Lucy had once told her.

And now *our bedrock* was shattering.

She went to the kitchen and swallowed still more aspirin. Water splashed out of the glass as she tried to bring it to her mouth. It wasn't Jed's ghost that haunted her. Nope. She'd thought about that and concluded that he wasn't the source of her anxiety. He was no better than a sled dog with rabies. When you grew up in a land of ice, where your exhaled breath froze to your face and survival depended on the fish you caught and the wood in your furnace, you developed a working relationship with death. Good people got killed and you blessed their spirits and cried. Bad people got killed and that was that. So it wasn't the thought of murder, but another sort of guilt that crippled her.

She sank down into a chair at her kitchen table, a table spotted with paint from craft projects, scarred from forks and butter knives, a dear old table that usually warmed her heart when she considered all the memories it held. But now it was just a slab of wood with dented metal legs.

How soon would they come, those policemen? How long before she had to face them? And what, oh what would happen to her babies when their mother was taken away?

In a half an hour, the sprites were awake. Nin was settling Marky into his high chair and busying herself with breakfast and dark thoughts when the light above the sink started blinking.

Someone was at the door.

Kids whooped and chattered around her. Cartoons romped loudly from the TV. Nin shook again, briefly but violently. *Our bedrock. Our bedrock that couldn't even stay awake long enough to call Josh and solidify our story.*

She unlocked the front door, expecting badges.

Instead she saw pink.

Two women stood in the doorway. One wore a neon-pink T-shirt that read PRACTICE CONSCIOUS SOLIDARITY. The other was Jo.

"Excuse me, madam," Jo said, "but my name is Josephine Adams. I work for Amway and I was wondering if I could come in and demonstrate some of our latest cleaning products for your home." Jo's hand rested on the handle of a vacuum cleaner.

And behind her stood half a dozen women, all adorned in some type of pinkage. They bore sponges and buckets and brooms.

"I don't get it," Nin said.

"There's nothing *to get*," Jo informed her. "We're coming in whether you like it or not. Here, consider this a search warrant." She shoved an envelope at Nin, then pushed her way inside. "Good morning, gang! Am I in time for oatmeal?"

Nin had no choice but to step aside as the women followed Jo through the door. They all greeted her as they came in, and without exception they were delightful with the children. Dazed by this sudden incursion, Nin fumbled the letter to her face. She read it slowly, as was her way, her lips moving as she absorbed each word. When she finally looked up, she saw the elves in full swing, attacking her house without preamble, a flurry of dustpans and cleaning rags. The munchkins loved it, and were soon hopping to and fro on small tasks designed just for them. Windows with layers of handprints, corners with cobwebs, bathroom tiles lined with grime—nothing was safe from the pink fairy creatures and their little pixie helpers.

"The painters will be here at noon," Jo said, toilet brush in hand.

"Painters?"

"You'll be dumbfounded by what a fresh coat of paint will do for this place."

"I am that way already." There were so many things she wanted to ask. But then again, she probably already knew the answers. How much was this costing? Jo would say don't worry about it. How did you find out about this letter from the Department of Health? I have my ways. Who are all these people? Women with nothing better to do, like me. Where did I ever get such a true friend?

To that one, she had no answer.

She folded herself into their beehive activity, counting her blessings.

Yet her guilt only grew. Here was Jo, above and beyond the call, and Nin had done nothing to deserve it. When the favor was in need of doing, the bedrock had been snoring. She needed to confess her delinquency, yet she didn't know how best to broach the subject, especially when Jo was up to her elbows in Nin's toilet.

Countertops shined. Windows squeaked. Mulberry air freshener filled the house.

Then the light blinked again. Another visitor had arrived.

Jo stepped into the pristine bathroom and shut the door behind her.

Nin worried a towel between her hands. Lucy finished her business on the stool, flushed, and said as she was zipping up her pants, "We're in trouble."

Jo took it in stride. "Keep your voice down."

"What kind of trouble?" Nin whispered.

"State cops showed up in town last night," Lucy said,

tucking in her shirt. "A whole team of them. Got in around six, started going at Jed's car like those painters outside are going at the siding."

"Why so soon?" Jo asked.

"Because we forgot to pick up a damn shoe."

"A *what?*"

Jo listened as Lucy explained the shoe discovery and related her conversation this morning with Hannah concerning Bottle's trip to the senator's house. They'd been messy in their abduction. They'd left behind a shoe. Those were the kinds of mistakes you made when push came to shove and you were only an amateur shover. Jo tested each new piece of information as Lucy delivered it, trying to determine the likelihood that it would be the piece that unraveled her life. The state police were already in town. So things were going downhill at a much greater rate of speed than she'd predicted.

"And here's something else you didn't know," Lucy said. "Oleoresin capsicum."

"I assume you're going to tell us what that means."

"Until an hour ago I didn't know either. But oleoresin capsicum is the primary active ingredient in pepper spray."

"So what? We tossed the can in the lake."

"Uh-huh. I know that. But about midnight last night I met this woman, a real beauty and kind of sweet on Terrell, I might add, and she happens to work in the Trace Evidence Section of the WVSP Forensic Laboratory."

"For God's sake, Lucy, just get to the point. There is a point, isn't there?"

"Two points, actually. One, they found a partial print on the Jaguar's door handle. I imagine it's yours. This print matches the one they got off Chuck's car at the Sheridan garage."

Jo leaned back against the door.

"Two, the chemical-analysis report arrived at Cantrell's office a short time ago, and behold, inside the Jaguar we have residue of oleoresin capsicum. Known in certain pink circles as asshole anesthesia. Or pepper spray. Which leads any logical person to believe that Jed was taken against his will. Shall I go on?"

"No."

"Furthermore," Lucy continued, her voice low but unyielding, "what was first a matter for county officials and the state cops is now a kidnapping. And for those of you who don't watch a lot of television, let me be the first to tell you that kidnapping falls under the jurisdiction of the federal government. In other words—"

"The FBI," Jo said.

"Winner. Give the girl a kewpie doll."

Jo tilted her head back, stared at the ceiling, and remembered the day she thought her daughter was dying.

It's only pneumonia, Joey. People live through that all the time these days.

But she's so small . . .

Sure, and so is a stick of dynamite.

The doctor said—

Phooey on the doctor. What does that old sawbones know, anyway? Look at me.

Jo looks up. Chuck stands only inches away. His chin is rough with beard growth.

What do you see? he asks.

Other than a face in need of a shave?

My face, your legs, who cares. So what do you see?

Faith.

Good answer. I may not be rich, but I've so much of that stuff saved up—

That you're living off the interest, Jo says.

That's right. So anytime you need to make a withdrawal from my account . . .

"So what do we do now?" Nin asked.

"Have faith," Jo said.

Lucy washed her hands. "Wish it were as easy at that."

"Nothing is easier."

"Listen to you. Is that Jo Adams I hear talking? Since when were you such a believer? I've known you since junior high, when your face was so covered with acne that you ran away from home for two days so as not to have to go to school. And who ran away with you?" Lucy accepted the towel from Nin and dried her hands. "And now here you are, turned into a believer when I wasn't looking."

"People change."

"I won't argue that."

"Chuck used to be a different man."

"I know. I was there."

"So maybe he went one way, and I went the other."

"Like ships in the night."

"Something like that." Jo opened the door a crack and checked the hallway. Satisfied that they were still alone, she shut the door again and said, "There's nothing to connect us to what the police found in the car, and as far as I know, no one saw us out that night. Hannah would have heard about anything like that."

"They'll find out," Lucy said. It sounded like a prophecy.

"A little optimism would be helpful here, Luce."

"What do we do if they start asking around?"

"Stick to the story. Look, there are over a hundred women, ages eighteen to eighty, filling up motel rooms and camped out in the city park. A lot of them are rather radical left-wingers, to say the least. I'm sure a few have rap sheets. Do you know what I saw on the way over here this morning? A

301

woman in pink camouflage. She was wearing combat boots, a black halter top, and pants done in a pink camo pattern. Now, I may be wrong, but I think the FBI will have plenty of names to check out before they ever think of getting around to ours. And thanks to the aforementioned ex-husband of mine, everyone in town is getting an earful of how AGNES is sponsoring some kind of secret terrorist operation, thanks to rumors that you started yourself on your mail route. Chuck heard those rumors and believed them, and now everyone else does too." She paused when she noticed the look on Nin's face. "What is it? Did I say something you don't agree with?"

Suddenly Nin was visibly shaking. "No, it's not that . . ."

"Nin?" Alarmed by the rare strain in her friend's voice, Jo went to her, Lucy jumped to her other side, and the two of them supported her just as her legs began to buckle.

"I didn't do it . . . didn't do it . . . slept too long . . ."

"Nin, you're not making any sense."

"I didn't phone Joshua. You told me that my Icky Errand was to get ahold of him and say certain things, so that he'd say we were at the hospital at the time of the . . . the . . ."

"Yes, so what happened?"

"I never called him." The fragility of her voice belied her size. Jo had never seen her like this. Her shoulders, ever ready to be leaned on by crying friends, trembled like rafters in a burning house. "Now when they come to ask us where we were that night, *we won't have anything to say.*"

"Shhh, now none of that." Jo gave her a squeeze. "It's not the end of the world."

"It's not the world I am worried about."

Lucy offered her some toilet paper. "Here, take care of those tears. What will your rugrats think if they see their mama crying?"

"It would have been a weak alibi at best," Jo allowed,

wishing she were as unfazed as she sounded. "It depended on ambiguity and Joshua's disoriented state of mind. But it was the only thing I could come up with on such short notice. Next time I'll be craftier in my duplicity."

Nin dabbed her eyes. "It was a good, fine plan. And I ruined it."

"All you're ruining is your eyeliner. The next step in getting through all of this is pulling yourself together. Consider that your new Icky Errand, pretending like you're nothing but sunshine and sugar. Can you do that?"

"I . . . guess so. I hope so."

"Not to add more fuel to the fire under our feet," Lucy said, combing her fingers through Nin's hair, "but I haven't told you about the dozen federal agents that are currently on their way."

"Only a dozen?" Jo asked. *Was that wry?* she wondered. She'd never really understood that word. Characters in books were always doing something wryly. She'd have to work on that if she were going to be a superheroine. "When can we expect them?"

"Likely they're already here. They'll set up a command center, my guess would be at the courthouse. And from there . . . I don't know. Cast the dragnet. Scour the countryside. Put the thumbscrews on anyone who looks at them sideways. Typical FBI kind of stuff."

A dozen agents. A massive manhunt. So the ante was upped again. Jo felt the tension ratchet a notch higher in her heart, but her mantle of calm remained, like gentle snowfall over rocky ground. "Well, that should make things interesting. Here I've lived all this time unnoticed, and suddenly I'm America's most wanted."

"You seem to be taking all of this a little unseriously," Lucy observed.

"No. That's just momentum in disguise. I call it antequity. But, if you'd rather have me freak out about something, then I could probably be convinced to get hysterical over all the details we've overlooked. If we left a shoe behind, I can't imagine what other little messes we forgot to clean up."

"There's one more *and*," Lucy said.

Nin hung her head. "Please, no more."

"*And* the senator is holding a press conference around five o'clock this evening. Cantrell expects he'll announce his son's disappearance and give the media the lowdown on what's being done to locate him. In other words, the sideshow this town has already become will soon be escalated to a national circus."

Upon hearing this final announcement, Jo gave herself a few moments to reflect. A press conference? So much for her big predictions about how long they had before the vultures began to circle.

She conducted a mental review of the converging disasters. Samuel Grady was receiving the vocal support of Native American groups from as far away as South Dakota. His congregation at Musket's place numbered close to thirty, with new members trickling in by the hour. He was surrounded on all sides by concerned Belle Springs citizens who might at any moment transform into a Sheridan-incited mob. As a victory display, Chuck had already called in his architect and building contractors, who were laying down the first surveys and driving posts into the ground, each one an undisguised metaphor for a nail in Grady's coffin.

Simultaneously, AGNES was attracting an army of students, misfits, hard-liners, artists, militia wives, free-speech advocates, and the occasional biker chick. They were coming out of the women's-rights woodwork. Yet more frequently they were coming from the mainstream; this morning they'd been joined by a former congresswoman from Pennsylvania, and just before Jo had arrived to recruit them for her cleaning festival here at Nin's, Rita Ingersol had announced the receipt of an unspecified monetary gift, the accompanying letter of support signed by no less than eight prominent Hollywood actresses. Pink pennants flew from car antennas. Mothers clad in super cerise gathered on street corners, chanted slogans from sidewalks, and bought up every scrap of posterboard in town, their placards turning Belle Springs into a forest of signs.

And if these various flammable elements set the city ablaze, then the press conference was certain to provide the wind to fan the fire. Senator Whitecross was so deeply entrenched in Washington, with so many ties to so many gargantuan entities, that he was one of those rare, insurmountable few who lived beyond the law. He'd been instrumental in the president's ascendancy to the Oval Office. Rumor had it that he was next in line to head the CIA. If there was a needle out there that he wanted, no matter how small, there wasn't a haystack that could hide it.

No matter how small.

Jo had never felt smaller. Yet at the same time, she'd never felt bigger. She stood in the center of the brewing hostilities between Sheridan and the Indians, as each side mobilized troops and prepared for battle. By necessity she'd entangled herself in Ingersol's holy crusade, which was further transforming the town into a militarized zone. And by killing a man in her resolution that enough was enough, she'd put herself in direct contention with the Federal Bureau of Investigation, H. Burgess Whitecross, and all the hydra-headed resources he had at his disposal. For someone who'd spent her life not choosing sides, she was making up for lost time exponentially.

Lucy and Nin were looking at her, obviously waiting.

"I suppose you two want me to say something like, the FBI doesn't know what it's up against. Or, the senator is going to find himself in for a fight."

"It would be reassuring," Lucy admitted, "even if it isn't true."

"Well, I can't say that. But don't place your bets quite yet. The wheel is still spinning."

"Watch it, Josephine. You may just make a believer out of me, too."

"Now *that* would be a miracle. In the meantime, though"—she straightened herself up and put her hand on the doorknob—"I'm going to go end a potential war by steamrolling some innocent natives and prying a small fortune out of my ex-husband, and if I make it through that with all my body parts still intact, then I'll see what I can do about getting us in the clear. You two will be all right until then?"

They nodded in unison.

"Good. Now let's go pretend we're invincible for awhile."

Chapter Twenty-three

Standing on the curb in front of Sally Fong's café, under clouds the same color as the oily apron in her fist, Tam made her decision to run away. She stood very still, cigarette hanging listlessly from her lip, wondering how far she could get on 600 dollars and change. The checking account she shared with Roy could be emptied as long as she got to the bank before three. And she had her tip money that was earmarked for Matthew's dentist bill.

"Screw the dentist." She dismissed him as easily as she dropped the butt to the street and flattened it with the toe of her cross-trainer; name-brand running shoes were the only dumb purchase she permitted herself. After tonight the dentist bill wouldn't matter. She would have shot Whitecross and maybe killed him had not Jo taken the gun from her, so Roy and the dentist and everyone else could consider her a missing person as of tomorrow morning. "Mother skips town with children," she said, imitating the headline. "Father too drunk to notice for three days."

She used the drive-through teller and cleaned out the account, except for thirteen cents, because she thought Roy would be especially rankled by that teeny amount. Thirteen cents sent a message, roughly translated as *kiss my ass*.

Then she went to Nin's for the boys. The chaos of painters and groundskeepers confused her, but Nin filled her in with the details of Jo's heroics. Tam hugged her fiercely before leaving. "You are so much my friend, Ningeogapik."

"We're going to get through this," Nin said in her ear.

"You bet we are. Come on, sir knights, into the truck."

She waved before leaving. She thought that waves were

funny things. So many times a wave is a throwaway gesture, like saying see ya later. But every so often your hand is so heavy that you know it's not a wave, but a signal that something good is over, that circumstance has intervened. The knowledge that she'd likely never see Nin again hurt more than she wanted to admit. If not for an offhand remark Nin had made a few months back, Tam wouldn't have had any notion where to flee. She'd never been farther west than Kentucky, and that had been the year Roy spent nearly a thousand dollars on their vacation to the Derby, because he said it was one of those things he'd wanted to do since he was a kid. He never bothered to ask if there was something Tam had wanted to do since she was a kid. But that was now very much beside the point. The *point* was a small fishing town on the coast of Prince William Sound in the Gulf of Alaska. Nin said the town consisted of little more than a post office, a grocery store owned by an old Russian and his wife, and a restaurant with rooms to rent upstairs. Tam hoped they were in need of an extra waitress.

"Have apron, will travel."

She started packing when she got home.

Not obviously, of course. She didn't want Roy to walk through the door and ask what the hell was up with all the suitcases. She was stealthy in her preparations, a spy in enemy territory, loading clothes baskets with what looked like dirty laundry but was actually the essentials of her flea-market wardrobe. If Roy looked closely enough, he'd see Brady's winter coat at the bottom of one of the baskets, along with long underwear and several favorite, lovingly abused action figures. But she was counting on Roy being his usual unobservant, uncaring, unhusbandly self.

In a blue flannel shirt she wrapped the only valuable thing she owned—a small statuette of an inkwell made of 14-karat gold. Her mother had won it as a prize in a national writing contest, three months before she died. She used to tell Tamaryn she was going to write their way off food stamps. Until now, Tam had resisted every urge to pawn the bauble, even when times got lean. Now she knew what she'd been waiting for.

The inkwell would fetch at least a thousand bucks, and that would get her and the boys to the high country, so long as the truck didn't break down along the way, which was a distinct possibility.

Damned fingerprints.

Hannah had called and told her about the prints the pigs had found. They could only be Jo's, because Tam had added a new Good Rule to the list: always wear gloves when pulling peckerwoods out of foreign sports cars.

She'd already given up trying to find remorse for her part in the murder. Maybe Nin was right and violence never solved anything, but there were PTA meetings and then there was action. You went to work and rotated your tires and talked to friends on the phone, but if you even once stopped living just to make the car payment, your life changed. Not always for the best, but at least it spiked your heart monitor and you were no longer living flatline.

"Mom, we're out of milk!"

"Go squeeze some out of the cow!" Tam hollered back.

"We don't have a cow!"

"That's because it jumped over the moon!" She sorted necessary clothes from ones the three of them could live without. What did people wear in Alaska? Earmuffs and animal furs?

"Mom, we never had a cow. You're just being silly."

"No, Brady, I'm being udderly ridiculous."

"What?"

She found Matthew's pajamas, smelled him in the worn fabric, and found there a remarkable peace. She pounced up and ran into the kitchen. "Where *is* that darned cow, anyway? I know I put it here somewhere."

She fixed Pop Tarts, cut them into little squares, smeared them with butter, and sat down on the living-room floor with her sons to eat them. They licked one another's fingers. It was sometime during this indoor picnic that her eyes settled on the guns.

Roy kept his hunting rifles in a glass-faced cabinet of hickory with brass hinges, the image of a bird dog and pheasant tooled into the wood. The case held a matching pair of 12-gauge shotguns, a lever-action .22 Marlin, and the revered Psalm 23, the bane of coyotes the county over. In the early years of their marriage, Tam had hunted with her husband. He'd prided himself in the fact that his was the only wife attached to his circle of quail killers who knew the proper application of Hoppes No. 9 gun oil. But that was long ago, a bond too superficial to withstand the wear and tear of the years. Tam hadn't fired a gun since then.

Though yesterday she almost had. But Hannah had saved her the trouble.

Oh, Jessler, why did you have to end up with the gun instead of me?

"Okay, squirts. Mom's got things to do." She tousled Brady's hair and headed to the kitchen to fill a paper bag with canned goods, hoping Hannah could find the strength to deal with what was coming.

"Hey, Mom," Matt said.

"Yeah, hon?"

"Are you cool?"

Tam was struck by the question. She considered it intently, one eyebrow raised, lower lip pinched between her fingers. "You know what? I think that maybe I am."

"Thought so."

"Anything else?"

He shook his head thoughtfully, then shrugged. "Nope." He went back to his afternoon cartoons.

Tam smiled. They would be okay, whether they ate their Pop Tarts in West Virginia or Alaska or from the backs of two-hump camels in Timbuktu.

She filled a sack with nonperishables, and later checked to make sure the key to the gun cabinet was still in the little basket on top of the refrigerator.

It was.

Satisfied that Nin was in capable hands, Jo returned to the front lines, resolved to hammer out a final armistice between the feuding factions and promptly thereafter hand Martin her resignation.

Something that smelled distinctly man-like occupied the seat beside her.

"So no two weeks' notice then?" Warren asked.

"Two weeks is a lifetime these days. You forgot your umbrella, didn't you?"

The first silver nickels of rain struck the windshield.

"I can't help but feel I'm missing part of the story," he said. "I don't know you at all, other than that you make terrific children and you renovate people's houses out of the kindness of your heart. But I wouldn't have guessed you'd be so . . ."

"Brilliant?"

"Well . . ."

"Sexy?"

"That too . . ."

"Really, Warren, if you were going to say *impulsive* then I must disagree. Impulses are things you follow without having a reason. You do them randomly, without any backstory behind them."

"Backstory?"

"Sure. Like this car. If you think I bought it capriciously, then you're overlooking all the events that led up to its purchase, all the backstory. I adore it, by the way." She honked the horn. "Send the salesman my regards."

"Send them yourself. Over dinner tonight."

"Dinner with an actual man two evenings in a row? Now *that's* impulsive. But while we're on the subject of car buying, don't you ever work anymore?"

"I try. But I was at the lot for six hours today and saw only two customers. The people of this little hamlet of ours all of a sudden have better things to do than buy subcompacts." He leaned forward and looked up at the dismal sky. "Though helicopters are apparently gaining popularity."

A chopper droned overhead, the second they'd seen in the last five minutes. It flew low enough that Jo could tell that this one was no television crew. The helicopter was black, with deeply tinted windows, and shaped vaguely like a killer whale.

Cast the dragnet. Scour the countryside.

Jo spent the remainder of the trip talking about what they might have for dinner, but thinking about being a fugitive from the FBI.

Things were happening with such falling-domino velocity that she had to act without much forethought, leap without any looking. At least the weather was on her side. The rain would eradicate any tread marks and footprints they'd left at the lake, and *hasta la bye-bye* to the signs of a struggle. Her plan now was a precarious one. Bring an end to the Sheridan-Musket affair while concurrently escalating the AGNES crisis.

How?

First, she would abdicate her role as neutral go-between and instead ram home the land sale so that construction could begin and its fruits enjoyed by all. *Step away from the birthing house, Mr. Grady, and nobody gets hurt.* Secondly, she'd fan Rita Ingersol's flame so that it turned into a media bonfire bright enough to convince the American viewing public that the pink-waving warriors were assuredly involved in the disappearance of the clean-shaven law student from Georgetown.

A week ago, had anyone asked of her such herculean tasks, she would have paid them a disinterested glance and gone back to her crossword puzzle.

"Looks like a raincoat convention," Warren remarked.

By now the Indian protesters had swelled to nearly a hundred, far too many to confine themselves to Musket's thin sliver of property. At least half of them in overcoats and hoods were camped out between the cars, which were parked helter-skelter along the highway. The Sheridan supporters enjoyed far more space to pitch their tents, and pitch them they had, from two-man pup tents to the huge canvas pavilion Chuck had rented just for the occasion. Inside they dispersed free coffee around the clock. Though the drizzle had halted the contractor's survey work, a gang of teenage boys was making good use of the flags in a game of tackle football. Their jeans were black with water, their enjoyment only heightened by the soupy conditions of the field. They paused in their game long enough to watch a blue-and-white CNN helicopter sink to the ground about fifty yards away, the down blast of its rotors flattening the long grass.

"This is getting a little out of hand," Warren said.

"Give me twenty minutes," Jo replied, "and I'll have either settled it or made it worse. And thanks for the hat." She'd brought along a windbreaker, but it was hoodless, so they'd stopped by Warren's place to pick up some headgear.

Jo had scanned his small collection of ball caps, most of them souvenirs from concerts of his past.

"Here," he'd said, handing her one. "A reminder of the youth I wish I would have misspent." In red embroidery across the cap were the words TAKE IT EASY. "What's the matter? You're not an Eagles fan?"

"No, it's not that. But I think 'Witchy Woman' would be more appropriate."

She stepped from the car and snugged the hat on her head. Rain began to drip from the bill.

She resisted the mad urge to run. Senator Whitecross was slated to go live at four-forty-five, which gave her just under an hour to pull off this bit of stage magic before the announcement of a possible kidnapping further agitated the two camps. Each glance at her watch only intensified the feeling that her life had become a race. As unlikely as it sounded, federal agents were not far behind her.

The crowd recognized her as she and Warren walked up the narrow causeway that led from the road to Musket's bastion. The lane on either side was cordoned with rope fences. Inside this barrier, Indians greeted her, most with mute stares, others by name. Just beyond the rope barrier, a quartet of indecently opinionated neo-vampires shouted that they wanted redskin blood. Their noses and cheeks were stitched with rings and jangling chains, and somehow they knew who she was.

"Jo-Jo shouldn't hang with peyote-eaters!" one of them yelled.

"They're all welfare-mongers, Jo Adams!" another cried. "Dirty drinking beardless welfare-mongers and their redheaded queen!"

"What's up with the freaks?" Warren asked, visibly disturbed.

314

"I get the feeling a little bird told them all about me."

"Watch out for your scalp, Jo-Jo!"

"Cripes. If I'd known you had friends like these, I wouldn't have invited you to dinner. Is it too late to retract the offer?"

"Samuel?" Jo ducked under his umbrella without being invited. "Mind if I join you? I have a proposal."

Samuel Grady looked like an owl with wet feathers. He'd traded his pinstripes for a clean blue chambray, but that was not the only change that had taken place since the last time Jo had seen him. His movements were clipped, a bird twitching at every creaking branch. Was he losing his nerve for this gambit?

"Dust-scratching, horse-humping Apaches!"

"How long has your fan club been here?" Jo asked him.

"They arrived at noon, with the storm clouds." Grady's voice, at least, had lost none of its resonance. "Soon they will lose interest and go back to where thunder sleeps when not shaking the earth. Does your proposal involve this man?"

It took her a second to realize he was referring to Warren. "Oh, him. No, he just came along for the delightful atmosphere. Can I ask you—"

A timber crack of thunder made her jump. Grady also started, and even the hecklers were shaken into silence.

The rain came down harder.

Jo nudged farther under the cover of the umbrella, so that she stood less than a foot away from Grady.

"How about I wait in the car?" Warren said, and he dashed off.

Members of both parties headed for shelter. Reporters hurried their equipment into vans. The last embers in barbecue grills spat out final notes of defeat.

"We seem to be getting very intimate, you and I," Grady said.

Jo detected the shine of amusement in his black eyes, but the avian uncertainty remained. Despite the theater he'd affected for the camera, he was not a showman, nor was he confrontational by nature. CNN was a more daunting venue than he'd been prepared for, and the goths with the tireless tongues were further dissolving his fervor for a fight.

"If Musket decides to sell," she said, "will you walk away?"

"I understood that he already declined the city's bribe."

"That's not what I asked. If he changes his mind and gives in to the greedy, materialistic pangs of his capitalist upbringing, will you and your troops remove yourselves?"

"They are not my troops. They've come of their own volition."

"You know what I'm getting at."

He shifted the umbrella to his other hand. Biding his time. Weighing his options.

"Samuel, I'm on a tight schedule here."

"Yes."

"Yes what?"

"If Peter sells, there is no reason for me to remain."

"What about defending ancient native burial ground?"

"Are you questioning my choice to leave, Jo Adams?"

Jo stamped out her rising smile as effectively as the downpour doused the charcoal. She'd given him a way to abandon ship without losing face, and he'd agreed. "Don't go anywhere. And keep my spot warm."

She became one more blurry form running through the rain.

Pete Musket had taken refuge under a tarp attached to the birthing house's flat roof. He was alone with his television set on the weathered flagstones in front of the building.

"Where is everyone?" Jo asked as she hustled under the

tarp. The water beat the plastic lean-to like a drumhead. "Where's Tenfeathers?"

"Someplace dry, I reckon."

"Of course. Are you sober?"

Musket fixed her with a rheumy gaze.

"Sorry. Forget it. I'm going to offer you a large amount of money, and only a drunk would turn it down. How long do you think you can stay out here without working? I made some calls. Your truck is one missed payment away from being repossessed, and I won't mention the rent and the IRS."

"Jesus." Musket scratched his face. "Are *you* sober?"

Jo smirked and put the phone to her ear.

Musket watched her intently.

"Hello, it's me. Where are you?"

"Standing in my tent," Chuck said, "asking myself why this woman is calling me when she's standing only thirty feet away."

Jo turned around. Through the shimmering curtains of rain, she saw him in the mouth of the pavilion. "Is that a chimney you have on that thing?"

"We have a portable stove. And a very important interview coming up. Is there something I can do for you?"

Yes, she thought, insanely. *You can be twenty-two again and recklessly compassionate.*

"No," she said. "I mean yes, there is."

She saw him put a hand on his hip, a sure sign that he was losing patience with her. "Jo, I really don't have time for your—"

"How much for Musket's land?"

"How much for . . . are you serious?"

More than ever, erstwhile lover of mine.

"Dead, Chuck. Dead. So how much?"

He took his hand off his hip. The rain slashed the ground. "That him with you now?"

"No, Chuck, it's Jimmy Hoffa. He's been hiding out in Musket's barn all this time. Now how much?"

"Well." He put his hand over the phone and yelled something into the pavilion, no doubt a command to quiet down. Then he said, "What's he asking?"

"No way. It's your call. Give me a figure."

He didn't immediately respond, and Jo wished she could see his face. She had always been able to read the runes of his eyes. He could withhold no secrets from her. But on second thought, she was thankful for the distance.

"Fifty thousand," he said. "It's worth half that."

"A hundred. And I don't care if it's only worth a dime."

"Get real. He has less than three acres of land, Joey. The Sheridan Corporation will not be extorted for one hundred thousand dollars."

"Spare us the drama. This is me you're talking to."

"Is it? I'm starting to wonder."

"A hundred thousand," she said again. She looked at Musket, who didn't protest. "No, check that. Make it a hundred and one."

"You call that negotiating?"

"No, Chuck, I don't. I have lost all ability to engage in any activity that bears even a middling resemblance to negotiation. So it's one hundred thousand for Pete Musket, and a grand to the shelter for battered women in Martinsburg. Take it or leave it."

She mentally counted the seconds. She got as far as seven before Chuck said, "It's worth that much just to get out of the damn rain."

They hung up at the same time.

Things sped up even more from there. Word spread. Journalists phoned their respective newsrooms. Shouts of protest sparred with cheers of triumph, but the duel was short-lived, pounded out by the storm. Though she meant to say farewell to Sam Grady, he slipped into his motor home without additional comment to either his followers or the reporters. Jo never saw him again.

She spent another half-hour at the site, giving her token comments for the papers, ignoring a few swan-song barbs from the Dracula wannabes, and by the time she slid behind the pony's steering wheel, there wasn't a part of her that wasn't soaked.

Warren, however, had dried up nicely. "I don't believe what I just saw happen here."

By then Jo had lost all sense of banter, wanting only a towel, a warm place to sit, and something to eat. She started the car. Though she should have been elated, she was only more wary, dreading sundown and the possible connections the investigators might make in the darkness. Even now the agents were out there, collecting bits of evidence too small for the human eye to see, talking to possible witnesses, making grids on oversized drawing pads and filling them with names. She hated to think how Nin or Hannah would hold up under even the most routine FBI questioning. And sooner or later, it was going to happen. Maybe even tonight. But she couldn't risk being seen with any of them, so they were all on their own. If she had a single prayer at that moment, it was that all five of them would be able to keep their balance until dawn, and wouldn't be frightened into revealing something small that turned out to be something big. But dawn was important. She had the feeling that if they made it safely to daybreak, the time of greatest danger would be over, and everything would be all right.

She was reaching for the gearshift when a fist banged against her window.

She unrolled the foggy window, revealing a face hidden within the cowl of a yellow slicker. "Greetings, my lady."

"Felix? I didn't know you were here."

"Martin sent me this morning. I just called him with the news. He said he's giving you his first-born child."

"Terrific. I'll pick it up one of these days when I'm dry. By the way, I quit. Tell Marty I'll see him around."

"No, wait. Charles told me to give this to you." His wet fingers poked something through the window. A photograph.

Jo accepted the picture and stared down into her own eyes.

It was the one that Chuck had taken of her seven days ago. It was a woman from a past life, only half-remembered. Like a person met in a dream.

". . . supposed to be dry by tomorrow," Warren was saying.

"Hmmm?" She broke eye contact with the stranger in the picture. "I'm sorry?"

"I was just commenting inanely on the weather." A change came over him as he looked at her, an expression of confusion and concern, like a man who's brushed up against someone in the dark and can't discern if they are friend or foe. "Jo, what's happening with you?"

"Everything."

Though he didn't look satisfied by the answer, he didn't press her, and they drove back to town with only the chatter of the rain to remind them they weren't alone.

Chapter Twenty-four

Hannah paced.

Up the ramp at one end of the hall, turn a one-eighty, roll back down.

Eight o'clock had come and gone and still no Terrell. The sun had dropped below the Appalachians, a storm-wracked night had descended angrily upon the town, Hannah had changed clothes twice since then, and though dinner was ready she had sustained herself on breath mints.

She sniffed her wrist. Was the scent fading?

Back up the ramp, pop a wheelie and pivot adroitly, speed downslope. Evel Knievel, eat your heart out.

She touched the left brake just enough so that she turned through the doorway to the bathroom. In front of the mirror once more. Another inspection. She'd chosen this summery cotton dress because it was the kind of thing she used to wear this time of year when she'd still been a whole woman. Back then, if it wasn't boots and Wranglers, then it was a simple knee-length jumper. She'd always had nice legs.

And hair, too. It fell in waves to her shoulders and smelled faintly of strawberries. Unfortunately there was a clock within sight, which only reminded her it was now eight-thirty and she was still alone.

Terrell was falling away from her. And that was no way for him to behave. Not after all they'd overcome. This day was horrible enough without having to deal with a second paralyzation; the accident had taken her legs, and losing Terrell was taking them all over again.

Eight-thirty-two.

Okay. Do something. Stay occupied. She went into her bedroom, where the windows were open and the chiffon curtains billowed like sails. She'd thrown wide the French doors. The awning above kept out the rain. Or at least most of it. Droplets speckled the hardwood floor. Other than the bed, the room was devoid of furniture. A can of paint and a roller on a long pole waited in the corner. Half the room was a shade whiter than the rest.

So paint then.

She picked up the can, thinking about the police. As soon as the senator had given his spiel this afternoon, the town had done another somersault. She'd kept the television off because it was all over the news. More manpower was en route from Quantico. More journalists right behind them. People with dogs were scouring the woods. The editors at all the big tabloids were probably already trying to decide if Jed Whitecross had been devoured by genetically altered, mutant orangutans escaped from a secret government lab, or killed by a mafia hitman last seen packing up his rifle behind a certain grassy knoll.

Was it now just a matter of time before someone zeroed in on the truth of what she'd done? What chance did she have against such forces? If it hadn't been for Jo's quick thinking, they'd probably already be staring at the world through prison bars. But Jo's diversion had kicked up quite a cloud of dust, the better to hide behind. One pink bandana tied to an antenna and some well-placed innuendo was all it took to lay a convincing false trail. Lucy had called and said the feds had interviewed Rita Ingersol and were eyeing her lieutenants with equal amounts of suspicion. Terrell was apparently keeping his sister well-informed of the very operation that was out to apprehend her. One more reason that Hannah was grateful for him.

See there? She'd gone for five or six seconds without thinking about him.

She returned the paint can to the floor. Resisted the desire to check the clock. Looked down at the strings where the dice had hung before she castrated them and threw them in the trash.

I killed a man. He's dead and can't ever come back.

And Terrell is standing me up.

The Hoofbeats pounded. They were excruciating. It wasn't simply that she was being dumped. She'd tossed in bed these recent nights, tasting the name *Hannah Campbell* on her tongue, and what was happening to her now was a lot worse than being dumped. As a matter of fact, she'd been so intent on directing her life toward a future with him that—

"Knock knock!"

Hannah caught her breath.

"I'm tired of getting rained on!" Terrell shouted from the front of the house. "So I'm coming in without being invited. Sorry about tracking in the water."

She heard the door shut.

Okay he's here so calm down take it easy he isn't lost just yet—

"I'm in here!" she called, hearing the strain in her voice but no longer worried about hiding it. "And who cares about the water! Just get in here."

"Bossy, bossy. Is that dinner I smell?"

She met him in the bedroom doorway.

He was drying his face with a dish towel. His uniform was wet. Diamonds of rain sparkled on his badge.

At the sight of him, the pang of longing was so forceful, so sudden, that it almost brought tears to her eyes. She tightened her fingers around the armrests to keep from reaching up to him.

"Hell of a day," he said.

She could only nod.

"And I'm afraid it's not over yet. They don't sleep, these FBI guys. I'm not sure if I'm cut out to be one of them or not. I'm not ruthless enough. Or obsessed enough. If Ingersol hired someone to do the job on Whitecross, then I feel sorry for those poor suckers. They don't stand a chance against this kind of posse."

Hannah wanted to be concerned by that. She wanted to be alarmed that the authorities were so ardent in their pursuit. But she could feel nothing past the ache in the center of her chest.

Terrell was looking down at her. "Say something."

She tried but she couldn't. She shook her head.

"Okay, I will."

Please don't! she thought. *Don't say there is no such person as Hannah Campbell. Because then I'll just be Hannah Half-Woman, and I think I will slowly die.*

"You see, uh, it wasn't until this Whitecross thing that I finally made up my mind," he began. "But I've done a lot of thinking lately. Yeah. A lot of thinking. About where we've been, you and I, all the stuff that's happened between us, all the things we said that we wanted to do before they put us away in the old folks' home where we'd *both* be in wheel-chairs."

Hannah remembered joking about that, and the memory almost tore her in half.

"Anyway, I haven't been able to get it off my mind. Get *us* off my mind. Honestly, Hannah, I'm scared. And maybe this will only make your life more complicated . . . well, probably not, but for what it's worth, I finally decided why I was scared in the first place." He pointed at her. "You."

It was too much. She hardly heard what he was saying, as consumed as she was by her need to fasten herself against him and erase the seams. She reached for his finger, needing to latch on to any small part of him that he'd offer—

He drew back.

Hannah inhaled sharply. *Oh please don't pull away from me!* Her eyes widened in surprise when he took a step in retreat. The first tear crept from her eye.

"Just hear me out," he said.

Hannah wanted to say *Don't do this to me!* But she couldn't speak. The ache crept from her chest to her throat, sealing it off. Maybe this was what they meant by the law of karma, that she had murdered a man and was now being murdered in return. If she could only turn around in the corridor of time as easily as she spun her wheelchair in the hall, she'd zoom back to the lake and keep Jed alive, not because he deserved to live, but for the simple selfish reason that she couldn't go on without this man who now stood in front of her, just out of reach.

"I was scared because I'm not good enough," Terrell said.

Every time Hannah blinked, she fanned fresh tears to her eyelashes.

"I don't know why I've always done that to myself. I'm sure I missed out on a lot of opportunities because I didn't think I measured up. Lucy's spent her life telling me otherwise, but it's not that easy. That's why I stayed around in these parts after high school instead of trying to be a cop in Baltimore. It felt too big for me. You know what I'm saying? Who was I to think that I could be a big-city detective, right?"

Hannah didn't want a cure for cancer. She didn't want an end to starvation in Africa, or even—if she had to choose— Penelope free from her coma. It was mean and it was self-centered but it was true. She wanted her arms around him. But she was afraid that if she rolled any closer, he'd turn his back on her and walk away for good.

"And do you know where I feel the most out of my

league?" He pointed at her again. "You."

What was he talking about? Hannah didn't understand. Had she missed something important? *Baby, what are you trying to say?*

"You are the prettiest girl in school, sweetness. You're the one everyone wants, the belle of the ball. But you're more than that. You're so . . . original. Things come out of your mouth that nobody else ever thinks to say. You eat up life in great big spoonfuls, and there are times I think I'm going to burst just needing you so bad."

He stepped toward her.

Hannah, stunned, stared up at him.

"There is not a man alive who wouldn't give twenty years off his life to call you his own. I see how you are with Nin's little ones . . . it's like that doorway between being a kid and being an adult never closed for you. You've still got it open, wide and fine. You cross through anytime you want, taking the best from both places. And I think to myself that if I ever saw you look on our own children that way, I'd be born all over again."

Hannah parted her lips but made no sound.

He sank to his knees in front of her. "Watching you, I realized that's what Jesus was talking about. Being born again doesn't mean letting some preacher dunk you under the water. It happens every time we go back through that doorway and shake hands with life, and remember why we're here and how damn fine it is just to breathe. That's what you do for me, sweetness. Each time I look at you."

Still unsure what was happening, Hannah watched in silence as he took her hands one at a time and tugged off her gloves. He placed them on the floor, and then did something very simple that dissolved the pain and saved her.

He entwined his fingers with hers.

Hannah smiled and sniffled and shook at the same time.

"You don't get it, do you?" he said, shaking his head in plain amazement. "You assume that I'm going to leave because I found something more right. But that's not true. I was planning on leaving because I knew that this was the rightest thing in the world, and I didn't think I deserved it."

Hold on. Was he saying that he planned on *staying*? All this time, had she been tearing herself to pieces for nothing? Did he want her as much as she wanted him? It seemed too good to be true. Yet here was her proof. Their fingers were locked, the Hoofbeats were fading, and Terrell had a look on his face that she'd never seen before.

He leaned forward, and Hannah eagerly met him, so that their foreheads touched. When he spoke again, she felt his breath on her lips. "I've got this plan, see," he said softly, "a plan that you and me are going to move someplace where nobody knows us. They won't know that I'm the son of a dirt-poor coal miner and you're someone who used to walk. We'll get us a pasture and a horse, and then I'm putting you up there on that horse, and don't you tell me you can't ride anymore, because I know that a person doesn't necessarily need their legs to get a horse to move. And I'm going to sit there on the porch and watch you do it, just ride yourself silly. And then I'll probably have to go inside and do the laundry and make dinner because once you're out there, I'll never be able to get you to come inside."

Hannah laughed through her tears.

"That's my plan, the whole thing, all that I care about."

Upon hearing this declaration and finally understanding what it meant, Hannah rejoiced. *Me, too! Me, too! All I care about is us!* She wanted to shout, whoop, sing out with the joy of someone narrowly escaping a fatal injury, but the flood of relief was so sudden that it made her feel light-headed. They were going to be fine. *Fine!* She'd fretted herself into a fit, and all along, he'd been crazy for her and just too self-abasing to say anything. Why did people do that to themselves? She felt her pulse in her fingertips—or was that *his* pulse? With the fading of the ache, the tides of desire were quickly rising. She had never wanted anyone so badly; she hadn't thought herself capable of such a hunger. Just as her sorrow had been a physical sensation, so too was her yearning. Her lips were still parted and she breathed through her mouth.

"I don't ever want to be without you," he said. "I want there to be a chair in my shower and gloves without fingers on my nightstand."

Hannah shuddered. She wanted to tell him how she felt but now her heart was knocking against her ribs, and she smelled his skin and felt his heat and—

"I read something the other day that reminded me of you. It goes like this." He cleared his throat. " 'I met a lady in the meads / Full beautiful, a faery's child . . .' "

—she squeezed his hands as hard as she could—

" 'Her hair was long, her foot was light / And her eyes were wild.' "

"Enough."

It was the first word she'd spoken since he'd appeared in the doorway. She'd never known a need so painful as this. Her body cried out from the pressure. She put her lips against the warm darkness of his ear. "There's a time to quote poetry to the woman you love," she whispered, "and a time to fuck her brains out."

A fresh spiral of wind tossed the curtains about the room.

Terrell seized her by the hair and kissed her.

Hannah made a sudden, senseless sound. She pulled him against her, tasting his mouth. She traded breath with him, so that when he exhaled, she swallowed his air. Her hands couldn't draw him in close enough, her mouth not open wide enough.

He broke contact. Hannah gasped audibly.

As if her words had released him from an old and tormenting confinement, he kissed her feverishly, down the pale curve of her neck, where he paused only briefly before moving his tongue all the way up her throat. The sensation made her shiver. When he reached her chin, she let the tides finally drown her. All she knew was the underwater feeling of immersion in another person, the weightlessness of swimming in him.

Terrell hooked his arms under her knees. She joined her hands around his neck, still kissing him, still uttering the same inarticulate noises.

He stood up and lifted her out of the chair.

The only time in her life that Hannah wasn't sitting was when she was lying down, or in the process of transferring herself to the bed, the toilet, or the van. When Terrell hoisted her up, she felt the change in her shoulders and spine. The unfamiliar placement of her own body weight dispelled what remained of her sense of reality. Nothing was real except the clicking of their teeth as they kissed, cannibalizing each other.

And then he let her go.

Hannah's legs dropped out from under. But she hung on. She kept her arms around his neck, her toes hanging inches above the floor. She anticipated his intentions and wanted to encourage him, to let him know that they were drowning together and whatever he did was all right, just do it, do it and don't be afraid, but she couldn't produce any words beyond a thin rasping in his ear. His hands traveled down her sides, her waist, and then there was nothing, no feeling at all, and she knew by this lack of sensation that he was at her hips and hiking up handfuls of her dress. She wanted to look, to confirm with her eyes that he was tearing at her underwear, snapping the slender elastic band, but her eyelids were seared shut and, besides, it didn't matter. Their thoughts were one and she knew what he was doing without looking.

He drove her against the wall.

She grunted. Again Terrell took her under the knee and brought her leg up around his waist, and this gave Hannah her opening. With one hand she reached down and her fingers tripped over his belt, and then she had the buckle loose but the button on his pants put up a fight and she raked at it until it parted and the zipper was easy and she plunged her hand into the furnace between his legs.

He leaned harder against her, using the wall to support her, kissing her and lapping her lips and neck and positioning himself between her knees. "Sweetness . . ." He spoke into the sweaty bend of her neck. "Is this okay?"

At any other time she might have laughed at such a ridiculous question, but she was beyond laughter, beyond everything but the rupturing agony of need, and she knew he didn't mean *Is it okay to make love to you?* but rather *Is your body okay for this kind of thing?*

"The sink may be busted," she panted, "but the plumbing still works."

That was all he needed. He adjusted himself. Secured her legs around him. And paused.

But only for a moment.

That first surge tore a cry from both of them. It was followed by a second of hesitation, and then the cadence began. Hannah's back slid up and down the wall, and she endured it for half a minute before losing herself in what felt like a lava bath from her own molten core.

She recovered, smiled radiantly, and stroked his face once before taking hold of her dress where it was bundled around her thighs. She wanted as much of her skin touching his as she could manage. In one fluid motion she pulled the dress over her head and let it fall to the floor. Terrell kissed her neckline and the sharp ridge of her collarbone. They used the wall for support, shifting enough so that her hands could dash behind her back, and after her bra was banished, she parted his shirt and pulled it down over his shoulders so that she could press her breasts against the black slalom of his chest.

But it wasn't enough. She wanted more. Terrell read the sway of her body and used the wall to hold her up while he fumbled blindly for her foot. First one shoe, then the other, and when she was fully naked she rocked against him with every muscle still capable of rocking.

He responded, adjusted his stance, and matched her rhythm. Completely submerged, they dissolved into each other, nearing implosion with each stroke, and for a time there was only the wind tossing the drapes, the thrusts, the sounds, the friction of her back against the wall—

Terrell called out incoherently.

Torrents of pleasure undulating through her, Hannah joined his outburst with her own. Her head arched back and rolled to the side. She opened her eyes just a little when the first bead of sweat dripped from her hair, and there, just over Terrell's shoulder, sat a chair with wheels. Hannah wondered who it belonged to, and why it looked so out of place sitting there alone.

Chapter Twenty-five

After stowing the last of Matt and Brady's clothes in the back of the truck, Tam jogged through the rain toward the shop, to steal Roy's favorite ratchet set. The inside of the metal-roofed building smelled like motor oil and distantly of beer. Tam closed the door so the light wouldn't be seen from the house, twisted the bulb in its socket until it flared to life, and went straight to the green plastic case on the workbench. She hoped the tools were something she'd never have to use; with luck, the Toyota would keep running without a hiccup, and she could pawn the sockets when she reached Alaska.

The case was so heavy that she had to labor it outside with both hands. She finally got it stowed in the truck bed, wedged in between the boys' two bicycles, which she'd decided at the last minute to take along. She was already disrupting their world enough as it was. Boys were never supposed to be bikeless.

She went back to the house, entered through the kitchen door, and saw that it was only nine-thirty. Could she maintain this charade until midnight? Roy was usually in bed by then on weeknights. She glanced into the living room. Brady slept on their sagging sofa. Matt sat on the floor, surrounded by die-cast cars, lining them up as if for parade inspection. And Roy, esteemed patriarch, sat on the edge of his easy chair, leaning over a TV tray and the fried chicken Tamaryn had surprised him with. Woman's oldest trick: allay a man's suspicions with supper. Gals had been deceiving men with food ever since the apple. You'd think they would have caught on.

"How is it?" she asked.

He nodded, still chewing, eyes on the baseball game.
Matt looked up at her. "Mom?"

"That's me."

"Is it too late?"

"Too late? You mean for an ice cream sandwich?"

"Uh-huh. Is it?"

"Normally, yes. But this time I'll make an exception."

"All *right!*" Matt went from sitting to running without
transition.

"Ain't it past his bedtime?" Roy said, wiping his mouth on
a paper towel.

"It's summer. Just eat your chicken."

"He didn't even finish all his dinner. I thought we agreed
that they don't get the good stuff if they don't finish all their
dinner."

"We did. You're right. I'm not fighting with you tonight.
If you don't want him to have the ice cream sandwich, you
can arm wrestle him for it."

Roy pried his eyes from the television and looked at her
guardedly. "Something happen to you today? You're acting
funny."

"Funny how?"

"I don't know. Different. You've changed."

"Changed? Well, I'll give you that. Once upon a time I was
captain of the varsity softball and track teams. My grades
weren't Harvard material, but I got offers from more than
one major university. I partied every weekend, I drove a
souped-up Jeep, then I got married. And bought a sewing machine."

Roy stared at her, obviously not understanding.

"Don't lose any sleep over it," she told him, dismissing the
subject. "It's just been one of those—"

A knock at the front door interrupted her.

"Now who the hell is that at this hour?" Roy grumbled. He put down his drumstick but made no move to get up. "You expecting somebody?"

Tam didn't hear him. Lately her life was a minefield, and she went around bracing herself for the next kaboom. She held her breath as she walked across the room, trying to decide which one of them would be standing there to deliver the message that Penny was dead. Would they send Lucy? No, these days Jo was running the show in person.

She opened the door and cops were standing on her porch.

Thank God she had her hand on the doorknob for support. *The fingerprints. They cracked open my juvey file and matched the prints of that fifteen-year-old to the ones on Jed's seat belt, and I don't want Roy raising my sons when I'm in prison. No, wait, that can't be right because I was wearing gloves—so what do they want?*

"Mrs. Soza?" Jason Reece, hat in his hands, smiled timidly. "I mean, Tamaryn, right?"

"What do you want?"

"Who is it?" Roy bellowed.

"Tamaryn, this here is Special Agent Lou Carlos of the FBI."

"Good evening, Mrs. Soza." Carlos was a handsome Latino with gray hair and an overcoat.

"Dammit, Tam, who the hell is it?" Roy got up from his chair.

"Is that your husband?" Carlos asked.

"In a manner of speaking."

"Excuse me?"

"Nothing. What's the matter?"

"Yeah," Roy said, pushing his way to the door. "What's the matter? You say you're the FBI? What do you want with me?"

"Mr. Soza, I'm Lou Carlos and this is Deputy Jason Reece . . ."

"I heard. Now what can I do for you?"

"You're a friend of Owen Selvey?"

"Maybe. I guess. We hunt together, if that's what you want to know."

"Can we come in out of the rain, Mr. Soza? We have a few questions we'd like to ask you concerning the disappearance of Jedediah Whitecross."

The doorknob again. It was saving her.

"Sure, what the hell. Town's really in a shitstorm over this, ain't it?" Roy opened the screen door and stepped aside. "We've got fried chicken and ice cream sandwiches. You boys are welcome to both."

They came inside, apologized for dripping water on the floor, and Roy said don't worry about it, Tam'll take care of it, and Tam didn't even offer a retort, because she was fully occupied with the doorknob. She was afraid that if she let it go, her knees would crumple the moment Carlos said anything about tire tracks or lake stones wrapped in sheets.

She stood there, waiting to be caught.

Jo stared for a long and intense moment at the chessboard, and eventually picked up her rook, jumped over two white pawns, and scooped them up in triumph. "King me," she said.

Warren raised an eyebrow. "Maybe we should go over the rules again."

"I know the rules. At least in a vague sort of way. But I don't have the patience this evening. And besides, what's a grown man doing with a chess set and no checkers? Really, Warren, I'm going to have to get some culture in you if this is going to work out."

"Hey, wine qualifies as culture, doesn't it?" He indicated the half-empty bottle of Dom. "And I think it's working out just fine, as a matter of fact. Whatever *it* may be."

"Do you happen to have that shiny watch in your pocket? I seem to have left mine back at the chateau."

"It's a few minutes before ten. Why? Is your carriage about to go pumpkin on you?"

"Can I ask you a question?"

"Shoot."

"Are you going to king me or not?"

Warren smiled. He reached into the bowl of cookie dough that sat opposite the wine bottle, pinched off a glob, and stuck it to the crown of the black rook. "This is crazy. You realize that, don't you?"

"I do. But when was the last time you made cookies after dinner and sat around on the floor eating the dough? Just because it's something you haven't done before, that doesn't make it crazy. Believe me. I know crazy when I see it. It's your move."

They played in comfortable silence, their legs folded under the coffee table, their hands roaming from wineglasses to bowl. Jo didn't know where the evening was headed, only that the rain slashing against the windows was a reminder of the tempest her life had become. Rita Ingersol had nearly 300 soldiers sleeping in motels, churches, and the guest rooms of local women sympathetic to her cause. The RV park was full of reporters, curious college students, and the long black bus belonging to the goths, whom Jo was beginning to suspect were under Chuck's employ. Now that the Sam Grady threat had passed, Chuck would probably sic his goons on AGNES. And then of course there was the legion of agents from the Justice Department, and they were certainly making better use of their time than sitting on their duffs eating chocolate chip cookie dough.

"You're doing it again," Warren said.

"I am?"

"Sometimes it's like you're not even here."

"Storms make me nervous."

He studied her as if expecting more, then shrugged as if to say it didn't matter. Perhaps he decided he was better off not knowing. "So what can I do to put you more at ease?"

"How about you just fill my glass and we'll see if we can make it through till morning."

Tam stood very still.

She leaned on the jamb between the living room and the kitchen, arms crossed in front of her, hands cupping her elbows, knowing that if they ever hooked her up to a polygraph, she was ruined. It was a wonder they couldn't see the vestiges of anger in her stance, or the desperation brewing in her eyes.

". . . so I'll briefly bring you up to speed on our procedure," Carlos said. He sat on the sofa next to snoozing Brady. It was the first time anyone had worn a suit and tie in this house in as long as Tam could remember. "I'm one of several agents tasked with locating the members of Owen Selvey's sportsmen's club. Each of us has been paired with a local officer to facilitate our search and keep us current on who's who in Clayton County. I've been teamed with Deputy Reece here."

Tam looked at Reece. He had declined a seat, and was still standing on the thin mat in front of the door. Every now and then he'd crouch down to answer one of Matthew's endless questions, which usually involved guns and sirens. He glanced over and caught Tam looking at him. He smiled tightly.

"You saw the condition of the hunting lodge?" Carlos asked.

"Damn right I did."

"What was your impression of the scene?"

"My impression?" Roy rubbed the stubble on his chin. No one had ever asked for *his impression* before. "Tell you the truth, I thought it was college kids. At least until Calamity Jane showed up in town."

"Who?"

"That Ingersol woman."

"Ah. Any idea why Ms. Ingersol would single out Owen Selvey, Gerald Fawles, and Charles Adams?"

"Other than just being an ornery bitch? Nope."

"Were you aware that a woman was assaulted here in town two nights ago?"

This sudden change of tack caused Roy to blink. He lost his train of thought. "Uh, yeah, sure. Penelope, her name is. Friend of my wife. Did she die of it?"

"No, sir. To your knowledge, was she romantically involved with anyone at the time?"

"You serious? Everybody knows that Whitecross was balling her."

"Of course."

"So he gets a little out of hand," Roy went on, "and whacks her a few times, maybe because he's drunk and doesn't know any better, and then Ingersol sends her lesbian leg-breakers out to grab him. You want my opinion, Mr. Carlos, I bet someone did a number on Whitecross out of revenge, probably the same someone who painted up Owen's cabin."

Tam found it remarkable that Roy had steered so close to the truth. She found it even more remarkable that she was able to stand here, an accessory to murder, while these men

338

discussed her without knowing it. What would she do if Lou Carlos stood up without warning and told her she was under arrest? How could she ever explain it to her sons if they had to watch her get handcuffed and led out to a police car? She was glad she hadn't eaten in awhile, because her head was pounding and the acid was tearing a hole in her stomach.

Reece squatted down beside Matthew again, talking softly. Carlos asked Roy if he knew of anyone whom he considered to be an enemy of Gerald Fawles. Roy said there may have been a few men who had it in for Gerald on account of him sleeping with their wives. Carlos asked for names and wrote them in a notebook when Roy recited them.

"What have you got there, son?" Reece asked.

Something in his tone set off Tam's alarm.

Reece picked up one of Matthew's toys and held it to the light. Except it *wasn't* one of Matthew's toys, and when she realized what she was looking at, Tamaryn almost lost control.

"Find something important, Deputy?" Carlos asked. Apparently he too had sensed the shift in Reece's voice.

Reece displayed a silver figurine of a jungle cat in mid-leap.

Tam struggled to keep her composure. She swallowed several times, fighting down the urge to cough. This wasn't happening. These men were not here in her house, Matthew didn't have the hood ornament from Jed's car, Reece was not staring at it as if it were a smoking gun.

Carlos held out his hand. "Is that what I think it is?"

"What is it?" Roy wanted to know. "Matt, what is that thing?"

Matthew looked back and forth between them.

Reece's face had lost all color.

Carlos examined the object. "It's Matt, right?"

Matthew nodded.

Leave him out of this! Tam screamed inside.

"Matt, where did you get this?"

Don't tell him, baby! Don't you say anything!

"I don't know," Matthew said. "Aunt Nin's, I think."

"Aunt Nin?"

"He means fat Nin Ryan," Roy said. "She runs the day care. She's not really his aunt."

"Is that where you found this toy?" Carlos asked, his eyes full of kindness.

Oh, sir knight, please don't!

"Yeah, I think so. She's got lots of toys. We get 'em mixed up all the time. I've got some other stuff from her house, too. Am I in trouble?"

Carlos gave him a grandfatherly smile. "Not at all, son."

Reece, however, was not so deft at concealing his thoughts. He stood up and swabbed his face with a handkerchief.

"Is that thing important?" Roy asked.

"It's all important at this stage, Mr. Soza. Do you mind if I hold on to this for awhile?"

"Hell, take it. Nin's brats have got so many toys they'll never notice one missing."

"Mrs. Soza?" Suddenly Carlos turned his attention on her.

She knew that if she spoke, her quavering voice would betray her. "Hmmm?"

"Was your friend Penelope also acquainted with"—he glanced at his notes—"Nin Ryan?"

Eat me, asswipe.

"I guess so," she said.

"Do you know Mrs. Ryan very well?"

She's one-fifth of my soul.

"We get along."

Carlos asked nothing more. He stared at the metal cat like a seer with a crystal ball. Then he abruptly got up and made for the door. "I want to thank you both for your time this evening."

"No trouble at all," Roy assured him. "You think fat Nin is in on this with Ingersol?"

"I don't think anything, Mr. Soza, and I'd appreciate it if you'd not mention what we discussed here tonight. We don't want to violate the integrity of our investigation, especially not when rumors are already so rampant."

Roy promised to keep his mouth shut and wished Carlos luck in nailing the Amazons who kidnapped Whitecross. That was the word he used: *Amazons*. Tam had never hated him more than she did at that moment.

"So there's our big excitement for the night," he said when they were gone. "I tell you, Tam, if this town is still standing this time next week, I'll be surprised. Any chicken left?"

Tam touched Matthew on the head on her way to the bedroom, not so much as if she were granting a blessing but hoping to receive one. She made it to the bed without blacking out, but she had to dial Jo's number three times before she got it right. Someone needed to get to Nin before the cops. They had to warn her. But even if she were prepared for their questions, Nin would knuckle under the first time she was asked where she was on the night of Jed's disappearance. Nin was no poker player. She'd be in jail by dawn, and the rest of them would shortly join her. They'd lose it all—Matt and Brady, Caroline, Terrell, all of Nin's little brood.

While she listened to the phone ring, she let the fear turn into anger, as she had always done, and its familiar flames soon cleared her head. Her personal plan hadn't changed. Get the boys, and then get out.

Oh, yeah. And get Roy's gun, just in case.

Erin O'Rourke

★ ★ ★ ★ ★

When her telephone rang, Jo was sitting on the floor next to Warren, their backs against the couch, talking about other rains they had known and other storms they had seen. Warren had spent a night in a Red Cross shelter during a hurricane in Florida. Jo had watched her family's chicken coop get carried away by flood waters when she was nine.

"Could you hand me my purse? That's probably my daughter."

"I hate cell phones."

"Life's too short to waste your hate on little things like that. Thanks."

"Okay. I'll hate the New York Yankees instead."

"Just shut up and have some more dough." She pressed the TALK button. "Hello?"

"If I have any more dough, you'll have to use a spatula to scrape me off the floor."

As soon as Tam's first sentence fell upon her ear—*"Nin forgot to get rid of the hood ornament that I knocked off of the dirtbag's car, and now the cops are on their way to her house"*—Jo knew the game was at last crashing to a conclusion. She listened in silence for a full minute, while Tamaryn, eerily calm, described the entire encounter with Carlos and Reece. Tam ended her monologue with a question that Jo wasn't able to answer: *"So what do we do now?"*

The only fitting reply, Jo realized, was *nothing.* There was nothing any of them could do to stop the wrecking ball from dismantling what was left of their lives. For awhile there, when she'd been concerned only with beating Warren at chess-checkers, it seemed as if they might get away with it, that their Icky Errands had sufficiently protected them. But now? Now they were no more than a few hours away from being charged with murder. Even if Nin didn't confess out-

342

right, she wouldn't make it through even the most rudimentary interrogation techniques.

"Stay put," she said. "I'll call you in a few hours."

"A few hours? Jo, in a few hours we'll all be in jail."

"Nonsense. It will take them longer than that to sort things out. So just lie to me and tell me you'll get some sleep."

After she hung up, Jo returned the phone to her purse, mistrusting her own icy composure. Was this what they meant by sangfroid? It was a word she'd never used before, and certainly not when describing herself. There must have been a fine line between calmness and fatalism, and she'd likely crossed over without realizing it.

"Who's sorting what out?" Warren asked.

"Say again?"

"You said it'll take them longer than that to sort things out. So who's them and what are they sorting?"

"Eavesdropper."

"Couldn't be helped. Your eaves are too close for me to ignore."

"I never talk about my eaves on the first date."

"Ah. Right." He nodded. "Good thing for me that this is our second date."

"It is?"

"Yep. So eaves are fair game." He gave her an authentic smile. It lit up his eyes. "Do you want to give Caroline a call, let her know we haven't fallen off the face of the earth?"

"I suppose that would be the responsible thing to do."

"Use my phone and give yours a rest. I know how expensive those things can be."

"Thanks, but I'm not calling her."

"You're not? What happened to responsible?"

"*That,* you dear man you, is the question on everyone's lips." She pushed herself up from the floor, aware of every passing second in the way that a candle is aware of the wind. Regardless of whether it was serenity or nihilism she was feeling, there was something else in her as well, a delicate tingling. Part of it she attributed to simple playfulness; it was nice to flirt again. But the rest of it was ineffable, to be acted upon but not discussed. She held her hand down to Warren and helped him to his feet.

They stood facing each other in *that place,* the one too infrequently visited, where nerves twist under the skin, feet try not to shuffle, eyelids blink.

Jo experienced none of these symptoms. Everything she cared for was about to come to an end. With luck she'd make it till noon before they came for her. These slender hours, then, were all she had. She placed her palm flat against Warren's chest, so that she could feel his heartbeat.

"What . . ." He cleared his throat. "What are we doing?"

"Whatever comes to mind." She moved closer to him. This feeling was one she hadn't known before. It was the acceptance of disaster mixed with the thrill of new beginnings, and the weird chemistry of the two empowered her. A smile played across her lips as she swayed in front of him, in a kind of dance.

"Jo." He stood very still. "Are you going to break my heart?"

"Not tonight." She pulled him down to the couch.

Chapter Twenty-six

"There was a time a woman could just buy a new hat," Lucy said to her reflection in the visor mirror. "Now our hair has to fend for itself." By the weak light inside the mail truck, she could barely see what she'd done to herself an hour earlier. Her hair lay close to her head, so short on the sides that it bristled. "Woman hits a certain age—*snip!*—off it comes. The road to menopause is paved with good-intentioned haircuts."

She flipped the visor up, put the truck into drive, and sped toward Nin's.

Or rather, she *intended* to speed, but a governor had been built into the engine, preventing the vehicle from breaking any drag-strip records. She'd never outrun the cops like this.

"Outrun the cops," she scoffed. "Listen to me, talking like some kind of fugitive. Ningeogapik, why did you have to go and keep that evil little cat?" As far as Lucy knew, West Virginia's courts had abolished the death penalty. But there was damn sure such a thing as life without parole, which was a concept so freakishly unreal that Lucy felt as if she were reading about it in a newspaper article, in which the words LUCY CAMPBELL were just meaningless typeface, and prison just an abstraction and not a real place with walls.

It was pushing midnight by the time she turned the last corner before Nin's house. Another night without sleep. Another night trying to—

Four cars were parked at the curb.

Lucy flattened both feet on the brake. "Oh, God. Oh, Jesus God . . ."

As she watched, car doors opened, umbrellas unfurled,

345

and dark figures advanced up the walk.

Roy was snoring by quarter after twelve.

Tamaryn softly closed the bedroom door and spent no more time second-guessing what she was about to do. You couldn't argue with the fire when it was the only thing lighting your path. She moved along the hallway by touch, one hand on the wall, until she came to the boys' room. One glance inside was enough to bolster her. She walked into the unlighted kitchen with the rain sounding like rocks as it struck the trailer's metal roof. Lightning cast the kitchen into a freeze-frame of objects she recognized, then it was dark again and she was standing on her toes at the refrigerator, and then she had the key.

She went to the gun cabinet. She worked in total darkness, liberating the Psalm 23 and two boxes of 5.56-millimeter ammunition. No plans yet on using the weapon, but plans change. If they tried to take her champions from her, the two princes who were everything she wanted to be but wasn't, then yes, plans could change very quickly.

She wrapped the rifle in a garbage bag to keep it dry and smuggled it outside to her pickup. She stowed it behind the seat. That completed, she went back inside and reviewed her mental checklist again, knowing she'd overlooked something that later on she'd kick herself for leaving behind. But there were just the boys, Tom and Huck, the only things life had ever leased her that she'd never missed a payment on. Her hands looked ten years older than the rest of her for all the time spent in diner dishwater, and don't even ask about her nails. But those hands served a higher purpose. Or *two* purposes, as it turned out.

She stole into their bedroom and whispered quiet, magic sounds in their ears, waking them up, soothing them, weaving a tale of midnight rides to secret places.

Jo lay in the black warm room, smelling their musk. Her body, buried under the duvet, was as relaxed and yet as primed as it had ever been. She felt his leg under her and the soothing rise and fall of his chest. Only minutes had passed since he'd huffed out her name at the apex of passion, and his breathing had yet to settle. Jo spent a short time in the languid void of the aftermath, eyes half-closed, finger resting on her lips, where the flavor of him lingered.

No other thoughts invaded her peace. She rolled against him and let her hand explore his geography, concentrating her search on his southern latitudes.

He sucked in his breath. "I don't think my batteries have recharged quite yet."

"Ah, the flaw in the species," she murmured.

"It's not my fault. That's how I was designed."

"I know. No one said men were perfect."

He shuddered at her touch. "It amazes me that you can just keep going without stopping."

"Girls rule," she said, smiling to herself as she slid on top of him.

"So you were at the hospital all night, is that correct?" Nin tried not to cry.

They'd shown up at her door fifteen minutes ago, three of them, one from the county and two from the FBI's field office in Pittsburgh. All the sprites were asleep, praise God, and Nin herself had been on her way to bed when the light above the door started blinking and a little chime sounded in the back of the house. She had thought it would be Jo, standing there in the rain to tell her that Penny had passed away. Instead she'd seen badges and photo IDs in slick leather wallets. More agents occupied the cars beyond the sidewalk, their glowing cigarettes visible in the gloom.

So many.

Now Nin sat very straight and very stiff, while they looked at her with their stone-carved faces, their shoes shiny with rain.

They know.

Yes, so it seemed.

So now what?

Nin asked herself what Jo would do. Not the Jo of a week ago but the eagle-Jo; Nin's grandfather said that the eagle's true nature was what it displayed at the highest point of its flight. The eagle-Jo would either lie to these men nonchalantly, or simply refuse to talk at all without an attorney.

That sounded wise. Ask for a lawyer. But wouldn't such a request simply appear as an admission of guilt?

"Mrs. Ryan?"

Nin tried so hard to focus, to keep herself together, to be the eagle-Jo.

"I asked if you were at the hospital all night."

"Yes, that is what I said the first time."

"Visiting your friend."

"Is that a question?"

He leaned forward, so that his elbows rested on his knees, his hands clasped in front of him. "I'm not trying to be rude, Mrs. Ryan—"

"*Ms.*"

"Pardon me?"

"I am no longer married. I am set free. And what you said is true. I went to the hospital to visit Penelope, because I thought she was going to die, and I still think that may be the case. That man . . . he tried to kill her."

"I won't argue that," he allowed. "But before I prosecute

him for what he did to her, I have to find him. You understand that, don't you? Of course you do. And I have reason to
believe that you have information I need if I'm going to locate
him and bring him to justice."

"Why do you think I know anything? I take care of children for a living."

"You were at the hospital the whole night? When did you
come home?"

Nin shoved up one shoulder in what she hoped was a shrug
of indifference. "You'd be better off asking my sister-in-law.
She was here baby-sitting while I was away. After what I'd
seen of Penny's condition, I wasn't much in the mood for
looking at clocks."

"What's your sister-in-law's name?"

Say nothing more.

Nin told him. One of them wrote it down.

"Don't take offense to what I'm about to ask you," he said,
"because I'm just going through the motions of my rather
thankless job. You don't even have to answer if you choose
not to do so. You're well within your rights to wait until you
have legal representation present. But I am the special-agent-
in-charge. They call me the SAC. And the thing about us
SACs is, we have a whole heck of a lot of men and women we
can boss around, but even *we* have to report to someone a
notch higher up the food chain. And this case being what it is,
that notch is none other than the Bureau's director, the top of
the heap. The director telephones Senator Whitecross every
few hours with an update. And this is just an assumption, but
I'm fairly certain that, as a member of the National Security
Council, the director has personally briefed the president on
this matter."

He let that sink in.

It sank deep.

At the mention of the president—the *president!*—Nin almost caved. The enormity of what she'd done was like the night sky, too big to comprehend, yawning above her and shrinking her to insignificance. She remembered a village elder who once told her that the universe existed because of her. Choices, he claimed, were little acts of creation. Nin had always thought him a charlatan. But, looking back at what she'd done, she reconsidered. You normally go about your days making only little choices, but if you are pushed hard enough, long enough, then the next thing you know, the streets are full of protestors, the nightly news is stirring up a furor, and the president is being briefed, all because you made a big one.

"So you can see why I'm under a little pressure here," he said.

Nin just looked at him and waited.

"My question is this: can anyone verify that you were at the hospital that night?"

Nin thought of her Icky Errand, left undone. "I was there. It's true. Ask her brother, Joshua. Ask her parents. Ask the doctors. I drank coffee at the nurses' station. Ask them. They will tell you it's true." Though she felt a little better by making such an affirming statement, she knew that her story would turn to dust when they set up a time frame and found that no witness could account for her during a four-hour span, just long enough for her to abduct a man off the highway, shoot him, and do to his body what her uncle did to his rabid dog.

"We'll check those people out," he said. "I appreciate your working with us on this. But I do have one item I'd like you to take a look at." He held his hand up, the man behind him passed something to him, and then he offered it to Nin. "Have you ever seen this before?"

An evil icon gleamed in his fingers.

It took Nin a moment to make sense of it. Then she knew. *Oh, what have I done?* She must have left it lying around, one of her babes had found it and made it a toy, and now . . .

Quietly, solemnly, Nin rose from her chair and left the room.

Lucy was still watching when they led Nin out of the house.

She'd been sitting there with the rain thumping the truck for over an hour, muttering to herself, talking to God, half-inclined to sell her sullied soul for a cup of coffee. The streetlights were blurry auras that provided just enough illumination for her to see the hatchback belonging to Nin's sister-in-law rattle up to the curb. Immediately men emerged from the surrounding sedans, two of them escorting Ramona to the front door. This drove Lucy slightly mad, wondering what was going on, how Nin was holding up, and why Jo wasn't here to wonder with her. She'd driven by Jo's on the way here, but her spiffy new car wasn't in the driveway. Lord only knew.

"They found us out, didn't they?" she said, though her voice could hardly squeak through the constricted flue of her throat. As she watched the raincoated men usher Nin down the sidewalk, she enveloped the steering wheel in her arms as if it were a life preserver. The silhouette in the window had to be Ramona, who'd been called to stay with the kids while their mother was in custody.

In custody. It sounded so far-fetched.

"Of all of us to get hauled off to the pokey, it has to go and be Nin." Nin the truthful, Nin the Good Witch, Nin the one who'd come along only because the others needed her. Nin was as far removed from wickedness as West Virginia was from the North Pole. And yet she was being helped into the back of a mud-colored car by men with shoulder holsters.

Lucy withdrew into the shadows of her seat as the cars drove past her like a funeral procession. When the last of them had gone, she was alone on an empty street.

"Think, Lucille, *think*." She tried the woman in the visor mirror again, but found no help there. "Them feet of yours want to leave some marks, well now's the time to get them moving."

If only Tam hadn't talked her into bringing the gun. In a way, all of this was Lucy's own fault. Had she not allowed herself to get carried away by indignation, she wouldn't be camped out here, strategizing in the driving rain.

There were preparations that needed to be made, if only to protect the children. That's what Nin would want more than anything. Whatever happened, Nin couldn't take the fall for this. Lucy refused to allow it.

"I may be a lost cause myself, but those darlings aren't losing their mama."

She got out of the truck and ran toward the house, cutting across yards with impunity. A blast of thunder made it seem as if she were running across a war zone, dodging incoming artillery. When she reached the door, she didn't bother knocking, just barged inside like a piece of the storm.

Burrowed deep in warm tunnels of sleep, Jo didn't come instantly to her senses when the doorbell rang. It wasn't until Warren moved that she began to stir, reluctant to part from the incubator heat of the bed and the incense of their mingled scents. Reality encroached in small increments, reminding her that time was not her friend. She wiggled her toes.

"Ooo coo haa bee," Warren said, his voice muffled by the layers of sleepiness and sheets.

"What did you say?" Jo asked, her mouth against his stomach.

Warren lifted the duvet and peered down at her. "Who could that be?"

"You've forgotten me already?" She poked him in the side.

"No, I mean at the door. Hear that?"

A gentle chime sounded throughout the house. Twice.

"It's for me," Jo sighed.

"Expecting someone?"

"What time is it?"

He threw a look at the clock. "Four in the morning."

"It's going to be a horrendous day."

"I'll try not to take that personally."

The doorbell rang again.

"Do you think it's Caroline?" he wondered. He slipped out of bed and searched in the dark for his pants. "You should have called her. She's probably worried sick."

Though Jo tried to hold herself in the sleep caverns for as long as she could, like it or not she was now fully awake. Her first clear thought was of a bounding feline form, a cat cast in chrome. She threw the sheets to the side and lay there with the bed cooling around her.

Warren turned on the lamp.

Jo crunched her eyes shut.

"A thousand pardons," he said. "Can't find the ol' trousers."

"Wear mine."

Once more the chime sounded. This time it was followed by a knock.

"Not much for patience, are they?" Warren finally got his pants fastened and hurried barefoot down the hall, turning on lights as he went. Then suddenly he turned around, ran back into the bedroom, and kissed her. "You're incredible, if you don't mind my saying so."

Then he dashed away.

Jo sat up, hair drooping in her face, enjoying the smile while it lasted. Earnestly she wanted to hold on to this feeling, this unalloyed appreciation of life. For the last twenty-four hours she'd acted on her desires without premeditation and in doing so found release. She'd quit her job—Martin had begged her to stay but she'd left before he actually got on his knees, the poor fellow—and though she wouldn't advocate such radical actions as a cure-all, there was something to be said for extreme measures.

She heard conversation from the front of the house, and though she couldn't make out the voices, her psychic talents for picking up Lucy's vibes told her everything she needed to know.

Is this the last day of my life as a free person? Instead of answering herself in what had become an introspective habit, she slid into Warren's shirt and fastened two of the buttons, though why she bothered with modesty at this point, she didn't know.

The woman at the door resembled Lucy Campbell, except her hair was radically short, her forehead was lined with concern, and she was soaking wet. Warren said something about hoping instant was okay with everyone, then wisely excused himself to the kitchen.

Lucy looked toward the kitchen, then at Jo's bare legs, then toward the bedroom. "Did I miss the latest update on your life and times?"

"There are a few details I need to tell you about."

"I guess the hell so!"

"Lucy . . ." Jo took her by the hands. "I can't promise that things are going to turn around for us today."

"I don't expect you to. They took Nin to the courthouse."

"I thought you'd say that. Have they formally charged her with anything?"

"Don't know. I went by Terrell's to plead with him for some info, but he wasn't there."

"Did you try Hannah's?"

"Just drove by there a few minutes ago. Saw his car beside hers."

"He spent the night?"

"Yeah, seems to be some kind of epidemic."

Jo grinned. "Stop looking at me like that. How did you find me here, anyway?"

"You weren't at home. So I played a hunch."

"I wasn't even aware that you knew where he lived."

"I know where everybody lives. I'm the goddamn mail lady. Now let's go outside and discuss this. Tamaryn's out there waiting. She's got the boys. She stopped by to tell me she was skipping town, and I convinced her to talk to you first."

"She's leaving?"

"As fast as she can."

"For good?"

"*Forever,* from what I understand."

"Where on earth does she think she's going to go that they won't find her?"

"Beats me. Maybe you'll have more luck with her. She's one step away from going off the deep end, and being even more stubborn than usual."

"Sugar and cream?" Warren called from the kitchen.

"Black," Jo replied, her eyes fixed to Lucy's. "The blacker the better."

"We've got to get out of here," Lucy said sotto voce.

"If we run, they'll know we're guilty."

"They'll know it anyway as soon as Nin confesses."

"Any takers for toast?" Warren hollered. He sounded far too normal to be part of these psychedelic events. "I've even got real butter!"

Jo yelled, "We'll pass on the toast, thanks!" To Lucy she said, "Okay, here's the plan." She invented it as she went along, a seamstress without a pattern but a needle, at least, that wouldn't stop. "You and Tam follow me to my house. We'll get Caroline to sit with Matt and Brady, and then we'll go to Hannah's and tell her what's happened with Nin."

"My brother's there, remember? You want him hearing all of this?"

"No, I don't want him hearing anything, but I do want at least a little bit of his help. He's the only way we have of keeping tabs on the police. It's imperative that we know what they're up to, so we can stay—"

"One step ahead of them, yeah, I got it. Fine. What about a lawyer?"

"For Nin? What about the woman who represented her during the divorce? What's her name? Upshaw, isn't it? Do you think she does criminal law?"

"She moved."

"What?"

"To Philadelphia. Or so says her forwarding address."

"All right then. Rita Ingersol."

"Who? Ingersol? She's a lawyer?"

"No, but I'm sure she can hook us up with a briefcase-carrying juggernaut."

"Then let's hope she also hooks us up with the money to pay for it."

They heard Warren whistling to himself.

"So that's it," Jo said. "I'll be showered and changed in fifteen minutes. Meet me at the house."

"Whatever you say, Josephine. I'm not about to start doubting you at this point."

They hugged and parted ways.

Jo met Warren in the kitchen. He stood at the sink, shirtless, hands in the suds.

"Last night's dishes," he said.

"Were you eavesdropping again?"

"I already told you. I can't stay away from your eaves."

She stood behind him and put her arms around his waist.

"This is not going to end well, is it?" he said after awhile.

"That's yet to be decided." She rested her cheek against his back. "You know, there were certain times when I used to say, 'Such is life.' Have you ever said that?"

"Sure. Everyone does."

"Then everyone's wrong. The bad stuff, the unfair stuff—such is *not* life. Saying that is just our way of pretending we can't change things."

He dried his hands. "I don't know how to respond to that."

"It's easy. The next time something really great happens to you, or the next time you see a child ride a bike without training wheels for the first time, or get a raise at work, or laugh, I want you to say, 'Such is life.' Can you do that?"

"Will it make any difference?"

"I'd like to think so, if enough people say it at once. In the meantime, though"—she turned him around and kissed him on the neck—"let me do what I have to do, and accept my thanks for the most spectacular night in the sack I've ever had."

He blushed.

She drank his coffee and used his shower, enjoying both as much as she could, for fear that she'd never come back.

Chapter Twenty-seven

Caroline looked scared. Jo could see it in her face, despite the girl's noble efforts to dissemble her emotions. She agreed to watch the boys, and a switch must have been thrown in her heart over the last few days, because she didn't even mount a medium-sized argument.

"Nin is in jail," Jo said, trying to be as succinct as possible. "And before you come unglued, let me save us both some time and give you the pasteurized, homogenized version of the story."

Caroline stood there in her nightgown and stocking feet while Jo provided her with a summary of events, edited for content. Was an omission considered a lie? She didn't fret over it, cleaving instead to her instincts, perhaps for the first time in her life.

"I'll have my cell with me if you need to reach me. Now I want you to call Hannah, tell her we're on our way. Oh, and don't be surprised if Terrell answers the phone."

Caroline's eyes widened. "Terrell? Are you *serious?*"

"Will wonders never cease, huh?"

"Well it's about *time* . . ."

They took Tamaryn's pickup. Lucy rode in the middle. Beside her, Jo turned so that she could get a look through the back window at the truck bed, which was loaded with laundry baskets and bicycles.

"You planning a trip?" she asked.

"Was."

"Anywhere particular?"

"Prince William Sound."

"Oh. Right."

"It's in Alaska."

"You're running away to Alaska?"

"I was supposed to be on the road an hour ago. Roy'll be awake by six."

"So you're going to be gone by then?"

"I don't know, Jo," she said, her voice hardening. "Maybe I should just hang around here and wait to be sent to the gas chamber. Running sounds a lot better than that, eh?"

"Sounds fine if we run out of options. Absolutely smashing, in fact."

"No gas chamber in this state," Lucy said for whoever was interested.

No one was.

When they arrived at Hannah's bungalow, the rain stopped. It didn't fade to a drizzle like static clearing from a television screen. It simply went from downpour to not a drop. The air it left behind was clean and scrubbed, striated with thin strands of mist.

Tam shut off the engine and the wipers froze in the middle of the windshield.

"Someone turned the faucet off up there," Lucy said. "Took pity on us."

"About time someone did." Tam was lighting a cigarette even as she climbed out of the truck.

Ensconced in her chair once again but feeling as if she were floating, Hannah said goodbye to Terrell and watched him drive away under the steel-gray clouds. He stuck his arm from the window and waved. Hannah, feeling slightly tipsy, blew him a kiss.

"Enough with the mush, Jessler, get in here!"

She rolled toward the sound of Tam's voice, but not too

quickly, as she didn't want to disrupt the spell she was under. Had there ever, *ever* been such an evening? Had two lovers ever feasted upon each other with such abandon? *Lovers!* Hannah adored the sound of the word. She would have liked to shape that word into a pendant and worn it around her neck for all the world to look upon and covet. Though she tried not to smile because the others were so dour and wouldn't think it funny, she couldn't prevent the occasional giggle from rising like champagne bubbles. She concealed her uncontrollable chuckles as best she could by coughing and clearing her throat.

Everyone was in her kitchen. Except Nin. And that was because Nin was locked up. But even this distressing development couldn't entirely dry Hannah's wellspring of joy. She'd spent last night making love to the man she wanted more than functional legs. It was hard to see beyond that. "Our spy," she said, trying to look serious, "is on his way to the enemy castle, though he doesn't see how it's at all possible that Nin had anything to do with what happened to Jed."

"We're all possible," Jo said, flipping through her address book.

"What does that mean, *we're all possible?*" Lucy asked irritably. "I don't even know what that means. But I *do* know that we have to get Nin out of there before she implicates us all, and we better stash the truck somewhere before Roy blows a gasket and further complicates our lives. The last thing we need is that ogre of a man getting in the way."

"We can put the truck behind the house," Hannah said. "If you drive down the hill, you should be able to fit through the trees and find a place to park that can't be seen at all from the street, if that sounds good to you."

Without a word, Tam left through the back door, keys in hand.

"Lucy, did they have a warrant for Nin's arrest, because they couldn't just take her in without getting a judge to approve it, and if there's no warrant, then she can leave whenever she wants."

"I'm not sure about a warrant. I just saw them taking her away."

"Hello, Rita?" Jo said into the phone. "I'm sorry to bother you at this hour but I have another little problem . . ." She walked into the living room, talking as she went.

"Let me ask you something," Lucy said.

Hannah poured herself a glass of apple juice. "Is this a Terrell question?"

"Do you honestly expect any other kind of question after you just shared a pillow with my little brother?"

"Well, no, but . . ." Hannah took a drink and licked her lips. "Why are you smiling?"

"Because I knew that no one could ever be good enough for him. And here you are."

Flushing, Hannah looked down at her glass.

"It's true. Bigger and better than I ever hoped. Do me a favor, will you?"

"Name it."

"Marry him."

Hannah laughed and tossed the hair from her face. She returned the juice carton to the fridge. "I don't think that's entirely up to me, but I'll be sure to say yes in at least three different languages if the proposal is made. Thanks, Lucy." She hit the wheels and two revolutions later she was meeting Lucy's embrace with her own.

"Don't thank me yet, child. You haven't heard the question." She dropped down to Hannah's level but didn't let go of her hand. "If by some Jo-produced miracle we make it out of this with our lipstick on straight, are you ever going to tell him what happened?"

Hannah's smiled dissipated. "Maybe you should ask me that again after I've had some time to think about it. Right now I'd rather just be happily inebriated, if I could."

"You bet. It's a fine way to be."

Jo came in from the living room at the same moment that Tam stepped through the back door. "Our attorney dilemma is no more," she said. "The old cerise is pretty super, after all."

"Rita has a lawyer on retainer?" Hannah asked.

"Better. There are members of AGNES who *are* lawyers, and apparently they make their living on cases like this."

"There ain't no cases like this," Tam said.

"Agreed. How's the truck?"

"Invisible. So what's next?"

"Follow our spy and storm the castle. Hannah, you'll have to drive."

"I'm headed that way. The queen of locomotion, at her finest." She zoomed through the house, chasing down her purse, her thoughts swimming between Nin and Terrell, Terrell and Nin, side to side, hot to cold. On one hand she wanted to turn on the radio and sing off-key with whatever was playing, and on the other she wanted to crawl into a corner and pray. How could the best day of her life also be the worst?

When she got outside, the darkness was losing its grip on the eastern sky and the van door was open and waiting.

"Like a tramp to her ramp," Tam declared.

"For the hoist I rejoiced," Hannah replied.

The machine rumbled her inside and Lucy slung the door shut.

"Shit!" Tamaryn yelled. "Look out!"

Hannah hit the brakes as a girl on a skateboard passed two feet in front of the bumper. The kid wore headphones over a pink beret.

Tam unrolled her window. "Hey, stupid, stay out of the street!"

Jo leaned forward and peered into the dim morning light. "Looks like she's going the same place we are. Hannah, you'd better hurry."

Tam's hands insisted on tapping, shifting, roaming, so she made two fists and held them against her knees. It was already after six. Roy was up and pissing battery acid by now. Going totally nucking futs, as they used to say in school. Which one of his caveman cronies would he call first? Or would he just cruise the streets, the mercury of his anger rising at every intersection? His hate for Jo being fairly well-documented, he'd likely go to her house right away, and that was the last place Tam wanted him to be. Because the knights were there, Lancelot and Galahad, two spotless souls that were hopefully learning by example the kind of man they shouldn't grow up to be.

"Real men are askers, right, Jo?"

"I'm . . . not sure I know what you mean."

"They ask, that's what I'm saying. About how your day went, what color of mini-blinds you prefer, why you like hugging so much. All the men who are worth anything, that's the most important thing to them. Asking. Don't you think?"

"I do. I think that a lot."

"Me too." She screwed her fists harder against her legs. "Me too."

The closer they got to the courthouse, the more she realized they were driving into pandemonium in the making. Knots of people had formed all over the grass, and the knots were beginning to tighten, forming bigger knots as their members shook hands and traded names. The signs were back with something to prove, bigger and more numerous than ever, their slogans usually done in pink, but red also holding its own. The letters of one sign had been drawn to appear as if they were bleeding: THICKER THAN WATER.

"Better pull over, Jessler. Won't be anyplace to park around the building."

"Just for the record," Lucy said, "when we were passing out sheets, I didn't have any intention of starting either a fashion trend or a civil war."

"Don't look now." Tam pointed down the street. "Thugs at ten o'clock."

They wore boots and one of them carried a Confederate flag. How many were there? Fifteen? Twenty? They were a mixed lot. Half of them looked like punk rockers brought back from the dead, with spiky hair and pale faces and even a couple of black capes. The rest of them, far more frightening, could have been straight from the Young Aryan Brotherhood.

"Skinheads," Lucy said.

They too had brought a sign. It bore only a single word: MURDERERS.

"Could this get any worse, because I really wish someone would tell me how this could be any more awful than it is, it's bad and somebody's going to get hurt, I know it, and it'll be our fault when it happens."

"No, Jessler, it won't be our fault. We're not pulling their strings, making them throw punches. We're not the ones who raised them to hate people. Now can you please just find a spot to park this tank?"

They ended up a block away. While they waited for Hannah, Tam and Jo walked to the other side of the van, looking off in the direction of the courthouse.

"I finally figured out what's different," Tam said.

"Different about what?"

"Us." She exhaled smoke through both nostrils. "You and me. Lucy and Hannah. Nin. Everything we do now, every decision we make, it all means something. Either we get caught or we go free. That's it. There are no little side streets, no detours, just those two whoppers. And every step we take puts us closer to one of those two. And it didn't used to be like that. Most of the things I did before"—she gestured vaguely with her cigarette—"take 'em or leave 'em. Like when I went shopping and found a sale on Granny Smith apples, ninety-seven cents a pound. Big deal." She thought about saying more, then frowned at herself. "Anyway, that's how it is."

"Here," Jo said. "Give me that."

"It's a little late to ask me to quit smoking."

"Who said anything about quitting?" Jo put the cigarette to her lips, inhaled, coughed. She took a second drag, and it went down easier this time. She handed it back. "Thanks."

Tam smirked. "Picking up a new vice?"

"Nope. Just wanted to see you smile, babe."

Jo and Lucy led the way on foot, and Tam faded back with Hannah a few paces behind them. With the parting of the rain, the clouds began to unlock and separate. Tam was thankful for the sun. Bad things happened in the rain and the dark. The sun made you believe you had a fighting chance.

"Let me ask you something," she said quietly, so that only Hannah could hear.

Hannah worked her wheels. "I'm listening."

"How was he?"

Hannah appeared pleasantly surprised by the question. "Both a savage and a gentleman."

"Thought so. Good for you."

"Don't speak too soon. The next time he and I are together may be when he comes to the prison for a conjugal visit."

"Yeah. Could be."

By the time they reached the courthouse, the preliminary shouts had already commenced. It was actually the pinkies who launched the first of the vocal attacks; the mere sight of the black-clad arrivals set their blood boiling. Tam counted five cops milling between the two parties, deputies imported from nearby counties. The pinkies kept to the grass around the building. The punks and skinheads stood in the street, prowling, like lions sizing up a herd of gazelle.

"We should hurry," she said.

"You're not waiting on me." Hannah stroked faster.

As they passed by the crowd, the weird thing was how often Jo was recognized. Random women bedecked in various layers of pink approached her, some just to introduce themselves, others to congratulate her for a variety of vague accomplishments. Tam felt like a bodyguard chaperoning a VIP.

"Hey, Hollywood!" Hannah called as a pair of women traded places behind a disposable camera, lining up beside Jo for a picture. "Can I have your autograph?"

Jo held up her hands and mouthed the words, *No pen.*

"Guess Ingersol is talking about her like she's the local Wonder Woman," Tam said.

"So maybe she is."

"Yeah. It wouldn't surprise me." On her way up the courthouse steps, she scanned the two bands of belligerents, but Roy wasn't among them. She knew it was only a matter of time before he appeared, demanding custody of the boys, in which case Tamaryn would have to kill him.

She waited at the door while Hannah took the long route up the recently built handicap incline, her eyes on the crowd.

★ ★ ★ ★ ★

Nin sat very still in a room without windows.

She was proud of one thing, and it went like this: the shakes had not come as a result of the murder she'd seen committed, but rather for failing her friends; indeed, she'd grown up in an inhospitable environment, and if you endangered the survival of those around you, they disposed of you. So Jed's death didn't bother her as much as it might otherwise have, as he was a threat to others. That very same environment had also taught her the incalculable worth of family. The shakes had seized her when she let her family down. But she was Nin the rock. Though the mountain might tremble, the ground below remains. She'd forgotten this, but hours ago when they brought her to this chamber, she'd remembered, and was now more pleased with herself than she'd been in quite some time. She had *recovered*.

"Do you want to tell us about this?" they asked her, displaying the hood ornament.

In response, Nin examined herself. She wore one of her newer housedresses, a nice floral pattern. Her arms, that Dan Ryan had once referred to as flab factories, were not quivering, nor were the feet in her shoes. The only part of her that wasn't comfortable was her fanny, and that was because the folding metal chair was too small, and she was cramped. There was nothing worse than being leaned on by federal agents when your butt was in a bad chair. Thinking about her posterior reminded her of the Ass Ends lingerie store, and all at once she felt like laughing. That proved to be her medicine. An instant later she recalled that she was Nin the constant, Nin the unmoved.

The policemen, knowing nothing of this, couldn't be blamed for thinking she was going to confess. "Ms. Ryan? Could you please talk to us?"

Nin turned her serene gaze upon them and said nothing.

And so it went.

Finally they brought in a woman, a state investigator called Charae, assuming that the simpleminded Eskimo lady wouldn't be so intimidated if there wasn't a man in the room. It was sad, how often grown men equated education with wisdom. Nin hadn't graduated high school. And look how she dresses, and how she sits and stares! Let us treat her as we would a child.

Nin felt too sorry for them to smile at their ignorance.

Charae explained Nin's rights, positive that Nin was unaware of them. Nin wasn't being charged with a crime, the men only hoped she'd say something that would give them a solid lead, and she'd frustrated them by remaining silent. Charae went on to say that Nin should contact legal representation as soon as possible, because at nine a.m. the FBI was going to ask for the necessary warrants to search her home and possibly arrest her. Then she asked if Nin needed a ride home.

Finally Nin spoke. "No, honey. Jo will come for me."

While she waited, she called home and made assurances that everything was under control, a statement which no one would have believed had they felt the intensity within the courthouse. The federal agents had commandeered an entire wing of the second floor, and even at the crack of dawn were tripping over themselves in an effort to get from fax machine to radio, from the parking lot outside to the helicopter on the roof.

As predicted, Jo arrived within the hour.

She pulled Nin close. "Have you eaten?"

That wasn't the question Nin had expected. "Only a fruit pie from the vending machine."

"Confab first, then breakfast." She led them all to the end of the hallway. The county assessor's office wouldn't open until nine, so it seemed a safer place. "There. Bathroom."

Tam kicked open the stall doors. "We're clear."

"I'll stay by the door," Lucy said.

Hannah rolled up beside Nin and took her hand.

Nin smiled down at her. "And how are you today?"

"Terrible and wonderful. You?"

"A little tired, but I'm used to that."

From beyond the window came the sounds of shouting.

"Better give us the condensed version," Jo said. "There aren't many sands left in the hourglass."

Nin told them everything.

"But I am better now," she concluded. "The shakes are all gone. Maybe they went away with the rain."

"They didn't fingerprint you?" Hannah asked.

"No."

"Did you have anything to drink during the interview?"

"Yes. They brought me water."

"In a glass, or was it a plastic bottle?"

"A glass. Why?"

Hannah looked at Jo. "They took her prints."

"You think?"

"Absolutely. They've got dozens of officers out marching through the woods and over every piece of grassland in the county, and they're all leading dogs, trying to catch Jed's scent, at least they were until it started raining, thank God, and screwed everything up. So now all they have is a print off the door handle, which happens to match the print off the Sheridan garage, and you can bet they already tried them against Rita Ingersol's and probably a lot of her helpers as well. Then Nin pops up, so they find some sneaky way of getting *her* prints to see if they're the same."

"They can do that? Take your fingerprints without asking you?"

"Legally? I don't know. But *can* they do it? Sure. You'd bend the rules too if you had the Oval Office insisting on results and the entire country watching you on TV."

"I didn't know," Nin said. "I should have been more careful."

"It wasn't your fault," Jo told her. "Besides, it works out in your favor, since they won't get a match with your prints. Now we just need to put together a plausible story about what you were doing with a hunk of Jed's car at your house." She hastily explained the legal counsel that AGNES was providing. "They should be calling this morning."

Somewhere down the hall, a window broke.

"We better get going before they bring this place down around our heads. We'll talk in the van, decide what to do next."

"I'm leaving," Tam reminded them.

"So you've said. Let's go. And Nin?" She gave her a thumbs-up. "You did well."

"I did nothing, really. Just sat there. But I am glad it turned out to be the right thing." She fell into step beside Tamaryn as Jo led them down the hall. Even before they reached the door, they heard the chants and the banging of what sounded like a tambourine. Nin had never personally seen a protest march or a public demonstration, and the first thing that struck her was the almost tangible emotion in the air—even before she was out the door. Two armed deputies hurried outside in front of them, one of them wearing what must have been a bulletproof vest.

The morning sun revealed a scene from someone else's life. Surely Nin had nothing to do with the 300 pink-waving individuals pressed up against a barricade made of sawhorses. And she couldn't have been responsible for the identical barricade on the other side of the street, behind which were jammed several dozen young men in jackboots and leather. The police officers who patrolled the no-man's-land in between these barriers carried nightsticks and looked terribly uncertain of themselves. One of them was Terrell Campbell. He was shouting through a megaphone to *Stay back! Everyone just make nice and stay in your own playground!* Unaccustomed to dealing with social expression on such a dramatic scale, the deputies looked ill-prepared to handle anyone who disobeyed Terrell's command.

"I think it's safe to say we hit a nerve," Lucy said.

At the end of the street, where the van was parked, three separate news teams were prepping their equipment. One man in a suit was already giving an interview. Nin recognized him as the SAC who'd brought her in this morning. Sheriff Cantrell stood behind him.

She followed the others into the crowd.

Because of Hannah's chair, they were forced to keep to the sidewalk, which put them within arm's reach of the sawhorse fence. Jo walked point—"Excuse us, pardon us, coming through"—with Nin in back, trying not to stare at the two women dressed in disturbingly familiar pink robes, garments that could have come straight from the bottom of a certain watery grave. Nin had dyed the fabric for the five original outfits, never dreaming they'd one day be all the rage amongst social deviants and political outcasts.

Suddenly the horde shifted. Nin lost her balance. Women pressed in around her, and everywhere there were pink headbands and pink lipstick, and they kept pushing, chanting now as a single voice. *"Jus-tiss! Jus-tiss!"*

Nin staggered off the sidewalk. Her knee struck the wooden crossbar of a sawhorse. Arms pumped the air around her. The heat from the bodies, the energy of their anger—

"Nin, where are you?"

"Jus-tiss! Jus-tiss!"

"Josephine?" She saw Jo swimming back for her. Nin displaced several of the protestors and worked her way forward. Her leg smarted.

Jo said something but it went unheard when the rowdies across the street let go with several air horns, and for a few seconds the masses fell silent. Many of them covered up their ears, such was the volume of the klaxons.

The horns faded. "Jo?"

"Don't fall behind!"

"I am trying not to!"

The voices rose again on both sides. The deputies gestured with their truncheons for people to keep back. A gang of men had jumped into a truck bed for a better vantage point, and they screamed obscenities, making frequent use of the word *murderers.* They were met with the words *oppressors* and *fascists,* hurled at them with such lung power that Nin wouldn't have been surprised if the men were blown from the truck by the gale. Terrell stormed through the middle of the melee, adding his own amplified voice to the mayhem, his words of choice being *tear gas.*

But no one took his threat seriously. Nin worked through the mob, but her way only became more difficult as people shoved closer to the barricade.

A sign clipped her across the brow.

"Ouch!" She put her hand on her forehead and it came away with blood.

Jo reached back and grabbed her by the arm. The others were out of sight, swallowed up whole.

More air horns, and now the intonation began again, slowly, picked up on the fringes of the crowd but building as more throats joined the beat.

"*Jus-tiss!*"

Nin didn't want justice at the moment. She only wanted to make it out of there.

And then, just when she thought she was nearly free, a girl with pink hair sailed through space. She landed on the concrete at Nin's feet, a tangle of boots and tube top. Nin pulled free of Jo's grasp, and before she even thought about it, she bent down, took the gamine under the armpits, and lifted her to her feet.

"*Nin, what are you doing?*"

The girl did a strange little move with her head, almost as if she were clearing it of debris. She looked at Nin, eyes like a child, then turned and ran into the street, screaming threats at the skinheads at the far curb.

"Honey, no!" Nin shouted.

Too late. The girl was almost there, her fingers bared like claws.

"Terrell, stop her!"

She never knew if Terrell actually heard her or just sensed the trouble at his back. Either way, he turned as the girl was sprinting past, her youthful face aged by hate, while the skinheads urged her to bring it on.

Terrell intercepted her. Almost.

He dropped the megaphone and backpedaled when the sudden weight careened into his chest. His back hit the barrier, directly in front of the men with their smooth white skulls and silver earrings. The girl wildcatted in his arms.

Nin didn't realize she was moving until she was halfway across the street. She was peripherally aware of Sheriff Cantrell and the FBI man sprinting toward her, and the deputies, and even Jo, running behind her. But then they disappeared as tunnel vision took over, and all she saw was Terrell pitching backward over the sawhorse, the girl thrashing on top of him, the skinheads swatting at her as she fell.

The girl raked one of them across the face.

He howled and recoiled. One of his friends swung in retaliation. Terrell was now on his back near the curb, trying to hold the girl and stand up at the same time, but the men enfolded him in their assault. The frenzy ignited the crowd around them. In a moment Terrell was lost from sight. Whistles blew. Sirens warbled to life.

Nin crashed into the ring of skinheads and sent one of them sprawling. And there was Terrell and the girl, with two men on top of them, arms flailing. Nin grabbed the nearest one by the back of the jacket and heaved, throwing him off the heap. But then she was hit from the side by a tidal wave of bodies, and everyone was shouting and kicking, and Nin toppled. She broke her fall with her hands, landing beside Terrell. His uniform was red. The girl was bleeding.

Nin pushed the man who was straddling Terrell's legs and punching the girl in the back. She put her weight behind the blow, sending him tumbling into the mass of kicking legs. Someone stepped on her foot. She winced but didn't quit, rolling the girl off Terrell and searching for the source of the blood. The girl's eyelids fluttered, her mouth open in a silent scream.

"Stay with me, honey! You hear me? You stay with me now!"

The girl's tube top had been torn away. Blood was smeared across her neck and chest. Deputies hurled themselves into the swarm, nightsticks swinging to clear a path. Nin ran her hands down the girl's body, talking to her as she worked, but if the girl had been cut then the wound had simply vanished, which of course wasn't possible, so that could only mean—

Nin turned her head.

Terrell held his stomach with both hands. Blood was everywhere.

"*No!*" Nin let go of the girl and put her hands on top of Terrell's. "*No, you got that, mister? No!*"

His eyes were closed, his lips moved. Nin put as much of her body against his as she could, as if by force of her own physical presence she could prevent the vital fluids from escaping.

"*I said NO!*"

She wanted to ask for a doctor, for someone to please call the paramedics, for just a little bit of help here holding this man's intestines inside his body. And maybe she did say these things. She wasn't sure exactly what was happening. She just kept thinking of Jed, lying on the ground just like this, cupping his guts and trying so hard not to die.

Chapter Twenty-eight

CHAPEL.

Breathing through her mouth, her body torqued by an occasional spasm, Hannah stared at the word on the door until the letters made sense. From far beyond the pain surfaced a dim memory. Five unknowing women marching through this very portal. Could it have been eight days ago?

After that, Hannah willed herself to think no more. Better to remain blank.

She fought with the door and let herself inside. The small sanctuary was empty. She batted her wheels and the chair obediently trundled down the carpeted aisle between the pews. The lights were soft here, not the revealing glare of those in the hall. And the smell was different, less institutionalized, clean but not antiseptic. A candelabra stood on the center of the altar. Hannah was thankful that no one had put a flame to the wicks. Fire was supposed to be comforting, and right now any promise of comfort was false.

She touched her eyes, but still found no tears.

Her body was holding back. That's what was so sickening. She couldn't cry, couldn't use the bathroom, could hardly even produce enough saliva to moisten her mouth. It was as if her mind had pulled a lever, shutting her down until the time came for release. But even this she could have endured, had it been her only test. Yes, it was making her ill, but she could deal with that. The words were killing her, though. Two words, like hammer strokes against her ear.

My.

Fault.

Had she not shot Jed Whitecross, surgeons would not have their hands inside Terrell's stomach right now. During the riot in front of the courthouse, he'd been stabbed when one of the skinheads pulled a knife. He'd been in the OR for nearly two hours. She'd heard one of the medics say that he'd never seen so much blood.

With trembling arms, Hannah pushed herself out of her chair.

She fell like a broken doll. Her legs were nothing—useless mush. She lay on the carpet with her face against the floor while the chair silently rolled backwards and bumped into a pew. She tasted carpet fibers on her lips. She waited to cry, *needed* to cry, but there was only the timpani beating of the two words and nothing more.

After an interminable amount of time, she crawled toward the altar.

She dug her elbows into the rug and dragged herself along, her mouth hanging open and her hair in her eyes. She inched forward until her head bumped the altar's wooden base. She rested her chin on the floor, then reached out, so that the fingers of one hand made contact with the altar. There she remained, alone with the sounds.

Myfaultmyfaultmyfaultmyfault . . .

"I'm really starting to hate this place," Jo said.

The four of them had taken over one of the glass-enclosed waiting rooms just off the corridor leading to the operating room. Magazines were fanned across the table and a coffee machine stood against the wall. No one read a magazine or drank any coffee.

Hands seemed very important. Lucy's dangled between her knees. She sat in one of the well-padded chairs but didn't lean back. She sat up straight, arms hanging through her legs.

Tamaryn had made fists of her hands and methodically tapped them together, knuckles against knuckles. She kept looking at the clock. Nin's hands were lined with dried blood. She held them palms-up in her lap and scrutinized them as if to read her fortune in their blood-caked creases.

And Jo's hands? Why, she was using them to hold the world together, of course.

That's what it felt like. The music had been building ever since they waved that first bat at Jed, and now it was reaching a crescendo, its notes so discordant they were finally shaking things to pieces. Jo had her hands full, throwing a stopgap here, mending a fracture there, but every time she turned to deal with one problem, another crack appeared behind her.

And what was worse? They'd lost their ace in the hole. A few hours ago, Jo had at least been able to console herself with the knowledge that they still had Terrell on their side. Even if Jed's corpse floated to the surface and they found themselves facing murder charges, Terrell would fight for them, would make phone calls for them, would maybe even lie for them. Jo didn't realize how integral he'd been to her confidence until he was gone.

"Tamaryn," she said. "You shouldn't be here."

"Where else am I going to go?" Tam replied without feeling.

"Roy could show up any second."

"You want me to say it again? Where else am I going to go?"

"I'm just saying . . ."

"I know. But I ain't leaving until I hear about Terrell. But I do need a smoke. Come with me, Luce?"

Lucy didn't move.

"Lucille?"

"Huh?" She shook out of her funk. "Sure. It's just . . .

that's my little brother in there."

Jo had never heard Lucy's voice sound so small. She and Tamaryn got up and left the room, as quiet as ghosts.

"Nin? Can I get you anything?"

Nin was silent a long time before responding. Perhaps she'd found a clue to the meaning of it all in the lines of her palm. When she spoke, it was in little more than a whisper. "Tell me about the answering machine."

Jo shifted in her chair, edging a bit closer. "What did you say?"

Nin lifted her head. "All those many long nights ago, on your front porch as we were all leaving the evening before painting the cabin, I wondered why you were doing this. Why you cared. You told me to ask you one day about the answering machine. So now I am asking."

Jo closed her eyes and there was Chuck at the kitchen table.

She comes through the door after work and finds him sitting in front of a microwaved meal, wearing only his torn chinos. His belly is a sandbag over his belt.

Long day? he asks.

They all are anymore. I thought you were working tonight.

Does it look like I'm working? They didn't need me. Said come back Monday.

Jo sheds her jacket and her shoes. Where's Sweet?

At a skating party or something like that. You're supposed to pick her up at nine.

I am? Why can't you pick her up?

She wants you to.

Jo curbs the next remark that comes to mind. It's Friday, and all week she's been looking forward to getting away, if only for a few hours. She hasn't seen any of her friends in two weeks. Work and home and vice versa. Lucy said she'd call and they'd set some-

thing up. Jo leaves the kitchen and goes into the dining room, where the telephone sits on the sideboard. She stops in front of it. Beside the phone is an answering machine. The NEW MESSAGE button isn't flashing.

Chuck?

Yeah?

Did Lucy happen to call?

Don't know. I haven't been here very long.

Well, did you check the messages?

Chuck doesn't respond.

And in that silence, Jo knows the truth. One day about a month ago she even caught him doing it. He didn't hear her come in, and when she walked into the dining room, he was erasing the tape. Maybe Lucy called tonight, but the tape has been rewound, and by this simple act, Jo is confined.

She wonders why she always feels as if she's running against rewind.

What occurs to her as she stands there is that thing about circus elephants. Supposedly the animal trainers are able to keep the elephants under control with only a slender string tied around their legs. The elephants feel the resistance, and from prior conditioning assume the leash is unbreakable.

She walks back into the kitchen, stares at Chuck's back.

What time am I supposed to pick her up? she asks dully.

Nine.

I better be there by quarter till. Sometimes they get out early.

Jo opened her eyes and said, "Let me start by telling you about a calendar. . . ."

The waiting-room door swung open. Dr. Cole stuck her head inside. "Ladies?"

Jo jumped to her feet. "How is he?"

"You mean Mr. Campbell? I don't know. No word yet.

I'm here about Penelope."

Nin stood up. "Penny? Is she . . . ?"

"She's awake." Dr. Cole smiled. "You look as relieved as I am."

"Thank You, Lord," Nin exclaimed to the ceiling. She put her hand on her chest and sighed.

"When did she come out of it?" Jo asked.

"Nearly an hour ago. We've already run a series of tests on her, and there's no sign of permanent damage to the brain. Her family is with her now. I'm sure she'd like to see you."

Is that true? Jo wondered. *When she learns that Jed is among the missing, will she want to see anyone at all?* Jo was happy that Penny had escaped the coma, but how could she face the woman, knowing that she'd murdered her boyfriend? Jed had nearly become a murderer himself, but Penny had pulled through and was probably fully prepared to forgive him even this offense upon her person.

"Are you coming?" the doctor asked. She looked bewildered.

"Yes. Yes, of course." They left the waiting room and followed Dr. Cole to the elevator.

Nin veered toward the exit sign. "I better get the others and let them know. They'll want to see her, and I don't believe Tam intends to stay around very long."

"I'll meet you there."

"Tell you what," Dr. Cole said. "While you're with Penelope, I'll run and check on Mr. Campbell for you."

"I'd appreciate it. Thanks."

"My pleasure."

"Keep him in guarded condition for me."

"Pardon?"

"Nothing." She walked away.

As she clipped down the hall, scanning the numbers on the

doors, she sent a bucket down into her well, hoping to reel in the feeling she'd had a few hours ago when she woke up in Warren's bed. Though already receding in her memory, enough of the heady experience remained that she smiled to herself—a true smile, despite Terrell fighting for his life and the FBI at her heels. She knocked on Penny's door. "Avon calling!"

Penny's parents greeted her, and they spent a few seconds hugging and wiping tears, then excused themselves so that Jo could be alone with their daughter.

Jo waited until the door closed behind them. Then she sauntered to the bed. "I said Avon calling. Rumor has it you could use a little eye shadow."

Penny, most of her face swaddled in bandages, smiled as best she could. "I'm glad you came."

"You think I'd ditch you?"

"I look like hell, don't I?"

"Yes. Like a woman who's fought off death and lived to tell the tale."

"You're supposed to lie to me and say I'm beautiful."

"Living to tell the tale *is* beautiful. Can I get you anything?"

"Your hand."

Penny's fingers were cold and her grasp was weak. Tubes snaked into her arm and the part of her face not covered in gauze was a lumpy brown landscape surrounding a pair of lusterless eyes.

"What's the matter?" Penny asked after Jo had been staring for awhile.

"You know when people say, 'It's a long story'?"

"Uh-huh."

"They don't know the half of it. Are you sure you don't need anything? Juice? Water? Shot of bourbon?"

"No, thanks."

"A date with that good-looking orderly down the hall?"

"No, Jo. Really. I'm fine."

Jo paused for a beat, then said, "They told you about Jed, didn't they?"

"A little. They said no one can find him. And the police think he's been kidnapped, but no one's called about a ransom. Is that true?"

"More or less."

"So it's not true. I got the impression they were holding something back. Jo, everybody else is lying to me. So you can't."

"I can't, huh?" She glanced at the little window in the door, but there was no sign of anyone lurking on the other side. "You're right, Pen. I only have time these days for truth. So here it is all at once. The cops believe that Jed was abducted as punishment for what he did to you. In fact, the whole thing has turned into anarchy. People from all over the Eastern seaboard are pouring into town and jumping to one side or the other of the line that's been drawn in the sand. Terrell got hurt when that line was crossed. Belle Springs is the top news story from here to California. Riot-control specialists have started arriving from Washington. The police still haven't found Jed, and I don't think they ever will. And since we're freebasing truth here, then I have to say that I hope they never do find him."

Penelope's pulverized eyes widened. "Why would you say that?"

"One reason? Because you almost died, that's why."

"But that doesn't make any . . ."

"What? It doesn't make *sense?* Is that what you were about to say? I have every right to hate the man for what he did to you. Hating, as it turns out, is the least I can do to him."

"You're a good person, Jo. Good people don't hate."

"I'm still a good person. But I dabble in insurrection."

"You don't understand . . ."

"What's not to understand? You've allowed yourself to fall into a pattern. You've been *abiding.* And I know that abiding has an inertia that's hard to resist, but if you just step back and—"

"Jo, Jed Whitecross did not do this to me."

"Please, Penny, let's just push on through the denial stage, okay?"

"No, really. It's true." Her eyes filled with tears. "It wasn't Jed. It was *never* Jed."

"What the hell are you talking about? Of course it was Jed."

"*No.*" She shook her head. "It wasn't."

Jo wrapped her fingers around the metal bed railing. "Okay, Pen, you can quit fibbing to me now, because I thought we agreed that truth was very important, and this particular bit of truth is even more important than you realize, so let's just stop kidding ourselves, alright?"

"Joshua did it."

Jo leaned all of her weight on the railing for support. "Penny. What are you saying?"

"My brother. My own *brother,* Jo. He's always been rough with me, all the time we were growing up, but lately it's been getting a lot worse—"

Jo breathed harder, each gasp a blade down her throat.

"—and after your party, when Jed found out that my brother hit me, he was so mad he said he was going to kill him, but I talked him out of it, told him it was okay, told him that Josh was going to get help—"

Jo swayed, her body bent over the bed, her mouth open but no more air coming in.

"—but I didn't want to say anything because he was my

brother. I've never once said anything to anyone about what he does to me. I know that's wrong of me, but you can't just do that to your own flesh and blood. He really just needs medical help. You know what I mean? Jo, what's wrong? Jo?"

Jo reeled back from the railing and bumped into the adjacent bed. "That's not true, it can't be true, Joshua did not put you in this bed, it was Jed, *Jed Whitecross goddammit.*"

Penny wiped her eyes and shook her head.

"It has to be Jed."

"Jo, it *wasn't.* But I wish it had been, I wish it was him instead of my own brother, but Jo, that's not how it happened, I'm so sorry . . ."

The room pitched like a rolling ship. Jo dropped to one knee, hanging on the bed.

"Jo, what is it?" Penny cried. "Jo, please!"

Lucy burst through the door. "What's with all the shouting in here?"

Jo lurched to her feet. She leaned in Lucy's direction and let gravity take over. Nin caught her just before she fell into the hall. "Josephine? Are you sick?"

". . . wrong one . . . it was the wrong one . . ."

"Wrong what, honey?"

"What's she talking about?" Tam asked. "Jo? What's up?"

Jo took Tam by the back of the head and pulled her close. The words tripped out of her, jagged and bitter. "We killed an innocent man. We killed a . . ." And that was it. Nothing else would come out of her.

She shoved herself free of their arms and ran blindly down the hall.

"Jo!" one of them yelled after her.

But Jo could not distinguish their voices, nor keep her legs from trying to outrun the truth.

★ ★ ★ ★ ★

Encased in walking shoes with padded drugstore inserts, Lucy's feet took over. She clipped to the junction of the two hallways and looked around the corner in time to see Jo disappear into the stairwell. In the opposite direction, she saw a sweat-stained surgeon heading her way— Terrell's doctor. Tam and Nin came running. And directly in front of her, just now poking his head out of the elevator, was Roy Soza.

"And me in the middle," she said. With Jo's abdication, Lucy was in charge. Or at least she felt that way. And now, as luck would have it, everything was going down at the same time. Terrell's operation was over and Jo had said they'd killed the wrong guy and Roy was coming this way. That settled it. First things first.

She spun around. "Tam, get back."

Tam saw Roy at the last second and ducked through the nearest door.

"Nin, do what you can with him."

"But what do I—"

"*Improvise.*" With that, Lucy took off and met the doctor halfway. She pulled up just short of a collision. "My brother is alive."

The doctor removed his green paper cap and nodded brusquely. "That he is. You're Lucy, right?"

The wind rushed out of her in relief. "Yeah. His sister. So he's really fine? Everything's shipshape, good as new?"

"I wouldn't say as good as new. The scar from our procedure will actually be far more pronounced than the one from the wound itself, but other than scar tissue, you won't be able to tell someone tried to play chop suey with his organs." He gave her a nominal smile. "I hope he won't mind living on pudding for a few days."

"Good God, the boy'll think he's died and gone to heaven. Can I see him?"

"Not yet, I'm afraid. You'll have to wait at least a few hours."

"Sure, I understand. It's not like I won't be able to find something to do in the meantime. Thank you. Thank you with everything inside me."

"You're welcome."

Lucy wondered if the surgeon was shocked by how quickly she scrambled away as soon as their conversation had ended. No, he was used to happy family members rushing off to trumpet the news, as giddy as children. But the last thing Lucy felt was giddiness. When she got back to the intersection, Roy was waving his arms truculently and Nin, may the spirits bless and keep her, was unflappable in the face of his ranting.

". . . and don't you tell me she *left*," Roy said. "I don't want to hear that from you, of all people. My damn wife did not leave me."

"Your damn wife sure did," Lucy snapped. She crossed her arms and stood beside Nin. If Roy was looking for a fight, he'd come to the right place. Lucy had to pull her hands tightly against her chest to keep them from tearing the man's eyeballs out. "Tam drove off around midnight, said she'd send me a postcard whenever she got where she's going."

"You can't tell me—"

"I sure *can* tell you, you sad little toad of a man. About the most worthless example of a husband I ever had the misfortune of knowing, that's what you are. If you cared half as much for Tamaryn as you do for your four-wheel-drive, you might have seen what a royal shit you've been to her for the last five years. Hell, I can't believe men like you still exist in this day and age. Think by now you'd have evolved into a higher life form, like an ape or something. Now get out of my face before I kick those teeny little gonads of yours into your brainpan."

She wanted him to argue. She wanted him to raise his hand, to twist his lip, anything to give her a reason to make good on her threat. Though too much was at stake for her to waste her energy on the execrable Roy Soza, she nonetheless stood there and waited for the invitation to pummel him.

He must have seen it in her eyes, because he backed away. His face was red and he twisted the bill of his cap in his hands. "This ain't over," he said.

"No. But it's close."

She turned to Nin after he was gone. "That was fun."

"I didn't think so."

"No, me neither." She ran a hand over her bristly hair. "Okay, this day has officially gone from bad to worse. We need to get somewhere and regroup. I'll go fetch Hannah and let her know about Terrell—doc says he's going to be fine. You and Tam wait here about five minutes or so, just to give Roy time to get on down the road, then meet me in the parking lot."

"What did Jo mean when she said Jed was the wrong man?"

"I don't know, but from the way it sounded, Jed wasn't the one who messed Penny up like that. We just assumed it was him. And now our assuming has got us into a whole world of trouble. Just try not to think about it, if that's possible. We can worry about it later."

"I am not sure I can make it until later."

"You and me both, sister. You and me both. Now go get Tam. I'll see you in a few minutes."

Nin hurried through the door Tam had taken, and Lucy turned and jogged down the hall to the chapel.

Chapter Twenty-nine

Jo sprinted across the street in defiance of the sign that warned her DON'T WALK.

A horn honked. Brakes squealed.

She'd cleared two blocks since leaving the hospital. A hacksaw blade raked her side as she ran, and people stared at her as she galloped by—but she didn't slow down. The sun threw her shadow out in front of her and she ran after it, as if by chasing something she'd feel like the hunter instead of the hunted. She cut through the alley behind the Book Nook, where she'd never again buy paperback romances for fifty cents apiece. From there she crossed in front of the Potomac Motel, no vacancies, just a parking lot jammed full of out-of-state cars, one of them with hubcaps painted carnation pink.

They were everywhere, these pink reminders of her unpardonable mistake.

Jo, Jed Whitecross did not do this to me.

She stopped after three grueling blocks. The stitch in her side was too vicious. She put her hands on her knees and panted, waiting for the pain to subside. Every time she inhaled, she saw another face: Penelope's as she said that her brother did it, Jed's as he pleaded for his life, Warren's when he asked if she was going to break his heart.

That's why Jed had screamed, *Why are you doing this?* Because he was innocent.

Her car was parked at Hannah's. How many more blocks? Four?

Ignoring the sting, she got herself moving again, not

knowing her ultimate destination, only trying to leave the faces behind.

Lucy was on her way to tell Hannah the good news about Terrell when she heard a man's voice hailing her.

"Lucy Campbell? Can I talk to you for a sec?"

Sheriff Cantrell was walking toward her at a brisk pace. His uniform was in dire need of pressing and his boots were scuffed. Behind him, three men in black suits broke their huddle and headed down various corridors.

Lucy sensed the danger like an animal smelling smoke in the forest.

"Lucy? I'm glad as all get-out that Terrell is going to pull through this."

"Is that what you wanted to tell me?"

"Uh, no. Yes and no, that is."

"Please, Sheriff, I'm a much busier woman than I seem to be."

"Right." He scratched his razor-burned chin. "Did your friends Jo and Hannah come here to the hospital with you?"

Lucy remained very still. "Why?"

"Special Agent Bonham would like a word with them."

"He'd like a word with them." Her voice was deadpan.

"That's what I said. Are they here?"

"If he'd only *like a word with them,* then why did he send so many goons?"

"Procedure, that's why."

"Procedure." She didn't know why she was repeating everything he said. "I don't think I believe you, Sheriff."

"Lucy, please . . ."

"Jo and Hannah aren't here. Your *procedure* just missed them. Are they in trouble?"

"Looks that way. You sure you haven't seen them?"

"Bo, I've known you for years. Why don't you do me a favor and tell me what's going on?"

Cantrell looked around uncomfortably, as if one of the men in dark suits might be watching. "Truth is, Lucy, the federal agents have found things."

"Things."

"Yeah. For starters, they found prints on Jed's car and Chuck Adams's garage, and they've been comparing them to just about everyone in the county. This morning they dusted Jo's desk at work. And they finally found a match."

Each of Lucy's breaths was less substantial than the last.

"And secondly, somebody reported weird tracks out at the lake. Tracks too deep to be washed away by the rain. At first I thought they belonged to some kind of cart, and I started thinking that maybe Jed Whitecross got dragged out to the water in a wagon or something. But it wasn't a wagon. Now I don't know why Hannah would be involved in this . . ."

Oh, God.

". . . but the FBI has warrants for the arrest of Josephine Adams and Hannah Jessler."

Slowly, Lucy began to turn around. If she didn't get away, she was going to incriminate them all. She walked away from the sheriff and prayed he wouldn't follow.

"Lucy, if you have any information on their whereabouts, you should let me know now."

Lucy cupped a hand over her mouth, turned the corner, and gathered speed.

Warrants.

She burst through the chapel door.

Hannah looked up. She was lying on the floor. "Terrell?"

"He's fine. Get up."

"Fine?" Her face brightened. "Fine, like he's going to be really okay? Did the doctors tell you that or is this you doing more wishful thinking?"

"He's in one piece, Hannah. Now let me help you up."

Hannah grabbed hold and together the two of them got her situated, with Hannah talking all the while. "Thank God he's okay. Can I see him now? When can I go in? I was so *worried*. Did the doctors tell you anything? Did he ask for me? Did they have to remove his spleen or anything? Does he even know I'm here?"

"Slow down, honey, before you blow a fuse." Lucy walked behind her, pushing her toward the door. "We won't be allowed in his room for awhile yet. He's sedated, you know. Man just got through surviving something that should have killed him. Takes a lot out of a person."

"I know. I've had my neck broken, remember?"

"Hiss-hiss. A little touchy this morning, aren't we?"

"I didn't mean to say it like that. I'm sorry." She reached back and patted Lucy on the hand. "I'm just strung out. All of these ups and downs . . . well, you know what I'm talking about. But maybe we could just hang around outside his room and wait for him to—"

"No, Hannah. I'm taking you out of here, right out the back door and into the parking lot and into that van of yours and then far away."

"Why? What's wrong? Has something happened?"

"They're coming for you. The cops. For you and for Jo."

Hannah twisted around in her seat so that she could see Lucy's face. "What are you talking about?"

Lucy started to jog. "They know you were out at the lake."

For a dozen revolutions of the chair's wheels, Hannah said nothing. Then she turned back around and placed her hands gently on the armrests. "We've got to find Jo."

"Missy, you're talking to the fastest rickshaw driver in Hong Kong. You just hang on."

★ ★ ★ ★ ★

Tamaryn swung from side to side, bouncing nervously, ready to tear a hole in the side of the van. She was sick of waiting around. She should have been on the highway hours ago, listening to the boys squabble on the seat beside her. When the door swung open, she sprang forward.

"Get down!" Lucy ordered.

Tam fell to the floor of the van without question.

"To the back!"

Tam rolled.

Hannah touched the remote control and the ramp began to lower.

Lucy climbed into the driver's seat. Two minutes later, Hannah was seated inside and Nin closed the door. Lucy misjudged the accelerator and caused the vehicle to lurch. "Damn! This is going to take some getting used to."

"No time for that," Hannah said. "Learn by doing."

"Yeah, whatever."

"Roy's still here, ain't he?"

"Nope. Special Agent Bonham. I don't want him to see us all together."

"Bonham?" Tam asked. "Who's that?"

"I know him," Nin said. "He is the special-agent-in-charge."

"He brought a few men along with him," Lucy said.

"*Lots* of them," Hannah added, a dismal note in her voice. "And they're looking for me and Jo."

Tam had no idea what they were talking about. Who was Special Agent Bonham? Apparently Roy wasn't the issue here, as she'd first assumed. "What the hell does a special agent want with you and Jo? Wait. Never mind." She lowered her forehead to the floor. "Shit."

Lucy applied too much brake, sending a jolt through the

van. "This is harder than it looks," she said. She eased down on the proper lever until the van moved smoothly through the intersection. "Just bear with me for a few more blocks. Unless I run us into somebody's yard before then."

"What happened?" Tam demanded. "Somebody tell me what's going on."

"Ruts," Hannah said.

"Huh?"

"Ruts from my wheels. They're going to match the ruts to my tire tread. And then they're going to . . . to . . ." Her words trailed away. She lowered her head.

Lucy said, "Bottle also told me they've got a match on Jo's prints."

Tam cursed silently. So much for sticking to the Good Rules. She had tried to live a decent life, raise her young knights, and keep in shape. Nothing more. Maybe on her report card for being an upstanding citizen she'd earned a few grades below a C average, but on her mothering report card, she thought she did fairly well, comparatively speaking. Her boys would grow up to be askers. Not takers. And certainly not ignorers. Their only fault was having a mom who one night got fed up with it all. Lying there facedown in the back of the van, Tam was brought to the brink of tears for the first time since the night Roy had violated her. Jo and Hannah would be taken into custody, and Tam wouldn't be able to let them take the fall alone. There were two things about it that she couldn't shake: the boys would grow up without her, and they would grow up under Roy Soza's roof.

"You want the worst news?" Lucy asked.

"Worse than us going down for murder?" She lifted her head and laughed spitefully. "Goddamn, I *gotta* hear this."

"Penelope told Jo that Jed never hit her. It was Joshua all along. Her brother."

Tam stared at her vapidly. "Bullshit."

Hannah buried her face in her hands.

Nin mouthed a quiet prayer.

Lucy kept her eyes on the street.

After thirty seconds of uncomfortable silence, Tam could stand it no more. "If any of you says that we capped a man who didn't deserve it, I'll lose it right here. Do you all hear me? If you tell me that we *murdered* and *sank* some innocent goddamn bystander, I will have a breakdown right here in this van. You got it? Huh? *Do you got it?*"

The only sounds for the remainder of the ride were the soft supplications from Nin's whispering lips.

The snapping of weeds against the undercarriage startled her from her daze.

Jo blinked, gasped, and jerked the wheel hard left. The car banked up the side of the ditch. The tires spewed dirt, then caught on the pavement and sent the vehicle zooming down the center of the highway.

Where was she going? She didn't know. First she was running and now she was driving, not with any destination in mind, just giving herself up to the flight because that's what you did when you were eluding pursuit.

If it hadn't been for Caroline, she might have been able to do it, to leave, to keep her foot to the floor and only stop to put gas in the tank. She'd drive to the Rockies or maybe the deserts of Arizona, liquidate her savings account and change her name. If she fled, perhaps she could take a little heat off the others, because the authorities would assume by her exodus that she was linked to Jed's kidnapping. Of course, it wouldn't be a mere kidnapping for long, because they had begun systematically to drag every pond, creek bed, and lake bottom in Clayton County, and from there they'd widen their search to the surrounding counties, if need be. Protestant Lake was not so deep as to prevent them from raising Jed's body when they trolled the water.

Shouldn't have been Jed down there in the first place.

"Shut up," Jo said, putting a hand to her forehead. Her hair was sticky with sweat.

Should have been Joshua instead.

"Please . . ."

Jed's mother must be losing her mind over this.

"She's not alone." Jo let up on the accelerator and unrolled the windows, hoping that the air would drive away the voices. The mid-morning sun was fully visible above the battlement of clouds, stenciling the shaggy hemlocks in gold. The trees marked the horizon line. Beyond them, the rest of the world waited.

PUSH LIFE.

Jo didn't realize where she was until she saw the sign. She'd been driving in a fugue state, subconsciously guiding the car while her thinking self was laden with thoughts of inadvertent self-destruction. It wasn't surprising that she should end up out here, as this place had occupied so much of her professional life as of late. The Indians were gone, as were the cars and tents. Paper cups and other bits of refuse clung to the tall grass. The ground was heavily marred by tire tracks, and the entire site had a look of exhaustion about it, as if the ground itself was worn out from overuse.

Jo hit the clutch and worked down through the gears. She turned onto the rutted track, passed a lone redbud marked for removal, took her foot off the gas pedal and allowed the car to roll the last few feet through the mud to the birthing house. The vehicle's approach disturbed a blanket of orange-winged butterflies, which lifted into the air, broke apart, and scattered like colored pollen in the breeze.

At the same instant that she shut off the motor, her telephone rang.

She'd been expecting this call. She played a little game with herself, guessing which one of them it would be. She put the phone to her ear and said, "Hello, Lucy."

"The shit is hitting the fan as we speak," Lucy said.

"Tell me about it."

"Where are you?"

Jo told her.

"What the hell are you doing out there?"

"Evading capture."

"They've got a warrant for your arrest. And Hannah's, too."

Jo lowered her head to the steering wheel. *So this is it.* "Where's Hannah?"

"Here beside me. So is Nin."

"And Tam?"

"Loading the boys into the truck right now. Jo, what do you want me to do?"

"For starters, tell Tam to come to me."

"What for? What good will that do?"

"She can take my car. Roy won't let her get very far before he freaks out and goes searching for her. He and his hunting buddies will be looking for her truck, not a yellow Mustang."

"Yeah, that makes sense. Hold on."

Jo heard her shouting instructions.

"Lucy? Any word on Terrell?"

"He's going to be fine."

Jo sighed. "Thank God."

"Tam's on her way. And the rest of us are right behind her."

"You're what? Why?"

"Where else are we going to go?"

"Lucy, I don't think that's a very good idea . . ."

"Girl, the sky is falling down around our heads, you understand that? They've got *divers*. You hear me? Divers down in the lakes. And when they bring him up, they're gonna find him wrapped up in two sheets. *Two*, Jo. And even Bottle Cantrell isn't dumb enough to think that the killer wore both outfits by herself. You and Hannah are their suspects. They want *both* of you. Which means Hannah needs to get the hell out of here. So I'm bringing her to you."

"Okay, okay, you made your point. Damn." She lifted her head off the wheel, waiting for an epiphany that wasn't coming. Surely there had to be some way of squeaking out of this, some tricky means of escape. "Where are you now?"

"Hauling ass in Hannah's van. We'll be there in a few minutes. So you can start pulling them rabbits out of your hat anytime now."

"Tam's going to need some money."

"We've given her everything we had between us, which wasn't much. Matt and Brady are scared to pieces. You know how good their mama is at covering up her emotions."

"Did you talk to Caroline when you stopped to get the boys?"

"A little. I told her about Terrell, and that Roy was on the rampage. I didn't know what to say about the cops looking for you and Hannah, but I had to say *something*. The girl's no dummy. She would've figured it out sooner or later anyway. Haven't heard her that worried since she was little. Told her that I'd have you call her as soon as you got off the horn with me."

"I'd better do that now. I don't want her driving around looking for me. You hurry up and get here, okay? I love you."

"Love you too."

Jo broke the connection and dialed her home number, still

no closer to conceiving any last-minute magic, but comforted by the fact that her fellow desperados were on their way.

"Mom, is that you?"

At the sound of that voice, Jo began to cry.

Less than two minutes later, Tam slammed the pickup door and ran to her.

They met in a hug.

"Jesus, Jo, this is *really* bad."

"Are the boys okay?"

Tam sniffled and nodded. "They're tough."

"Like their mother. Now I want you to listen very closely to what I'm about to tell you. It's not much of a strategy, but it's the best I could come up with on such short notice. Next time you decide to run off and leave your husband, I'd appreciate a few days' advance warning."

"I'll keep that in mind."

"You do that. So here are my keys. I want you to take my car. I don't think you'd make it very far in yours without being seen by Roy's goons. But the switch won't dupe them for long, so we have to make provisions to get you another car somewhere down the road."

"And how are we going to do that?"

"One of us will have to meet you."

"Meet me where? Come on, Jo, you can't send Lucy halfway across the country to bring me a car. If she leaves, the cops'll only assume she's involved with Jed's disappearance, and we can't afford that right now. She and Nin need to seem as innocent as possible."

"Fine. We'll have someone else do it for us. Caroline or Warren . . ."

"You really want to let them in on it?"

Jo fought down a surge of frustration. She took a breath

and tried again. "Look. I'm doing the best that I can here, okay? So cut me some slack. Our only other recourse is renting a car. You can take all the cash and credit cards I have. So drive for a few hours, leave the pony in a crowded parking lot, rent a car, go for awhile and then ditch the car and take a bus. After that you can use the money to buy a cheap used car. You pay cash for it, then . . . do whatever."

Tam smoked and fidgeted.

"What? Say it."

"Nothing. I'll do what you said. It's just . . . I'll never see you again, will I?"

"Never's an awful long time. Don't worry about that right now. Just go."

Tam nodded just as a helicopter appeared.

Her stomach leaden, Jo turned toward the sound. The chopper had just crested the sawtooth line of hemlocks, a harsh shadow against the sun. It seemed to be flying straight at them.

"Not yet," Tamaryn croaked. "Not yet, you bastards."

"Mom?"

"It's okay, Matt," Jo told him. "Just stay in the truck."

"Goddammit, Jo." Tam slumped against her, pressing her face against Jo's neck and clutching handfuls of her blouse. "It's over . . . we killed him . . . we killed him and they're going to take my babies away from me. . . ."

Jo could do nothing else but put her arms around Tam and watch the helicopter close the distance. After all of her planning, after her quick work with the Icky Errands and her faith in happy endings, still it hadn't been enough.

Four blasts from a horn signaled the van's arrival. It whipped sideways onto the gravel track, its rear end edging perilously close to the culvert before sliding back to the road. Over the howl of its engine and the lamentation of the wind,

Jo heard the haunting call of sirens.

There were a few seconds between the time the van shimmied to a halt and the moment Lucy said, *So where's that rabbit, Ms. Houdini?* that Jo supposed she could have called it quits. It didn't seem fair, to be given so little time to render such a monumental decision. But then again, fairness hadn't shown its face since all of this started a week and a half ago, so Jo wasn't about to mourn its absence at this point.

She watched the van pull up beside the truck. Doors swung open.

What was it that Tamaryn had said this morning? Every choice they now made was an important one. They weren't mulling over which earrings to wear with a certain outfit or trying to choose between one-percent milk and skim. Their actions, like those of a soldier in a trench or a surgeon during an operation, were arrows pointing at life and death. And in those extremes Jo found a titillating clarity. Her perspective on herself and her own towering significance had never been so clear.

Feet jumped from the van. A ramp descended.

The choice, then, pared to the bone, was this: give up and face the consequences—the courts, the public outcry, the loss of friends and children, the complete abandonment of this extraordinary freedom—or don't give up and let the game play out. Surrender or . . . or what?

It was the *or what* that she wasn't sure about. Tam had made it sound so simple. *Either we get caught or we go free.* But that wasn't where the arrow was pointing. There was no *we go free.* Barring intervention from a divine partisan, they wouldn't be able to slip away unseen, not against this size onslaught. Jo might have been able to smuggle one or two of the women to a safe haven, but not when there were kids and wheelchairs to be considered. Lucy was the only witch in the Crazy Coven without any familiars tying her down, and she wouldn't budge if budging meant leaving the others behind.

Had she one of her mother's magazines to consult, Jo probably could have found a pithy proverb reminding her what all good abiders did when armed agents were closing on your position. But she had no counsel other than her own.

Nin brought the wheelchair close enough that Hannah was able to reach out and take Jo's hand. Jo sought in their eyes a trace of doubt, the smallest hint of reluctance. But their faces were stark and without pretense. They saw the same two arrows. They were waiting for Jo to select one or the other.

"So where's that rabbit, Ms. Houdini?"

Two police cruisers were speeding down the highway, followed by a convoy of unmarked sedans.

"Everyone get inside," she said.

"Inside where?" Hannah asked.

Without taking her eyes from the onrushing cars, Jo pointed at Pete Musket's birthing house.

Chapter Thirty

"We can't go in there, Jo, there's no way out and we'll be trapped, and besides we have Matthew and Brady with us, and what are we supposed to do with them?"

The lead squad car slowed down and turned onto the track.

"The boys will be fine," Jo said, hoping that was true. "Trust me, Hannah."

"So you have a plan then?"

"Everybody get in there, *now.*"

The women scattered.

Tam ran to the truck. "All right, sir knights, pile on out of there. Brady, hon, you've got to put some zip in it 'cause Mom's kind of in a hurry here."

"Are the cops after us, Mom?"

"Yeppers, Matt, I think that they are."

"Cool!"

The expression on Nin's face was unreadable as she shoved the wheelchair through the flattened weeds. The soft earth oozed over the tires and clung to the spokes. Had Nin been a lesser woman, she couldn't have forced the chair over such terrain. Hannah assisted as much as she could, cranking the wheels so that the muscles stood out on her upper arms. She bit her lip tightly between her teeth.

Lucy reached inside the van and brought out a shoebox. Mumbling to herself, she dashed for the low stone building.

Having yet to move an inch, Jo watched them jostle inside. First Nin and Hannah, the chair barely fitting through the narrow door frame, trailed by Tam and the boys and the oblong black parcel Tam carried under her arm. Lucy stopped on the threshold and looked back. "I'm still expecting that rabbit, you know."

Jo cast one last glance at the line of cars barreling down the track, then followed Lucy through the door.

"They're searching my truck."

Tam and Jo stood on either side of the window. Jo peeked through a narrow strip where the glass wasn't layered in ages of dirt, fully realizing the absurdity of her actions. *I'm taking cover and watching the cops surround my hideout. Jesus.*

"They look a little confused," Tam said.

Jo silently concurred. Confusion seemed to be the order of the day. Evidently the FBI wasn't prepared for such a contingency, having failed to anticipate that the two suspects and their ditzy girlfriends would lock themselves in a tumbledown antebellum stable. Jo turned from the window and conducted a speedy survey of the building's interior.

There wasn't much to see. The birthing house was a single room with a nine-foot ceiling, its walls great slabs of river rock cut from the Potomac a year before Richmond was named capital of the Confederacy. The smoke-blackened rafters were eight inches thick and festooned with hooks, strands of rope, and a section of rusty chain that served no identifiable purpose. The door was iron-shod oak. The floor was comprised of smooth flagstones, joined at their edges by the same black mortar that cemented the walls. A layer of straw covered much of the floor, and a metal trough was bolted to one wall beneath a hitching post. Racks of wooden shelving, now mostly rotted, held a few dirty glass jars and a coffee can full of roofing nails. What appeared to be a combination stove and blacksmith's forge squatted like a troll in the far corner. The stovepipe had been patched with muffler tape. Nearby was a grungy sleeping bag, a battered lantern, and a coal scuttle holding several empty liquor bottles.

A thin patina of dust covered everything. The four windows, two in the front and two in the back, provided the room with a uniform gray light.

"Mom, I think I need to pee."

"Me too, Mom," Lucy said.

"I think I already have," Hannah added.

"Brady, you'll just have to go over there in the corner. I know it's a little strange, but it'll be okay. Here, give me your hand."

Jo used the hem of her shirt to clear a peephole near the bottom of the window. She got down on one knee and sighted through the small opening she'd made.

She counted fifteen . . . no, sixteen people. Those in suits—presumably Bureau agents—had discarded their jackets, their shoulder rigs distinct against their white shirts. Bottle Cantrell stood amongst them. He looked lost.

The noise of the helicopter intensified as it came to rest on the very spot Chuck's fancy pavilion had been standing only yesterday. Three men disembarked. Jo recognized one of them as Special Agent Bonham. He'd ridden in the back of the ambulance with her when they'd taken Terrell to the emergency room. He had kept Terrell talking by inquiring about his sex life and laughed good-naturedly when Terrell, through his oxygen mask, asked him for a job.

Bonham kept his head down until he was clear of the chopper. He was instantly beset by the other agents, many of whom pointed at the birthing house as they apprised him of the situation. They stopped gesturing when Bonham started to speak. One by one the agents peeled away from the group as they received their instructions.

"So they're actually, truly surrounding us," Jo said.

"What?" Lucy nudged her out of the way. "Let me see this madness for myself. Maybe I'll start believing that it's real."

"Be my guest. Though it's probably best if we stay away from the windows as much as possible." She pointed to the stove in the corner. "I'd say that's the safest spot."

"Safest for *what*?" Hannah asked. Her face was white, save for two perfect red circles of distress high on her cheeks. "What's happening here, Jo, and don't tell me we're going to sit in here until they get tired of waiting because I don't think that's ever going to happen. This is what they mean by *laying siege*. It's the kind of thing you see on the news, and in case you forgot, it usually doesn't have a very happy ending."

"All will turn out for the best, honey."

"No, Ningeogapik, it won't. Let's stop kidding ourselves here, can we do that? I shot Jed Whitecross. I *shot* him. We're not watching this on TV or reading about it while we wait for our clothes to get dry at the laundromat. This is *us*."

"Mama, what's Aunt Hannah talking about?"

"Nothing, Mr. Brady Lee Soza. You know how she gets sometimes."

"Mom, are the cops mad at us?"

"No, Matthew, the cops are not mad at us. They just . . ."

"Just what?"

"Here comes some more of them," Lucy reported.

Jo sprang to the far window and wiped another porthole near the bottom. As she watched, three unmarked cars turned off the highway, followed by a state trooper. Bonham held a cell phone in either hand and was walking the perimeter as he alternated between them. Though he'd directed his men to assume sentry positions around the building, his orders apparently didn't include an obvious display of firepower; the men stood in their shirtsleeves, their ties wagging in the summer wind.

"Imagine what's going through that sucker's head," Lucy said. "Bonham's got himself half a dozen housewives holed up in a shack, with the television cameras on the way. Knowing the government's history with standoffs, that poor schmuck is wishing he'd called in sick this morning. You better believe he'll play this just as delicately as he can."

"We're not housewives," Jo reminded her.

"No, but that's what the evening news will call us."

"I don't want the evening news to call me *anything*," Hannah said. "I just want this to be over, is that too much to ask? What are we doing here? What are we waiting for? This is only going to get worse as more of them show up out there, and I don't see how it does us any good to lock ourselves in this smelly dump, waiting for them to tell us to come out with our hands above our heads."

"Consider the alternative," Jo said.

"I have."

"And?"

"And I don't want to go to jail for murder. But that's what we did, isn't it? We murdered someone who didn't even deserve it."

"Murdered who, Mom?"

"Jessler, can you please shut the hell up."

Lucy kept her face to the glass. "They're moving fast, aren't they?"

Jo had been thinking that very thing. She didn't know how often FBI agents trained for this kind of scenario, but if the alacrity of their actions was any indication, they'd played through standoffs before. However, they had probably assumed their adversaries in such an event would be left-wing militia freaks with machine guns, not five middle-class women who bowled two Saturdays a month. *A standoff? Is that what this is?* Bonham directed his people to park their vehicles at certain points around the building, forming a loose circle with the birthing house in its center. Someone climbed into Tam's pickup and backed it out of the way. They did the same with Hannah's van.

"Never leave your keys in the ignition," Lucy said, not taking her eyes from the window.

A hundred feet of muddy, well-traveled ground now stood between the birthing house and the nearest car. A fire truck pulled off the side of the highway. A second helicopter appeared, this one painted with the call sign of the NBC affiliate out of Washington.

Brady hiccupped loudly, a prelude to tears.

Nin touched Jo on the arm. "Whatever we do, we need to get the little ones out of here."

"I know." Jo left her post at the window and went to the stove, where Tam was crouched in front of the kids, maintaining a continuous stream of chatter in an effort to keep them occupied. "Hey, folks. Mind if I join you?"

"Aunt Jo?"

"Yes, Brady?"

"How's come the policemen are here?"

She glanced sidelong at Tam for approval. Tam nodded.

"They're here," Jo said, "because your Aunt Hannah and I broke the rules."

"You did?"

"Uh-huh. And now they want to talk to us about what we did wrong."

"Are they gonna make you stand with your noses in the corner?"

"Don't be a dummy," his brother chided him. "The cops are here to put them in jail."

"They *are?*"

"Well, we're still working on that whole jail thing. But in

the meantime, it would be for the best if you two went outside for awhile. I'm sure Sheriff Cantrell will tell you all about his police car if you ask him nicely. Maybe he'll even let you play with the lights. You'd like that, wouldn't you?"

Tam pinched her lips together and dabbed a hand across her eyes.

"This is really weird, Mom," Matt said.

"I know it is, baby. Come here." She folded both of them into her arms.

Jo returned to the window, ostensibly to give them a few moments alone. The truth of the matter was that if she stayed there any longer, her fledgling resolve would surely fracture; giving up the kids was far too great a price. She wondered what Caroline was doing at that moment, how worried she must be. *I'm so sorry, Sweet!* If there was one message she could have sent her daughter, it would be to impart the dangers of living life by rote. For years Jo had simply been going through the motions. Like everyone else. But in the space of a week she'd become a woman of passion and covert derring-do.

"Hannah," she said. "Can you please stop pacing?"

Hannah slammed her hands on the wheels. "Excuse me for being a little nervous."

"You and all the rest of us."

"It's just that I can't help but think that I've already lost him, you know what I'm talking about? Because I don't see how you're going to squeak us out of this mess, and even if we do, I'm still going to have to explain to him what happened with Jed, and he's too good a man to let me get away with murdering someone, so if you could just tell me how we're supposed to—"

"JO ADAMS!"

The voice shook the dust from the rafters.

Through the hole she'd cleared in the window, Jo saw Bonham with a bullhorn to his mouth. When the helicopter passed overhead, he scowled at it and angrily waved it away. Behind him, more vehicles lined up along the highway. Additional Bureau agents, county deputies, and camera-bearing journalists advanced in a steady stream.

"Twenty-six, twenty-seven . . ." Lucy counted.

"JO ADAMS AND HANNAH JESSLER!"

"Mom, what's that guy want with them?"

"*Jo, what do we do?*" Tam demanded.

"Hannah, what's your number at work?"

"Huh?"

Jo ripped the phone from its leather sheath at her waist. "What's the number of the dispatcher's office? Hurry up!"

Hannah rattled it off, and Jo dialed.

"Mommy . . ."

"Shhh, now. It's going to be alright. Would your number one mom lie to you?"

". . . and the cameraman makes thirty-one," Lucy said. "Lordy, what my kinfolk are going to say when they see my face on Dan Rather. Do you think old Dan'll be able to pronounce Nin's name correctly?"

"I do not want him to have a reason to pronounce it at all."

"Esther?" Jo said into the phone. "Esther, this is Jo. I need you to patch me through to Sheriff Cantrell."

"Jo Adams?" Esther asked.

"Yes, Jo Adams, now get Bo on the line, *please.*" She cupped her hand over the telephone and said, "We've got to be ready for anything, so stay alert. It's going to get a little sticky from here on out."

"As if it isn't sticky already," Lucy said.

Jo returned her attention to the window. She knew the moment Cantrell got the call. One of his men shouted at him from a squad car, and the sheriff turned around just in time to catch the phone—Jo heard the sounds of him fumbling it to his ear.

"This is Cantrell."

"Good morning, Bo."

"Good morning to you too. Who is this?"

"I'm watching you right now. That's kind of strange, don't you think?"

"*Jo?*"

"I need to talk to Agent Bonham."

"Jo, what in Christ are you doing in there?"

Cantrell had suddenly drawn a crowd.

"Just give me to Bonham, will you?"

"*Shit.* Here. She wants you." He held out the phone.

Though there were too many people in the way for Jo to see his face, she knew it was Bonham on the other end when he said, "Didn't I meet you in an ambulance only a few hours ago?"

"What's your number?" Jo asked.

"Pardon?"

"Your number. What's your cell number?"

He gave it to her.

"I'll call you," she said, and pressed the END button. She turned away from the window to gather her thoughts.

"Now what do we do?" Hannah wanted to know.

"I wish people would stop asking me that."

"Who else are we going to ask?"

Jo stared at the floor and tapped the phone against her chin.

"Are they gonna arrest me too, Mama?"

"Of course not, you silly goose. You haven't done anything wrong."

"What about Dad?"

"No, this is one crime your father isn't guilty of."

"What?"

"Never mind. Just be brave for me, okay? Just for awhile longer."

"You're thinking something, aren't you, I can tell that your wheels are turning, and let me just say that I am *really* happy about that, because you had me wondering there for a bit if we were actually going to squirm out of this one."

"New arrival," Lucy informed them. "One shiny new Lincoln, trailing the biggest-ass pink flag you have ever seen. Can't be sure from this far away, but I think that's Rita Ingersol and her ladies-in-waiting."

Jo tried to recall the instant when everything had changed. Had it been Lucy donning the pillowcase in the hospital church? Tamaryn handing out cans of paint? Or mere minutes ago, when Jo herself had chosen between the two arrows? *It doesn't matter now, you saucy moll. Just do what you can with what you've got. Just make do.* Like sandpaper on the soul, guilt had rubbed away her veneer. What she exposed beneath that protective covering surprised her.

"Remember the cat that caught fire at the barbecue?" she asked.

The others traded glances.

"Do burned cats ever learn not to wave their tails near fire?"

"Is this like some kind of Zen riddle?" Lucy ventured.

Jo pondered it in silence for awhile, then sedately dialed Bonham's number.

Nin listened to Jo's half of the conversation from her position on the floor beside the furnace—a crude iron box with a hinged grate and legs like metal tree stumps. She thought it looked rather like a boiler from an antique and decidedly malignant steam engine. The mildewed bedroll indicated that someone had at one time slept near the spooky coal-eating oven, a proposition that Old Nin might have found unsettling. New Nin, on the other hand, had been hardened in a kiln of her own, and was frightened only by the thought of her little fairies growing up without her. She held Brady on her lap and hummed in his ear.

". . . not going to waste your time or mine explaining myself," Jo said.

While Jo spoke with Agent Bonham, Lucy kept her vigil at the window. Hannah was biting her thumb. Tamaryn unlaced and then retied Matthew's sneakers, and tucked his shirt in, and smoothed his hair with her hand. Nin's heart cried out to her.

"Do you insist on pressing me for an answer to that question?" Jo asked.

Do not press her, Nin would have liked to tell him.

"Then I think the consensus here, Bonham, is *no.* We're not coming out."

Nin waited for the rebuttal. Surely Hannah would protest.

Or me, Nin thought. *What about a protest from me?*
Well?

She blamed her silence on her belief that Jo's store of self-made sorcery was not yet depleted.

"You heard me. Hannah Jessler and I are not coming out."
Lucy snapped her head around.

"The others?" Jo looked at each of them in turn. "Hostages."

"Hostages like hell," Lucy spat.

"Hang on a minute, Bonham." She covered the phone with her hand.

"Speaking just for me," Lucy said, shaking her finger, "I'm nobody's hostage. I'm here of my own free will. And don't think you're gonna make yourself some kind of hero by staying behind while we all go free, because I won't put up with that kind of thing."

"Me neither, Jo," Tam said. "We're all in this together. So let's just get Matt and Brady out of here and then we'll talk about it."

"Jo's right, Tam," Hannah said. "You're all innocent. I pulled the trigger on that man. Maybe it was an accident and maybe it wasn't. But either way, it's me that they're after, me and Jo. You three take the boys and leave."

Tam shook her head forcefully. "Not without you."

"Nin?" Jo looked her in the eyes. "What about you?"

"I am as much to blame as anyone. We are all responsible for what happened. The finger on the trigger is irrelevant."

Jo went back to the phone. "Bonham? Apparently our hostages have changed their minds. They're staying, at least until Hannah and I talk some sense into them. But we're sending out Tamaryn's kids—"

At the mention of this, Tam choked back a sob.

"—so tell your shooters to stand down. Let me repeat that for the record. Matt and Brady Soza are going to walk out of this door in one minute. If they are mishandled in any way, we will open fire without regard for who or what is in the way. Am I understood?"

Nin realized that New Nin had nothing on New Jo.

"Are we *armed?* I don't know. Ask Roy Soza how armed we are. I'm not a hundred percent sure, but there's a garbage bag in here that I think might contain something that's recently gone missing from his gun collection. Bye for now."

She pitched the phone to Lucy, and in two strides she'd cupped Tam's face in her hands. "Easy, don't cry. I don't think I've ever seen your tears, and I don't want to start today, because that just might be more than I can take."

Tam nodded but didn't speak.

"Are you sure this is what you want?"

Another nod.

"Then let's do it."

As soon as she backed away, Tam dropped to both knees and swept Matthew into her arms. Brady leaped from Nin's lap and flung himself at his mother. She spoke to them, but too quietly for Nin to hear, for which Nin was thankful. Already she was dabbing her cheeks with the back of her hand.

"Well, that sure put them into a tizzy," Lucy said. "Must have been the word *hostages*. Bonham's shouting at them right and left and at least half of them are now ducked down behind their cars. And shoot . . . there must be twenty people talking on phones. Who the hell do you think they're talking to?"

"Let's go, Tam."

"Okay, sir knights . . ."

"But, Mom . . ."

"No buts, Matthew. You're just going outside with Sheriff Cantrell for a few minutes while Mama stays here and takes care of a little business. Can you both be extra special brave for me? Hmmm? Can you?" She shepherded them to the door, holding their hands. "All right. Here we are, going to head outside like big strong men, right? You'll walk out side by side." She drew their hands together, linking them.

Hannah cried softly into her sleeve.

Tam kissed their joined hands. "And don't you forget"—her voice cracked—"don't you forget to always hold hands when the going gets tough. Do that for your mom, okay? Tell me you'll always stick together, no matter what."

"Mom, don't talk like this . . ."

"Oh, Matthew."

"We'll see you again, right Mom?"

"I'll try, Matty, I will really, really try."

Jo opened the door. She closed her eyes and pinched the bridge of her nose.

"Mama, I don't want to go."

"God, Brady, just go, just go, baby, please just go and be strong for me . . ."

Nin stood up and caught her just as she began to fall.

"Come on," Matt said to his little brother. "We better go. I love you, Mom."

Tam exploded into loud, convulsing sobs.

The boys stepped out together under the sun.

"Don't let go of each other's hands!" Tam yelled.

Jo slammed the door.

Tam crumbled. Nin, a terrible hollow carved in her chest, eased her against the wall, trying to say the words but not finding any. Tam slid down the wall to the floor. She clamped her hands over her mouth and nose and froze that way. Even the tears on her face seemed to solidify, like drops of glass.

Chapter Thirty-one

Ten minutes passed.

Jo sat cross-legged on the floor. There was no sound but the occasional sniff.

The window was just above her head. If she opened it, she might be able to relieve some of the heaviness; like the bottom of the ocean, the room's pressure was such that they were all in danger of implosion.

Nin, with a mother's prestidigitation, produced tissues from nowhere. Perhaps they came from one of the floppy pockets of her housedress. She dispersed them without a word.

Jo's telephone rang.

No one started at the sudden sound, or made any move to answer it. Their eyes traveled to where the phone rested beside Jo's knee. She wondered how many times Bonham would let it ring. Indefinitely, to be sure. Or at least until the batteries expired.

"If that's for me," Lucy finally said, "I'm not here."

Lucy's voice released a bit of the tension in the room. Jo was able to make her hand lift the phone to her ear.

"Yes?"

"We have the children. They're fine. Real troupers, both of them."

"They take after their mother."

Tamaryn looked up sharply. Her eyes were dry, but also empty. What spark had once lived there was gone.

"We're waiting for your next move, Jo. Truthfully, you've got us all a little nervous out here."

"You ought to try it from my side of the wall."

"Yeah. I hear you. You are planning on coming out, aren't you? I don't mean to be pushy or anything, but I wouldn't want the men to get it into their heads that you're going to refuse to give yourselves up. And the press, too. You know how they are. So can I tell them you'll be out in a moment?"

"Tell them whatever you want."

"Please, Jo, you've got to work with me a little."

"No. No, Bonham, I don't think we do."

"We have a warrant for your arrest. Your fingerprints were found on the Jed Whitecross vehicle. We also have castings of tire impressions taken from the road leading to Protestant Lake. Maybe they'll correspond with the tread of Miss Jessler's van. And maybe the other set of castings will match her wheelchair. In other words, we have strong reason to believe that you are both somehow involved with the disappearance of Jed Whitecross. But of course, you wouldn't know anything about that, would you?"

"What makes you think I do?"

"Call it a hunch. Can I be frank with you, Jo?"

"Only if you hurry. I need to have another girl-to-girl talk with my friends. So make it quick."

He lowered his voice, as if he didn't want to be overheard by his fellow agents. "Jo, if you don't give me a little something to go on here, you know what's going to happen. It's now eleven o'clock. I have been ordered to bring this situation to an end by no later than noon. The powers-that-be want to avoid a media spectacle at all costs. You got that? *At all costs.*"

"What are you trying to say?"

"Call it off, that's what I'm trying to say. Call it off, or in fifty-nine minutes, we will come in and get you."

"That could be messy."

"Only if you let it turn out that way."

Jo looked at her watch. "What time did you say it was?"

"It's two minutes after. You have less than an hour."

Jo adjusted the slender hands of her watch accordingly. "We'll be in touch." She put the phone down to find them all staring at her. "They're sending in the commando team at twelve."

She expected a reaction. A groan. A quip. Something. But they just kept on staring.

Jo scooted around so that she was facing the window. She hung her watch from the head of a nail that protruded from the casement. She watched the hands sweep away another minute.

Fifty-seven to go.

Hannah thought of dying.

Ever since the men had begun surrounding them, she'd speculated on the possible outcomes. There seemed to be only three. One, they were arrested, she was convicted of murder as soon as the body was found, and everyone else kept quiet, stayed free, and grew old. Two, they were arrested and evidence was found to convict them *all* of murder. Or three, they weren't arrested. But the only way that was going to happen was if they were dead.

Talk about the Hoofbeats.

Hannah wouldn't allow herself to pace, so she settled for rolling an inch forward, an inch back. Her fingers gripped the rubber treads when they should have been touching Terrell's eyelids, coaxing him from his slumber in a hospital bed. The thought of losing him almost crushed her beneath its weight. She had to talk to him. *Had to.*

"May I use the phone?"

She waited for an admonishment that never came. Jo

simply tossed the phone to her.

She knew the hospital's number, having called it many times during the course of her job. She held the phone with both hands, though it didn't help much. The tremors rippled through her. She kept her voice under control when she asked for Terrell Campbell's room, and she did okay when a nurse answered and said that, yes, he was awake but really too tired to talk. "This is Hannah Jessler," she said steadily. "If there's a TV in the room, I'm sure they're talking all about me."

"Hannah . . ." The nurse was nonplussed. "I don't understand . . . I thought you were—"

"Just give him the phone, lady."

The next voice she heard was his: "Sweetness?"

That's when she lost it. "Baby, I'm so sorry."

"Sorry I got skewered by a skinhead, or sorry for whatever the hell you're doing now?"

"Please, just listen to me . . ."

"What *are* you doing by the way?"

"Resisting arrest."

He said nothing. She could hear him breathing.

"You sound good," she said. The tears streamed down her face.

"Kept hearing bits and pieces," he said gruffly. "Kept hearing crazy things. Crazy things about my Hannah shutting herself in some damn chicken coop and telling the FBI to piss off. So I threw a fit and got them to wheel in a boob tube. And lo and behold."

"I'm sorry."

"Stop saying that."

"What else am I supposed to say?"

"That you're coming out of there right now."

"I can't do that."

"You can and you will."

"It's not that easy. Not anymore. Things are . . . different now."

"I cannot lose you, Hannah. You hear me? I don't know what happened between Jo and Whitecross. From what they're saying, she did something to him, maybe the worst kind of something. I don't know what to think or who to believe. But I do know that I don't want you messed up in it."

"A little late for that, lover."

"Yeah, I noticed. I guess my sister's in there with you?"

Hannah looked at Lucy. "She is."

Lucy said, "Tell him I'll talk to him in a minute. Got to get a few things straightened out first."

"Terrell, Lucy said—"

"I heard. I don't understand, but I heard. Damn, sweetness, have you all lost your minds? Is that what's happened? If you're trying to protect Jo, then let me be the first to tell you that this is a bad way to go about it."

Hannah panned her eyes from Lucy to Jo. Now, *there* was an expression she'd never seen before. Jo's face was contemplative and confused, reluctant and unwavering. In the space of those few seconds, Hannah made her decision. "I think I need to go, Terrell. We don't have a lot of time here."

"Says here on the news that you have weapons in there. That true?"

"Not weapons, plural. Weapon, singular. But don't tell anyone. It's probably best if they're not sure how many guns we have."

"Probably best? *Probably best?* Hannah, listen to yourself . . ."

"Thanks for giving me legs for awhile, lover. That means more to me than you'll ever know. Now tell me that you love me, you black stallion."

"Hannah . . ."

"Fine. Don't tell me. I've got to go."

"*I love you.* God, do I love you."

She smiled. "Thanks. I'll never forget. Here's your sister."

She threw the phone to Lucy.

"How is he?" Nin asked.

"Grumpy." Hannah blinked back the moisture in her eyes. "Grumpy and perfect." She sat there trying to recall the feeling of his hands on her face, but she was numb, as if the paralysis had finally claimed those parts of her it had missed the first time around.

Lucy sat down on the sleeping bag, the phone to her ear. "Hey, little brother."

"*Sis, don't do this.*"

The ache those four words ignited in her caused her to open her mouth in quiet agony. She leaned her head against the wall and stared at the ceiling.

"Sis, you there?"

"I'm here. But don't you fret. Hannah's going to be just fine. You'll see."

"I'm talking . . . about you. About . . . you and me."

"Now don't you cry on me, mister. Don't you dare do it. I can't handle that, no sir, I can't."

"Good, then maybe you'll . . . you'll give this up and come home."

"Jed Whitecross is dead, Terrell."

"What? He's dead?"

"That's a fact."

"But . . . but how do you know anything about—"

"Hush up and listen to what I'm saying. I thought Jed hit Penny. I assumed it was his hand that put her in that coma. But I was wrong. It was Joshua. *Joshua,* you got it? So you tell them that, and they can lock him up."

"Lucy, I don't give a damn about that. You're my . . . my *sister.*"

Lucy began weeping so hard that she almost dropped the phone. "I got to go now, little brother."

"No."

"We make a promise, we make it true."

"I don't want to hear that."

"You've got to finish it, Terrell, or the magic doesn't work. Now. We make a promise, we make it true."

"You for . . . please, please, Lucy."

"We make a promise, we make it true."

"You for me and . . . and . . . me for you."

Lucy fell over on her side, the phone spilling from her hand. Tam lay down behind her and held her close, saying words that Lucy couldn't hear.

"We have forty-one minutes left," Jo said.

"He'll fall apart without me," Hannah said, mostly to herself. "He needs me too much."

"Then why aren't you rolling on out the door?"

"Well, for two reasons, I think. First of all, if I went out there, they'd use me against you. Somehow they would. They'd call and tell you that you better give yourself up, otherwise they'll put me away, but if you come out peaceably then the prosecution will go easy on me." She swung her gaze toward Tamaryn. "And you, Tam, you'd probably confess to the murder and go to prison for the rest of your life to keep me free, wouldn't you?"

"You know the answer to that already, Jessler."

"See there? That's my first problem."

"Mine too," Nin said. "My peeps need me, as Terrell needs Hannah. Yet still, I would die any manner of death if it would save one of your lives."

"But reason number two," Hannah said, "has nothing to do with Terrell." She studied the straw-covered floor for a few seconds. "Even if all of you decide to get up and walk out of here and surrender"—she shook her head—"I don't think I can follow you. I can't spend the rest of my days locked up. Maybe I could have before all of this started. Maybe I could have a week ago. But not now. Things have changed."

"Yes, they have," Lucy agreed, sitting up and wiping her nose. "They most certainly have."

"So what do we do then?" Tam asked. "Jo? They want you and Hannah, but the rest of us ain't about to leave you in here to take the fall while we go free."

Jo took her time standing up. She swatted the dust from her pants. "Correct me if this summary is wrong, but it seems like we need to get some people out of here, but in leaving, they become leverage to be used against whoever stays behind."

"It's what you call a paradox," Lucy said.

Nin also came to her feet. "I believe it would be best if we all left as one and faced the outcome together."

"That can't happen," Hannah said, still shaking her head.

"But, Hannah . . ."

"I can't, Nin. I love you so much for that look you have on your face right now, but I can't go to prison for the next fifty years. This chair is all the prison I can stand."

Helping Lucy up from the floor, Jo said, "No one's going to prison."

"But, Jo, you agreed that if Tam and Nin and Lucy leave then the cops'll use them to force us out, and that's true, that's exactly what'll happen, so I can't see how we can make this work."

Jo stood there for a moment, as if in meditation. Then she went to the corner opposite the stove and used her foot to clear away the straw, revealing a trapdoor. "So, Lucille. Here's your rabbit."

Lucy bent down and tapped twice on the door, then looked up. "About goddamn time."

"Nin . . ." The veins stood out in Tam's neck as she strained to lift the door. "This sucker's stuck solid. I'm gonna need some help."

"Gladly. Excuse me, Lucy." Nin had never considered herself exceptionally strong. Physically endowed, yes, but not brawny. By contrast, Tamaryn was built like one of the women Nin saw in the magazine advertisements for home gyms. Nin had never been self-conscious about her size. She hadn't been overly teased as a child, nor was she prone to dieting anxiety as an adult. What difference did the shape of the vessel her soul chose to inhabit make? "Can we both grasp the handle at the same time?"

"I think so. How's that feel?"

Nin put the fingers of her right hand through the metal ring and gripped her wrist in her left hand. Tam also grabbed the ring, and though it was an awkward posture for both of them, Nin was able to brace herself sufficiently by squaring her feet. "I am ready when you are."

"Onetwothree, *go.*"

Nin heaved upwards.

The hinges didn't look very old. It was likely that someone had replaced them a few years ago. Still, they were stubborn. The trapdoor rose three hard-fought inches before the hinges finally gave up the fight. The door swung up to expose a cellar-smelling shaft that dropped eight feet into a limestone burrow. Stagnant water rested in the bottom of the pit.

The five of them stared down into the darkness.

Lucy whistled. "You care to explain this, Jo?"

"There isn't much to explain. I've been spending a lot of time out here lately. I've never been inside this place until today, but Pete Musket told me all about it. I think the old guy sort of had a crush on me. Otherwise I doubt he would have parted with this little secret."

"What is it?" Hannah asked.

"A tunnel for runaway slaves."

"No kidding?"

"So Musket said. It's apparently shored up with boards from one of the area mines. He told me it runs over two hundred feet, which puts it well inside the woods. And effectively out of sight."

"The air will be stagnant," Nin said.

"If there's any air at all," Lucy said.

Tam dropped a stone and watched it *plunk* into the water. "Where does it come out?"

"Beats me. I wasn't too concerned with it at the time, so I didn't ask."

"What if it doesn't come out anywhere?" Tam asked. "What if it just stops at a dead end? Then what are we supposed to do, just crawl all the way back here? And now that I mention it, how are we supposed to get Jessler's chariot down there, anyway?"

"She'll have to leave it here," Lucy suggested.

"I will carry her," Nin offered. She knew that she could.

"No," Hannah said, and everyone looked at her. "I'm not going."

Tam grabbed one of the handles on the back of the wheelchair. "The hell you're not."

"Haven't you heard a word I've said? I can't go to jail, Tam. I'm already imprisoned enough as it is. You know what I've learned these last few days? A person can only give up so much of their freedom before they're better off—"

"Don't you say dead," Lucy warned.

"YOU'VE GOT THIRTY MINUTES REMAINING!"

"I'm gonna go out there and ram that thing up his ass," Tam said.

Nin put her hand on Hannah's shoulder. "Jo, even if we do use this tunnel, and even if we find an opening at the other end, how does this help us? Will we walk all the way back to town? And after our thirty minutes expires, however this turns out, the police will find the tunnel, learn we escaped and they'll still arrest us. Won't they?"

"You're likely to have a rough time of it for awhile," Jo admitted, pressing numbers on her phone. "Between the reporters and the cops, you won't be able to think straight, much less get a decent night's sleep. But unless they find direct evidence putting you at the site of Jed's murder, then they can't touch you. Rita's attorneys will make sure of that. That's how the whole plan works. The only thing they've got is the fact that Jed's hood ornament was found at Tamaryn's house, and that's circumstantial. And when they eventually bring Jed up from the lake, they're only going to find two sheets wrapped around the body. *Two.* And as for getting back into town from the mouth of the tunnel, that's my second magic rabbit."

She went back to the phone. "Hello, Rita. Jo Adams. If you're within earshot of anyone you don't trust, then just listen and don't talk. But I need one more favor. And it's a biggie."

"Hannah," Lucy said. "You're not serious about staying."

"Actually, I think maybe I am."

"Dammit, don't *say* that! What about Terrell?"

"He has you. He's always had you. He'll be all right."

"I'm sending them out as soon as possible," Jo said. "Can you be there to pick them up?"

Lucy wagged her finger as if she were scolding a child. "Now you listen to me, Hannah Jessler. Terrell's more of a man when he's with you." A pleading note entered her voice. "You've given him whatever it is that makes a person think highly of themselves. When you're by his side, that boy is seven feet tall."

"But *Lucy* . . ."

Jo hung up. "Two of Rita's people will be waiting on the old woodcutter's road. You know where that is?"

She directed the question at Nin, who wanted to lie and say no, I don't know anything about any woodcutter's road, so let's call it all off and sit here and face the end together. And she might have, had it not been for her math. Her sum would never be the same, once she traveled down that dark passageway. She would leave too many numbers here behind. She decided something, right then and there: people are not totals, but little additions of everyone around them. So by going down that tunnel, she lost a good portion of who she was. But the rest of her calculation was six children strong. Her future was down that shaft.

"I am familiar with the road," she said, and it was settled.

Tam had been crouching at the trapdoor, but now she stood up and looked Jo in the eye. "You can't expect us just to go and leave you two here. I won't do that. You know I won't."

Jo had anticipated as much, this typically Tam-esque response, but that didn't make it any easier to do what she was about to do. "It's the only way."

Tam aimed her heat at Hannah. "Jessler? Please tell me you don't agree with this stupid, stubborn woman."

"Tam, don't you see? I can't let them put me away."

"Do you hear what you're saying, honey?" Nin asked her.

"You're talking about *dying*."

"Wrong," Jo said. She paused, letting them think their thoughts, letting them get a good hard look at her so that hopefully they'd believe the lie she was about to tell. "The only chance that Rita and her people have of not being noticed when they pick you up from the end of the tunnel is if we provide some kind of distraction. It's imperative that we keep their eyes on this building at all times. Our main objective is keeping you three from getting arrested."

"Let me see if I got this straight," Lucy said. "You want Nin, Tam, and me to belly-crawl down this smelly hole, and you two will keep the cops off our backs until we're safe."

"It's the only plan I've got."

"And then what? You two are giving yourselves up?"

Jo shrugged. "Barring intervention from heaven, yes, that's exactly what we'll do."

Hannah nudged her chair closer. "But, Jo . . ."

"No buts. Once we know the others are safe, you and I are giving ourselves up and hoping that AGNES has some fantastic lawyers on retainer and that public opinion will pull us through." She felt her face growing warm, as she'd never fibbed to the Crazy Coven, never once in her life. "But the rest of you have to go, because there are cameras out there, and the last thing we want is Nin's face on the nightly news. Everyone will assume she's some kind of fugitive, and she'll lose the kids. Do you understand what I'm saying? Tam can't afford to be seen with us, either. The public will make her guilty by association. It's all about appearances. So you three should be as far away from here as possible when Hannah and I put up our hands and give up. Now then." She pointed to the pit at their feet. "Shall we?"

They all looked down at the hole.

"So this is it?" Tam asked, throwing up her hands. "This is

what it comes down to, Nin and Luce and me just leaving you two here, after everything that's happened?"

They stared at one another and waited for someone to say yes.

"TEN MINUTES!"

"You have to go," Jo said.

The five of them stood in a cluster, in what Tam thought was like kittens clumped together for warmth. Tears tracked freely down Lucy's face. Jo leaned against Nin and whispered something that made Nin smile and cry. Tam sank down in front of the chair and held up her hands. Hannah gave her a double high-five, and they locked their fingers together.

"Can I tell you a secret, Jessler?"

Hannah cleared her throat and nodded. "Yes."

"I always wished . . . hell." She dipped her head to their joined hands and wiped her eyes across their knuckles. "I always wished I could be like you."

Hannah hiccupped through her tears. "Goddamn you, Soza."

Tam laughed halfheartedly and threw her arms around Hannah's neck. She had never hugged anyone so tightly. She smelled Hannah's hair and perspiration and perfume. *God, this is killing me.*"

Before she lost the will to leave, she pulled away.

Lucy, standing behind the chair, breathed on Hannah's ear. "You just remember now, child, before you were ever my sister-in-law, you were my sister."

"I'll never forget, Lucy, I'll never ever forget." She held on until Lucy backed out of reach, leaving Hannah holding on to nothing.

Tam helped Nin down the shaft, thankful for the act of physical exertion, anything to keep Hannah's little sobbing sounds from driving too deep. Nin's elbows scraped the earthen walls. Dirt trickled down around her. She dropped the last few feet, splashing heavily into the water.

Tam used her lighter to put a flame to the lantern. She handed it down. "Did you hurt yourself? Can you see the tunnel?"

Nin was nearly too big to navigate within the narrow space. She had to put the lantern aside to manage the contortion, and even then she could barely fold her legs beneath her when she got down on her knees.

"One of the advantages of being an underfed slave," Lucy commented. "They could build their secret passages really skinny."

"I am facing the tunnel. I only wish there were a light at the end of it."

"You *are* the light," Lucy said. "Now get a move on."

Nin looked back up, the lantern light imbuing her face with a ruddy glow.

"What are you staring at?"

"You," Nin said.

"Well, it's just a new hairdo, that's all."

"No, Lucy. That is *not* all. God bless you." She shoved the lantern in front of her and proceeded slowly into the mouth of the passage.

Tam looked at Lucy. "You're next."

"Yeah, I was afraid you'd say that."

Jo brushed a hand over Lucy's stubby hair. "How's your heart?"

"Same as yours, I suppose."

"That'll teach you to wear pillowcases on your head."

"Kind of took on a life of its own, huh?" Abruptly she sat down on the edge of the shaft and dragged over the shoebox Jo had seen her take from the van. "Best three hundred and twelve dollars I ever spent."

Inside the box was a pair of shoes.

Lucy removed her thick-soled walking shoes and slid her feet into the leather dreams.

"How are they?"

"Still too damn cheap for these walkin' feet of mine. But they'll do."

Tam helped her lower those shoes into the water.

"Now don't you be too long, Jo Adams!" Lucy ordered.

"Not far behind you, sister." Jo's voice was lined with lead.

Lucy vanished down the tunnel.

Which only leaves me, Tam thought. She looked at Jo and didn't know what to say. Fancy words had never been her strong suit. In softball she could turn a double into an in-the-park home run, and she could raise damn good kids, but she couldn't make poetry around the ache in her throat.

Jo stepped close, took Tam's head in her hands, and kissed her on the lips. "Push life."

Tam held very still for a moment, then kissed her back and jumped down the hole.

She landed in frigid water. The world stank of limestone and burning lantern oil. She had pledged that, once down, she wouldn't look back. The way ahead of her was claustrophobic. The darkness was thwarted by the lantern some twenty feet in front of her, though Nin blocked most of the light.

She kept her pledge. She walked low so as not to dislodge one of the support planks. She heard Nin huffing for breath. The walls pressed down around her. The air was rank and difficult to breathe. But the odor was something to think about other than the pieces of herself she was leaving behind, and so she was thankful for the foul smell. But after only a dozen steps, she could no longer contain her grief. Tears blotted out the lantern light. Tamaryn staggered onward. She made no sound, but her body shook.

Jo finished replacing the straw over the trapdoor. She lifted her head when Bonham's voice pierced the white-hot wall that misery had constructed around her mind. "YOU HAVE FIVE MINUTES REMAINING IN THERE!"

Hannah rolled to the window. "Where did they all *come* from?"

Jo tottered over and peered outside. Cars were everywhere, and behind the cars were men—men in body armor and riot helmets, men with knee pads and compact submachine guns, men with sniper rifles on bipods and two of them in silver suits with fire extinguishers. The news people had been confined to the far side of the highway. Their cameras and telephoto lenses lined the pavement. Air coverage had increased to three helicopters.

Hannah looked up at her. "You lied to them, didn't you?"

Jo didn't answer. Instead, she picked up the phone. She knelt at the window, eyes on the watch that hung from the nail in front of her face. The hardest thing she'd ever done in her life was say goodbye to Tam and Lucy and Nin. Seconds later, this was surpassed by the nearly unbearable torment of listening to Hannah cry. And now there was this phone call, and the voice that answered.

"Adams residence."

"Good morning, Sweet."

"*Mom?* Mom, what's happening? What's going on?"

"Listen to me, Caroline. This is the most difficult conversation I've ever had, so listen close. I killed Jed Whitecross."

"What? You didn't kill anyone. Why would you say that?"

"It was more or less an accident, but that's what happened. Hannah and I killed him. We killed him because we thought it was his fault that Penelope was in the hospital. And because of what we did, the police are here to take us in."

"No shit, Mom, I'm watching it right now!"

"I've never heard you say shit before."

"You're lecturing me *now?*"

"No, I'm not. I've said it a few times myself lately. In one minute and forty-five seconds, those men out there are coming inside. I don't know what's going to happen when they do. So I'm calling to tell you how proud I am of you, the decisions you've made, the woman you've become."

"Wait, you're going too fast. You're not making any sense. Are you saying that it was you all along, painting houses and messing up Dad's car?"

"Hard to believe, isn't it? Your old ma's a late-blooming dissenter."

"It was you? You really did that to Jed? You *murdered* him?"

"Don't forget your promise. You swore to back me up, whatever choice I made." She ran her hand through her sweaty hair. "God, there's so much I want to tell you right now. But I can't sort it all out. Unless you have a family to support, don't ever take a job just for money. There's not a greater personal disservice than that. And always vote for the candidate who had to pay their own way through school."

"Mom, I'm not listening to this. I won't. You're acting . . . you're acting like a child."

"Sometimes I am a child. But that's okay. It's allowed. You should do it more often. Oh, and only marry the man who it would kill you to be without."

Caroline started to cry. "Mom . . ."

Jo put her hand flat against the wall, as if by doing so she could keep herself from breaking apart. "Depending on how things work out today, you may end up living with your father for awhile, at least until you go off to college. You can tell him what I did to his car. But don't let him convince you that the world is as ruthless a place as he thinks it is. There was a time when he could see all the stuff worth saving out there, but all the unhappiness in the air wore him down. Don't ever be worn down. And drop in on Warren from time to time. He's one of those things worth saving."

"Mom, I love you, I love you—"

"I love you too, in a way that you won't know until you have someone like you to call a daughter. But it looks like I've only got about a minute and a half until this goes one way or the other, so I need to go."

"I said I'd back you and I am, Mom, really I am. But I don't understand it at all because it seems like such a load of *shit*. So there. You heard me say it twice in the same day."

The moisture hurt Jo's eyes. Water can be sharp sometimes. "Goodbye, Sweet Caroline. You are the best thing I ever did."

"Mommy, please."

Hardest of all was hanging up.

When she lifted her head, she found Hannah had rolled up beside her.

"Company's coming," Hannah said.

"Looks that way."

"We're not just providing a diversion, are we?"

"A diversion's part of it, yes."

"But that stuff about giving up . . ."

"I had my fingers crossed when I said that."

Hannah nodded. Her face was empty of everything but resolve. "Tam brought something."

"Show me."

Hannah hoisted the black plastic bag, unwrapped it, and pulled out a rifle.

"Is it loaded?"

Hannah deftly extracted the magazine, spilled a box of ammunition into her lap, and began jamming in shells. Her eyes were now dry and hard, like the desert floor.

Jo glanced at the watch. "Forty seconds."

Hannah rammed the loaded clip into the rifle. They heard the rush of movement outside. The shouted words. The boots.

"Here." Jo held out her hand. "Give it to me."

"You sure?"

"Just tell me what to do."

"My father taught me to ride a horse and shoot a gun," Hannah said. "If he could only see me now." She worked the bolt. The noise rang sharply against the stone walls. "I'm not sure, but I think it fires as fast as you can pull the trigger."

Jo accepted the rifle, wondering why it didn't seem like a profoundly stupid thing to do. She moved away from the window and slid against the wall. She raised the stock to her shoulder and pointed the barrel at the door. She had no intention of shooting anyone. But neither had she any intention of surrendering. She hoped the others would forgive her for her fib.

Hannah slid down out of her chair and crawled over, dragging her legs. With some effort, she positioned herself so that she was sitting beside Jo, so close that their bodies touched.

Jo thought of the elephants then. She didn't know why.

But then again she did. Say by chance the elephant gave a tug and snapped its tether. Was it ever capable of being tied in such a manner again? She should have checked the encyclopedia about that. Put that on the to-do list.

She felt Hannah's fingers tighten on her arm.

The hands of her watch touched twelve.

Even in the back of the car a quarter-mile down the road, Lucy heard the gunshots.

They seemed to be without end. Not once in real life had she ever experienced the rattle of automatic fire, but that's what the cops were using, pouring it into the birthing house. Lucy closed her eyes immediately so as not to see the others' faces—Nin's open shock, Tam's searing fury—and in the darkness of her mind she saw Jo standing beside her in the hospital chapel. Jo said, *We better cut some eyeholes in that thing. Kind of hard to follow our truth if we can't see where we're going.*

Taking Jo's advice, Lucy opened her eyes. And kept them open.

Epilogue

Penny stood at the window and watched the leaves fall.

"First day of winter," said a voice from behind her.

And so it was. Penelope could remember little of the preceding autumn, with her days running away from her the way the brown leaves tumbled down the street in the wind. As the trees had been bared to the icy touch of frost, so too had her inner self been exposed to the harsh weather of police inquiries and television interviews and her name on the tongue of strangers. The hard part wasn't the publicity—"A little fame never hurt anyone," her new roommate liked to say—but rather the constant awareness that Penny herself was the cause of the madness and the reason that people were dead.

"I saw the letter on the coffee table, Pen. Don't you even want to open it?"

Though Penny didn't watch TV anymore, she'd heard about the protests in California and that riot at the women's clinic down in Mobile. One of the national news magazines had named this the Year of Flags and Fists. Penny hadn't picked up a newspaper in weeks, and maybe she never would again. Finally she drew herself from the window and turned around.

Caroline Adams was standing there with the letter in her hands. "It's from Nin, postmarked Alaska." She gave the envelope a wave. "It's addressed to both of us."

"Could you read it to me, please? But I don't want to hear it if it's not good news."

Caroline did as instructed, prying into the envelope with her usual exacting manner. She'd moved in with Penny the day after Penny was released from the hospital. Though Caroline was several years younger than she, Penny felt like the girl's little sister, always needing the comforting word and the morning sprinkle of optimism. Caroline had not been broken by her mother's death. If anything, she'd been elevated by it.

" 'Dear Penny and Sweet,' " Caroline began.

Penny turned back and gazed from the window, letting Nin's words flow over her.

" 'For the moment, I am alone. I just switched on the sign in the day-care window. The sprites are still snoozing in their beds in the apartment upstairs. It is early, just past six in the morning. Yet guess what? I feel as fresh as the cold breeze. My favorite room here in the day care is one that I call the Jamboree Room. It has lots of open floor space for games like balloon volleyball and indoor tag. I tell you, girls, life grows so big in that room that it nearly takes the roof off, like popcorn rising in an air popper.' "

Penny couldn't help but smile faintly. With an unprecedented outpouring of public donations, Rita Ingersol had purchased a former dentist's office and put Nin in charge of converting it to a first-class child-care facility. According to Nin, there were plans to bring in a counselor one day a week to help those children who needed it, and an unused room in the back would soon be a drop-off for clothes and canned goods, to be distributed to the needy. Riding a tidal wave of national support, the AGNES legal team had kept Nin and the others out of the courtroom. Now that the police inquiry was well behind them, the women had settled into the next chapter of their lives. Nin's life, past and present, had always revolved around children.

Caroline continued. " 'One entire wall of the Jamboree Room is done in mirrors. The lower portion of the mirrors is usually smeared with fingerprints, but yesterday Sheila came in to do the cleaning. Sheila is my best employee, and also my friend. We've even gone out once or twice, to drink champagne for no reason at all and talk about the men who happen by.' "

"That doesn't sound like Nin," Penny said.

"Does that surprise you?"

"No. Not really." Nin was one of her champions, someone who'd gone the distance for her and sacrificed so much on her behalf that Penny couldn't comprehend the scope of the woman's heart. "She deserves champagne."

" 'Tamaryn will drop off the boys in a few minutes. Two nights ago she came over to celebrate. Her divorce is final. The court was going to make Roy pay a large amount of child-support, but you know Tam. She said the only time she'd accept a blankety-blank dollar from him was if she was going to use it to wipe her butt. Except she didn't say butt. Though she still works at the little diner here, she's also serving as part-time athletic director down at the YMCA. I believe she will soon be hired on permanently.' "

"Good for her," Penny said, mostly to herself. Often she'd lain awake at night wondering what Tam had said to Jed that day at the lake, what kind of words she'd used. Though repulsed by what had happened, Penny wished she could have seen Tam's face. To know that someone was enraged on your behalf was strangely comforting. People standing up for you was nice.

" 'Lucy has accepted a position at a bank. She has a desk. This is very important to her, though I do not fully understand why. She told me that her walking days are over. She says the old feet of hers have earned their rest.' "

Penny thought, *I miss Lucy delivering my mail.*

" 'Terrell works for the city police department.' "

At the mention of Terrell's name, Penny tensed. Here the guilt lay the deepest. Of all the awful things that had happened, the one most difficult to live with was Hannah's death. Hannah, who had never harmed anyone, Hannah, upon whom Terrell had built the foundation of his future—she was gone and it was Penny's fault. If only Penny hadn't kept quiet. If only she'd spoken up when her brother first hit her, then Hannah would still be alive and Terrell wouldn't be a walking ghost. She learned many lessons in the last several weeks, none of them greater than this: Speak up.

" 'Lucy says that Terrell was invited to visit the FBI field office in Anchorage, but he said no. His police car is a four-wheel-drive truck, and he is already very popular here in town. Everyone seems to like him. And for some reason, he has taken to wearing a cowboy hat.' "

Caroline paused, and for a moment Penny thought the letter was over. But then Caroline turned the page over and said, " 'Penelope, Terrell has asked me to tell you to be strong. That man has faith in both of you girls, and he knows that Hannah is out there somewhere, cheering you on.' "

"Stop already," Penny said, her head bowed.

"There's more."

"I don't care."

"You think this is any easier on me?" Caroline grabbed a tissue and blew her nose, then finished the letter. " 'There is one problem with the Jamboree Room. I can never come here without feeling that something is very different about me. I think it has to do with the mirrored wall. I look at myself, but I can see no change. I have not lost weight. I dress as I always have. And though Lucy talked me into getting a perm—forty-five dollars!—I look very much the same. About a week ago I stood in this same spot and decided that it was the size of the mirror that makes the difference. The bigness of the mirror. I am not sure how to explain that, but there you have it.' "

Penny stepped away from the window and faced her friend. They had an appointment in Washington today, inescapable guilt notwithstanding. Penny's coat waited by the door. She had but to slip into it and be invincible. Perhaps the letter was perfumed with a bit of Nin's strength.

" 'On some days I cry,' " Caroline read. " 'Many years ago Dan came home and found me crying as I folded clothes. He asked me what was wrong. I said it was nothing. And that was true. But Dan couldn't understand that. He got angry and said that something was wrong and I simply wasn't telling him. I wanted to tell him that sometimes I cry and it doesn't have to be because of anything. Maybe there is a man out there somewhere who understands that. Maybe one of you two will meet him. If you do, hold on tightly. Now I must go, because the first of the children have arrived. I admire you both. Love, Nin.' " Caroline grinned as she read the next line. " 'P.S. Your Aunt Tamaryn says that if you bawl like a couple of sissies when you read this letter, she's going to drive down there and smack you around.' "

Caroline folded the letter and put it away. "So what do you say? We've still got time to join the convoy to the capital. They won't want to leave without us."

"I guess you're right."

"Never thought you'd be a figurehead, did you?" Caroline shouldered her school backpack, which was crammed with hundreds of pamphlets to be distributed in the streets of Washington. "Come on. If nothing else, the fresh air will do you good."

Penny knew that was true. She retrieved her laptop, in which she had begun a hesitant chronicle of her experience, not so much because publishers were asking for it, but simply so she could get her feelings out in front of her and in doing so separate them into manageable portions.

"Are you up for this?" Caroline asked in the doorway.

Penny nodded, and that felt good. "Yeah, I think maybe I finally am." She grabbed her coat on the way out the door. It was solid pink.

July 28–December 2, 2001
Stillwater, OK

About the Author

Erin's parents are a poet and a hunter—one a pacifist, the other a Marine veteran of Vietnam. Perhaps as a result of this contradiction, Erin's been unable to find any vocation satisfying outside of writing. It seems to be the only activity capable of containing the heart's opposing forces.

Erin's first birthday was spent in the Shriners' Hospital for Crippled Children. Since then, Erin has waited tables, fought grass fires, protested the death penalty, taught children to read, touched the Rosetta Stone, and received a letter from Ray Bradbury. Somewhere along the way Erin picked up a few college degrees which have yet to be put to practical use.

Currently a full-time volunteer with the AmeriCorps program, Erin teaches language-arts skills to the youth of the Otoe-Missouri tribe in Red Rock, Oklahoma. Erin has also been seen charting the paths of barn swallows and calculating the escape velocity of fictional planets.

DEMCO